Four Brothers On the Train

Book 6

JEL JONES

(Sequel to Four Brothers In Love)

ISBN 978-0-359-16366-3
Published by Lulu

Lulu Press, Inc.
627 Davis Drive – Suite 300
Morrisville, NC 27560
www.lulu.com

Chapter One

Catherine opened her eyes at seven o'clock the next morning with a stiff neck. She frowned as she grabbed the back of her neck with both hands, almost falling out of the straight back chair where she had slept all night. She noticed that any movement of her neck from side to side caused her mild discomfort. Therefore, slowly she lowered her hands from the back of her neck and stared at her watch, noticing it was seven a.m. She was still quite tired considering the many times she wakened during the night hoping Fred would walk through the door. The vaguest sound of an airplane in a distant or a vehicle passing down the highway, Catherine eyes blinked opened. Therefore, she stared over at the comfortable looking sofa and thought of lying her tired achy body there for another hour of sleep. But quickly that idea faded as she became more and more alert, realizing she needed to head back to Franklin House to let the family know that Fred had abandoned the car and apparently his job. And although, she was well aware that she had to inform of Fred's confession to Antonio's murder, she dreaded delivering that piece of stunning, unbelievable news. Nevertheless, she slowly stood from the chair and grabbed her neck again with both hands, squeezed and massaged her neck for a moment with her fingers, and then slowly stretched both arms above her head and yawned. She was trying to shake the sleep away, which she noticed had swiftly vanished, suddenly giving in to the anxiousness and worried feeling in the pit of her stomach that had consumed her since Fred's disappearance. Still racking her brain of what to do, dreading heading home, she slowly stepped across the room and dropped heavily on the sofa. She rubbed her neck for a while as she sat in disbelief that Fred had left her to face the music without his personal confession to law enforcement. She wondered for a while trying to figure out if there was any other way around confessing Fred's crime. She didn't want to be the one to make a confession that he had promised to make. She felt it would make it appear that he was trying to escape his punishment when deep down she wasn't convinced that he had disappeared for the sake of not facing the authorities for his crime. She entertained the thought of remaining up at the lake house for a while longer in hope that Fred would return. But that idea along with all the other thoughts that dashed through her mind seemed hopeless. She was forced to face the cold hard facts that without the presence of Fred to vouch for himself, all other efforts were hopeless. That realization was like a punch in the stomach as she slowly stood from the sofa, wiped her eyes with her fingers, grabbed her purse and headed through the kitchen toward the back door to leave.

Almost in tears, Catherine felt weighed down with concern and worry of Fred's whereabouts as she locked the back door and then headed across the backyard toward her car. Somewhat in a daze she noticed the limo parked two car length from her car. Seeing the car lifted her spirits for a second as she wished Fred was lying asleep inside the car. She hurried toward the limo and stood back and stared at it for a moment before peeping inside to find her thought was just wishful thinking. If nothing else, she was hoping for some sign or clue of Fred's whereabouts, but all she noticed was that he had been responsible in making sure all the limousine doors were locked.

Catherine headed home more confident that Fred had actually skipped town to keep from facing his day in court. However, she racked her brain wondering where he had gone off to. The lake area covered ten acres and she felt Fred was hiding out on the lake.

Catherine arrived at Franklin House and unlocked the front door feeling wearily. She stepped inside feeling unsure of what she would say. It was eight o'clock and she knew she would find everyone gathered in the dining room for breakfast. Therefore, she quickly stepped into one of the guest bathrooms to wash her face and hands; afterward, she hurried into the dining room and took a seat in her regular chair. Everyone appeared to be just gathering into their seats, but it was apparent that Catherine was the last to be seated at the table. Nevertheless, no one seemed curious or inquired about Catherine's night away from Franklin House. But after everyone said good morning, Veronica raised an eyebrow noticing how unkempt Catherine looked dressed in the same attire from the day before. Catherine threw a quick glance toward Veronica, hoping Veronica wouldn't asked her any questions. But Catherine's nerves were obvious from her trembling hand as she lifted her glass of orange juice to her mouth. Veronica discreetly noticed Catherine's nervousness and figured it was due to the stress of having to give her statement about Antonio's murder. Therefore, she didn't mention her nervousness or unkempt attire. But when Catherine carelessly knocked over her coffee cup that spilled into the white tablecloth, Veronica, Amber and the four brothers looked toward Catherine and noticed that Catherine had tears in her eyes. Immediately Veronica buzzed Natalie to come into the dining room to take care of the spill, but as Natalie hurried toward the table, Veronica held up one finger to get Natalie's attention.

"Catherine spilled her coffee, but please leave it for now," Veronica said in a whisper and nodded toward Natalie.

Natalie nodded and headed directly out of the dining room.

"Aunt Catherine, we are so sorry you are going through this," Rome said. "But please don't worry. We'll make sure everything works out fine for you."

"That's right, Aunt Catherine, our attorneys have assured us that your case will not be that much of an issue with their expertise," Britain assured her. "Apparently, what's working in your favor is that you honestly don't remember committing a crime."

Paris eyes showed compassion as he nodded and touched his Aunt's shoulder. "That's right, Aunt Catherine. We all know you're worried, but your case of temporary insanity is quite sincere. Besides, you loved Antonio and didn't want to see him harmed. And we're aware how you think you may have harmed him because of your fiery anger for him on that morning. Plus, you confessed to heading to the hospital to harm him. But, you have no memory of it; and none of us around this table." He pointed to them all. "Actually, believe you were the one who took Antonio's life," Paris meaningfully stated.

Veronica nodded toward Catherine as Sydney noticed how his Aunt kept looking at her watch and sort of glancing about the room. "Aunt Catherine, I guess you are not hungry at all," Sydney observed. "Are you looking for someone? Do you need Natalie for something?" he asked.

Paris figured she was probably concerned about the authorities showing up at the door. He touched her shoulder. "Aunt Catherine, no authorities are coming to the house to talk to you if that's what you think," Paris told her. "They'll only question you and take your statement when we all take you to the station to give your statement."

Catherine turned to her right to look in Paris's face and she nodded as he finished what he was saying to her. Because she heard him but had no idea what he was saying since her mind was consumed with thoughts of Fred and trying to find the right words to explain to them what she needed to tell them.

Then Sydney who were seated to her left said assuredly. "That is absolutely correct, Aunt Catherine. No one is coming here to question you. You'll only be questioned when you're ready to give your statement. In the meantime, only our attorneys and the seven of us which includes you, knows about your statement and that you plan to give it."

Catherine picked up the white cloth breakfast napkin and dried her eyes. Then she turned to her right and looked at Paris again. "Have you seen Fred this morning?" she asked in an anxious manner.

Paris was caught off guard and quickly shook his head and looked toward his mother and brothers and they all shook their heads. He was surprised to be asked about the staff whereabouts when she was in charge of them. "No, I haven't seen Fred." He paused looking this Aunt, caught off guard and surprised she had asked him about Fred. "I don't usually see him stirring before we leave for work."

Veronica drew an attitude and had become annoyed that Catherine for asking Paris the whereabouts of one of the staff members that Catherine supervised. Yet, she held her irritation and spoke calmly. "Catherine, why are you asking Paris about Fred? Isn't it your job to keep up with the staff?" Veronica calmly said and held up one finger. "Besides, if you don't feel up to driving yourself to the library and want Fred to drop you off, I can send him a quick message to place you on his agenda. What time do you want me to tell him to drive you there?" Veronica asked. "I'll send him a message now."

Catherine jumped up from her seat and held up both arms. "No, don't send him a message. I changed my mind."

"Okay, I won't send him a message, but you don't have to be so dramatic about it. I guess this whole situation really have you in a bad way."

Catherine nodded as she dropped back in her seat. "I'm sorry about my behavior," she mumbled as she glanced across the table at Amber. She felt just awful that Rome's new wife had to witness her going through so much turmoil and such an ordeal. "I'm a wreck and I'm so afraid it's going to get worse."

"I'm sorry you are going through this rough patch, Aunt Catherine," Amber said politely. "But just try to hold on to what Rome and his brothers are saying. They believe all will work out fine for you. So, I wholeheartedly believe it will all work out just fine as they're encouraging you it will."

"Catherine, I agree hundred percent with Amber. It all will work out fine," Veronica assured her. "But you need to cancel your schedule for the library today. The sooner you can go in to give your statement, the sooner our attorneys can get your case off the ground. That will start the process, so we can have this nightmare behind us." She lifted her juice glass to her mouth and took a sip of orange juice.

Catherine stared at Veronica for a moment, and then stood from her seat. "You'all have to excuse me." She stared down at the blueberry pancakes on her breakfast plate. "My stomach is in knots and I can't eat."

Veronica threw Catherine a solid look and pointed to her chair. "Catherine, please just keep your seat. No one is making you eat, but you need to be seated and pull yourself together. I realize you are having a rough time of it, but right now you're disturbing everyone's breakfast."

The four brothers continued to eat their breakfast, trying not to appear too taken by Catherine's unusual behavior. And after Catherine hesitantly too her seat, she pushed her breakfast plate aside. She had stood at her seat in an effort to get everyone's attention to tell them all about Fred's confession. But Veronica telling her to be seated was all it took to destroy her courage to say what she needed to say. She shook her head as she stared down at the spilled coffee on the table in front of her. She wasn't shaking her head at the spill she was shaking her head at what caused the spill. Her raw nerves and clumsiness.

"Catherine, after breakfast we all need to meet in the library for a discussion," Veronica announced as she exchanged looks with her sons. "You are in a weird way and it's understandable, to a point. Although, your behavior concerns me. Instead of taking you to the authorities to give your statement, we may need to get you to a doctor first," Veronica seriously suggested.

Catherine's eyes widened, and her stomach tightened at Veronica's remark. It made her more aware of her strange behavior and it made her realize that she had to pull herself together and find the courage to inform them of what was going on. Therefore, she pulled out her phone and buzzed Natalie. And within a few minutes Natalie appeared in the dining room.

"Natalie, I buzzed you," Catherine quickly said. "Please bring out a fresh pot of coffee and another stack of pancakes."

Natalie nodded and headed out of the dining room, but not before she discreetly glanced toward Veronica. But Veronica was busy passing the blueberry syrup to Britain.

After Natalie stepped out of the room, Rome smiled looking toward Catherine. "Aunt Catherine, I'm glad you found your appetite."

Catherine nodded. "Yes, I have found my appetite and my senses." She held up one finger. "And after I get some food in my stomach and a full cup of coffee, I have something to share with all of you."

Veronica nodded, looking toward Catherine. "Very well." She was pleased to see that Catherine was pulling herself together.

After Natalie stepped into the dining room pushing the serving cart that held one pot of coffee and a plate with a stack of pancakes, before she could

7

remove anything from the cart, Dillion rushed into the dining room unannounced. He had a frantic look on his face as all heads turned to look toward him as he walked quickly across the room toward the table where they were seated. He stood close to the back of Britain's chair as he glanced at Britain and then at Veronica.

"I'm sorry to barge in and interrupt your breakfast, but I just got a call from Fred and he's in big trouble," Dillion said breathless.

Catherine's heart skipped a beat because she thought Dillion meant that Fred was in trouble with the law.

Veronica held up both hands. "Dillion, please calm down and explain to us what you mean by your statement."

"I mean he's in real trouble."

Britain softly touched Dillion's arm and then pulled out the kitchen chair to the left of him. "Come, Dillion, and have a seat and get your bearing."

Dillion looked at Britain and nodded as he anxiously took a seat at the nice elegant dining room table that seated twelve. After he was seated Veronica motioned to Natalie to pour Dillion a cup of coffee. Natalie placed a cup and saucer in front of Dillion along with a napkin and a spoon, and then she lifted the coffee pot and filled his cup with coffee.

Dillion placed his hand over the cup, shaking his head. "Thank you, no sugar or cream. I take it black."

Natalie nodded and then busied herself pouring coffee into their cups.

Dillion's hand shook as he lifted his cup to his mouth and took a long sip of coffee. He lowered his cup and glanced at the stack of pancakes that Natalie were placing on a plate in front of Catherine. He stared too long at Catherine's food. Britain and Natalie both observed how Dillion's eyes lit up at the sight of the pancakes. Britain smiled toward Natalie and then pointed at the empty placemat in front of Dillion.

"Natalie, I think Dillion would like to try a couple of your famous blueberry pancakes."

"Sure, Mr. Britain," Natalie said and then placed two pancakes on a plate and placed in front of Dillion.

Paris passed the blueberry syrup down to Sydney and Sydney passed over the butter dish to him. Then Dillion smiled as he took his fork and knife and dug into the pancakes. "Thank you so much for this fine breakfast," Dillion smiled toward Britain. "I didn't get a chance to grab any breakfast before I received that call from Fred," he said as he took his fork and placed a piece of pancake in his mouth.

Just then it dawned on him that he didn't have time to sit there and enjoy a leisurely breakfast as he forked down a couple more bites and then turned his coffee cup up to his mouth and finished it. And before he could say anything else, Veronica looked toward Dillion and smiled. "Did you enjoy your pancakes?" she asked.

Dillion nodded. "Yes, I sure did. Those were sure delicious blueberry pancakes. I ate them without the syrup," he said, smiling.

"That's good, but now that you have calmed down with some food and a cup of hot coffee in your stomach, could you please tell us what this trouble that Fred is in," Veronica inquired.

"Fred called my phone a few minutes before I walked in here," Dillion explained in a more relaxed tone. "He said he fell at the lake house and hurt his foot," Dillion explained.

Catherine's eyes were wide with anticipation as she stared across the table at Dillion. "Is that the trouble you were referring to?" she asked.

Dillion looked toward Catherine as if she had caught him off guard. He wasn't sure what she had just asked him. "I'm sorry Miss Catherine, but what did you just ask me?"

"When you rushed in here you said Fred was in trouble," Catherine said in a rude tone. "Is he in trouble or just hurt his foot?"

Everyone at the breakfast table was surprised by Catherine's rude manners toward Dillion. Suddenly the room became extremely quiet as Veronica gave Catherine an irritated discreet stare. "Catherine, please just let Dillion say what he has to say."

"I was just inquiring to be clear if the hurt foot is the trouble he was referring to when he walked in and announced to us that Fred was in trouble," Catherine quickly added.

Veronica threw a quick annoyed glance toward Catherine as she held up one finger in hope that Catherine would keep quiet as she looked toward Dillion. "Dillion is that the trouble you wanted to relay about Fred is that he injured his foot?" Veronica asked.

"Yes, Miss Veronica. He told me that he left the limousine parked in the back parking stall at the lake house. Then he took a walk on the grounds. He's somewhere on the lake house property but he's not sure where he is," Dillion anxiously explained. "He also hit his head and knocked himself out," Dillion relayed. "He's up at the lake house lying in the woods where he laid all night unable to move because he hurt his foot so bad until he can't walk."

The four brothers gracefully stood from their seats to leave the room. But they paused as Rome leaned down and kissed Amber on the cheek and whispered near her ear. "Have a nice day, Mrs. Franklin. I'll call you later."

She looked up at him, smiled and touched his arm. "You to darling. I love you," she said in a low voice.

"I love you too," he said in a whisper and gave her a quick kiss on the lips. Then he looked toward his brothers and nodded. They all nodded back at him and then Rome stepped near his mother's chair.

"Mother, we are all heading up to the lake house right now," Rome informed them. "If Fred is lying in the woods unable to walk, he's in pretty awful shape."

"We will also call EMS and send them to the lake house," Sydney said to his mother. "Although, we don't know the exact location of Fred, if they are in the vicinity that will help him get quicker medical attention when we do locate him," Sydney said, realizing he had to cancel his plans to move up to the lake house today. He would have to postpone his getaway until things settled down in his household.

"Dillion we need you to come along with us." Britain patted Dillion's back as they all headed out of the dining room together. "You said the limo is parked in one of the back-parking stalls at the lake house. We'll need you to drive it back."

"Sure, Mr. Britain, whatever I can do," Dillion assured him.

"Thanks, Dillion. You can ride with me," Britain said as they all headed toward the exit of the large room.

Veronica, Catherine and Amber paused their meals and looked toward the five of them as they headed out of the dining room. And within five minutes of the four brothers and Dillion heading to the lake house, Amber lifted her juice glass to her mouth and took one last sip just as Natalie stepped back into the dining room. She filled all their cups with fresh hot coffee and as she started to head out of the room, Veronica stopped her.

"Natalie, I know you are concerned about Fred, but don't worry. The boys are headed to the lake house and they have a medical team meeting them there. They will get Fred home safely," Veronica assured her.

Natalie nodded and some of the worry lines smoothed out of her face. "Thank you, Miss Veronica," she said and headed out of the room.

Amber took two sips from her coffee cup and exchanged looks with Veronica and Catherine. "I'm going to head upstairs. I have a conference call coming through in ten minutes," she glanced at her gold and diamond Swiss watch. "After the call I have a full schedule this morning."

After Amber left the breakfast table, Catherine felt awkward sitting there alone with Veronica. However, she managed to finish her meal while sitting there hoping Veronica wouldn't question her about anything. She desperately wanted to leave the dining room, so she could sneak outside and follow the four brothers to the lake house. She wanted to find Fred before any of them. She needed to talk to him and find out if he was still turning himself in. She had been weighed down with worry and didn't sleep well because she thought he had skipped town to get out of turning himself in. She was pleased he hadn't left town, but she was suspicious of his sudden injuries. Now that he had confessed to her and promised to turn himself in to make it easier on her, suddenly out of the blue he's inured. She couldn't think of a time since Fred employment at Franklin House that he had injured himself. Plus, Catherine was aware that his injuries meant he would get special treatment and special care from the Franklins.

"Catherine why are you sitting there like a frog on a log?" Veronica asked as she lifted her coffee cup and took the last sip of coffee. I'm so sick of your sour mood. You need to do something about it. There's especially no excuse for the rudeness you displayed toward Dillion. "

Catherine nodded. "I know, and I plan to apologize to Dillion for that."

"Well, see that you do." Veronica slight shook her head and then lifted one finger toward Catherine. "Something just came to my attention."

"What?" Catherine curiously asked.

"Right before Dillion rushed into the dining room with the news about Fred, you had just announced you had found your appetite and your senses. I take it, you had something to share with all of us," Veronica reminded her. "Was that a bunch of hot air for my son's benefit or do you care to share it?"

Catherine stared at her speechless. She couldn't share anything with Veronica because what she was going to share wasn't the facts anymore that Fred had confessed to Antonio's murder then abandoned the limousine at the lake house and skipped town. That information about Fred abandoning the car and skipping town wasn't true.

"So, what in the world were you talking about?" Veronica insisted. "Whatever it was it had to be important. You seemed quite serious."

"It is serious," Catherine said as she tried to think of some lie to tell Veronica to get her off of her back."

"If it's so serious, what the hell is it?" Veronica insisted.

"I'm done at the library. I told them I couldn't volunteer anymore of my time," Catherine stated.

"Catherine, that is very serious. You love that library and how a section of it is named after Ryan. Why would you stop volunteering there?"

"I do love it there and the help I'm giving is needed. But I have so much on my mind lately. I can't seem to concentrate while I'm there," Catherine admitted. "However, once things settle down. I'll call and have my name put back on the schedule," Catherine assured her.

Veronica nodded. "I just don't understand you anymore. You go from spending nearly every evening at the library to walking out completely."

"I just said I'll get back on the schedule when some of this chaos fades out of my life." Catherine stood up from the breakfast table to leave.

"Catherine, where are you off to?" Veronica asked.

"I'm headed to the library," Catherine quickly said by force of habit.

"Catherine, you're not making any sense. Why are you going there? You just said you're no longer on the schedule."

Catherine realized she was stuck, by not having the library as an excuse to flee Franklin House, she had painted herself in a corner. She glanced around and forced a smile. "I guess you're right. I'm not headed to the library."

"That's good because Amber has decided that she's ready to move things into the east wing," Veronica said.

Catherine nodded. "Okay, that's good. What do you need me for?" Catherine asked.

"I need you to instruct the staff and see to them tidying up the area along with placing fresh linens on all the beds."

"Okay, I'll do that now and make sure they change all the linens and fresh up that part of the house," Catherine quickly said. "But, if you're looking for me later, I won't be around. I'll probably be off site running errands."

Chapter Two

Catherine managed to leave Franklin House after she instructed Mrs. Bradley to tidy up the east wing and change all the linens on all the beds in the east wing. But she didn't have a minute to spare and couldn't take a quick shower or brush her hair or change out of yesterday's clothing. She felt so out of sorts and had never spent a hectic uncertain day like the one she was having. The fact that she needed to get to the Lake House and find Fred first was all that echoed in her mind. Nevertheless, she tried to push some of the dread from her thoughts now that Fred hadn't left town as she dreaded he had. She was trying to convince herself that all had a chance to work out. Yet, she was anxious as she drove down the highway enroot to the lake house. The four brothers had a twenty-minute lead ahead of her. But she was hoping against hope that she could locate Fred before any of them. Since she desperately needed to have a conversation with him before he spoke to anyone. She mainly wanted to know what he was thinking and if he was still in favor of confessing to his crime and turning himself over to the authorities.

Hopeful and anxious, when Catherine pulled into the driveway at the lake house her eyes widened with surprise and her jaw dropped with disappointment when she didn't see the four brother's car parked in the driveway. She shook her head with a deep sigh as she slowly drove her car to the back-parking lot of the summer cottage. She found that the limousine had been driven away as well. She wondered where they could have headed. She needed to find them and didn't know where to head next. Anxious and concerned, she put the car in park and dug to the bottom of her purse to locate her phone. She pulled the phone out and quickly dialed Natalie's cell number.

Natalie answered her phone as usual on the second ring. "This is the Franklin Residence. May I help you?" she said, although she could see the call was from Catherine.

"Hello, Natalie. I'm calling to see if there's an update on Fred's condition."

"Yes, Miss Catherine. He just arrived here. He sprang his ankle and can't walk on it. But he wouldn't go to the hospital. They all tried to convince him including me, but he was firm almost like he had a fear of going to the hospital. So, Mr. Rome and Mr. Paris took him up to one of the guest rooms and he's receiving medical care onsite at Franklin House. Mr. Britain called the family doctor and the doctor is enroot here to patch Fred up."

Catherine didn't want to search through the big house to find which guest room Fred was in. But she pondered in silence on the other end of the receiver, wondering if she should ask Natalie which room he was taken to. Then she figured how she had no choice but to ask. She needed to get to Fred as soon as possible to speak to him.

"Did you need anything else, Miss Catherine?" Natalie asked.

"Yes, Natalie, do you know which guest room they took Fred to?"

Natalie was silent for a moment as if the question had caught her off guard. She wondered why Catherine wanted to know. But thought nothing of it as she answered. "Yes, they took him upstairs to the ocean blue room."

"Thanks, Natalie, for the update. I'm sure Fred is going to be okay. I'll be home soon to check on him," Catherine said.

"Don't worry yourself, Miss Catherine. Fred is okay. I'm sure you have plenty to do other than worry yourself about Fred."

Chapter Three

The moment Catherine arrived home she headed straight upstairs to the ocean blue room to find Fred. Hurrying up the staircase, she was anxious and breathless and quite relieved that she didn't have to figure out which room he was tucked away in.

She noticed that the door was ajar. She gave it a slight push with both hands and then stuck her head in the door. Fred stared across the room at her with surprised eyes as if he hadn't expected her to pay him a visit in his sick bed. He had a bleak look on his face as he laid on top of the covers with a white thin blanket covering his legs. At Catherine arrival, he appeared to be engrossed in watching TV. But the instant Catherine stuck her head in the door, he took the remote that was already in his hand and turned off the set. Then he nodded toward her and beckoned for her to step inside. Catherine glanced over her shoulder and looked both ways down the hallway and then stepped into the room and slowly closed the door behind her. She walked toward the bed with both arms in the air, shaking her head in confusion and disbelief. "Fred, what happened?"

He pointed to his sprung foot. "Isn't it obvious what happened? I had an accident," he dryly mumbled.

"Come on, Fred. It's me, you're talking to."

"What are you getting at?" he asked seriously.

"I'm getting out how you have never had an accident since you have worked here. You have never been laid up at this estate," Catherine stressed strongly. "Then all of a sudden, you have to come clean about how you lost it and murdered Antonio! Now you're injured and cannot walk." She paced back and forth at the foot of the bed. "I know I'm coming on strong, but I have been going out of my mind climbing the walls wondering where you were. I thought you had left me to face the music on my own," Catherine said and then look toward Fred.

Fred was looking down as if he was in deep thought. But Catherine wondered why he didn't correct her and reassure her when she said she thought he had left her to face the music on her own. "Fred, did you hear what I just said?"

He glanced up with distraught eyes. "I'm sorry. What did you say?"

"I said, I thought you had skipped town and left me here to face the authorities on my own without your true confession."

Fred frowned. "I'm sorry I worried you," he protested. "But I couldn't help what happened."

Catherine threw up both hands. "Maybe you couldn't. But it seems so convenience for you, to say the least. Because when I left you at the lake house you were just fine. Plus, I was under the impression that you were going to follow me back to the estate at a distant. But I guess you changed your mind and decided you would take a walk instead."

Fred nodded. "That's exactly what happened. My plans were to follow you back. But I just couldn't. I needed to be alone and think for a while. I had made up my mind to do the right thing. But I still needed to think about it. That's when I decided to take a walk to clear my head. I walked and walked until I lost count of the time and before I realized it, it had gotten dark outside and I had no idea where I had wondered off to. My thoughts were all over the place and somehow I mis-stepped and injured my damn foot," he distraughtly grumbled. "As if I don't have enough problems." He raised both hands. "Now I'm laid up with a bum foot."

Catherine put both hands on her hips and stared at Fred with stress on her face. "Fred, things seem to be going from mad to worse." She shook her head in distress. "So, how bad off are you? What did the doctor say?"

"It's not as bad as it could have been."

Catherine shook her head. "Is that what he said?"

"No, the doctor didn't say that. That's what I'm saying. The doctor just said it sprang and told me I'll be off my feet for a while," Fred frowned in a frustrated voice. "But I'll tell you this much. I might have to hop around, but I be damn if I be laid up."

Catherine noticed the pair crutches near the bedside table. "I guess those are your temporary legs that you'll be getting around on." She pointed to the crutches.

He nodded. "Yes, those are my new pair legs for now," he said jokingly with a dry laugh.

"I'm glad one of us can find something to laugh about," Catherine grunted. "We are both in hot water if that slipped your mind."

Fred jaw dropped at Catherine's comment. "I know we are both in hot water and that wasn't laugh. You know as well as I do that I have nothing to laugh about. That was a damn frown turned upside down," he stressed. "I'm doing all I can to keep my composure under all this pressure." He held up both hands. "And no need to remind me that I drove myself into this horrific situation. But surely you can believe me when I say, I'm not really in a joking mood. I'm just trying not to crack under pressure," he firmly admitted.

She held up both hands. "Look, I don't want you to think I'm not compassionate about what has happened to you. I feel bad and I'm sorry you injured your foot. But your injury is temporary; and frankly, I'm too worried about the fate of my life to be too concerned about your foot right now. So, please just tell me," Catherine stressed. "I need to know if you're still turning yourself in as we discussed."

Fred nodded. "Yes, that's still the plan."

Catherine nodded. "Okay, if it's still the plan. When is your true confession to the family and the authorities supposed to take place? I seriously need to know since I'm in limbo and can't keep putting the family off. They want to take me to give my statement and I can't give my statement until I know what you're doing," she fussed.

Fred held up both hands. "Catherine, I still plan to do what I promised. However, I need to get my bearings and be on my own two feet when I come clean," he strongly stated.

Catherine shook her head in disappointment and turned her back to him and looked across the room toward the closed door. She felt stuck. She turned around to face him and inhaled sharply. "Okay, Fred. But I just hope the authorities doesn't figure out our involvement before we have the opportunity to go into headquarters on our own and give our statements," Catherine said and then quickly looked around toward the door.

They both could hear footsteps on the marble floor headed down the hallway coming in the direction of the ocean blue guest room where Fred was residing. They both kept their eyes glued to the door and then moments later someone knocked softly twice.

"Come in," Fred said.

The doorknob turned, and Mrs. Leola Bradley walked in carrying a tray of food. She seemed surprised to see Catherine standing there. "Hi Miss Catherine, Natalie asked me to bring up this lunch tray to Fred."

"That's fine, Leola. Is there a reason Natalie pulled you from your work to do her's?" Catherine asked, with crudeness. She wasn't normally rude or unkind to the staff. But her nerves were raw. She was running on empty with a lack of sleep and stressed to the limit with what she knew about Fred.

Leola stared humbly at Catherine but didn't comment as Catherine softened the frown on her wearily face. "I guess Natalie is busy with other work," Catherine commented in a softer tone. But she was hopeful that Leola would volunteer Natalie's whereabouts, since she was curious to why Natalie didn't bring a food tray up to her own husband.

Leola felt awkward as she walked across the large room and placed the food tray on the right bedside table. Then she stood next to the bedside table with her hands folded in front of her as she looked toward Catherine and slightly smiled. "Miss Catherine, Natalie is busy finishing up lunch for the family," Mrs. Bradley said as she glanced at her new Seiko watch, noting it was 11:30. "It's just thirty minutes before lunch is served. Remember, Helen isn't here. She works at Taylor Gowns during the day. She only works in the kitchen with Natalie for dinner preparations," Mrs. Leola Bradley reminded her.

Catherine nodded solemnly as Leola Bradley continued. "Besides, Miss Catherine, I don't know if you know, but everybody is home today."

"What do you mean everybody is home?" Catherine asked. She didn't notice any of the four brothers' cars when she arrived at the mansion. Then she thought they could have garaged them since they were home for the day.

"Mr. Rome and his brothers brought Fred here and we were told that they won't be going in to Franklin Gas today," Mrs. Bradley explained. "That's why Natalie hands are full. The original schedule was lunch for three, but it was changed at the last minute to seven. Then of course, she had to take time to prepare a lunch for Fred," Mrs. Bradley politely said as she headed across the room toward the door. When she grabbed the doorknob, she looked over her shoulder. "Miss Catherine, I almost forgot. Natalie is looking for you. Should I tell her you're in Fred's room?"

Catherine swallowed hard since she didn't expect Mrs. Bradley to be so talkative. She didn't want Natalie to know that she was in Fred's room. But she couldn't tell Mrs. Bradley not to relay her whereabouts. "Please do and would you please wait right outside the door," Catherine politely requested.

Catherine held up one finger to Fred letting him know that she would return to finish their discussion just as soon as she spoke to Mrs. Bradley. She quickly walked across the room and stepped outside into the hallway where Mrs. Bradley stood waiting for her.

"Leola, I mean this with the greatest respect. Please do not take orders or chores from any of the staff, especially Natalie," Catherine said politely. "I know you were only trying to be helpful, but Natalie is being paid to deliver food trays, not you. I have noticed that this isn't the first time that Natalie have had you do some of her work."

Mrs. Bradley didn't understand why it was such a big deal to Catherine that she had delivered a food tray to Fred. "Its okay, Miss Catherine. I didn't mind doing it."

"I know you didn't mind doing it, but I mind and don't want you doing other staff worker's work. You and Natalie both have worked here at Franklin House for many years and if Natalie feels she needs more help in the kitchen, all she has to do is just say the word. In the meantime, please don't do any more chores for other staff," Catherine firmly stated.

Mrs. Bradley nodded. "Okay, Miss Catherine. I'll do as you have requested," she said respectfully and then turned and headed down the long hallway toward the staircase.

Catherine stood there and watched as Mrs. Bradley walked down the hallway. She wasn't really looking at Mrs. Bradley, she was just standing there looking into space trying to put everything in perspective regarding her situation. Then she grabbed the doorknob, snatched the door open and stepped back into the guest room.

When Catherine stepped back into the room, Fred had a more alert look on his face as he sat up in the bed with the food tray on his lap. He was sitting there enjoying his egg salad sandwich, cup of chicken soup, cup of mix fruit and glass of milk.

"You're right Catherine," he said to her as she stood against the closed door with her hand on the doorknob.

"About what?" Catherine asked.

"About everything," he sadly mumbled. "While you were in the hallway with Leola, I thought about what you said. I have put you in a tough spot. The morning I stepped into Antonio Armani's hospital room and lost my head, I shot my life to hell!" he admitted in disgust. "Now I have you tagging alone." He looked don't at his tray of food on his lap and shook his head. "I'm so disgusted with myself. I have lost my appetite."

"Well find it. Fred, there's no time for self-pity! If I can stomach the pressure without sleep or a shower or a change of clothing on my back, I'm sure you can suck it up too!" Catherine strongly urged. "Besides, you need to eat for your strength and to keep a clear head of our debacle."

"I guess you're right. But I feel like I can't open my eyes from a disturbing nightmare. Yet, I know I have to do the right thing and get your neck off the chopping block and take my punishment." He lifted the glass of milk and took a sip. "I guess what bothers me the most is the disappointed faces I'll have to contend with, especially Natalie's and the Franklins."

Catherine glanced toward the ceiling and sighed. She looked toward Fred shaking her head. "That's a given. They'll all be shocked and disappointed just as I was when you confessed to me."

"Yes, that's a given that cannot be avoided," he said staring across the room into space for a moment. Then he looked at Catherine with sad eyes. "Nevertheless, the longer we hold off the greater the risk of everything hitting the fan without our input. Either way it looks bad for me. But it will really look bad for you as well if you don't reach out to the law before they reach out to you," Fred said as his slightly shaking hand lifted his glass of milk to his mouth as he slowly took another swallow.

"Fred, I'm glad you realize that. I stepped out of the room for a second and you wised up quick," Catherine said as a small smile showed at the corners of her mouth, relieved at what he had just said to her.

He nodded as he took a bite from his sandwich. He chewed his food and then placed the sandwich back on the dish. "Why are you standing against that door?" he asked.

"I can't visit you much longer. I have already been in here longer than I should. I won't be able to explain such a long visit here in your sick room. By-the-way, which you are not really ill. You just have a sprung ankle that you're not suffering any pain from."

"I was in a lot of pain before the doctor gave me that pain shot."

"I don't care how the pain left. My point is that you're not in pain or suffering." Catherine pointed out. "Besides, everyone knows there's no reason for me to hang out in your sick room longer than a few minutes."

"Don't fret about it," Fred suggested. "I doubt if anyone has time to give a rat's butt about how long you spend in this room."

Catherine stared at him with narrow eyes. "I beg to differ."

"Well, I still don't think you should worry about that. You're just wind up tight right now. Otherwise, you wouldn't worry about who's going to care or question you about how much time you spend in this room talking to me. You're my boss, remember? Maybe you have instructions for me that takes longer than a few minutes."

Catherine shook her head still leaning against door. "Fred, you would be surprised to know, who needs to know what. But I think you already know who I'm referring to."

He slowly lifted his glass to his mouth and took another swallow of milk. "I guess you are referring to Miss Veronica."

"Of course, I am. Believe it or not, she's my boss," Catherine said.

"What do you mean, she's your boss? You don't have a boss," Fred seriously reminded her.

"You're right. I don't actually have a boss," Catherine agreed. "Nevertheless, when you actually think about it, Veronica relationship toward me is not much different than a boss toward an employee."

Fred lifted his sandwich from the dish with both hands and took another bite as he looked toward Catherine. "She does control the money."

Catherine inhaled sharply. "Yes, that and she's the head of this house."

Fred nodded. "That is correct, and I guess you are concerned about her questioning you about spending so much time up here with me."

Catherine raised both hands. "I'm glad you finally get. That's exactly my concern. I can easily say I dropped in here to check on you. However, I can't explain away thirty minutes of hanging at your bedside. On that thought, I need to take off this instant."

Fred held up one finger and then placed his lunch tray to his right on the bedside table. "I'm afraid you can't leave just yet," he said humbly, looking in Catherine's eyes. "I haven't finished telling you what I decided."

"That's right, you haven't. But I guess I sort of assumed what you have decided since you said during the course of our conversation that you don't think it's wise to put this off. Plus, before I stepped into the hallway with Leola, it appeared you were about to tell me that you have taken a hold of your senses and don't plan to make me wait until your foot heals before you give your statement to the authorities."

Fred slowly nodded while looking down at his hands folded in front of him. "That's right, Catherine. While you were out there talking to Leola, I wake up to this disastrous situation that I created. The predicament I have put you in. I can't lie here in this immense fancy blue room and pretend all is well," he sadly stated as he shook his head. "My right foot is sprung but the rest of me is working just fine. Therefore, I think we should stick to the plan to do the right thing. You can let Miss Veronica and the four brothers know that you would like to give your statement here at the mansion."

Catherine nodded. "Okay, I'll do that. But what about you?"

"I'll be present in the room along with the rest of the staff and the Franklins; and after the authorities take your statement I'll speak up and allow them to take mine. Then it will all be over. You'll be able to rest at night and I'll be able to look myself in the mirror while I pray every day to be forgiven for my odious crime against another human being."

Chapter Four

The occupants of Franklin House were anxiously anticipating the arrival of the authorities who were due to arrive shortly after dinner. Catherine had asked for a family and staff meeting combined where she informed the family and the staff that she had asked Rome to request the authorities to Franklin House. She emphasized that she wanted all the family as well as all the staff present during her conversation with the authorities. She wanted everyone to hear her statement so there could be no misunderstanding or speculation about what she knew and the extent of her involvement. She explained to the staff that the statement she was giving contained important information regarding Antonio Armani's death and she wanted to relay everything she knew to law enforcement. She also shared that she had chosen to give her statement in the comfort of home because it would make her feel less nervous and more at ease to be surrounded by family.

Unbeknownst to the rest of the family, one of the main reasons Catherine had requested the authorities to Franklin House was for a convenience to Fred. He had promised to give his statement directly after her. Nevertheless, she didn't share that vital information with the family that Fred would be giving a statement. She didn't want the family to know Fred's dreadful crime until he was actually confessing it.

In privacy Veronica had called the Barrington Hills Police Department and asked the Police Commissioner, who she knew quite well, since they attended all the same fundraisers, to keep Catherine's statement out of the press. Although he couldn't ease her worries. He informed her that he would put forth the effort, but he couldn't promise since public statements couldn't be tucked away under lock and key. They had a way of taking on a life of their own and always ended up in the public domain. Therefore, Veronica sat boiling with private contempt for Catherine, beside herself with subdued anger over Catherine throwing the family in the middle of a possible scandal.

Noticing that the entire family seemed quieter than usual, and much aware of everyone's stress level due to the expected arrival of the law enforcement, Natalie served a very casual no fuss meal:

Home Baked Deep-Dish Pizza
Home Baked Thin Crust Pizza
Mixed Green Salad
Mixed Fruit Cup
Hot Tea, Iced Tea, Coffee and Coke

Catherine sat at the dinner table barely eating her meal as everyone around her appeared more at ease, enjoying their dinner. She poked in and out of her salad eventually eating all the cherry tomatoes, cranberries and slices cucumbers out of the salad. But she didn't touch the rest of the salad, and only took one bite from her slice of pizza as she sat there staring down in her dinner plate. She had a defeated look on her face as if she was moments away from shedding tears. Veronica glanced over at Catherine, noticing the weary look on Catherine's face and fidgeted dinner behavior, but didn't share much sympathy for Catherine since she was livid with Catherine for involving the family in such a predicament.

Although Catherine was surrounded by family that loved her dearly, she still felt alone since only she and Fred knew the entire story behind Antonio's murder. Therefore, she felt quite uneasy about giving her statement since it was no longer accurate that she didn't remember what happened. She recalled everything and knew it wasn't her who took Antonio's life. Yet, she had promised Fred that she would give her original statement and then he could give his statement afterward. She wondered could she keep her word, or would she tell the whole truth, which she actually wanted to do during the questioning. Deep down she wasn't sure what she would say until law enforcement questioned her.

Rome and Amber exchanged discreet looks among each other as they noticed Catherine's gloominess. Desperately wanting to lift his Aunt's spirits, Rome caringly looked across the table at his Aunt as he slowly lifted his glass to his mouth and took a sip of Coke. "Aunt Catherine, we know you're nervous, but just tell them exactly every single thing that you remember, and I believe everything will smooth out for you."

She nodded but didn't look toward Rome. She knew if she did what Fred had asked she wouldn't be completely honest. She was torn over her decision.

"We'll all be right there with you," Britain assured her, taking his knife and fork cutting the cherry tomato in his salad bowl in half. "They'll come take your statement and leave, and that will be that," he forked a piece of tomato into his mouth.

"What if they arrest me after I give my statement?" Catherine asked, looking toward Britain. "After hearing my statement, it does make me appear guilty." She pushed her plate aside and placed both elbows on the table to hold up her face.

"Aunt Catherine, if you are arrested and charged for something that we all know you couldn't have done. Their hold on you won't stick. Besides, we're banking on our attorneys to completely clear your name," Rome assured her. "I don't think and I'm sure no one else at this table think you'll be arrested. However, if it happens, we still don't want you to worry." Rome nodded toward Catherine. "I would be willing to state my professional reputation on the fact that you're hundred percent innocent of that heinous crime that befallen Mr. Armani." Rome said, exchanging looks with everyone at the table and then looked back at his Aunt. "Besides, no one at this table believes you are cable of such a horrendous crime."

"I just hate the thought of handcuffs and spending anytime in a jail cell," Catherine admitted as she wiped a tear from her right eye.

Veronica took a sip of hot tea, holding the cup with both hands. Then she placed the cup back on the table and looked toward Catherine with irritated eyes. "Catherine, could you please get a hold of yourself. You knew this was coming. Besides, at one point you were willing to throw your whole life away just to come clean to the authorities. So, could you please cut out the drama and deal with this debacle of your own making," Veronica said firmly, holding back her anger. "Do I need to remind you that you have involved this entire family in the middle of a situation you created? We're all here giving you support, and you need to collect yourself before the Officers arrive."

"That's true, Aunt Catherine," Sydney remarked. "If they see or sense extreme nervousness about you, it may not work in your favor."

"Otherwise, Catherine, if you don't pull it together and act like a grown up while the authorities are here questioning you, they could throw the book at you on suspicion," Veronica snapped of irritation, and then stopped herself, lifted her tea cup to her mouth and took another sip of tea while looking disappointedly across the table at Catherine.

Catherine looked across the table at Veronica with sad exhausted eyes. Although, she felt less irritable since in the midst of all the chaos of preparing for the house call from the police department, she had managed to grab a few minutes for a quick shower and a change of clothing before dinner. She held her head up straight and gave Veronica a serious stare. "I know this is a situation of my own making and I greatly realize how I have involved all of you in the middle." She glanced about the dinner table apologetically eying them all. "But at this point, all I can say from the bottom of my heart is how deeply sorry I am for suturing all of your lives in the middle of my debacle." She raised both hands and stared seriously at Veronica. "However, this is my neck on the chopping block and I get to be a basketcase. I'm only human and as of this evening my life may never be the same after I give my statement to the authorities," she firmly stated, and then looked toward Rome. "I know you and your brothers truly believe in my innocence and I believe in my own innocence. But it doesn't mean the authorities will."

Rome sympathetically nodded while looking toward his Aunt. "Aunt Catherine, we're painfully mindful of how sometime innocent people are found behind bars."

Veronica nodded as some of the anger and disgust for Catherine faded from her eyes. "Catherine, Rome has a point how innocence doesn't always find justice. And I guess you have a point about freaking out with everything that's on the line for you," Veronica said calmly. "But I'm pleased to finally hear you say that you believe in your own innocence. Up until now you never shared that you believed in your own innocence. Do you remember the events of that morning and now know it wasn't you who sneaked into Antonio's hospital room and committed that revolting crime?"

Catherine mouth fell open and she didn't know what to say to Veronica. She was on the spot, but she couldn't tell what she knew. It would blow Fred's cover. And just as Catherine went to comment, they all looked toward the double French doors as Natalie softly opened them and entered the dining room. She had an anxious look on her face as she headed across the dining room floor in the direction of Veronica's chair at the head of the table. She was walking quickly carrying the cordless house phone in her hand.

"Miss Veronica, I know you don't usually take calls during dinner, but this is an urgent call from the Barrington Hills Police Department," Natalie anxiously informed her as she passed Veronica the phone.

Chapter Five

Veronica put the phone to her ear as everyone at the dinner table looked toward her in wonder of why the Barrington Hills Police Department was calling. They all figured it probably had something to do with their expected visit from Officers Ford and Fields as they all paused with their meal until Veronica finished her phone call.

"That will be fine," Veronica said, slightly smiling. Then she hung up the phone and passed it to Natalie who stood behind her left shoulder.

Natalie took the phone and walked quickly out of the dining room to leave them to their meals. Veronica exchanged looks with everyone around the dinner table. "It was nothing really," she said casually. "The department just called to let us know that the two officers that are heading over to take Catherine's statement will not be arriving at 8:00 as they had original intended. They'll be arriving sometime between 8:15 and 8:30."

After the wearisome dinner was over and as they all headed out of the dining room, Paris glanced to his left as he was getting out of his chair and noticed Natalie at the serving counter. He casually walked across the room to the serving counter and tapped Natalie on the shoulder. "Natalie how are you?" he kindly asked, smiling.

"I'm fine, Mr. Paris," Natalie smiled up at Paris. "Is anything the matter?" she curiously asked, wondering why he had approached her.

He smiled. "Everything is fine. I just need your help with something if you're available," he politely said.

"Of course, I'm available. What do you need?"

"I was hoping you could assist me in pouring a glass of wine for everyone? We'll be gathering in the library awaiting the authorities."

Natalie smiled looked up at Paris and touched his arm. "Mr. Paris, you go right ahead with the rest of the family. I'll take care of the drinks," she nodded.

"I merely thought you could maybe assist me," he quickly replied. "You're busy with your chores and I don't want to take you away from your work," Paris kindly said.

"Mr. Paris, you're not taking me away from anything. I think you know how much I love my job; and waiting on your family is my job," she said laughingly. "Therefore, go right along in the library with the rest of your family. I'm aware how weary and on edge all of you probably are awaiting those dreadful cops to drop by," she thoughtfully said. "I'm right behind you, but I'll stop off in the living room to fetch the wine from the bar. I'll pour all of you a glass of wine to help you all relax," Natalie said, walking along side Paris.

"Thanks, Natalie," Paris said and then paused in his tracks. "After you serve the wine, please gather the rest of the staff and join us in the library before the authorities arrive," Paris said and then proceeded on to the library.

Natalie stopped in the living room at the bar and poured glasses of wine for them all. She placed the wine filled glasses on a serving tray and slowly made her way to the library. The two French doors were opened when she reached the library as she carefully carried the serving tray with both hands. She entered the library to find them all seated about the room. She carefully placed the long silver serving tray on top of the fireplace mantle and then proceeded to hand them each a glass of red wine. The four brothers, Veronica and Amber took their glasses and thanked Natalie. But Catherine took her glass and didn't look toward Natalie as she seemed preoccupied staring into space with worry. But Natalie was aware of Catherine's stress level over giving her statement. Therefore, Natalie gently patted Catherine on the back as she stepped away to head out of the room.

After Natalie left the room it dawned on Catherine that she had completely ignored Natalie. She shook her head, realizing she was absorbed in her misery and emotions of her situation. Plus, she was greatly concerned about the whereabouts of Fred. She looked all about the large room and noticed he wasn't presence in the library. She sipped her wine and paced about the room as everyone seemed collected sitting about on sofas and chairs. Although, she felt apprehensive about Fred keeping his word to show up and give his statement. Then it registered in her mind that the staff would join them shortly. Her mind eased when she figured Fred would show up in the room when the rest of the staff joined them. Catherine had specifically asked that all staff be present for the sake of it not appearing inappropriate to have Fred in the room without other staff members. Her nerves tightened when all staff joined them, and Fred was not in attendance.

It was 8:15 and Natalie had replaced all wine glasses with cups of hot tea along with a tray of lemon cookies on the coffee table. The Franklins and their staff sat sipping on tea and nipping on cookies while off and on glancing over at the two French doors. Finally, when the doorbell sounded they all sort of took a deep breath, sat up straight looking toward the two French doors with anticipation of what Catherine's fate would be after giving her testimonial. Dillion was waiting in the living room area to answer the door. He escorted the two officers through the big house into the library; and the moment he escorted them through the two French doors of the library, he immediately closed the doors and then showed them across the room to where Catherine was seated.

They all stood when Officer Fields and Ford stepped across the room among them. Rome reached out and shook their hands. "Thanks for coming at our request. We greatly appreciate you fitting us into your schedule," he glanced to his left to Catherine and nodded. "My Aunt Catherine especially thank you both for coming out to the house. She has a statement to make and was a bit apprehensive about doing so." Rome continued to look toward Catherine. "But she feels much more at ease here among family." Rome looked toward the two officers. "That's why your house call means a great deal to us."

"We were pleased to come at your request," Officer Fields said and then he exchanged looks with the other officer.

"Please take your seats," Officer Ford politely asked.

They all took their seats and Rome pointed toward two comfortable chairs that were placed out for the two officers. "Please be seated," Rome encouraged them.

Officer Ford glanced at his watch and then looked toward Rome. "Thank you, Mr. Franklin. But we won't be here long. We have another meeting that we need to get to when we leave here. Therefore, we'll get right to the point," Officer Ford said, looking toward Catherine.

"Miss Franklin, you are Catherine Franklin, is that correct?"

Catherine nodded. "Yes, I'm Catherine Franklin."

Officer Ford nodded and smiled. "I recognize you, Miss Franklin; and has gotten to know all of you great people quite well," he said politely. "Yet, do to protocol, I had to ask you to acknowledge your identity."

Catherine nervously smiled. "I understand."

"Anyway, as we said. We won't keep you good people long," he said looking in Catherine's eyes. "We must ask you if your pending statement have anything to do with the murder case of Antonio Armani."

Catherine nodded nervously. "Yes, Officer Ford it does."

Catherine stood before the officers beside herself with nerves as she secretly with boiling anger wondered where Fred had taken off to. He had promised to gather with them when the authorities arrived. She discreetly inhaled sharply wondering why the officer had asked her that question.

Officer Ford and Fields exchanged looks and nodded at each other, then they looked at Catherine. "We saw your name on the list as one of the visitors at the hospital that morning. That's why we figured your request to give a statement was probably in regard to that case. But listen up good people." Officer Ford exchanged looks with all the Franklins and the staff as he raised both hands. "We appreciate your willingness to get involved with the community and tell us what you know regarding this case. And don't think you wasted our time. We didn't mind making the trip over here. However, we are here to relay that we closed the Antonio Armani case earlier today."

Catherine discreetly grabbed her mouth with both hands to keep from shouting in excitement. For a second, she thought she had not heard Officer Ford correctly, but as she kept looking at the officer and listening, she realized she had heard him correctly. However, that realization caused her to breakout into an instant sweat as she inhaled sharply wondering if Fred had made his way to the authorities to confess and were now in custody. She folded her arms across her waist and shivered at the thought of Fred going solo to the authorities against their original plan. Catherine was worried how the news of his crime could blindside the family if it came out in that way. Although, she figured if he had gone to the authorities it would explain his absence. He had promised to be at the gathering to confess and give his statement directly after she had given hers. But he had not shown up. Catherine wondered, but thought better of that idea. She knew the officers knew that Fred was their chauffeur. Therefore, it dawned on her that they would share the news with the family if by chance they had Fred in custody. But Catherine stood there on pins and needles waiting for Officer Ford to share more information.

Rome stepped forward and reached for Officer Ford hand to shake it again. "Thanks again for making the trip here out of courtesy. We greatly appreciate your efforts."

"Don't mention it Mr. Franklin. We know we didn't have to make the drive out. But we chose to do it out of courtesy for your family. We wanted to show our appreciation for your involvement. Besides, one favor deserves another. We greatly appreciate your family continued generous donations to the precinct."

"We're pleased to help," Britain said, as he Paris and Sydney stepped over to shake the two officers' hands. "We're pleased you were able to close the case," Paris said.

Officer Ford nodded with a pleased look on his face. "Yes, we caught a break this afternoon when the person who murdered Mr. Antonio Armani came forward on her own and confessed to the crime."

Catherine swallowed hard as her heart raced to hear it was a female. She was especially relieved that it wasn't Fred in Custody. But she was still uneasy and didn't feel out of the woods. She knew that Fred had confessed to the murder. So, she couldn't feel comfortable even though someone else had confessed to the murder. She felt herself trembling from nerves and didn't want to appear too suspicious in the officers' presence. So, she took a deep breath and tried to gather her composure as she glanced over at Veronica who caught her glance. She noticed the relieved look on Veronica's face.

Veronica stepped forward and shook the officers' hands. "Officer Ford and Fields, as my sons just said. We greatly appreciate your efforts to drop by to let us know the case is closed," Veronica smiled. "I cannot tell you how relieved we all are to hear this news. Because it's absolutely great news that you have finally apprehended the person who killed my ex-brother-in-law?"

"Yes, Mrs. Franklin. We're at liberty to say the case is closed. Plus, the person apprehended is a female that we have in custody. However, that's where our shared information ends," Officer Fields stated.

"However, I will share this one bit of information. Pretty much every word of the statement of the person being held is going to make the front page of the local news. She gave her full statement to ABC news." Officer Fields exchanged looks with Officer Ford and then paused before he spoke.

"It turns out it was a nurse on duty who was involved with the deceased. She came forward this afternoon and confessed to her crime of fatally stabbing Mr. Armani too death." Officer Fields paused and exchanged looks with Officer Ford, who looked at him for a moment, then nodded his approval.

Then Officer Fields nodded toward everyone and held up one finger. "So, it appears we have decided to enlighten you further into the case."

Veronica nodded. "Thank you. We'll appreciate whatever information you are allowed to share with us."

The two officers exchanged looks with each other again, as if they were debating whether to share their information with the Franklin family. But Officer Fields nodded. "Yes, Mrs. Franklin, we know your family has suffered over who took the life of your sister-in-law's ex-husband. Therefore, we'll share with you that the nurse who confessed to taking Mr. Armani's life, declared in her statement that the murder weapon was found onsite in Mr. Armani's hospital room; and she admitted to a motive of retribution vengeance against lies and stolen money along with broken promises made by the deceased that he would marry her, and they would leave town together."

Chapter Six

During breakfast on Saturday morning, Catherine appeared more at ease with obvious lightness about her that a heavy burden had been lifted off of her shoulders." She picked up her butter knife and tapped it against her water glass. She had a relieved look on her face as she exchanged looks with everyone at the table. "Listen up everyone. Now that the real killer is behind bars, I have something I need to tell all of you," Catherine seriously stated and then looked at Veronica. "I know I should have mentioned this before now and it will come to all of you as a shock, but Fred asked me not to say anything."

Veronica eyes widened with surprise and suspicion. "Catherine, what should you have mentioned? What does Fred have to do with it?"

Just then, Natalie rolled the serving cart into the room and as she placed a platter of blueberry wafflers on the table, she had a solemn look on her face.

"Natalie is anything the matter?" Veronica asked. "You seem sad and not quite like yourself this morning."

Natalie placed a pitcher of orange juice on the table and stepped over to the serving cart and looked down at the large bowl of mix fruit.

"Natalie, I asked if everything is okay," Veronica insisted.

Natalie lifted the bowl of fruit and placed it on the table and then wiped both hands on her apron. "I'm okay, Miss Veronica."

"Pardon my assumption, but you don't look okay," Veronica told her.

Natalie held up both hands. "You're right, Miss Veronica. I'm really not okay; and I might as well tell you and the family what's going on," Natalie sadly mumbled, looking toward Veronica.

Sydney held his knife and fork about to cut a portion of his waffler but seeing the crushed look in Natalie's eyes and hearing the sadness in her voice, he placed his silverware back on the table and placed his focused-on Natalie.

"Natalie, you have us all concerned right now," Sydney caringly commented. "What happened to put such a dim look on your face?" Sydney asked.

She took the back of her hand and wiped a tear. "It's Fred."

"What about Fred, is his foot in a lot of pain?" Sydney asked.

Natalie took the back of both hands and continued to dry her falling tears. "No, Mr. Sydney. It's not his foot; and I really appreciate your concern. But there's nothing anyone can do to fix this."

"What is it, Natalie?" Veronica asked. "What needs fixing?"

"Fred left me," Natalie sadly informed them.

"What do you mean, he left you?" Veronica quickly asked. "His foot is sprung, and he can't even walk, but he has left you?" Veronica inquired.

Natalie collected herself and grabbed the handle of the serving cart. "Yes, he left me. We've been having some problems. But he never gave me any indication that he was thinking about leaving. It's a complete surprise to me and I wouldn't believe it myself if he hadn't left a note telling me his plans to catch the 8:00 o'clock train to Las Vegas. He emphasized in the note that he no longer wanted the marriage. Then in his last sentence he asked me not to bother contacting him since it was impossible for him to return to Franklin House." Natalie raised both hands. "Whatever that is supposed to mean."

Everyone at the breakfast table exchanged looks of surprise. Veronica felt it defiled logic and was completely out of character for Fred. "Natalie, we are deeply sorry Fred left you so abruptly. It just doesn't sound like Fred."

"I'm sad, Miss Veronica. But I realize marriages breakup all the time."

"Yes, they do. But, I'm referring to his actions and method. He has always been dependable for years. It's hard to believe he just packed up and left you and his job without the courtesy of resigning or talking to me or one of my sons," Veronica said confused as Natalie stood motionless with sad eyes.

"I know Miss Veronica. Helen and I are stunned by his actions," Natalie sadly admitted as she slowly rolled the serving cart out of the dining room.

They all had stunned looks on their faces but stayed mum as they busied themselves with their meals. Then Paris looked to his right at Sydney who sat next to him. He knew how close Sydney was to Natalie and it moved him to see how visibly disturbed Sydney was by Natalie's news. He discreetly watched as Sydney pushed his uneaten plate aside and lifted his orange juice glass to his mouth to take a swallow.

Then Paris looked toward the head of the table at his mother and caught her attention. Veronica lifted her coffee cup and was about to take a sip but placed it back on the table when she noticed Paris looking toward her about to say something. "Mother, something doesn't add up with the sad news Natalie just dropped on all of us."

"I agree," Sydney quickly added. "This all strike me as odd."

Veronica nodded. "I think we are all in accords; and I'm sure it doesn't add up to any of us at this table. Fred is one of the most reliable individuals I know. It just doesn't make sense and defiles logic that he would take off without personally letting any of us know that he was leaving the premises and his job," Veronica sighed.

"Natalie did say he left her because he no longer wanted the marriage. Maybe he didn't really leave his job and plan to notify someone about his plans to work and live off the premises," Amber suggested as she placed a piece of waffler in her mouth.

Rome turned to wife and nodded as he tapped the top of her hand. "Your theory is as good as any. But it still doesn't sound like Fred. Regardless to the trouble in his marriage. It's not like him to be irresponsible and leave his job high and dry. Plus, to do it in such a desperate sneaky way," Rome explained to Amber as he reached out, lifted the orange juice pitcher and poured juice into his glass. "Bottomline, what Natalie just walked in here and told us about Fred and how he left here without a word to anyone just doesn't add up."

Catherine took her fork and tapped it on her juice glass and they all immediately looked curiously toward Catherine. She looked toward Amber and Rome and nodded. "Rome, your bottomline is right. It doesn't add up and it's not like Fred. And I'm sure Natalie realizes that something is off with what Fred has done. His foot is seriously injured, and he can barely get around even with the crutches. But at this particular time, he decides to take off across country to explore a new life. And keep in mind, if you will." Catherine lifted her coffee cup to her mouth and took a sip, then placed the cup back on the table. "Fred is doing this without his final paycheck or one word to his boss." Catherine slightly shook her head. "This has desperation written all over it."

Veronica held up one finger. "Catherine, we are all in accord with you. We know it's a desperate act on Fred's part. But it's not going to do any of us any good right now to spoil our breakfast trying to puzzle our brains as to what could be going on with Fred. But make no mistake, we will get to the bottom of this," Veronica said assuredly.

After Veronica spoke, they all nodded and dug back into their breakfast. But Catherine wasn't done. "Excuse me, but I have something more to say." Catherine took her fork and tapped it on her juice glass again.

Veronica was annoyed how Catherine was disturbing everyone's meal. "Catherine, please just let it go for now. We all feel just awful about what's going on with Natalie and Fred. But we don't need to puzzle our brains at this moment to figure it all out," Veronica firmly stated.

"Just give me a moment. What I need to say is vitally important and we don't have to puzzle our brains," Catherine anxiously said. "This is what I was about to say before Natalie brought in the rest of the food. Remember, I was about to say something to the family when Natalie walked in?" Catherine looked toward Veronica.

Veronica nodded. "Yes, we remember. Just say what you need to say."

"Well, what I need to say and what I was about to say before Natalie walked into the room is about Fred. I'm not surprised he took off the way he did. I wondered about him when the authorities showed up last night. I was disappointed that he wasn't around after he had promised to be. It makes sense to me now why he didn't show up."

"Catherine, what is this all about?" Veronica firmly asked. "Apparently, you know something that the rest of us don't. So, spill right now."

"That's what I'm trying to do," Catherine sighed impatiently as she stared toward Veronica. "If you'll just please allow me to finish speaking."

"Sure, go on. You have everyone's attention," Veronica stiffly uttered.

"Fred didn't want to leave Natalie or Franklin House," Catherine seriously relayed as she exchanged looks with everyone at the breakfast table. "Believe me, he left because he felt he had too," Catherine admitted.

"Aunt Catherine, what is this all about?" Sydney was very curious. "Why did he feel that way? Did Fred tell you he was breaking up with Natalie and quitting his job?"

Catherine shook her head. "No, he didn't tell me that," she said, suddenly feeling uneasy about sharing everything that needed to be told.

"Maybe he didn't tell you that. But it's apparent he shared some information with you," Veronica curiously inquired. "You seem to know why he left these premises. So, did he tell you what was going on with him?" Veronica firmly asked.

Catherine nodded. "Yes, Fred told me what was going on."

"He told you, but apparently not his wife," Veronica quickly added.

"It was a reason for that. He confessed to me," Catherine said in a low voice as she looked down in her breakfast plate, feeling more and more uneasy about sharing Fred's secret that they both had kept from the family.

"He confessed what to you, Catherine?" Veronica insisted.

Catherine kept looking down in her plate and didn't comment. She kept weighing her options, wondering if sharing the information was the best choice to make.

"Catherine, I asked you a question. Did Fred share with you that he was quitting his job and leaving his wife?" Veronica strongly inquired.

Catherine stared at Veronica and discreetly shook her head. Then she inhaled sharply. "No, Veronica. Fred didn't tell me anything like that. I had no idea he was thinking about quitting his job or leaving Natalie."

"Okay, if he didn't confess that, what did he confess that makes you feel you know why he up and left these premises?" Veronica firmly asked.

"Yes, Aunt Catherine, we are all wondering what he said to you," Sydney politely commented. "Your exact words were: Fred didn't want to leave Natalie or Franklin House, but left because he felt he had too," Sydney reminded her of what she had said to them.

Catherine sadly looked toward Sydney. "I'm sorry to tell you this, Sydney and I'm sorry to tell all of you this. Because it's really awful news and there's no soft way to put it." Catherine took her napkin and wiped her mouth. By now, she had them all at the edge of their seats waiting to hear what she had to say about Fred. Sydney heart raced hoping it wasn't too disturbing.

Then all eyes were on Catherine when she held up both hands. "Everybody, I'm sorry to say, but Fred confessed to me that he went into Antonio's hospital room and stabbed him to death."

After a moment of silence, Veronica asked irritated and confused. "What are you talking about, Catherine? You mean, Fred confessed to murder? The very same murder that you thought you had committed?"

Catherine nodded. "I know it sounds crazy, but yes. He actually thought he killed Antonio. He has been consumed with guilt and in a bad way ever since that morning."

"But Aunt Catherine, if he told you this, that would have put you in the clear," Rome quickly interjected. "Is there a reason why you didn't mention any of this?" Rome exchanged looks with his brothers and then looked at Amber with confused eyes.

They were all stunned and confused by the information that Catherine was relaying to them.

Veronica shook her head. "Yes, Catherine, why are we just hearing something like this? You were walking around in the dumps thinking you had murdered the man but had somehow forgotten. Now, on the other hand, you tell us that our very own trusted chauffeur had confessed to you that he murdered your ex-husband," Veronica sighed.

"This is all quite unbelievable," Amber stated, shaken by the news.

Rome turned to Amber and touched her arm. "Are you okay, Sweetheart?"

Amber nodded. "Yes, I'm okay. I'm just stunned to hear this."

"I'm sure you are," Rome softly said as he reached in her lap, grabbed her hand and held it firmly. "We're all stunned to hear such news about Fred."

"Yes, it's very unbelievable," Veronica agreed. "However, none of this non-sense leaves this room. Although, they have the actual killer behind bars, just a hint of this would make for sensational press."

"I agree with that," Catherine nodded. "I can see the headlines displaying me and Fred as two assumed murders moonlighting at the Franklin mansion."

"Catherine, please. This is no joking matter. I'm actually highly disappointed in you. I'm sure your nephews are as well, that you would keep a major secret as this from the family. Especially with how we were all so worried about you. Because when Fred confessed to killing a man, you assumed at the time that his confession was valid. You had no way of knowing that he hadn't actually killed anyone. Therefore, when he confessed that to you, you should have confided in all of us right away. As much as we care about Fred, he wouldn't have been welcomed here in our home as a cold-blooded killer. What you did at the time was criminal by keeping his secret. Furthermore, you put this entire family in danger," Veronica fussed.

"How do you figure that?" Catherine asked.

"Catherine, I'm sure you know a tad about the law. The part where protecting a criminal from the authorities, is called aiding and abiding which is also a crime. Plus, when I say you put us all in danger, it simply means, what if Fred had snapped and was no longer aware of right and wrong. We all could have been in danger as you sat on his secret!" Veronica firmly said.

Catherine wiped tears from her eyes. "I feel awful about not mentioning his confession. But he was scared, and he asked me to keep his secret."

"Of course, he was scared and asked you to keep his secret. He didn't want to face the music for his crime," Veronica snapped. "You could have promised him that you would keep his secret, but then you should have made a beeline here to tell us. Because if all this had turned out to be true, Fred would have needed our help personally and professionally; and maybe he wouldn't be on the run right now."

"I wanted to tell you guys, but I didn't have the guts. He had confessed to me that he lost his head and stabbed Antonio because he was thinking of me. He said he followed me that morning because he had a feeling that I was headed to the hospital to harm Antonio after he spied me taking the knife from the kitchen. Apparently, he saw when I dropped the knife and he grabbed it and rushed into Antonio's room to do what he thought I had intentions of doing," Catherine regretfully explained.

"I have never heard anything as stupid as what you are saying," Veronica fussed.

"It might sound stupid, but it's what he told me. Besides, I was shaken and afraid for myself. Therefore, I was quite relieved when Fred confessed to a crime that I thought I had committed. His confession took a lot off of my shoulders and in a weird way I was thankful to him. Therefore, the last thing I was thinking about was turning him in. I knew he needed to face his crime and punishment, but he had convinced me that he would do just that. He is the main reason why I asked for the authorities to come here to the house. Fred had promised to give his statement after I gave mine. He especially asked me not to mention his name to the authorities during my statement, because he had promised to give a statement right after me."

Britain nodded. "That's too bad that he took off like that."

"Yes, it is too bad. But he took off because he got cold feet and had no idea that he was in the clear. At least with me, I could have gotten off on an insanity plea. But Fred was looking at first degree," Catherine pointed out. "That's why he got cold feet and sneaked out of the house and hopped a train to Nevada." Catherine held up both hands. "Good for me that they found the real killer. Otherwise, Fred left me holding the bag."

"Aunt Catherine, it is so hard to wrap my head around that kind of confession from Fred," Paris said looking toward his Aunt.

"I know it sounds crazy, but Fred honestly confessed and thought he had murdered Antonio. He was dead serious when he confessed to me. He told me that he found the knife I dropped and then he went into Antonio's room and stabbed him."

Sydney shook his head in distraught. "This is too unreal for words. Fred confessed to murder? Natalie will be devastated when she finds out." Sydney looked toward Catherine. "It doesn't sound like Fred and besides from that, what reason did he have to harm Antonio Armani?"

"I'm sorry to say, but Fred didn't have a motive to harm Antonio. His excuse to me was that he was doing it to help save me from myself. He thought I would find the knife and attempt to stab Antonio. He felt I would be throwing my life away. He stepped in for me and put his own livelihood at risk. But based on the reports, he apparently stabbed Antonio's pillow and not him. Now, he's on a train to Las Vegas, Nevada away from his family and job for something he thinks he has done."

"Maybe he didn't do it. But the facts remain that he attempted to do it or thought he did it," Veronica firmly pointed out. "That disturbing, very alarming fact doesn't sit well with me regarding one of my employees," Veronica sharply stated.

"It's a big mess but you shouldn't blame Fred. You should just blame me. If I hadn't lost my head and took a knife to the hospital in the first place, Fred wouldn't be in this predicament right now," Catherine humbly admitted.

"Catherine, as much as I would like to agree with you and throw all the blame for all of this mess on your shoulders, I cannot blame you for it all. Fred Madden is a grown man and you didn't hold a gun to his head forcing him to take the actions he took. He made a choice to break the law without the forethought of the possibility of any repercussions," Veronica seriously stated.

"I know you are right. But I still feel like I'm the blame for his troubles. He got sucked into my mess and if anything happens to him while he's on the run like this, it will be my fault for putting all of this chaos in motion." Catherine wiped a tear with her napkin.

"Don't worry, Aunt Catherine," Paris said. "We'll find Fred and get him back home."

Catherine solemnly looked toward Paris. "That's admiral of you guys to want to do so." She held up both hands. "But none of us know exactly where he is. All we know is what he said in the note he left for Natalie."

"That's true, Aunt Catherine. However, it is a start. We know that apparently he took a train to Las Vegas, Nevada," Sydney added. "We'll try to trace his steps from there."

Paris lifted his orange juice glass and took a sip. "Of course, we realize it's not going to be easy to figure out his exact destination once he's in Las Vegas. But somehow, we'll find Fred and get him back here to Natalie and his job where he belongs."

Rome nodded. "Yes, we'll make whatever calls necessary and then we'll take the same route and try to trace Fred's footsteps to catch up with him."

"Why do you need to take a train? I do not like that idea at all. Just call or text Fred and let him know that all is well," Veronica suggested.

"Mother, we have to think like Fred," Britain quickly uttered, feeling quite anxious. "I'm sure he won't be answering any calls or text messages from any of us. Stating the real killer has been apprehended will just make him think it's a ploy to lure him back into the custody of the authorities. Therefore, I think we should take the first available plane to Las Vegas. We'll arrive in Las Vegas before Fred's train," Britain said, looking toward Rome.

"That's a genius idea and it sounds perfect," Sydney said, nodding toward his mother. "That will give us plenty of time to land in Las Vegas and make a beeline to the train station and be there waiting for Fred's arrival."

"Smart thinking," Rome agreed, exchanging looks with Sydney and Britain. "Arriving at the Las Vegas's train station before Fred's train arrives is an excellent idea; and most likely our best way of catching him before he gets absorbed and lost into the city."

Veronica nodded with relieved eyes. "That sounds more like a feasible plan that could actually work if all is as it seems. Meaning, if Fred actually took a train to Las Vegas." She lifted her coffee cup and took a sip with a weary look on her face. "But in all likelihood, I'm sure he probably did since he went through the trouble of leaving Natalie that note," Veronica said assuredly. "Now, the way it stands with the four of you taking the first flight out to Las Vegas, the odds are in our favor of locating Fred, updating him on the Antonio case and then getting him back here to Franklin House where he belongs."

Rome leaned over and kissed the side of Amber's face, then nodded toward his mother and glanced at his watch. "We need to get to the airport as soon as possible." He stood from his seat, exchanging looks with his brothers.

Britain and Paris quickly took last sips of juice, water and coffee and then took their napkins and wiped their hands and mouths before getting out of their seats to leave the breakfast table. Sydney stayed seated and quickly typed a text message to Starlet:

Good Morning, Miss Precious,

I hope your morning is starting out well. My morning just hit an unexpected turn of events. Everything that was on my agenda for today has been wiped clean and will have to be rescheduled. Therefore, my plans to get away to the lake house just fell through as well. As vital as my get-a-way is, an urgent family matter just literally popped up during breakfast that cannot be rescheduled or ignored. At the moment, I'm just finishing up breakfast and about to head upstairs to pack an overnight bag to take off to Las Vegas with my brothers. This is a vitally important trip. I'll fill you in on the matter when I return, which should be tomorrow, if all goes as planned.

Just an update on my retreat: I still plan to proceed with my plans. Probably within a couple days of my return of this trip. Although, I really need the retreat, this delicate family emergency is something I wasn't willing to let my brothers handle without my assistance.

Love, Sydney.

After Sydney hit the send button on his phone, he glanced up and nodded toward his mother. "I just sent Starlet a quick note to let her know the retreat at the lake house is off for now," he said standing from his seat and heading toward the head of the table to his mother's chair.

"That's right, you were planning to head up there today," Veronica recalled. "I know this is something that you feel you need to do, but the fact that it's delayed is okay with me; and I'm sure it will be okay with Starlet. I do not want you up at that lake house in isolation," Veronica stressed with concern. "Now that your plans have been delayed, I seriously hope you'll reconsider your retreat location."

"Mother, I seriously don't think I'll do that. However, I understand your concerns and I will think about it. But I'm making no promises that I'll change my retreat location. Right now, the lake house seems like my best bet for complete solitude," he kindly uttered.

"I hope your brothers or Starlet can talk you out of trying to rough it during your retreat. I agree and understand you need this time away from the family, so you can think and put things in perspective," Veronica sincerely uttered. "But during your retreat I want you to be able to free your thoughts and get some relaxation."

"Mother, I'm sure I'll get some relaxation at the lake house," Sydney said.

"Sweetheart, I seriously doubt you'll receive any relaxation according to your agenda. If you insist on staying at the lake house for several days on your own, fending for yourself. You'll be tackling unchartered waters and unfamiliar territory. You'll have to make your own meals, make your own bed and wash your own clothes. If it gets too cool out, you'll have to make your own fire," Veronica solemnly explained as she slowly lifted her coffee cup to her mouth and took a sip of coffee. "You have never done any of those things."

Sydney stood there smiling down at his mother. "Mother, I love you for your concern. But you worry too much. Maybe, I haven't done any of those things, but I don't think I need a lesson in housekeeping to feed and care for myself for a few days," he said jokingly. "I think I'll survive."

"You shouldn't have to survive. You should take a normal retreat where you can think and relax at some decent resort. That resort in Hawaii that your father and I used to visit before any of you were born," Veronica suggested.

"Mother that resort may not still be in operation if it was that long ago," Sydney politely said as he glanced over his shoulder toward the exit.

"That was quite a number of years. But, I do believe they are still in operation," Veronica quickly said, hopeful that he was showing some interest in her idea of a resort. "I wouldn't mind calling and booking a stay for you."

Sydney shook his head. "No, Mother, please don't. I haven't decided to give up the notion of the lake house yet. I still might very well retreat there. However, as I promised, in the meantime, I will give it some thought about another retreat location." He leaned down and kissed the side of his mother's face. "I need to get upstairs and pack my overnight bag, so I can be ready when my siblings are ready to head to the airport," he said glancing at his watch.

"Sweetheart, before you leave the dining area, I would just like to thank you for accompanying your brothers on this last-minute unexpected trip to look for Fred. I greatly appreciate you cancelling your retreat to take this trip with your brothers, since I realize just how important your plans were to you," Veronica softly uttered as she patted his arm.

"Thanks, Mother, but you don't have to thank me. This is something I want to do. I wouldn't feel comfortable allowing Rome, Britain and Paris to take the trip without me."

"I just wanted you to know that I realize how important your plans were and that you wanted to start your retreat today. Plus, I know you made a special visit to Starlet last night to inform her that your retreat would start today," Veronica acknowledged.

Sydney smiled. "Yes, Mother, those were my plans. But locating Fred and getting him back to Franklin House is a vitally urgent matter at the moment," he said as he leaned down and kissed the side of her face again and then headed out of the dining room.

Midway out of the room, Sydney glanced over his shoulder and waved goodbye to Catherine and Amber and then swiftly headed across the floor toward the double French doors to exit the dining room. He walked promptly down the hallway to the living room and hurried across the living room floor toward the staircase. Then he dashed up the staircase and down the hallway to his room to quickly pack an overnight luggage. Afterwhich, with overnight bags in all of their hands, Sydney and his brothers met in the library for a conference call. They spoke with Rome's assistance as well as Rome's secretary and informed them of their overnight trip out of town on a family matter. They informed the two staff persons that they would not be back into the office until Tuesday. They also informed them that Sydney's agenda hadn't changed. He was still on an indefinite work leave until further notice.

After they ended the conference call, a substitute limousine driver was ready and waiting and took the four of them to O'Hare Airport.

Chapter Seven

Ten minutes after the limousine carrying the four brothers pulled out of the driveway, Catherine, Veronica and Amber were still at the breakfast table.

"Catherine, before the police informed us that someone confessed to killing Antonio, I understand why you thought you could have murdered him and blocked it out. But I guess I'm still unclear on why Fred thought he had murdered Antonio?" Amber asked.

Catherine could sense how confused and shaken Amber seemed about the news regarding Fred. "I'm sure it's all quite confusing. But he told me that he found the knife I dropped and then he went into Antonio's room and stabbed him in order to do me a favor."

"But why would Fred do something like that?" Amber was bewildered. "He seems so mild-mannered and easy-going."

Catherine nodded. "He is mild-mannered and easy-going. He just got caught up in my craziness."

"That may be so." Amber discreetly shook her head. "Yet, Fred doesn't strike me as a vehement person who could harm anyone." Amber looked toward Catherine. "Besides, what motive would he have had to want to harm your ex-husband?" Amber perplexedly inquired, quite shaken by Fred's action.

Catherine took her napkin and wiped her mouth and hands and just as she was about to reply to Amber's question, Amber looked at Catherine and raised one finger as she lifted her coffee cup and took a small sip of coffee. "No need to answer that question. I guess this is all sort of moot since we know Fred really didn't harm anyone. But it's eerie that he attempted to and thought he had," Amber softly commented.

"I agree with you, Amber." Veronica nodded toward Amber. "It's extremely eerie. Therefore, Fred will have a lot of explaining to do and face much scrutiny by me before he'll be allowed to remain on here as our chauffeur," Veronica stated assuredly as she lifted the coffee pot and poured more coffee into her cup. "The authorities may have a confession out of the real killer, but I have a problem with the fact that Fred, while in his right mind was willing to take someone's life in cold blood."

Amber raised one finger. "Excuse me, Mrs. Franklin," Amber said browsing through her smart phone. "I'm looking for the local news about Antonio's murder. The two officers stated last night that the person's statement would make the morning news. It will most likely explain what happened and we won't have to speculate," Amber said as she clicked through her phone for the local news.

She smiled. "I just pulled it up."

"That's good," Veronica said as she held her coffee cup to her mouth, sipping her coffee slowly. "Please, read it aloud to us, dear."

Amber nodded. "Sure, I'll be glad to read it aloud."

The Northwest Herald reports:

On Friday, May 23, 2014 at 1:30 pm in the afternoon, Nurse Jessica Hanes confessed to first degree murder of Antonio Armani. Nurse Jessica Hanes who were on duty at Barrington Hills Memorial the morning Antonio Armani were stabbed in his sleep, made her way to the Barrington Hills Police Department and confessed of her own free will to the cold-blooded murder of Antonio Armani. She stated that she killed him over a love affair that went terribly wrong after she learned that Mr. Armani had planned to leave town with another woman other than herself. She was under the assumption that she and Mr. Armani would leave town together and be married. She admitted that what drove her to her confession were the many sleepless nights and the fact that she had become suicidal and feared for her life. She admitted that she could no longer live with herself for taking the life of the man she loved. She chose to bypass a trial by jury and asked to be sentenced and sent straight to prison. Her request comes on the heels of another resident, Raymond Ross who also requested to bypass a trial by jury for the charge of two counts of attempted murder of his wife, Mildred Ross and Antonio Armani. Mr. Ross was sentenced and sent straight to prison as he requested.

Jessica Hanes confessed that she was so enraged with disillusion after learning of Mr. Armani's plans that when she walked into his hospital room and found a pillow on his chest with a butcher knife sticking out, she immediately thought he had been killed. Then she lifted the pillow and pulled the knife from the pillow and noticed that Mr. Armani was very much alive lying asleep in his hospital bed. In one quick mad rage she took the knife with both hands and repeatedly stabbed Mr. Armani. Afterwhich, she took a Kleenex and alcohol from the bedside table and wiped the handle of the knife and then dropped it on the floor. She then screamed at the top of her lungs and other hospital staff rushed to Mr. Armani's room to find Nurse Jessica standing over Mr. Armani dead bloody body screaming with both hands holding her cheeks. She stated that she gave a false statement and said she had walked into the room and found him in his deadly state. The authorities found her original false statement believable, and Nurse Jessica may have escaped her crime and punishment if her conscience and ethics hadn't taken control and forced her to confess."

After Amber read the news report, Veronica looked toward Catherine and shook her head. "It's unbelievable the life Antonio Armani led. I'm not a bit surprised that a woman ended up taking his life. He didn't seem to have a heart where they were concerned."

"He had a heart for one," Amber commented. "Apparently he was deeply in love with Courtney and Kenny Ross's mother."

Silence fell over the breakfast table for a moment, and then Amber realized that her comment could have bothered Catherine. "Aunt Catherine, I hope I didn't offend you by saying Mr. Armani loved the Ross lady."

Catherine shook her head and smiled toward Amber. "The truth is the truth. My head is no longer in the sand. He always loved Mildred Ross. I just never wanted to accept or admit it," Catherine glumly mumbled.

To break the tension, Veronica lifted the meal bell and then exchanged looks with Amber and Catherine. "Would either of you care for more coffee or juice? I'll ring Natalie to bring in a fresh pot of coffee and more juice."

Amber politely shook her head and held up her coffee cup. "I'm still working on my first cup. This will do me for now."

Catherine held up her cup. "I'm good too. Besides, if I put anymore caffeine in my stomach I'll be climbing the walls," she said edgily.

"Okay, I won't ring for Natalie. We'll finish up and get dressed for the fundraiser at noon," Veronica reminded them. "Besides, when the fellows took off it put a damper on our meals and I've pretty much lost my desire for food."

"I have lost my appetite as well," Amber said looking across the table at Veronica. "Plus, the thought of Rome and the others all hopping a plane together makes me sick in the pit of my stomach. I'll be a basketcase until they're all back here safely."

"I know, dear. I didn't really want them all to hop a plane and track down Fred," Veronica lifted her coffee cup and took a sip. "But Fred needs to be located and they were determined to take a shot at tracking him down."

Amber nodded. "You're right. They all seemed quite determined to find Fred. And I really hope they do." Amber held up one hand. "Before I forget. I'd like to respectfully decline the fundraiser this afternoon," Amber politely said as she turned her juice glass to her mouth and took the last swallow.

Catherine spoke before Veronica. "Sure, it's fine if you don't care to attend. It's for a good cause but I think our absence will not hinder the function. I feel like you Amber. I'm too worried about the fellows to get dressed and attend some function," Catherine stated.

"I'm incline to agree," Veronica nodded toward Catherine. "I'll write a check for a hefty donation from the family and have it delivered to St. James."

Just as Veronica made that statement, Amber lifted her glass of ice water and took a sip as her eyes showed a great deal of worry. Then she took her fork and poked in the scrambled eggs not attempting to eat them.

Veronica noticed. "Amber, dear. I know you're concerned about the fellows and how they took off in a flash in search of Fred but try not to worry too much. I wouldn't want you to make yourself sick. Rome and his brothers will see after each other. They'll be just fine," Veronica assured her.

Amber nodded. "I'm sure they'll be just fine. I'm just afraid of airplanes and flying across the sky," Amber softly admitted. "I really don't want to have this fear of flying. It's not something I used to fear. I have flown to many cities all over the world from the time I was eighteen years old. Now, at this late age in my life I'm apprehensive about flying."

Veronica nodded. "It's understandable considering the devastation you have faced. But it will probably pass in time," Veronica encouraged her.

"I doubt it will pass. I have felt this way ever since Rome and I returned from our honeymoon and received the awful news about my girls. I've noticed how this fear comes over me whenever I hear the word airplane or someone discussing taking a flight. Also, during my stay at Shady Grove it was confirmed by my doctor that I've developed a fear of flying," Amber explained. "It's an awful scary feeling that comes over me and makes me feel helpless."

"Thanks for sharing that with us and I'll make sure to be careful not to mention those words in your presence. However, if it's okay, I would like to mention them now just to make a point," Veronica said seriously.

Amber nodded. "Sure, say whatever you like."

"What I'd like to say is, having a fear of airplanes and flying is nothing to be ashamed of. As I said before, it's understandable given your history. You've some terrible memories attached to planes. You lost your first husband, your children and your ex-mother-in-law to plane crashes. So, with that much pain wrapped up into plane flights, I feel your fear is well founded." Veronica looked toward Catherine. "Wouldn't you agree, Catherine?

Catherine sat there staring down in her plate as if she was preoccupied and hadn't heard a word Amber and Veronica had discussed.

"Catherine, I asked you a question," Veronica firmly said.

"I'm sorry," Catherine said, still looking down.

Irritated with Catherine's rudeness, Veronica snapped. "What are you sorry about?"

Catherine glanced toward Veronica as if she was oblivious to what Veronica's question was. "I'm sorry, but I wasn't listening."

"That, we can both see. What's going on with you, Catherine?"

"It's really nothing." Catherine took her napkin and wiped her mouth.

"Don't tell me it's nothing," Veronica mumbled, taking a sip of coffee. "Clearly, something got you preoccupied and looking out of sorts."

Catherine pushed her plate aside and grabbed her face with both hands, shaking her head. Veronica and Amber looked at her waiting to see if she would say anything; and after Catherine didn't speak, Veronica asked.

"So, what has you wind up so tight? Catherine?"

"I guess I feel pity and sorrow for Natalie."

"And why is that, Catherine?"

"You know why," Catherine quickly said.

"Maybe I do know why, but I still asked you a question and would like an answer: which is, why are you feeling pity and sorrow for Natalie?"

"I guess because it just dawned on me that she's in the dark. She doesn't have a clue to why her husband actually left here. I'm wondering how we are supposed to face Natalie, knowing what we know and why Fred actually took off the way he did?" Catherine said in a whisper as she glanced about making sure Natalie wasn't in earshot of her conversation. "We all know Natalie believes Fred left here and quit his job because he's unhappy with her."

Veronica nodded. "Yes, you are right. We do all know that, Catherine."

"Well, don't you think one of us should have a talk with her, so she won't think the worse about her husband?" Catherine whispered her suggestion.

Veronica looked toward Amber and smiled. "Sweetheart, I don't mean to be rude, but this one here." She pointed toward Catherine. "Makes it almost impossible not to be rude." Veronica held up both hands and glared toward Catherine. "Please get over your pity and sorrow and don't go lay any of this on Natalie. Can you do that, Catherine? This is a big mess we're dealing with! And you're right in the middle. So, suck it up and deal with it! Leave it alone and let it play out. Besides, there's nothing we can say to Natalie at this point."

Amber lifted her water glass and took a small sip of water. She wasn't sure whether she should say anything since she could tell Veronica was quite heated with Catherine, but she spoke. "Well, I have every confident that Rome and his brothers will track down Fred. They'll get him back and maybe Natalie won't have to know the whole vulgar story unless Fred tells her."

"Did you hear what Amber just said?" Veronica firmly asked. "That's my point exactly. But maybe Natalie won't have to deal with what we know that you shared with us. After the boys find Fred and get him back home, there'll be no need to upset Natalie with all of that mess that Fred got himself tangled up in. He escaped ruining his life by the skin of his teeth and I think Natalie can live without that dark piece of information," Veronica sharply stated.

Chapter Eight

Rome, Britain, Paris and Sydney were seated in that order on a long wooden bench waiting for the train from Chicago to pull into the Las Vegas train station. At 6:00PM that Saturday evening, they were standing on the platform as the train was slowly pulling into the station. They watched as the long train came to a complete stop and the trainman opened the door and placed a step stool for the passengers to step off the train. They watched the passengers un-board the train and after most passengers had stepped off the train at their stop, they finally spotted Fred stepping off the train on crutches with one piece of luggage. He also had a small black bag on his shoulders.

He headed into the waiting room and took a seat on a bench as he placed his suitcase and overnight bag on the concrete floor in front of his seat. He had a lost look on his face as he grabbed his face with both hands and then looked toward the high ceiling before he let out a deep sigh. The four brothers didn't want to startle him as they slowly walked over to his bench and took a seat on either side of him.

Rome gently patted his back. "Hello, Fred, I'm sure you are shocked out of your mind to see us," he said seriously.

Fred was too startled to say anything as he stared at Rome to his left. Then he realized he was surrounded by the four brothers. He knew he wasn't dreaming but he was stunned that they had beat him to his destination.

"We are so glad we caught up with you. Thank goodness you left that note telling Natalie where you were headed," Rome said. "Otherwise, this would be a much different story and we wouldn't have been so lucky," Rome gratefully relayed as his brothers and Fred looked toward him listening.

"Thank God for planes and how they can sail across the sky at 600 miles an hour. That's 500 miles an hour faster than a train. Therefore, we hopped the first plane into Las Vegas this morning and that's how we were able to beat you to this location," Rome kindly explained.

Fred finally collected himself. "Seeing all of you here sort of threw me for a loop," he said irritated, shaking his head. "I wished you boys hadn't bothered. I didn't ask you to come after me; and I didn't go through all that trouble of leaving just to be found. It's ridiculous that you took off after me after Natalie told you what I wrote in my note. I left because I wanted to leave!" Fred firmly admitted as he stared across the station into space.

"Fred, did you really want to leave Franklin House?" Sydney asked.

Sydney's words caught Fred's attention. "I'll be on the level with you. My reason for leaving is complicated. But I can tell you all right now that I have no intentions of returning to Illinois. The four of you wasted good money on your trip out here," Fred said nervously.

"Fred, how are you?" Paris asked.

"Well, I thought I was okay to the best of my ability until the four of you showed up." Fred held out both hands. "I know you mean well. But chasing all this way out here for me will prove to be a waste of your time and money."

"We don't think we wasted any money," Paris said, nodding toward Fred. "You're like family to us and we would hop a plane anywhere if we thought you needed us."

"That's my point. I appreciate that you all care enough to be concerned about me. But Natalie never should have mentioned the note or told you about our personal business. I know she owed you an explanation since I had left your employment. But she was just supposed to say I left and that was it. She definitely wasn't supposed to tell you my destination," Fred stressed seriously.

"Natalie was very concerned and worried about you, Fred," Paris told him. "And, she actually did you a favor by telling us your whereabouts."

"How do you figure that? I left town and I wanted to be left alone. I wasn't expecting to have any of you butting into my personal business right now. I left because I wanted to get away from everything," Fred explained.

"Fred, I see you and I hear you. However, it doesn't sound like you and none of what you have said rings true," Britain politely acknowledged, looking Fred in the eyes. "I can't believe you would leave Franklin House in the middle of the evening without alerting any of us. You have worked for Franklin House longer than we have been alive. You have never been anything except dependable and reliable. The Fred we know would never skip town without a word to any of us," Britain seriously stated.

"That's true, Fred." Sydney stood from the bench and patted Fred's back. "We know something isn't right and we want to help you. We came here to give you our support and let you know that regardless to what is going on with you, you can count on us to be there for you," Sydney assured him. "So, please confide in us and tell us what's going on. Let us know why you really packed up and left home?"

"The four of you have a heart of gold and I don't have the nerve to tell you the truth. But clearly you all know something is not quite right with me."

"What is it, Fred?" Sydney asked. "Just tell us. We won't judge you."

Fred rubbed the back of his neck with his left hand. "Well, I might as well tell you, I guess. You flew all the way out here to track me down. I'm sure you're not planning to head back without some kind of explanation. Besides, it's obvious how the four of you care; and I'm damn blessed to be a part of such a compassionate group of people. So, you know what? Damn right I'll tell you," Fred said as he looked from one to the other. "Here's what happened and why I left Franklin House. I left a note for Natalie, but it didn't give any details other than me taking a train to Las Vegas. Here's the thing that I'm ashamed of. I'm running from the law. I left Franklin House because I was too much of a coward to stay and face the music for the crime I committed."

The four brothers remained silent at Fred's confession. Fred wondered why they didn't sigh or ask what crime. Then it dawned on him that they were probably just displaying their normal politeness. Therefore, he continued. "I'm sure you'all are wondering and waiting to hear what crime I'm referring to. So, I'll get right to the point," he said and paused, exchanging regretful looks with each of them. "I'm the person who walked into Antonio Armani's hospital room and stabbed him while he was asleep in his bed."

They were all still silent as Fred looked at them, eyeing them for any sign of outrage or disgust. But when none of them groaned, sighed or seemed surprised or irritated by his statement, Fred humbly continued. "I didn't want to harm that man and I had no motive what so ever to do what I did. Yet, I did it under the hair scheme assumption that I was somehow helping someone else," he admitted and looked toward the gray cement floor. "I don't get it. I know you boys are always polite, but I figured you would be outraged and stunned or at least surprised at my confession of taking someone's life. Antonio Armani was once your uncle, married to your Aunt Catherine."

Rome exchanged looks with his brothers and they all nodded at each other. "Listen, Fred. You're right. We're not surprised by any of what you have told us. We made the trip out here because we're aware of why you left home."

Fred jaw dropped from Rome's words. "Wait a minute." He held up both hands. "The only person who knew was Catherine. I guess her conscience got the better of her and she ratted me out. I should have known I couldn't escape my crime. I was insane for a split second to do the crazy thing I did, now my life is over, and I have to accept that," Fred humbly grumbled. "I apologize from the bottom of my heart that I have thrown you young fellows in the center of my mess. You are all upright citizens and didn't deserve to get caught up in such an alarming situation!" Fred roared angrily, shaking his head in disappointment of himself. "What a sorry ass no brain son of a bitch I turned out to be to get your family tangled up in this criminal shit! Which will probably end up being the scandal of the year!" Fred threw the unopened water bottle he was holding and slammed it on the cement floor, bursting the plastic bottle, spilling water across the waiting room floor.

"Fred, please calm down," Rome calmly and politely suggested. "Things are not quite as bad as you think. Although, we are aware of your attempt to murder Antonio Armani, we are also aware that your attempt failed."

Fred grabbed his crutches and hopped up from the bench. He was startled by what Rome had just said to him. And although Rome was seated on the bench next to him, he needed to stand and look Rome eye to eye. "What do you mean my attempt failed?" he asked with shockingly disbelief. "I know you boys would never stoop to tricks to get me back to Illinois. But where did you get your information? I know I didn't imagine walking into Antonio Armani's room and stabbing him to death. That one act haunts me every hour of every day since I lost my head and committed such an unforgiveable hideous crime."

"The way we know your attempt at whatever you tried to do when you walked into Antonio Armani's room failed, is that we have confirmation from the police department," Britain said. "Yesterday afternoon the authorities arrested the person who murdered Antonio Armani," Britain told him. "We were all stunned to hear the authorities' information, since we thought, and we are aware that you are privy to this information, that Aunt Catherine thought she could have been the one to stab Antonio. Although, we never actually thought she had done it. She was torn and unsure, all set to give her statement and go to trial to prove her innocence," Britain candidly explained.

Fred stepped away from the bench hopping on his crutches. He was dumbfounded and astounded by the information that Britain had just shared with him. But after hopping a few steps away, he turned to face them being propped up by his crutches. "I know you fellows don't lie. Therefore, maybe that police officer lied to all of you just to make you guys think I was off the hook. Then you could get me back in their jurisdiction."

"Fred, you have our word. This is on the level. The authorities are not after you. They have closed the case," Rome assured him.

Fred glanced about the large waiting room and spotted people standing in line at a carryout bar stand buying beer and different alcoholic beverages. He pointed toward the line. "I need a drink. Could one of you do me a favor and step over there and buy me a cold bottle of beer?" Fred went in his pocket but before he could pull out his wallet. Sydney headed toward the stand.

"What kind of beer do you want?" Sydney glanced around and asked.

"Budweiser or Old Style," Fred replied, grinning.

They all stood up from the bench and hung around answering and sending text messages as they waited for Sydney to return with Fred's beer. But when Sydney returned he had five beers instead of one. He handed Fred and each of his brothers a cold bottle of Budweiser beer.

They were not beer drinkers and preferred vintage wine. Nevertheless, Sydney knew his brothers wouldn't object as a courtesy to join Fred in a drink. "I figured we could all use a drink about now," Sydney said as he twisted the cap off of his bottle of beer and dropped the top in the nearby trashcan, then turned his bottle to his mouth and took a sip.

"You have never been more right, little brother," Paris smiled as he turned the bottle up to his mouth and took a swallow. Then held up one finger. "Fred, when you walked into Mr. Armani's hospital room, did you place a pillow on top of Mr. Armani's chest?" Paris asked, taking a seat on the bench.

Fred nodded. "Yes, I did," he said as he turned the beer bottle up to his mouth and when he lowered the bottle it was half empty. "I couldn't stomach it otherwise," Fred admitted and dropped down heavily on the long bench.

Sydney leaned forward from the opposite end of the bench and nodded toward Fred. "That's the thing that saved you. Apparently, the knife didn't reach through the pillow that you placed on Mr. Armani's chest."

"That's correct," Britain nodded, seated next to Fred as he patted Fred's back. "What Sydney just told you came from a direct statement from Jessica Hanes, the nurse who confessed to the murder of Antonio Armani."

Fred turned his beer bottle up to his mouth and finished it. "That hit the spot and took the edge off. A huge load lifted from my shoulders. Someone up there must love me." He pointed one hand toward the ceiling." I tell you all, from the morning I walked into Mr. Armani's hospital room until now, my life has been one big pile of nerves, guilt and rage for myself."

"We're glad that's over for you," Britain said and then glanced at his watch. "We need to flag a taxi and head to the airport. Our flight back to Chicago is only two hours from now." Britain turned his beer bottle up to his mouth, took a swallow and hopped off the bench to drop the half-finished bottle into the large trashcan at the end of the bench.

"Britain is right. We need to head to the airport," Rome said.

Then they all stood from the bench and threw their beer bottles into the trashcan and headed across the room toward the exit. When they didn't see Fred walking along side of them, they glanced over their shoulders and saw him still seated on the bench. They walked quickly back over to the bench and before they could say a word, Fred spoke, holding up both hands. "You fellows might as well know why I'm still seated. I'm taking the train back. I've a fear of flying. That's why I took the train here. But you have my word I'll board the next train to Chicago. I know you'll land there before the train arrives, but you have my word I'll return to Franklin House to my wife and my job."

They were surprised to hear Fred was afraid of flying as they stood speechless for a second. Then Rome held up one finger. "Fred, could you please excuse us for a moment?"

Fred nodded as they stepped away from Fred to discuss their dilemma. "I believe he will take the train back," Rome said.

"I believe he will take the train back as well," Sydney said.

"I think we all believe he'll take the train," Rome said. "But, I think it would be rude to fly all this way to track him down just to leave him to head back on his own."

"So, I guess you are suggesting that we should cancel our flight and accompany Fred on the train back home," Paris said, smiling.

Rome nodded. "Yes, that's my suggestion."

Paris nodded. "It sounds fine by me. Besides, I think it's a neat idea since none of us have had the pleasure of riding a train."

"And in this case, Mother can't talk us out of it," Sydney said, smiling.

Britain smiled. "But she won't be happy about it."

Rome exchanged looks with his brothers. "Okay, we all seem to be in agreement. So, that's what we'll do. We'll cancel the flight and make reservations for five to Chicago on the train," Rome said, smiling. "You know, we might end up making somebody's news afterall."

"What do you mean?" Paris asked.

"I think four brothers on the train will be considered news to one Franklin matriarch," Rome said jokingly.

Paris and the others laughed as Sydney shook his head. "I agree, it will be big news to Mother."

"Maybe we'll just keep this bit of news from Mother until we have arrived home," Britain said jokingly. "Although, on second thought, she'll have a fit if we don't call and let her know."

Chapter Nine

Comfortably seated on the Amtrak train headed to Chicago in first class seats, they knew they would obtain some decent rest since Rome had purchased sleeping cars for the five of them. It was 9:00 PM when the train pulled out from the Las Vegas train station, and ten minutes into the trip, the conductor walked into their private car.

"Good evening and welcome aboard. Can I offer any of you a newspaper or a complimentary beverage: tea, coffee or soft drinks?"

They all smiled and shook their heads politely as the conductor continued. "Our dining car is three cars back where dinner is being served. The evening special is Baked Chicken and Rice," the conductor informed them, as he slowly headed down the aisle to exit the car.

"Thank you, Sir," Sydney politely said just as the doors closed at the conductor's back.

Rome and his brothers along with Fred got out of their seats and headed straight to the dining car for dinner. They were all quite hungry since up until now they hadn't found one minute to spare for a meal.

Seated in the dining car at a square table draped with a white tablecloth, the four brothers felt comfortable with an impressive look on their faces. They were not sure what to expect but they were rather pleased with the accommodations. The dining car was set up similar to a regular restaurant, serving hot freshly cooked dinners and not package meals. They all ordered the evening special: Baked Chicken and Rice with Broccoli.

"So, Fred, how do you feel?" Sydney asked, just as the waiter placed a bottle of beer at Fred's plate.

The waiter was a tall, slender African American male with soft brown eyes and long brown braids hanging to his shoulders. "Four glasses of white wine coming right up," the waiter said to Britain and held up one finger. "However, I checked with my boss and he has never heard of that wine you mentioned. But, if you still want the white wine, all we have is Sutter Home."

Britain nodded with understanding eyes toward the waiter. "That's fine. We'll take whatever you have."

"Okay, in Sutter Home whites, let see what we have," the waiter said as he pulled a wine list from his front pocket. "We have Chardonnay, White Zinfandel and Moscato," he said looking at Britain.

"I'll take the Chardonnay," Britain nodded.

"I'll take the Chardonnay as well," Sydney raised his finger.

"I'll take the Moscato," Rome nodded.

"I'll take the Moscato as well," Paris raised a finger.

The waiter was dressed in all white attire with a neatly folded white cloth napkin draped across his right arm. He nodded at them, jotted down their drink order and just as he walked away, Fred lifted his beer bottle to his mouth and took a quick swallow. He looked toward Britain shaking his head and smiling. "You fellows need to come down to earth with the rest of us," he said and took another quick swallow from his beer bottle. "I'm not trying to be rude. But the wine you asked that waiter for is not something they sell on trains or planes. That wine is not even carried in bars, restaurants or liquor stores. It's purchased and owned by a select few." Fred nodded toward Britain.

"Thanks for the enlighten update," Britain said politely. "However, this we know. It was a slip of the tongue and after I ordered the wine, the moment the waiter stepped away, it dawned on me that it wouldn't be available here," he said casually.

Sydney smiled toward Britain. "It's easy to forget it's a collectible when we have it so often for dinner at home."

Just then the waiter returned and placed a glass of Sutter Home white wine at each of their plates; and before the waiter stepped away from the table, Fred tapped his arm to get his attention. "I'll take another bottle of Budweiser," Fred said anxiously.

The waiter nodded and stepped away from the table. Paris exchanged looks with his brothers and then reached across the table and tapped Fred's arm. "We can see you're still sort of uptight. We were hoping you would try to relax more," Paris suggested.

Rome nodded toward Fred. "We understand how you probably feel off course right now. We can only imagine the kind of stress you have gone through," Rome caringly stated.

Sitting next to Fred, Sydney tapped his shoulder in a friendly gesture. "It will get better in time. Take it from someone who has been stressed out to the extreme," Sydney compassionately encouraged him.

"I'm sure you're talking about the Jack Coleman incidents," Fred said.

Sydney nodded. "Exactly, I was stressed to the extreme and I'm sure that's the kind of stress you're dealing with now. But just give it some time," Sydney said, and then lifted his glass to his mouth and took a sip of wine. "I'll admit, you do have a long road ahead of you. But once you go through the proper channels to get your life back on track, things will fall in place and come back together for you," Sydney assured him.

"Sydney is right," Rome nodded in agreement. "Things will eventually smooth out and get better."

Fred turned his beer bottle up to his mouth and took the last swallow, placing the bottle back on the table heavily. "I hope that time comes around soon. I'm about as stressful as I can get right now. I have a lot of music to face when I get back home. Natalie will be standing at the head of the line to chew me out for taking off the way I did," he inhaled sharply. "Of course, she'll want some answers." He shook his head in disgust of himself. "It was a coward's way out and I'm ashamed of my actions."

"Fred, we understand how you feel," Rome stressed seriously.

Fred shook his head. "I don't know how you can."

"Well, we sympathize with your situation and can understand how stressed you are right now," Rome said in a low voice that only they could hear. "You're worried about coming clean with your wife, of course. Plus, let's not forget the answers Mother will demand. But, on top of all of that, your main stress load is carrying around the kind of guilt you have for all that time." Rome lifted his wine glass to his mouth and took a small sip of wine. "We can't even begin to imagine how you have coped with thinking you had committed a ghastly atrocious crime. It would have anyone stressed to the extreme."

Fred opened his mouth to comment but held back his statement when the waiter arrived with their meals, placing a hot baked chicken dinner at each of their plates. And as soon as the waiter stepped away from the table, Rome glanced at Fred to hear his comment, but Fred was now preoccupied smiling at the dinner in front of him. He didn't look toward Rome, he just quickly rolled up his shirtsleeves, picked up his fork and dug into his meal.

Paris lifted his glass and took a sip of ice water and then took his knife and fork and sampled the baked chicken. "This is really good," he nodded.

"It's either really good or we're all really hungry," Fred cheerily commented from the influence of two bottles of beer.

Rome nodded toward Paris. "I'm incline to agree with you. This meal is quite tasty; and of course, I won't tell Natalie, but this baked chicken and rice is in competition to hers," Rome said, smiling. "However, with that said. Honestly, I haven't met a cook yet that can out cook Natalie Madden." He smiled and nodded toward Fred.

"Don't you boys know that's why I have stuck with Natalie all these years," Fred said laughingly. "The way she cooks, I'd be a fool to leave her."

"Her food is fabulous. But of course, we're not buying the line you're trying to sell us about sticking with her because she's a good cook. We know you love Natalie and your life at Franklin House," Rome said seriously. "That's why we're doing all we can to make sure we get you back to Natalie and that life." Rome glanced at his watch. "Brothers of mine," he said, smiling, exchanging looks with all of them. "There's no way around letting Mother know we're headed home on a train. Of course, she won't like it but she still has to know."

"You're right," Britain smiled as he lifted his glass to his mouth and took a sip of wine. "I think we were all kidding around about not telling her."

"This is really a pleasant trip and we'll have to work on getting Mother to take this trip on the train," Sydney said, smiling. "We can surprise her with a train trip to Las Vegas for her birthday or some other occasion."

Paris nodded as he forked a piece of broccoli in his mouth. He chewed his food and then said. "I like that idea. It's something different; and of course, Mother will protest at first. However, we'll convince her and get her on the train and I think she'll find it neatly refreshing with all the convenience of home at her fingertips," Paris lifted his wine glass to his mouth and took a sip. "Let's plan something and make it happen," he suggested.

"The idea of a train trip to Vegas for her birthday that Sydney suggested is a great idea," Britain smiled in agreement. "Let's work on making that happen for her next birthday."

Fred grinned and raised his hand for the waiter. "Good luck with that surprise. I know your mother and convincing Miss Veronica to take a train will be like pulling teeth. That will be a hard sell for sure," he said just as the waiter stepped over to their table.

"What can I get you?" the waiter looked at Fred.

Fred pointed to his empty beer bottle. I'll take another one."

"One Budweiser coming right up," the waiter said and stepped away.

"Fred, please order whatever you like," Rome encouraged. "It's on us."

"Thank you, because after this meal before I retire to that sleeping car you bought me, I need to knock back a few more of these." He pointed to the beer bottle.

"Fred, we are pleased we found you and no matter what, we wouldn't have given up until we did," Paris said. "However, on the serious side. I'm sure you know, Mother will be insistence on getting to the depth of why you attempted to do what you thought you had done. Although, we sympathize; respectfully, we would like some answers," Paris stressed politely. "In your sober mind you were willing and ready to take another person's life. That within itself doesn't sound like you. But the facts are the facts and you indeed entered Mr. Armani's hospital room with the sole purpose of ending his life," Paris seriously stated. "Aunt Catherine explained that you chose to commit the crime to protect her from committing a crime. Yet, it still doesn't ring true or add up to much of an urgent reason to be motivated to attempt such an unspeakable act other than in self-defense or temporary insanity."

"That's true, Fred," Sydney added. "We accept how destroyed and out of her mind Aunt Catherine was. Although, she didn't commit a crime, and even if she had, it'd have been proven as temporary insanity. She was actually out of her mind for a moment with anguish considering what she went through and how she suffered at the hands of Mr. Armani," Sydney explained. "We're not privy to all the details, but the same goes for the nurse who took his life."

Fred pushed his plate aside. He had only eaten half of his meal. He placed both elbows on the table and nodded toward Paris. "Everything you're saying is right. No jury in the world would have convicted Miss Catherine. You see, I know how awful Antonio Armani treated your Aunt. He was a bastard to name all bastards," Fred said rather loudly.

"Keep your voice down, Fred," Rome politely suggested. "This is a pretty tightknit place and we need to stay respectful and make sure we don't get too loud. Otherwise, we could be asked to leave the dining car."

"They won't ask you to leave. They'll just escort me out," Fred sadly said.

"Nobody is going to escort you out of here. Everything will be fine. You can enjoy your beer, just keep your voice down. That's all you have to do," Rome suggested.

Just then the waiter placed another Budweiser at Fred's plate and after the waiter stepped away, Rome continued.

"But, before we finish our meals and head to our sleeping cars, we would very much appreciate your explanation of your state of mind that lead you to almost commit an awful crime. We are all here for you, but we need to know what's going on with you to get you the proper help you might need."

"That's right, Fred," Britain nodded. "We want to help you. No one can go through what you have gone through and come out on the other side unscathed," he stressed sincerely. "We want to get you the proper help you need. And just to be clear, in order to keep your job at Franklin House, we're sure Mother will insist on some kind of counselling or treatment for you," Rome stated seriously.

Fred exchanged looks with them all. His eyes were sad with a solemn look on his face. "I'm sort of lost for words because I know I messed up. But one thing for sure I can tell all of you right now," Fred stressed in a low voice. "I'm not out of my mind or off my rocker. I made a huge mistake. It was a poor judgement call. But I have worked many years for Franklin House before any of you were born. I can place my hand on the bible and assure you, I'm not some sociopath out to take the lives of others." He held up both hands.

"Fred, we're not accusing you of being out of your mind or a sociopath. We would never think that of you," Britain strongly stressed. "All we know is what we know. Which is, we know you're a good man; and we know what you set out to do. We just need your explanation, so we can make sense of this. It seems too extreme to have you in the middle."

Fred placed both hands on his chest. "Okay, here's what happened," he said solemnly. "On that morning, I was out of my mind with rage for Antonio Armani. He had treated your aunt like she was dirt beneath his feet. I couldn't take it how he was treating her. He was conning her, but she couldn't see it."

"Fred, with all due respect. How were you privy to how Mr. Armani was treating Aunt Catherine?" Paris curiously inquired.

"Just take my word that I knew." Fred shook his head. "That's all I can tell you. I'm not at liberty to get into details about how I know what I know," Fred said anxiously.

"Fred, you need to trust us and be totally on the level," Paris insisted. "We can't help you and go to bat for you with Mother unless you're completely open and share with us all that lead up to what you thought you did."

"I know you're right. You decent young men have put your lives and jobs on hold just to hop a train with me. You could have easily boarded a plane back." He held out both hands. "But here you all are. You're sitting here with me on this train. Your first train ride ever just to accommodate me because I'm scared stiff of flying," Fred caringly stated.

When Fred said that, Rome instantly thought of Amber and her recent acquired fear of airplanes. He wondered if she would ever get over her fear, so they could travel abroad more, and maybe take another trip to Italy. But he wouldn't pressure her. He felt her fear of flying was understandable given the devastation she had faced from plane crashes.

"Plus, you give a damn to have raced out to Las Vegas in the first place to try to track me down. I'm grateful as hell and I will be completely open and share it all," Fred assured them. "However, in order to be completely on the level and completely open, I need to share a secret with all of you. It's a huge secret that I wouldn't breathe a word of if it wasn't for this incident. You fellows are so straight-laced and about doing the right thing. So, I hope you'll keep my secret. No good will come from the person hearing this secret that I don't want to hear it. So, here it goes. I'm in love with your Aunt Catherine."

They all kept their composure but didn't comment after his confession of love for their Aunt Catherine. But they shifted in their seats and swallowed hard but couldn't erase the surprised looks on their faces from his admission.

"I can see how surprised all of you are to hear what I just told you. But you wanted me to be completely open and honest."

Paris nodded. "Yes, we do want you to be completely open and honest. So, please go ahead. We're listening."

"Mr. Paris. I don't plan to hold any details back. But I do feel vulnerable sharing my feelings for Miss Catherine. Hell, I know I shouldn't be in love with her, but I am. It's a long story. We liked each other as kids but never got together." He held out both arms. "Anyway, I'm sitting here, and I can read your silent thoughts. You are all thinking about the fact that I'm married to Natalie, but I have confessed love for Miss Catherine. Here's the answer to that. Yes, I'm married to Natalie and that's the way it's going to stay. As far as my feelings for your Aunt. I have always loved her and probably always will."

Rome nodded. "Okay, Fred, we get it," Rome said, trying to move the story along minus all the awkwardness of him mentioning his feelings for their Aunt Catherine, who is actually his boss that he calls Miss Catherine. "You're a married man with feelings for someone else, but nothing will come of those feelings. Is that correct?"

"That is absolutely correct," Fred agreed nodding.

"Okay, please continue," Rome urged nodding toward Fred.

"I know hearing this is awkward and freaks you fellows out. Never in your wildest dreams did you ever think one of your staff members were at the head of so much chaos. However, I need to make one thing very clear. I had to rat out Miss Catherine in order for any of this to make any sense to the four of you," he stressed strongly. "This confession is hard to make." Fred turned his bottle up to his mouth and finished off his beer.

Because the days leading up to Mr. Armani's murder, I had secretly followed Miss Catherine and knew all about her secret meetings with Antonio Armani. But I give you my word. I will not follow another soul, Miss Catherine or anyone else."

"Thanks Fred. But please continue," Rome urged. "Mr. Armani had promised Miss Catherine that the two of them would leave town together. Although, Mr. Armani had promised to leave town with Miss Catherine, he had been lying to her from day one. I knew all of this. His intentions were to leave town with Mildred Ross all while he was meeting with Miss Catherine. He was only meeting with her to con her out of money, so he could leave town with the other lady. I wanted to warn your Aunt. But I couldn't let her know I knew what I knew. I couldn't let her know that I had been basically spying on her."

Paris nodded. "Fred, I'm glad you can acknowledge the truth about spying on Aunt Catherine. However, what you were doing was a complete breach of trust toward her."

"Mr. Paris, you are absolutely right. I knew what I was doing was sneaky. But it came from a good place in my heart." Fred touched the center of his chest with one finger and after a moment of silence he continued. "I have secretly loved your Aunt for many years. Therefore, I'm sure this is a shock to the four of you. I'm sure Miss Catherine didn't share any of this information since she would have been too embarrassed to do so. But every word is the truth. Sitting here with the four of you. Being candid and on the level about the stuff that I have to put on the table in front of you. It's hard as hell; and frankly I'll be honest and just say, I thought about not being on the level about my feelings for your Aunt. But I realized I had to come clean about Catherine in order to come clean about myself. I don't want you young men thinking I'm out of my head or some would be murder on staff at Franklin House. I was driven to do what I did. I was drove by rage and disgust of Antonio Armani's foul inhuman treatment of Miss Catherine! I couldn't bare for her to throw away the rest of her life on a man who had taken most of hers. Therefore, when I saw her take that knife from the kitchen that morning, my instincts told me she would probably head straight to the hospital to harm Mr. Armani. So, I followed her; and in route to the hospital, I finished off an entire half pint bottle of Gin. When I reached the hospital, I'll admit that I wasn't in my right sober mind. I was conscience enough to stick to the plan of stopping Catherine from doing something she would regret. But I wasn't thinking too clearly or walking too straight. Nevertheless, I continued to follow her inside the hospital until she dropped the knife out of her coat pocket without knowing it. When she stepped away from that spot and wasn't looking, I quickly grabbed the knife and hid around the corner. She went back outside I assume to look for the missing knife. But while she was outside looking for the knife, I sneaked into Antonio Armani's room, threw a pillow over his chest and stabbed him," Fred said in a whisper and then looked about to see if anyone was paying attention to his conversation.

The four brothers kept their composure but swallowed hard with disbelief of Fred's confession and explanation of his attempted crime. Fred had always been a good worker and they wanted to keep him on staff, but they knew it would take some time for them to digest his huge error in judgement and file it away to the far corners of their mind. They also had serious doubts if their mother would ever see Fred in the same light; and they were wearily she would dismiss him of his services at Franklin House. Nevertheless, they felt he deserved a second chance and would try to convince Veronica to keep him on staff.

Fred exchanged an apologetic look with the four brothers, then turned his beer bottle up to his mouth and finished a fourth of the bottle. After he lowered the bottle he frowned and shook his head. "Well, fellows, that's my disgusting story. I know it's horrible and unbelievable that I could lose my head and stoop so damn low to commit such an appalling act. But that's what happened, and I feel about as low as I can," Fred grumbled in disgust of himself. "Any damn lower, I would be six foot under!"

Before one of the brothers could comment to Fred's confession and explanation, just then a waiter was walking by, Fred held up one hand and stopped the waiter. He ordered another beer; and fifteen minutes later they were all still seated in the dining car watching Fred knock back bottles of beer. They had no real knowledge of Fred's drinking habits other than their observation of him having a couple drinks at some of their family social events. At their family functions where the staff were invited, were their only opportunity to socialize with Fred with an exchange of food and drinks with Fred. At Rome and Amber's wedding they recalled Fred having only one glass of champagne. However, on this evening, Fred had stepped outside of his usual mode of drinking. He was wallowing in guilt and disgust of himself, trying to fade out his thoughts. The four brothers had discussed among themselves that they wouldn't interfere with Fred's drinking during the duration of the train trip. They knew his mind was saturated with worry; and felt a few drinks might help to ease some of his stress. However, after watching him drink bottle after bottle with no end in sight of him ceasing to order bottles of beer, they were having second thoughts. They knew they were taking a risk by not cutting off his bar tap. Since they had no idea how he would behave intoxicated. They had no insight on how the alcohol would affect him mentally or physically. They were not sure if he would just fall asleep or if intoxication would make him difficult to deal with.

Paris touched Rome's arm after Fred appeared to be falling asleep at the table. "Look at him," Paris said to his brothers. "Don't the three of you think he looks tired and drained?"

Britain and Sydney nodded as they both glanced at the end of the small square table at Fred. "Yes, he does. He has definitely had his fill," Sydney solemnly commented.

"He looks completely out of it," Britain regretfully acknowledged. "Maybe we shouldn't have encouraged his drinking."

"I'm not sure we encouraged it," Rome added. "We just didn't discourage it, which maybe we should have, considering he could find himself awfully hungover by sunrise."

"That's true," Britain nodded. "But hopefully he won't wake up sick on this train tomorrow morning, which he very well could," Britain regretfully admitted. "This kind of drinking is most likely out of his normal routine."

Sydney nodded. "You're probably right. Other than tonight, I cannot recall a time I have seen Fred drink more than a couple drinks at our family functions that he has attended."

"Well, keep in mind, that's at our functions," Rome commented. "We have no idea how Fred drinks at his own personal functions or during his time away from the estate. He very well could be a much heavier drinker than we know," Rome pointed out, exchanging serious looks with his brothers.

They all nodded in agreement as Rome continued. "Nevertheless, on second thought, we shouldn't assume anything of Fred. We'll stick with the facts of what we know, which is: Fred isn't usually a big drinker," Rome nodded toward his brothers, lifted his bottle of water and took a sip. "And although his drinking tonight is quite alarming, we have to keep in mind what he's going through and how stressed out he is. Afterall, he thought he had taken someone's life, and he was fleeing his family, his job and everyone he knew," Rome strongly relayed.

Paris nodded. "You're right. Fred has been through a lot. What he's going through is quite substantial. It's probably more shattering than anything he has ever dealt with." Paris glanced at Fred. "I think we should probably just get him to his sleeping car," Paris strongly suggested.

Rome, Britain and Sydney nodded in agreement as they looked at Fred, noticing his demeanor. Fred appeared half asleep and oblivious to what was being said and going on around him as he gripped his beer bottle with both hands. He was looking down toward the white table cloth in front of him that was spoiled with beer rings and spilled beer.

Rome looked at Fred with sympathetic eyes. "Okay, we'll do that, so he can get some rest and sleep it off," Rome agreed.

"I don't want any rest!" Fred quickly grumbled, widening his eyes to appear more alert. "I heard what Mr. Paris said. But I'm not falling asleep," Fred strongly protested. "I know I've been sitting here quietly. But I didn't want to interrupt your chatting. But to prove I'm awake and fully alert, I have a funny tale to share with the four of you," Fred grinned and tilted to the right a bit with his eyes half closed, and the movement of his shoulders leaning too far to the right quickly jerked him back awake. He grinned and held up one wobbly finger. "Listen to this. Have any of you boys ever been so damn horny for a woman, but let her slip through your fingers?" Fred exchanged looks with the four of them with half opened eyes. "Of course, you have. Well, listen to this. My one shot to get it on with Miss Catherine when we were kids blew up in my face after my business wouldn't work," Fred grinned, slurring his words. "I was one dumb ass teenager to let her get away. But believe it or not, your Aunt Catherine had promised to be good to me. I even kissed her hand." He shook his wobbly finger at them. "Here's the kicker. I even had a chance to see her naked, but I botched that too!"

Suddenly you could hear a pin drop as the four brothers stared stunningly at Fred. His unexpected statement had left them speechless. Fred was wobbling at his seat as if he would fall to either side as he held up both hands. "I guess you boys don't believe I had the opportunity to see Miss Catherine with no clothes. I wouldn't lie about a thing like that."

Other passengers in the dining car sighed in displeasure of Fred's loud disrespectful language.

Rome stayed collected as he held up one finger. "Fred, please keep your voice down. You are disturbing the other passengers," he politely requested. "Better yet, don't speak," he firmly suggested.

"I'm sorry, Mr. Rome. I guess I was a bit too loud?" Fred said in a slurring whisper. "Just listen fellows. I'm not finished. Your Aunt Catherine and I were in her basement and that damn girl pissed me off! The little tease was teasing me! You guys know that wasn't right. It's a bummer when a girl promises and then renege! Have a girl ever promised one of you and reneged?" Fred shook his head. "I shouldn't have asked you that. Based on what Helen said, the four of you have women chasing you down the street, mailing you their underwear." Fred held up one wobbly finger. "I believe it. Women go for men who are not chasing them. You boys don't chase girls. They just fall in your laps. That's what Helen said. You know Helen, don't you? My freckle face daughter that none of you look twice at. Natalie and I told her it would help the family if she could snag a rich boy little one of you. But I'm realistic. Helen isn't pretty. She took after her mother that's for sure." Fred turned his beer bottle up to his mouth and took a long swallow, then grinned. "I got off track, but I remember now. I was talking how your Aunt reneged on letting me jump her bones. She told me, she was afraid someone would come downstairs."

Rome tapped the table in front of Fred to get his attention. "Fred, we realize you have had a lot to drink and probably oblivious to what you're saying. However, you're being disrespectful toward Aunt Catherine, obnoxious and loud," Rome firmly said to him. "You definitely need to stop talking or change the subject of your conversation," Rome strongly advised. "We do not need or want to hear anything about your teenage years with Aunt Catherine."

Fred stared at Rome with his mouth open. "What's the problem? Did I say something out of line? You boys know I wouldn't disrespect Miss Catherine or any of you."

Rome nodded. "We do know that, Fred. However, the problem is you're being controlled by alcohol. Your words are unfiltered and impolite. Therefore, whether you are in agreement or not, we need to get you to your sleeping quarters, so you can sleep off some of the alcohol in your system," Rome firmly suggested.

Fred shook his head. "I don't think so, Mr. Rome. I don't plan to spend any time in those small quarters. No sleeping car for me."

The four brothers looked at Fred but didn't comment as he continued. "I can see all of you are looking at me as if I just said I'll go jump off a cliff. But I'm just letting all of you know, I won't be sleeping in my sleeping car."

"But you need to get some good sleep," Rome seriously and politely said. "So, you'll sleep off all the booze you have put in your stomach."

Fred shook his head. "I don't care about getting a good sleep because with all the stuff that's on my mind, I wouldn't be able to sleep anyway," Fred seriously stated slurring his words. "So, just don't worry about me. I'll be okay because I plan to stay awake all night."

"We wouldn't recommend that, Fred," Rome seriously stated with frustration. "Well, I guess it's your business if you stay awake all night. Nevertheless, the four of us feel we should get you to your sleeping car. Besides, with your language and loud talking, you seem..."

Fred rudely cut Rome statement off. "I seem what? I'm not wasted, and I'm not smashed by a long shot. It takes more than several bottles of weak beer to kick my ass!" Fred said laughingly, but in a low voice. "See, I'm sober enough to know to keep my big mouth low." Fred held up both hands. "Fellows just let me stay here and drink. I'll behave. I promise I'll watch my language. Better than that, I won't talk at all. How is that for a deal?"

Rome nodded toward Fred and then exchanged looks with his brothers and they were in agreement to hang out a tad longer in the dining car with Fred. Therefore, they sunk back in their chairs and got the waiter's attention. They each ordered hot black coffee. They had finished off two glasses of wine, which was usually their limit after dinner. They had a long train ride ahead of them and didn't want to risk waking up with a headache or a stomachache. Therefore, they sipped their coffee and sort of chatted among themselves as Fred sat quietly drinking his beer. Then fifteen minutes after Fred said he wouldn't talk; the four brothers were stunned again when Fred cursed out loud for no apparent reason. "Got damn," Fred said as he stared down at the beer bottle in his hand.

"Fred, what's the problem?" Paris quickly asked. "You promised not to speak and disturb anyone."

Fred nodded. "I know what I said. But this is a free country; and I should be able to speak if I want to. Don't you young men agree?"

"Sure, but you have had a lot to drink and we don't want you disturbing the other passengers," Paris told him.

"That's right, Fred," Britain firmly stated. "If you plan to talk, you need to watch your language," Britain stressed strongly. "It's women and children in this dining car."

Fred laughed. "I'm sorry, Mr. Britain. I know I shouldn't curse like that."

"Well, why did you?" Britain definitively asked.

Fred blinked his eyes a couple eyes as if it was hard to keep them open. "Well, to tell the truth. I'm still sitting here thinking about your Aunt Catherine. I was imagining her with nothing on but her birthday suit. I can really go for her if she would give me a tumble."

The four brothers kept their composure but shifted in their seats. They could see Fred was still talking through his booze. They tried to overlook what he was saying. But Fred wouldn't let it go. "The four of you are looking at me like I said something improper. What's improper about visualizing a naked lady? You boys get me. I just want to roll in the hay with Miss Catherine."

Rome stood up from his seat. "Fred, that's enough talk like that about Aunt Catherine," Rome assertively said. "Plus, we'll do you the favor of not mentioning this discussion to you tomorrow. You're talking through your booze. But we can put an end to your talk right now."

"Come on, boys. Why you want to put an end to my talk? I'm sure you know how I feel. You may be gentlemen. But got damn. Come on and give me a break!" Fred said rather loudly. "We're all over twenty-one. Hell, I'm sure you all get as horny as the next guy!" Fred grinned, slurring his words as he almost fell out of his chair as he turned his beer bottle up to his mouth and took a swallow. "There's no reason to shut me up. Besides, I'm just getting started."

"No, Fred, I'm afraid you're done," Paris said as he and Sydney got out of their seats and went and stood on either side of Fred, holding his arms, helping him out of his seat at the table. "Besides, you were falling asleep at your seat and being a disturbance to the other diners."

"Yes, Fred, we're getting you out of this dining car before we all get kicked out," Britain added. "Your language is over the top disrespectful and you're talking much too loud."

Fred stood there at his chair with Paris holding one arm and Sydney holding the other. But he stiffened his body and wouldn't move from his spot. He widened his drunken red eyes and stared at Britain. "Says who? I'm not bothering anyone!" He looked at who had his left arm. "Mr. Sydney knows I'm not bothering anyone. Tell your brothers I'm not disturbing anyone."

"I'm sorry, Fred," Sydney said. "I can't vouch for you. You're being all those things Britain mentioned. You're not yourself, Fred. You're intoxicated and need to be in bed."

"You guys are bursting my bubble. You're no damn fun to hang out with," Fred grumbled. "I'm a grown man and if I want to drink and get wasted that's my damn business! Why do the four of you have the need to usher me to bed?" Fred fussed loudly.

"Fred, you need to calm down and make some steps out of this dining car," Paris determinedly said. "If you don't let us usher you out of here, what Britain said will come to past. They'll kick us all out of here and off this train in the middle of nowhere. Do you want that?"

Fred shook his head. "No, Mr. Paris, I don't want that. I just don't understand why you're ushering me out of my dinner chair. You both have me by the arm and you want to usher me to my sleeping car when I'm not ready for bed, "Fred fussed.

"Fred, you have had too much to drink. You're incoherence and doesn't seem to grasp what we're saying or trying to do." Rome looked Fred in the eyes. "We're not saying you have to go to bed. You just have to leave this dining car," Rome authoritatively told him in a low voice.

"But I'm not done drinking," Fred growled.

Rome nodded. "That's fine. If you want to continue drinking, we can't stop you. But you'll have to do your drinking in your sleeping quarters, so you won't disturb other passengers," Rome firmly said. "Seriously Fred, they won't allow disturbance on this train."

"Have it your way boys. You're the boss anyway! Hell, I'm just trying to ease my nerves."

"We understand how you must feel, Fred," Sydney caringly acknowledged. "Nevertheless, this is a public train. The way we act and behave can affect the other passenger's trip. They paid their fare for a pleasant trip and shouldn't have to be disturbed by someone else's bad day," Sydney politely pointed out. "Besides, you weren't just being loud with vulgar language. You were also falling asleep in your chair."

"Here you come with that falling asleep crap again. How many times do I have to say I wasn't falling asleep," Fred grumbled, pointing to Rome. "Mr. Rome know I wasn't falling asleep. I think I was talking about the good old days with Miss Catherine and how much I would like to get her in bed," Fred slurred with his words. "I'm a man and that's where my mind is right now. It's on your Aunt Catherine. I have never known such a good-looking woman; and you know what? That damn Armani guy messed up your Aunt Catherine's head. She doesn't even know she's fine; and I'm starting to think she hates me," Fred said as they finally managed to escort him at least two feet from their dinner table. "That's probably the reason she wouldn't give me a tumble and let me make any headway with her? Maybe a billionaire has no use for a chauffeur and any other measly soul who's in my category of earning $70,000 a year or less," Fred stumbled and slurred his words. "I think that's what my salary is. Well, it used to be my salary. I just forgot I don't have a damn job anymore! Do I guys?" Fred slurred his words. "Only the four of you know if I still have a job. So, what's up? Do the cat have your tongue? You guys need to correct me and help me out if I'm off the mark," Fred managed to say clearly.

Just then an upscale looking expensively dressed elderly couple walked passed them frowning. The elderly lady stared at them and pointed her finger. "Young men, you should be ashamed of your vulgar language."

"Sir, Madam," Britain politely spoke. "We're sorry for the disturbances. We're headed to our sleeping car now."

"Well, see that you stay there!" The elderly lady fussed. "I don't know what this world is coming to. You look like such fine young men. But you have zero manners."

Fred opened one eye and half opened the other. "Grandma, who are you? You don't know who you're talking to. These boys can buy this whole damn train and the tracks too!" Fred slurred with his words.

"I don't need them to buy the train. I just need them to respect it with some decent manners."

"These four young men are poster boys for good manners! Grandma, what the hell make you think they're not?" Fred rudely grumbled. "Lady, you don't know us from Adam!"

"Fred, please stop being so rude and disrespectful," Rome insisted.

"But she can't talk to my boss like that," Fred growled and then accidentally dropped the bottle of beer he was carrying in his hand.

When the bottle fell to the floor of the dining car, the Conductor instantly was standing there. He had a serious look on his face as he looked at the elderly lady and the old man. He could see that the elderly lady appeared greatly upset and shaken. Then he looked at the four brothers as they were trying to hold up a drunken Fred. "What seem to be the problem? We received complaints about loud disrespectful language being used in the dining car coming from your table."

Rome held up one finger. "I'm Rome Franklin and these are my brothers, Britain, Paris and Sydney." He pointed to his brothers. "This man is Fred Madden. He's profoundly intoxicated and we're trying to get him to his sleeping car. We apologize for his language and conduct."

"Is Mr. Madden the person from your table that was disturbing the dining car?" The Conductor inquired.

Rome nodded. "That's correct. But it's our fault for allowing him to indulge in so much beer."

"How is it your fault?" The Conductor asked. "Who is this man to you?"

"I beg your pardon?" Rome didn't hear the Conductor's question since the elderly couple was chatting out their complaints loudly at Rome's side.

The conductor slightly raised his voice. "I said, who is this man to the four of you? Is this your father?" The Conductor firmly asked.

They shook their heads. "No, he's not our father, Sir," Rome replied.

"Well, who is he? We have quite a number of complaints that he was sitting at your table talking loudly and using distasteful language. We can't have that kind of rudeness displayed bluntly on the train. Therefore, if his conduct continues, we'll have to ask him to exit the train and find another mode of transportation back to Chicago. To allow him to stay onboard displaying such disrespectful talk and behavior, it shows disrespect to the other passengers," the Conductor candidly explained.

"Yes, it shows disrespect!" The elderly lady continued to fuss. "That's why we didn't finish our dinner. It was enough to make me sick in the stomach the way they were engaging in vulgar conversation at their table next to ours."

The Conductor looked at the elderly lady. "We received a number of complaints pertaining to what you just said. But I don't think we'll have any more trouble out of Mr. Madden tonight. Nevertheless, I'll have your dinner charge reversed to re-appear as a credit on your credit card as a token of our apology for your disturbed dinner?"

The elderly man elbowed the elderly lady. "You gave out incorrect information. It wasn't the young men conversation. It was their father doing the talking and they were trying to tone him down and when they couldn't, that's when they decided to take him out of the dining car," the elderly man said with conviction. "I was paying attention and heard their conversation."

"Well, you never told me it was their father when I chewed out the young men," the elderly lady snapped at the elderly man.

The Conductor looked at the four brothers. "So, they're saying this man is your father. But you said he's not your father. So, I'll ask again. Who is this man to the four of you?"

"As we said, his name is Fred Madden. He's not our father, but he's very close just like family to us," Paris politely explained. "He's our very dependable and reliable chauffeur." Paris patted Fred's back and nodded as he exchanged looks with his brothers. "We are aware of how this looks and how he looks at the moment. Because he's quite intoxicated and seems like trouble and a handful. But honestly, we have known Fred all of our lives. He's really a good guy. And we do apologize for his loudness and intoxicated behavior, but he's just going through something quite significant right now."

They all nodded in agreement as Sydney spoke. "That's right. Fred is going through something and that's why we went against our better judgement to allow him to drink as much as he wanted."

"So, he's your chauffeur?" The Conductor pointed to the four of them as Fred held his head to one side oblivious. "Who did you say you are? The four of you do look familiar."

"We're the Franklin brothers," Britain answered. "We might look familiar to you due to our resembles to our father. The late Ryan Franklin."

"That's it. You'all are a split image of the late movie star, Ryan Franklin. He was one of my favorite actors," the Conductor said excitedly. "So, the four of you are Ryan Franklin's sons?" The Conductor smiled excitedly. "What a small world. It's a privilege to have the four of you on Amtrak."

They all nodded and smiled. "Thank you, Sir," Paris graciously said. "This is our first train ride."

"Well, I hope you're enjoying it." The Conductor glanced at Fred. "Other than keeping your troubled friend out of trouble."

"We're really sorry about the disturbances he caused," Rome apologized. "From here on in until we reach Chicago, we'll keep him sober. There'll be no more vulgar language in the dining car in connection to him. You have our word."

"That's fine. Go on and get him to his sleeping car. In these cases, the person isn't allowed back in the dining car during the duration of their trip. But we'll make an exception in this case. Therefore, if you want to bring him in for breakfast tomorrow morning, feel free to do so."

Chapter Ten

The next morning, Fred and the four brothers enjoyed a simple breakfast in the dining car of toast, fried eggs fruit and coffee. During their meal Fred didn't mention his drunken behavior or disrespectful language. He appeared not to have any memory of the conversation he had engaged in about their Aunt Catherine. The four brothers decided between the four of them that it would serve no good purpose to tell him about his drunken behavior and disrespectful talk about their Aunt. Therefore, it was like the incident hadn't taken place.

The train ride had been an experience that the four brothers had not gone through. For the most part, they thought it was enjoyable. But they were rethinking their idea about repeating the long trip with their mother for her birthday. The trip had drained a lot of energy from them; and after experiencing the very long train ride from Las Vegas, Nevada, they were more than pleased when the train pulled into the Chicago Union Station. They exited the train quite relieved to be back in Illinois. The four of them and Fred walked through the newly remodeled station and headed straight outside where a substitute limousine driver was waiting for the five of them.

The moment they walked through the front door at Franklin House, Veronica was waiting anxiously seated in the living room. She stood and watched them walk across the room toward her and after she hugged her sons and shook Fred's hand, she insisted on a family meeting with Fred before he had an opportunity to freshen up or visit with Natalie. It was already a quarter to 3:00 and dinner would be served at 6:00 o'clock. Veronica wanted Fred to have a clear understanding of where he stood at Franklin House after his botched attempt at taking another's person's life. The four brothers, Veronica and Fred met in the library behind closed doors.

Amber, Catherine and Natalie were not surprised by the immediate meeting as the three of them sat in the living room sipping hot tea. Catherine and Amber had asked and invited Natalie into the living room to join them while they sipped hot tea and waited for the family meeting regarding the Franklin House employment of Fred to end.

They decided to invite Natalie because Catherine figured Natalie was beside herself with concern and confusion of why Fred took off from her and his job so abruptly. She was no doubt filled with questions she wanted to ask Fred to get to the bottom of his out of character behavior.

"Miss Catherine, I can assume the meeting is probably about whether Fred still have a job here," Natalie softly mumbled, looking toward Catherine. "Is that correct? Do you think the meeting is about his employment status?" Natalie nervously asked as she nervously lifted the white China teacup to her mouth and took a sip of tea.

Catherine looked toward Natalie and nodded with solemn eyes. She felt regretful and guilty for indirectly being the reason behind Fred's current predicament.

"Natalie, I will not lie or sugar coat this situation and what's taking place right now," Catherine said and paused with a long stare toward Natalie and then sadly shook her head. "I'm deeply sorry to say this. You have no idea how sorry I am. But I believe Fred's job is on the line; and I believe that's exactly why they're having the meeting with Fred."

Natalie swallowed hard after hearing what she expected Catherine to say. She paused and digested the realization of the situation before she solemnly stated. "From my humble viewpoint, it seems like they went through a lot of trouble flying all the way out to Las Vegas to find him just to get him back here and give him his walking papers," Natalie said and inhaled sharply. "I just wonder why they even bothered looking for Fred if that's the case?" Natalie asked, irritated and confused.

Catherine and Amber discreetly exchanged looks with each other. They knew the exact reason why the four brothers had flown out to Las Vegas to track down Fred. The consensus was that they needed to locate him and inform him of the closure regarding the Antonio Armani case, revealing he wasn't facing any murder charges. They wanted him to be updated on the whole story and now they needed the whole story from him.

Amber leaned forward and lifted her cup from the coffee table and slowly lifted the cup to her mouth and took a sip of tea while Catherine was looking into space as if she was in deep thought.

"Miss Catherine, you and Miss Amber didn't comment, but I'm quite curious about that. If Fred was going to lose his job, why go through the trouble of getting him back here?"

"Natalie, I know you have a lot of questions, but I don't have all the answers and zero authority. I hope Fred will be able to keep his job but it's not up to me. Veronica has the final word," Catherine kindly explained. "But Natalie, you have to keep in mind the big picture of this situation. Fred took off and abandoned his position without notice."

Natalie nodded. "I understand and realize that's grounds for dismissal. That's why it's off to me and doesn't make much sense that they chased across the country after Fred. It seems odd that they would chase after him, find him and bring him back to town just to tell him he's fired."

Catherine looked at Natalie with solemn eyes. "Natalie, I believe they chased after Fred because that's who they are."

Amber looked toward an anxious Catherine and nodded. "I agree. That is who they are." Then she looked toward Natalie. "But I can also see Natalie point of why chase after someone to return them to their job to tell them they're no longer needed. But the principle of it," Amber explained. "But the bottom-line. They figured after thirty years of service something had triggered Fred's motive to flee the state and they were determined to find him and get to the bottom of his issue, so they could possibly help him. Wild horses couldn't have kept those precious men from going after your husband and making sure he was okay," Amber politely explained.

"Miss Amber, you are probably right. After thirty years on the job this is the first time my husband has brought chaos and disruption to halt the flow of things here at Franklin House. I hope they can get to the bottom of this issue and get some answers out of Fred. I'm his wife and I'm as much in the dark as the rest of you, maybe even more," Natalie solemnly explained while sitting on the edge of her seat in wonder.

"Natalie, try not to worry," Catherine encouraged. "The meeting will be over soon, and you and Fred will get a chance to talk. Veronica gave me permission to give you an hour off of work after the meeting is done – so you and Fred can have some time to talk."

"Thank you, Miss Catherine. But if Fred loses his job over all of this, I won't be upset with anyone except Fred. He brought this on himself," Natalie sadly admitted.

Amber held up one finger. "If Rome and his brothers have anything to say about it, I'm sure Fred will get a second chance to keep his position here."

Catherine nodded. "That's so true. If a solution can be brokered, they will figure it out. But in this situation, they may not have any say. Unfortunate for Fred, I think Veronica hold all the cards and will be the sole decision maker in this case," Catherine pointed out.

The three of them sat there in hopeful thought that Fred would be able to remain at Franklin House.

Chapter Eleven

Suddenly the library felt foreign to Fred. He felt awkward in a room he had frequent for over thirty years as he sat in a side chair holding his hands. He had a panicky stomach as he nervously looked straight at Veronica trying to read her mood as she was busy pouring a few drops of cream into her cup of hot tea. She reached out and placed the small crystal creamer pitcher back on the coffee table and then looked straight at Fred.

"So, Fred, you have just explained how and why you did what you did on that morning and we are so pleased you are okay, and the situation turned out in your favor the way it did. However, business is business and you are hired here for a service you provide us in return for a salary. Trust and reliability are key in maintaining your position here. Therefore, I guess you need to explain why we should give you your job back? Afterall, you did leave without notice," Veronica seriously pointed out.

Fred looked from Veronica to each brother and he held up both hands. "I know I messed up big time and I'm grateful to know people like your family who cared enough to drop everything and get to me. You have my word that I have learned my lesson. What I did was irrational and stupid. It could have ended up changing my life for the worse forever," Fred humbly explained. "I think back, and it seems like someone other than me who attempted such a criminal act. But if you give me another chance and allow me to step back into my old job, remaining here on the premises with Natalie, you have my word that this will never happen again. I will keep my nose clean," Fred strongly promised.

"Fred, a lot is riding on my decision. If you don't know I have no issues with your work performance. I have an issue of trust and safety where you are concerned. You took the law into your own hands disregarding us all. You could have thrown this family into a whirlpool of a scandal. My issue is, are you stable enough to make the right decision if your back is against the wall again? Will you consider this family, or will you just act on impulse and think of the moment? That's the million-dollar question to whether I'll allow you to stay on here or not," Veronica seriously stated.

Fred nodded with a solemn look on his face. "Miss Veronica, I understand your concern, but I can answer that million-dollar question. The answer is no. I will not just think of the moment, I'll think of this family," he anxiously answered as worry showed in his eyes. "I just want you to know, sitting here having this meeting with all of you, it has dawned on me how blessed I am to be employed by this incredible family. Mr. Rome, Mr. Britain, Mr. Paris and Mr. Sydney treats me with much kindness just like Mr. Ryan used to treat me. Plus, living in this big magnificent house is like a dream for me, Natalie and Helen," Fred said as he glanced about the room. "I realize if I'm dismissed, me and my family would have to move out of our two bedroom living quarters on the lower level. My wife and daughter are good workers here and haven't done anything wrong. They shouldn't get kicked out of here and lose their jobs because of me," Fred humbly stated.

Rome looked toward his mother for acceptance to reply to Fred. Veronica looked toward Rome and discreetly nodded her approval.

"Fred, we need to correct you on something," Rome politely uttered. "If we don't keep you on, it has nothing to do with Natalie and Helen's positions. They are free to continue their employment here as long as they like," Rome assured him.

"That's right, Fred," Paris added. "Your status will not affect theirs."

Fred eyes widened with curiosity. "But we'll have to move. Is that correct?" Fred looked toward Paris.

Paris solemnly nodded. "That is correct," Paris said, and then he held up one finger. "But listen Fred. That is only true, if we do not allow you to step back into your position here," Paris said and paused. "Yes, you will have to move off the premises if you're not reinstated back into your staff position. But once again, Natalie and Helen will be free to continue living on the premises. But most likely they would choose not to live onsite if you're not with them," Paris projected.

"I don't understand why I can't just continue to live in our quarters if you let me go, especially since my family would still be working for you," Fred said confused.

Veronica raised one finger toward Paris and Rome to allow her to answer Fred concerns. "Fred, you are absolutely correct in your assumption in a normal situation where one member of a husband and wife team is let go, that person can usually continue living on the premises with their spouse. Most of the time that individual lost their job due to their job performance. Therefore, in your case, Fred, if we let you go, it will be because we feel you are a danger and a possible liability to the property. You need to bear in mind why we're having this meeting. It has to do with your state of mind and the fact that you were willing to commit cold blooded murder. Have you really taken the time to think about that, Fred?" Veronica firmly asked.

Fred nodded. "Yes, Miss Veronica. I have thought about it and I'm sick in my stomach about it. How can I prove how deeply sorry I am over all of that?"

"Okay, Fred, there is one way we'll be willing to give you a second chance and allow you the run of the property again," Veronica said.

Fred perked up and smiled. "Okay, thank you. What is that one way?"

"I would like to have you checked into Shady Grove to be evaluated and after the doctors have treated you, if they send you home with a clean bill of mental health, we'll welcome you back into your Franklin House position," Veronica seriously uttered.

Fred eyes widen, and his mouth fell open. "I'm willing to do pretty much anything to get my job back because I need the pay and the roof over my head. I have worked at Franklin House for so long until I wouldn't know how to work anywhere else. This job is my life and means everything to me," Fred strongly admitted.

"Fred, it didn't seem as if it meant everything to you when you sneaked out into the night and headed to Las Vegas," Britain reminded him. "You are saying all the right words, but there's a trust issue and a stability issue regarding you. We all love you to death and would love to keep you on," Britain caringly stated. "But it does come with conditions."

Veronica nodded toward Fred and then leaned toward the coffee table and lifted her cup of tea. She lifted the cup to her mouth without looking toward Fred, she sipped her tea. "Your possible reinstatement does come with a condition just as Britain pointed out. However, you haven't commented on my requirement."

Fred shook his head. "I'm assuming you're referring to having me committed to Shady Grove." He held up both hands. "I would do anything for this family. But checking into a crazy house is where I draw the line. I'm not out of my head or nuts if that's what you all think." He touched his forehead. "I know I did something crazy but I'm not crazy."

Veronica leaned forward and placed the cup and saucer back on the coffee table. She exchanged looks with her sons, and then looked toward Fred and nodded. "I guess this meeting is done. Fred is not in favor of checking into Shady Grove. And doing so is the one condition he needs to honor in order to be reinstated back into his position here," Veronica seriously said as she looked in the faces of all of her sons.

The four brothers desperately wanted Fred to keep his job. They believed in second chances, but they knew their mother was dead set against giving him his job back if he didn't meet her conditions. Therefore, they needed to get through to him and stress the urgency of her conditions.

"Fred, what's the big deal with checking into Shady Grove?" Sydney asked. "It's a fabulous state of the arts facility. They'll check you over and you'll be there for a while, of course; and I'm sure you'll receive a clean bill of mental health and end up with your job back in no time," Sydney encouragingly said to him.

"I'm sorry, but I have a problem with places like that. I know Miss Amber stayed there. But Miss Amber suffered a breakdown. And I don't belong at a place like that. If I end up there I'll never hear the end of it. Besides, that place is so damn expensive I couldn't even afford a glass of water from there," Fred pointed out.

"Fred, do you understand that your refusal to be evaluated at Shady Grove means an immediate dismissal?" Sydney asked. "You would have to leave the premises today."

Fred sat looking toward the floor and he didn't comment as Paris talked.

"Fred, we want you to completely understand," Paris said. "So, do you understand that it's not a choice, but a requirement?" Paris asked.

"I guess I do not understand that part." Fred got out of his seat with one crutch under his arm, hopped over to the coffee table, he looked at the silver teapot and the silver coffee pot and decided to continue drinking coffee. He poured more coffee into his cup.

They all watched him in silence as he dropped two cubes of sugar into his cup and then lifted the cup to his mouth and took a sip. "I do want to keep my job here, but I should have a choice about whether I want to be used as a guinea pig at some nut house," he exchanged looks with them and laughed.

"Fred, this is not a laughing matter and Mother is quite serious about her requirements," Paris told him. "We all met briefly in the den when we first arrived home and we asked you to wait in here while we had a short discussion. In full disclosure, Rome, Britain, Sydney and I recommended to Mother to reinstate you back on here at Franklin House. We informed her that we spoke with you in-depth on the train and we shared with her our opinions that we feel you have learned a hard lesson. We also stressed upon her all your loyal qualities and how you have been completely reliable for the family over the past thirty years," Paris exchanged looks with his brothers and then looked back toward an anxious Fred. "Yes, we went to bat for you, Fred. However, Mother stressed upon us that under no other circumstances regardless of your past work history, an evaluated at a mental facility is required without an exception. So, Fred, just in case you felt we had some say so in this matter to help keep you on. We do not. You either choose to accept the evaluation or you will not be reinstated," Paris politely explained.

"Thinking about being confined in a place like that gives me the creeps. I rather wear a foot monitor or anything else other than to be committed in a crazy house," Fred said with a nervous grin.

"Fred, your language is uncalled for and downright rude," Rome said firmly. "Referring to Shady Grove in those terms doesn't make it so. My wife stayed there and the staff there helped her tremulously. It's a wonderful facility and well known all over the world," Rome informed him. "You mentioned a concern for the cost, but we would definitely pay for your stay at Shady Grove."

"In that case since it's a requirement with no exceptions, I may have to say my good byes to your family," Fred said, shaking his head. "You folks don't know my side of the world. If I were to check into a facility like that I would never be able to live it down. Everybody I know and those I don't know would be gossiping about my stay there. They would all say I'm out of my mind and would probably stop talking to me or associating with me. I'm worried once again that my predicament could affect my wife and daughter and cause them to lose some of our friends as well," Fred said with a choked-up voice.

Veronica didn't comment as she sat there and sipped her tea. She wanted Fred to stay on, but she was prepared for his departure and had already spoken to Dillion and his wife, Leola. Dillion had agreed to accept the chauffeur position and Dillion's duties would be handed over to a new hire. Nevertheless, she hoped Fred would do what's needed to keep his position at Franklin House.

"Fred, if we understand you correctly, it sounds as if you have a hang up with mental institutions, but even more than that   your greatest concern is how others will perceive you if you are committed for an evaluation at Shady Grove," Britain politely stated, looking toward Fred. Then Britain exchanged looks with his Mother and his brothers as he looked back toward Fred and continued. "Okay, Fred, what do you think of this idea?" Britain asked as he turned to his left and lifted his coffee cup from the chair side table and lifted it to his mouth and took a sip. Then he got out of his seat, stepped over to the coffee table and grabbed the sugar bowl. He removed the crystal lid and removed one cube of sugar and dropped into his cup; and then placed the sugar bowl back on the long elegant silver tray that sat on the coffee table.

They all looked toward Britain as he took his seat and lifted his coffee cup to his mouth and took a sip. Fred especially wanted to know what idea Britain had in mind. "Okay, Fred. Here's what I have come up with; and you can let me know what you think of it," Britain said and then he was silent a moment as if he was pondering some thoughts. "What if we checked you into Shady Grove in secret? You would of course have to inform Natalie and Helen. But you could let them know it's a secret because you don't want the news to get out. We would, of course, keep your whereabouts a secret and not inform any of the staff," Britain kindly explained. "We would just relay to the staff or whoever seeking you out that we gave you two weeks leave of absence for personal reasons. The two weeks leave of absence for personal reasons is true. You could spend that time at Shady Grove and afterward step back into your job," Britain suggested, hopeful Fred would agree.

"It sounds like a better plan that I could live with. It's just hard as hell to keep anything under wraps. If the news got out, I would be devastated." He held up both hands. "But on the other hand, it might just work. I could check in for the evaluation and the silver lining would be keeping my job and my home," Fred pondered with a slight smile.

"Fred, you need to be aware of what Mother said about Shady Grove. She was quite clear in her statement, that after your evaluation, if the doctors there give you a clean bill of mental health then you would be reinstated back into your position here," Paris made clear.

Fred nodded, sitting straight with a serious look on his face. "I understand completely. But I'm not concerned about their evaluation and my mental status report. I'm confident that all my marbles are in place. I just need to go through this process and get it over with, so I can get back to work."

Veronica looked toward Fred's foot. "Hopefully by the time you checkout of Shady Grove, your foot will be back intact and you'll be off the crutches and able to drive again. At your current state, even if you had your job back, you cannot drive the limo with your foot the way it is," Veronica respectfully reminded him.

Fred smiled. "I know, and I can't wait for it to completely heal. But before you end this meeting I would like to ask when I am expected to check into Shady Grove?"

"I have made arrangements with the facility for your arrival this evening. Your arrival time is scheduled for 4:00 o'clock." Veronica glanced at her watch. "However, I was assured that if you arrive sometime after 4:00 but before 4:30, you would still be processed and checked into a private room. It's 3:00 o'clock now. That gives you enough time to spend some time talking to Natalie, but since we're pushed for time to get you to the facility on time. It's best not to spend more than fifteen minutes filling Natalie in. She can of course get some time off to visit you tomorrow or whenever you like. After you're done talking to Natalie, the boys will personally escort you and get you checked into the facility," Veronica assured him.

"I'll speak briefly with Natalie and I'll let her know what's going on, especially about the required condition of being evaluated at Shady Grove in order to keep my job here. But that's as far as I'll go with the information I'll share with her. She would kick me out for sure if she knew about everything: what I tried to do to Antonio Armani and why," Fred anxiously explained. "All of that I would like to keep from her. There's no need for her to know. It was a stupid mistake that I'm trying to put behind me."

"Fred, what you do in your personal life is your own business as long as you're not putting this family at risk. Therefore, if you choose to keep secrets from your wife, that's your business," Veronica seriously remarked. "Whether we think it's wrong or disrespectful doesn't matter. It's not our place to interfere in your personal life and tell Natalie things that should be told to her by you," Veronica nodded toward Fred. "Although, I'm sure Natalie will want some more answers about why after thirty years you jumped up, packed up and left this job and your marriage."

"I know, and I'm ready for her questions. I'll tell her what I can. But I don't want her to know about what happened and I would greatly appreciate it for no one casually mentioning any of it."

"Fred, we're not going to say anything to Natalie. You are aware that Catherine knows. Plus, Amber knows," Rome reminded him. "I'll speak to Amber and make sure that she knows you don't want any of this mentioned. The incident regarding Mr. Armani as well as your stay at Shady Grove."

"I'm sure Miss Catherine will not say anything, but thanks for saying you'll mention to Miss Amber not to mention any of what's going on with me."

Veronica and her sons stood from their seats and then Fred stood and propped himself against his chair. He remained against the chair as he watched them all headed toward the double French doors to exit the library.

Paris glanced around and then glanced at his watch and nodded toward Fred. "We'll ride along with you when the driver takes you to Shady Grove. We'll meet you in the front driveway at 3:30 on the nose," Paris said.

"Wait a second," Fred said as he grabbed his crutches and slowly headed across the room where they all stood midway to the double French doors.

"What do you need, Fred?" Veronica asked. "The time is ticking. You need to have a conversation with Natalie before you leave the premises for Shady Grove. Besides that, they would like to get you checked in at the facility, so they can head back for dinner which will be served at 6:00," Veronica softly informed him.

"I know time is tight. I'll call Natalie right away and have her meet me in here. But I'm wondering about that driver that picked us up from the train station and who plans to drive us to Shady Grove."

"What about him?" Veronica asked. "Besides, you already know Sam Westwood. He works for Charles Taylor. He's just filling in until you can get back to work. Charles asked him, and he was willing to pull the double duty, driving for us both until all this is straightened out," Veronica explained.

"Yes, I know Sam. He's a good man. We are not close friendly buddies, but I think you know that he and I know each other pretty well. I'm just worried about him finding out my business. If he drives us to Shady Grove and everyone returns from the institution except me, he'll put two and two together and figure out I was committed to the facility," Fred sighed with concern. "And as I said before, I really do not want anyone I know to know about this aspect of my personal life. What I'm about to embark upon is very private to me and I would like to keep it private," Fred stressed strongly.

They all stood there in silence for a moment, then Rome looked at his mother. "Mother, I can cancel the driver. I'll notify Sam and cancel the trip. This way he won't be privileged to it."

"If you do that how will you get Fred to the facility?" Veronica asked, and then answered the question herself. "I guess we could call the agency and have a limo sent here for this matter. At least it would be someone who doesn't know Fred. That would put him more at ease about not being recognized by someone he knows."

Paris shook his head and his brothers agreed. "If we do that it would seem odd to Sam who's filling in. It wouldn't make sense to him that we cancelled our limo trip that he was scheduled to drive, just to order an agency limo to make the drive."

"Paris is right," Sydney agreed. "It would be too confusing for Sam and as well as the other staff. They would be wondering and discussing a car and driver showing up here when we already have a car and driver," Sydney politely explained.

Rome and Britain exchanged looks with each other and nodded. "Mother, that's more than a possibility. It's a probability that the staff curiosity would spin out of control into a lot of whispers about what it all means. Therefore, the best we can do to solve this situation of keeping Fred's trip to Shady Grove private is to take him there ourselves," Rome suggested.

Fred had a surprise look on his face and Veronica's jaw dropped. "I do not like that idea of any of you driving the work limousine to haul someone else around." She looked toward Fred and shook her head. "No offense meant to you, Fred."

Fred nodded. "None taken since I get you. I don't think it looks good for them either. If we're worried about the staff wondering what's up. Seeing Mr. Rome behind the wheel of the limo while I'm sitting in the back is more curiosity for the staff to gossip about. Maybe Mr. Rome could just ask Sam to keep quiet about my stay at Shady Grove."

"Fred, that's out of the question. I know you mean well and trying to come up with a suitable suggestion but that one won't do," Rome kindly disagreed with his suggestion. "It's a thing called integrity. We'll do all we can to keep your stay at Shady Grove private because it's your request. However, we won't ask anyone else to keep your stay a secret."

Fred frowned a bit confused over Rome's statement. "Mr. Rome, I guess I'm a little confused that we can't ask Sam to keep my stay at Shady Grove to himself. You did say you're going to ask Miss Amber not to mention my stay at Shady Grove to any of the staff or why I left town to Natalie," Fred quickly reminded him.

"Fred, that's different. Amber is my wife. Sam is staff and shouldn't be asked to compromise his principles," Rome said.

"I'm not trying to be difficult," Fred tried to assure them. "I guess I'm just trying to understand how can keeping a secret about my stay at Shady Grove compromise Sam's principles? I guess I'm not clear on that."

Rome glanced at his watch. He knew it wasn't enough time to get into a deep conversation with Fred to fully explain what he meant. "Fred, I'm sorry if you're confused. My intentions were not to offend your suggestion."

"That's right, Fred," Paris added. "I'll just give you a quick example of how Sam can compromise his principles in this situation. He can be untruthful to his wife. Maybe she'll ask him about his day and he'll leave out the part about driving you to Shady Grove to be committed for an evaluation. He would withhold that information from his wife, indirectly lying to her, which is a big deal," Paris politely, yet strongly relayed. "When two people have pledged to be completely open and honest, the omission of information is a breach of trust. Because a lie by omission is still a lie," Paris politely explained.

"Mr. Paris, I get you. But if we can't get Sam, and the staff will be curious about another driver; and it won't look properly for one of you to drive to limo. That still leaves us high and dry without a driver," Fred said in a defeated voice.

"It doesn't leave us high and dry because we're sticking with my suggestion to drive you," Rome said and looked toward his mother and nodded. "Mother, it will be fine. I know it doesn't look proper for one of us to drive the limo. However, there's nothing wrong with driving our own car with Fred sitting in the back." He held up both hands. "However, before you make a remark that five of us cannot fit in any of our cars comfortably. I know this and suggest that I drive your Bentley. If that's okay with you, Mother."

Veronica nodded with approval in her eyes. "Sure, take the car and drive him there. That's a splendid idea. This way Fred private business will be kept private," Veronica softly said as she and her sons headed out of the room.

Chapter Twelve

Fred immediately called Natalie after the Franklins exited the Library and within six minutes she was opening the double French doors and walking into the library. Then she turned right around and stepped back over to the doors and slowly shut them tightly before heading across the room toward the side chair where Fred was seated. He looked at Natalie and smiled as she took a seat in the side chair next to Fred's chair.

"Talk to me, Fred," Natalie said nervously. "The first thing I want to know is do you still have your job, or did they fire you?"

Fred shook his head and smiled. "Can you believe it, I'm still apart of the staff and I'm not out of the door yet!" Fred grinned.

Natalie narrowed her eyes at him and wondered what he meant by that statement. "If you're not out of the door yet, do you expect to get kicked out of the door at some point?" she seriously inquired.

"What I mean is, Miss Veronica is going to allow me to keep my job under one condition." He held up both hands.

"Okay, what condition is that?" Natalie asked.

"I have to check into shady Grove and allow them to evaluate me."

Natalie eyes widen with surprise of the requirement. "What makes them think you need to check into there? I wonder," Natalie mumbled annoyed.

"I'm not sure, but Miss Veronica made it crystal clear that after my stay at Shady Grove if the facility gives me a clean bill of mental health, then I'll be reinstated back into my old job," Fred explained anxiously. "I'll tell you I hated that idea at first and I still do. But they agreed not to mention my stay at Shady Grove to any of the staff or anyone else. Just myself, you, Miss Amber, Miss Catherine and the brothers will know about my stay at that insane asylum."

Natalie shook her head in frustration of Fred. "After thirty years of having the Franklin's trust. You have messed that all up. But you are one lucky man that Miss Veronica chose to find a way to reinstate you. Frankly, I don't think you deserve all the kindness they are throwing your way," Natalie fussed. "Afterall, you did such an inconsiderate thing when you left these premises on the spur of the moment without any regard for anyone else or thinking through your consequences," Natalie angrily snapped. "I'm so angry and upset with you Fred until I could scream."

"I realize you are very upset with me, but I want to beg your forgiveness for being such an inconsiderate bastard. I had no business messing up my good thing here by packing up and heading for parts of unknown. That was the craziest thing I have done so far!" Fred shook his head in disgust of himself. "As we get older we are supposed to get wiser, but it seems I'm slipping the other way." He glanced at his watch.

"You'll get no argument from me disputing you were an inconsiderate bastard. I agree with everything you just said. Because God knows what you did was out of character and one big fool ass thing for sure," Natalie seriously fussed with a sharp edge as she looked Fred in the face. "I see why Miss Veronica is having you committed to Shady Grove. Something is seriously wrong with you to jump up and leave home as you did."

"Natalie, what can I say? I know I messed up and I'm damn ashamed about! But I can't undo what's been done! I can only move forward never to do it again," Fred said assuredly and then glanced at his watch again.

"Why do you keep looking at your watch? You just got back are you heading out again?" Natalie sniped.

"Yes, I am heading out," Fred said with a solemn look on his face. "They are taking me to Shady Grove at 3:30."

Natalie eyes widen with surprise. "I see, but I didn't think they would check you in so soon. I figured maybe tomorrow."

"I figured never," Fred joked. "But it is what it is; and I realize how lucky I am. They are looking out for me and giving me a second chance after I made a major error in judgment. I walked away from my marriage, you and my daughter!" Fred raised both hands. "On top of that, I walked away from this job! I left the Franklins up the creek without a chauffeur. If that wasn't inconsiderate enough, I left my job without notice. It all adds up to look like I was missing my good sense," Fred said with disappointment in his voice.

"I agree that you were inconsiderate and what you did was quite dumb. It was grounds for dismissal. But I don't see how it's grounds to commit you to a mental institution. That part I don't get. Do you get it, and if you do get it? Please explain it to me."

Fred looked toward the floor as if Natalie inquiring mind was making him nervous.

"I know you said it was Miss Veronica's one condition that you had to meet in order to keep your job. But it just doesn't make sense to me. You are many things, but out of your head I don't think is one of them. I know you crossed the line and abandoned your job and your duties; and you need to earn their trust again of course. But committing you to a mental institution as a requirement to keep your job. That seems a bit harsh. They act as if you're a danger to this household," Natalie spoke with irritated confusion. "Fred, I know you want to keep your job. But what do you think? Do you think the requirement is too harsh? Miss Veronica is treating you as if you went out and tried to kill someone!" Natalie shook her head. "And we both know that's not true! Therefore, if you ask me, I think the requirement is too severe. But you haven't told me what you think."

"What difference does it make, Natalie? This is her requirement and whether I agree or not. I don't get a say in the matter if I want to keep this job. You think it's too harsh of a requirement and I think it's a bit too much as well. But on the flipside, after I broke their trust showing no reliability for my position I don't expect them to give me a slap on the wrist. That would be too lenient," Fred explained, hoping she would drop her inquiry into their motives to send him to Shady Grove.

"For someone who hates mental institutions, you seem quite indifferent about this whole thing. Plus, what I also do not get is the four brothers going along with Miss Veronica decision to have you committed to Shady Grove. They are fair to a fault and they would never go for such a decision unless they also felt it was warrant," she stressed with a heated tone. "I love my job here, and Miss Veronica and her sons have always treated me like part of the family. However, I think it's a bit odd that Miss Veronica is treating you as if you're dangerous. Sending you to Shady Grove for a mental evaluation means she doesn't think you're stable enough to be on staff here and live under her roof. What you did was irresponsible and misguided but you're not unstable. I would like to speak to her on your behalf if that's okay with you. It may not help, and she still may not change her mind about sending you there. But I don't think it could hurt. She has a lot of trust and faith in me. She may give you your job back without the condition of checking into Shady Grove."

"Natalie, you're the last person that should talk to Miss Veronica on my behalf. As you said, she has a lot of trust and faith in you and I don't want to put you in the middle of the mess I made. So, please just do me a favor and leave it alone. As you said before, Shady Grove is a world class place. I can't do any work right now with my foot injury anyway. I'll just look at this stay as a retreat spot to help me heal. Once I have spent my time there we can get back to normal. She'll receive the report that I'm mentally stable and that will be the end of it," he strongly convincingly explained.

"It will be the end of it for you. But Fred, something in the pit of my stomach is telling me I'm not getting the whole story about this predicament you're in. That's why I'd like to have a talk with Miss Veronica. Maybe she can tell me something she has noticed about your behavior that I have missed."

Fred threw up both hands. "Natalie, please let this go. Miss Veronica is my boss and she's your boss. We need this roof over our heads and we need to keep our jobs. I don't want you to rock the boat. It's not worth it. Maybe sending me to Shady Grove isn't warrant. But Miss Veronica is probably pretty peeved with me and if I didn't have thirty years under my belt and the praise of her sons, I'm sure I would be out of the door already! What I did was foolish and irresponsible. Put yourself in her shoes. Would you have much trust for an employee who would walk away from his duties at the spur of the moment without notice? She doesn't see that kind of behavior as normal, I'm sure. And maybe it wasn't something dangerous in your eyes, but we both know how Miss Veronica thinks. She would walk through fire to protect her family. If she feels I pose a threat in any way to her family, she's doing what she feels is best. Bottom line: I broke her trust and now she's unsure about having me on her premises," Fred strongly stressed as he observed Natalie's facial expression. "I see that look on your face, Natalie. You still don't get it. But doing what I did, sneaking out in the night and leaving you that note the way I did, Miss Veronica probably feels as if she cannot trust me anymore. She may give me my job back, but it will always be in the back of her mind how I left here without notice once, and that I could easily do it again."

Natalie rubbed her finger across her chin as she listened to Fred pleading with her, trying to convince her that Veronica was not too strict in her request to send him to a mental facility. "Fred, I'm listening to you and you seem too okay about all of this. It just seems so unlike you to be okay with something like this. That makes me even more curious."

"Natalie, you are mis-reading me. I'm not okay with it. I'm just grateful and considering my actions toward this family I feel lucky with the current arrangements. So, please, can we just drop this; and can you try to find it in your heart to be thankful that they are giving me another chance."

"Okay, I won't say anything to her to try to figure out her motives behind sending you to Shady Grove. I'll let it go for now. But it will all eventually come out in the wash. Then you and I will both know why Miss Veronica felt it was necessary to send you off to Shady Grove for an evaluation," Natalie calmly assured him.

Fred heart raced in his chest and he hoped her words were not true. He never wanted Natalie to know the whole story about his feelings for Catherine and how those feelings drove him to seek vengeance against Antonio Armani, to the point of attempted murder, then running scare that forced him to leave his home and job. He would keep that information from Natalie at all cost, he thought as he looked at Natalie with solemn eyes.

It was clear from the look in Natalie's eyes that she was upset with Fred and confused and not pleased regarding Fred's situation.

"I can see from the look on your face, Natalie that you're distraught over all of this and just plain ticked from every angle with me. Nevertheless, I think you realize just as much as I do, just how damn lucky we are right now," he humbly acknowledged. "You may not know this, but they told me this during the meeting. They explained to me that if I wasn't rehired, I would have to move off the premises."

"What do you mean by that?" Natalie jaw dropped. "In that meeting, they told you that we would have to move out if you lost your job?"

Fred shook his head. "No, they didn't say we. They said I would have to move out. You and Helen would still be allowed to stay in the servant quarters. But they explained that many times when something like this occur with families. They all move if one member has to leave," Fred explained, realizing he shouldn't have mentioned that.

"I'm really puzzled now because usually when a family member is let go and another is still employed at the residence, that person can remain living on the premises with their spouse or family," Natalie deeply sighed.

"Maybe you're right, but it probably depends on why that person was fired," Fred said. "You have to keep in mind that they didn't find fault with my work performance. They found fault with my irrational personal actions and my peculiar bizarre behavior."

"Whatever, I'm still confused that Miss Veronica feels you need to be evaluated at Shady Grove; and that the four brothers would support it," Natalie grumbled.

"Listen, it's what Miss Veronica required but Mr. Rome and his brothers told me themselves that they didn't support the decision to have me committed to Shady Grove. They told me that they went to bat for me and asked their mother to just reinstate me on my word that I would not abandon my position ever again without notice," Fred explained. "So, please be clear that the brothers had nothing to do with the decision to ship me out to Shady Grove. It was all their mother's idea. I guess I messed up so big that she thinks I'm nuts! But you have my word, Natalie, I'm deeply sorry for all the worry I put you and Helen through. Please let Helen know how sorry I am."

"It would be best if you told her yourself."

"Well, I can't do that because I'll be leaving here shortly. So just tell her I'm sorry and I never meant to worry either of you. Can you please do that for me and make her understand how I didn't mean to worry anyone."

"Of course, I'll tell her you're sorry. But how do you expect for me to make her understand when I don't even understand myself," Natalie fussed.

"Listen, Natalie. I just hope you can forgive me, so we can move forward from this big mess."

"Fred, when you left me that note, it made me feel unwanted as if you just didn't want any part of our lives together," Natalie sadly mumbled.

"I know I hurt you, but I'm paying for it all right now," Fred firmly mumbled. "Since in order to keep this job I have no other choice but to accept the accommodations of a mental facility. Being behind doors in a place like that is going to make me feel about two feet tall."

"I'm sure you'll survive. Besides, Fred, you are very aware of Shady Gove reputation; and know as well as I do. It's not your typical mental facility. It's a world class facility that caters to the very rich. I read it's like staying at a resort. Miss Amber raved about the place," Natalie encouraged him.

"Just for the record, you won't hear me rave about it," Fred assured her.

"I know you have to leave soon, but I need you to answer me one question," Natalie said with serious eyes.

Fred nodded in wonder of what she needed him to answer. His heart pounded from anxiety. He hoped she hadn't overheard or caught wind of the real reason the Franklins were committing him to Shady Grove.

"So, what's your question? I need to head out front and wait for Mr. Rome and his brothers. They are taking me to the facility themselves, so all the staff and Sam Westwood won't find out about my personal business of being committed to Shady Grove. It would really bother me for anyone to find out about my stay there. But I'm pleased to say, my stress level is near zero since I feel that won't happen," he said with confident.

"My question is quite simple. I just want to know, and I want an honest answer. Do you still want to be in this marriage or do you still feel the way you felt the night you left me that Dear John note?" Natalie seriously asked.

For a moment, the room fell completely quiet as Natalie stared at Fred with anguish and disappointment in her eyes. Natalie was waiting to hear Fred's answer to her question. But, he didn't appear to want to answer her.

"Fred Madden. I'm waiting for an answer to what I asked you. It's not a complicated question. As I said, I just want an honest answer, which only you can give me. You either want to be in this marriage or you don't. So, which is it?" Natalie asked.

Fred shook his head. "My goodness, Natalie. I just told you how deeply sorry I am. What more do you want from me?"

"I want you to answer the question. Can you do that?"

"What difference will it make whether I answer the question or not? You'll believe what you want anyway. Damn, Natalie. Maybe Shady Grove is the right place for me, considering I had to be out of my mind to leave a good woman like you."

"Fred, I don't care how you spin your lies. It just doesn't make any sense to me that you would pack up and take off at the spur of the moment if you really didn't mean what you said in that note to me. I'm aware that you had a lot going on that day. You had just injured your foot at the lake house. But what else was going on with you? Did you have one too many drinks or did something else happen that you haven't shared with me?" Natalie argued.

Fred nodded. "Hell yes, I was drinking. Plus, I was upset about my foot and a number of other things."

"I guess you were stone out of your mind and in the process, you alienated me and put our livelihood in jeopardy," Natalie fretted.

Before Natalie could finish what, she was saying, they both looked around from the click of the double French doors opening. It was Helen. She was smiling hurrying toward them. She headed straight to Fred where he was seated and threw her arms around him.

"Dad, you came back. I'm so happy you came back with the Franklins. Mom was worried sick about you. But she wasn't sure if you would come back," Helen said as she sat on the arm of Fred's chair, still rubbing his back. "Whatever possessed you to take off and leave us like that?" Helen hopped off the arm of the chair and noticed the solemn look on her mother's face. "Dad, why did you take off and leave that hurtful note for Mom?"

"Listen, Helen, I messed up big time. I wasn't thinking straight, and I can't tell you how much booze I had put in my stomach. I'm just glad to be back and get this second chance with the Franklins."

"So, I guess Miss Veronica is giving you your job back? You are beyond lucky. Especially, since you abandoned your position without notice. I'm sure without a doubt, it was her incredible compassionate sons that went to bat for you. They probably convinced Miss Veronica to give you a second chance," Helen assumed.

"Are you just getting here from Taylor Gowns?" Fred asked.

Helen nodded. "Yes, Dad. I went to our quarters and put my purse and jacket away, and then headed straight to the kitchen to start my food preparation duties for Mom."

Helen looked toward Natalie. "Mom, I thought I would find you in the kitchen preparing dinner. But when I didn't see you, I headed to the living room where I found Miss Veronica and Mr. Britain. I asked did either of them know your whereabouts and Mr. Britain told me that I could find you and Dad in the library. But he and Miss Veronica seemed to be in a serious discussion and I got the feeling that it was about you," Helen said with a curious look on her face. "Like I said Dad, you are so lucky how the Franklins have decided to overlook the fact that you went AWOL on them.

Fred and Natalie swallowed hard with anxiety as Helen went on and on. They stood there mute as she continued, all smiled. "It's great how they are just taking you back into the fold overlooking your abandonment and your desertion to just keep you on. Plus, what really astounds me is how they personally dropped everything to fly across country looking for an employee." She held up both hands. "Dad you are so lucky." Helen exchanged looks with Fred and Natalie. "Because seriously, who does something like that? Something so considerate and caring other than the angel heart of the Franklin brothers? Those guys are every woman's dreams. How I wish I was someone they would notice but I'm not," she said, shaking her head. "But at least, I'm smart enough not to daydream about either of them. That's what happened to Courtney Ross. She went batty over a Franklin man she couldn't have," Helen smiled, still shaking her head.

Fred had deep sorrow in his eyes as he looked at his daughter. "Helen, my dear. You're right. I know I'm lucky to have the compassion of the Franklins," he said and paused in her eyes for a moment, dreading to say what he had to tell her. "But dear, you need to know I'm not completely out of the doghouse with the Franklins," Fred informed her as he grabbed his crutches and stood from his chair.

Helen exchanged looks with her mother and then looked anxiously at her father. "Dad, what do you mean by that? They went searching for you and gave you your job back. What else is there?" Helen curiously asked.

"I'm allowed to stay on here at Franklin House and keep my job under one condition," he humbly said as he glanced at his watch. "I need to make my way out to the front driveway."

"What's in the front driveway?" Helen curiously asked.

"The brothers will be out there waiting for me in the next ten minutes."

"But Dad, why would they be waiting in the driveway for you?" Helen inquisitively asked. "You definitely cannot chauffeur them anywhere as long as your foot is the way it is," Helen was curious.

Fred nodded. "That's right. I'm not able to drive right now and for the next two weeks I won't even have to worry about trying since I'll be on a leave of absence. But do me a favor and don't really share this information with anyone," Fred said, headed toward the double French doors to exit the room.

Helen walked toward the exit door, alongside him. "Dad, I think everyone pretty much knows about how you injured your foot. Taking a leave of absence until your foot heals makes a lot of sense."

"Helen, the leave of absence is not about my foot. It's about my head. The one condition to hold on to this job is to be committed at Shady Grove and if the doctor send me home with a clean bill of mental health, I'll be reinstated back into my old job. It will be as if I never took off. But I have to get through this hurdle first," Fred seriously explained.

Helen was surprised to hear but Fred didn't have time to continue talking with his daughter. "My goodness, Dad. Is that where you're headed?"

Fred nodded. "Yes, it is. Your mother will continue filling you in." He glanced over his shoulder as he opened the doors to walk out. "Remember what I said. Keep this to yourself. I don't want every Tom and Harry knowing my personal business."

"Don't worry, Dad. I won't breathe a word," Helen assured him.

Helen and Natalie stood and watched until Fred walked through the double French doors and were completely out of view.

Helen looked at her mother and shook her head. "What's happening to his family? I feel like I can't wake up from a nightmare." Helen dropped down in the side chair where Fred had been seated. She grabbed her face with both hands and stared at her mother in wonder. "Mom, do you think Dad really need to be committed to Shady Grove for a while? Is he okay or not?"

"Don't ask me, dear. I'm as confused and in the dark as you are. Your father and I talked before you walked in and I still don't know any more about why he's in the predicament he's in than I knew before the two of us talked."

"Did he tell you why he packed up and took off like that?" Helen curiously asked. "Because Mom, to do something like that is a desperate act. And I know in his note he stated how he wanted to get away from the marriage."

"Yes, it does sound desperate. But your father isn't saying much about what he should say much about. He's saying a lot about nothing, which means he's only saying how he knows he messed up and he just want to make a mends," Natalie deeply sighed. "He's giving me a bunch of rhetoric that just doesn't add up! And every time I think about all of this I get a cold chill straight up my spine. Your father was a prominent part of the Franklin staff and he chose to blow that up; and for what? He said he was drunk and maybe he was, but I don't buy that as a reason for all this madness. He was so lucky with the odds on his side. Because what if the Franklins were not the type of people they are. Meaning, what if they hadn't dropped everything and went in search of Fred. He would still be out there somewhere; and we don't know if he would have chosen to return on his own or not," Natalie stressed. "And after further consideration, I think Shady Grove is exactly where he should be. The choices your father made were definitely odd. Plus, if there's more to the story, I'm not sure if we'll ever know."

"More to what story, Mom?" Helen asked.

"More to the story of why he packed up and left this estate in the first place. I'm wondering did he do something on the job that he shouldn't have done. The more I think about it the more I think your father was desperate when he left here. And I think it has something to do with the Franklins. Something he did that he shouldn't have done; and I think that's why they went after him," Natalie said with conviction.

Helen stood front the chair. "Mom, you're probably right. Because otherwise, why would they assumed his note to you were not what he truly intended. Now, we need to find out what he did to the Franklins. It must be sort of major that it made him leave his family and everything behind, including free housing in a mansion along with a thirty-year position that pays him extremely well," Helen seriously stated.

"Plus, we need to keep in mind, he's being evaluated at a mental facility," Natalie pointed out. "The Franklins are very smart, wise and fair people. Therefore, if they feel Fred needs to be evaluated at Shady Grove, they must have a darn good reason." Natalie cringed. "I hate to think of what his sin could be against this family that warrant him to be committed to Shady Grove," Natalie curiously wondered as she quickly glanced at the small silver clock on the library fireplace mantle. "We need to head toward the kitchen and get busy," Natalie reminded Helen.

"So, Dad's stay at Shady Grove is a secret?" Helen asked as she and Natalie headed out of the library.

"Yes, that's the way your father wants it. And the Franklins agreed to his privacy. Therefore, no other staff member or anyone else who comes here or calls for Fred will know about his whereabouts. The Franklins will simply tell the other staff members that your father is on a leave of absence until his foot heals," Natalie explained as they headed down the hallway toward the kitchen. "They are incredible folks and they even honored your father's request not to be chauffeured to Shady Grove by Sam Westwood. He knew if Sam drove them there and everyone returned from the facility except your father, Sam would have known your father was left there for some reason. In that case, to put your father's mind at ease, the Franklins decided to drive Fred to Shady Grove themselves," Natalie shared as they headed for the kitchen.

"That's amazing. When you say they, I'm sure you mean Mr. Rome, Mr. Britain, Mr. Paris and Mr. Sydney. Dad is really blessed the Franklins care as much as they do for him. As busy as they are, they are taking the time out of their schedule to drive Dad to Shady Grove and make him feel at ease and comfortable with the arrangement. This is especially generous considering, he has most likely done something majorly over the top to disappoint the Franklins," Helen said as they stepped into the kitchen.

"I think we should change the subject, dear. I want to hear what's going on with you. So, tell me. Have you heard anything else from Oliver Bartlett?" Natalie asked as she and Helen stood at the sink washing their hands.

Helen shook her head and smiled. "No, Mom, I haven't heard from Oliver in a while and I don't expect to hear from him. He's seeing Trina Ross now," Helen announced while drying her hands on her white apron.

"Is that Courtney Ross's sister?" Natalie asked, drying her hands on a hand towel that's pinned to her white apron.

"Yes, Mom. Trina Ross is Courtney's younger sister."

"When Mr. Rome dated Courtney, I heard mention of a brother named Kenny," Natalie said as she opened the refrigerator and removed a package of celery and carrots and placed them on the long solid white marble countertop. "He might be a nice young man to go out with?"

Helen nodded. "Yes, Kenny can be nice; and he's a good-looking guy. But he has a serious issue he needs to fix."

"What's his problem?" Natalie curiously asked.

"Mom, I'm sad to say, but Kenny Ross is a drunk. It's also rumored that he uses women for their money, expecting them to pay his way," Helen said, as she pulled two cutting boards out of a drawer and passed one to Natalie.

"That's too bad, sounds like you wouldn't mind talking to Kenny if he would sober up." Natalie stood at the counter chopping up celery and carrots.

"That's a moot thought since Kenny Ross is never going to give up his booze," Helen said lighthearted.

"That's too bad about Kenny Ross throwing his life away on booze," Natalie caringly stated. "I'm also sorry that you and Oliver didn't make it."

"I'm sorry too. But he's with Trina Ross now. And guess what, Mom? Trina works at Franklin Gas and she also works part-time at Taylor Gowns with me," Helen said lighthearted and then paused to think. "I guess she still works for Taylor Gowns. I haven't seen her in a while. But no one has mentioned that she's no longer working there."

Natalie nodded. "Well, in that case, I'm sure she's probably still employed there," Natalie assumed.

"Another thing, Mom. I didn't know this at the time, but I found out later after Wally Simpson married Pamela Taylor," Helen said as she stood at the counter peeling potatoes.

Natalie placed her knife on the cutting board and looked at Helen. "What did you find out after that Simpson boy married Don Taylor's daughter?"

Helen shook her head in disbelief. "I found out that Trina Ross was dating Wally Simpson while he was engaged to Miss Pamela. I never heard her say it, but I heard it through the grapevine. To make a long story short, after Wally married Miss Pamela, Oliver told me that he met a downhearted Trina and they hit it off and now they're dating," Helen said disappointedly.

"I'm sorry to hear that. I remember well what a huge crush you had on Oliver Bartlett," Natalie caringly said. "You two had become fairly good friends. I recall him showing some interest in you."

"Yes, Mom. I liked Oliver a lot; and I am disappointed that things didn't work out and go any further for him and me. But he chose Trina Ross; and I'm okay with that. I work with Trina and can't really be upset with her. She really is a decent person. She's nothing like her batty, loony sister, Courtney."

Chapter Thirteen

The last day of May was a grim overcasted looking morning as Courtney slowly drove up to the Taylor's mansion. She sat in her car with her head lying on the steering wheel for a few minutes before she killed the engine and exited her car. It was at the crack of dawn and she didn't appear a bit hesitant about ringing the Taylor's doorbell. No inside lights were on which made it apparent that Sabrina and the rest of her family were all still in bed. Yet, very boldly without reluctance, Courtney strolled up to their front door and rang the doorbell. After a while when no one answered the door, she glanced at her diamond Gucci watch that Rome had given her last Christmas and shook her head at the time. She thought to herself. "It may only be seven in the morning. But I'm sure their Cook should be stirring about in their big kitchen, preparing for their Saturday morning breakfast. They'll probably consider my early morning timing as rude, but I consider it as a smart way to catch Sabrina before she gets up and out."

She rang the doorbell a couple more times, and when no one answered the door, she knocked on the front door a couple times. Starlet heard the doorbell and she heard the vague knock. She sprang up in bed and glanced at her bedside clock. She was startled by the early hour and who could be ringing their doorbell and knocking on their front door at the break of day. She quickly threw her covers back and hopped out of bed. But she stood wobbly by the bedside rubbing both eyes with the back of her hands as she yawned. Still not fully awake, she dropped back down on the side of the bed and grabbed both cheeks for a moment as she continued to hear the knocking at the front door. Therefore, she willed herself off the bed still half asleep and walked across the floor and looked out of her bedroom window. She was instantly alerted at the sight of Courtney's car parked in the driveway. She figured something was the matter as she then grabbed her long blue satin robe from across the foot of her bed, threw it on and hurried out of her room, down the long hallway and then strolled down the staircase. When she made it to the bottom of the staircase, she glanced to her right at the tall white grandfather clock in the corner of the living room and was surprised by the early hour as she held her robe tightly around her hurrying across the living room floor toward the front door.

Courtney had just reached her car and pulled opened the driver's door, when Starlet swung open the front door. Starlet grabbed her mouth and yawned with sleepily looking eyes. Courtney smiled at her as she slammed her car door shut and hurried back up the walkway to their front door. The big house was quiet as Starlet and Courtney's voices floated up the staircase and down the hallway to Sabrina's bedroom.

"Hi Starlet. I was just about to leave. I didn't think any of you were up and about yet," Courtney said, smiling with a solemn look on her face.

"You were right. We were all still asleep. Your knocks woke me. I hopped out of bed and looked out of the window and saw your car. You look sad. Is everything okay?" Starlet grabbed her mouth and yawned again as Courtney stood there at the front door with both arms wrapped around her.

"I'm okay," Courtney mumbled.

"That's good. But what's going on? What's so urgent that it would bring you knocking at our door at seven o'clock in the morning?" Starlet asked as Courtney stood there looking anxious. "I know my question may sound a bit rude and I don't mean to be impolite, but I'm still half asleep; and paying a house visit at the crack of dawn is very bad-manners within its self."

"I know it's early, but I need to see Sabrina. Is she home?"

Starlet nodded. "Yes, she's home."

"Good, may I please come in?"

"Sure, you can come in." Starlet stepped aside as Courtney stepped inside. "But she's still in bed," Starlet said politely as she closed the front door. "I know you said you need to see her, but can it possibly wait until later in the day?" Starlet suggested. "Once again I'm not trying to be rude to you. But I'm not usually at my best manners at the crack of dawn after being awakened from a peaceful sleep," Starlet said slightly jokingly. "But I'm curious about something and don't mean to be too inquisitive."

"What are you curious about?" Courtney looked toward the staircase.

"How did you and Sabrina manage to broker such a close friendship?"

"I don't know what you mean? We're just friends," Courtney mumbled.

"I know Sabrina thinks you're her friend, but I get a different vide from you. I'm not convinced that you're my sister's friend," Starlet said honestly.

"Well, I'm glad it's not left up to you who Sabrina chooses as a friend."

"I know it's not left up to me, and I'm not trying to be rude to you. But there's something that's not right about your behavior. It seems heinous."

"Well, that was very rude to say something like that to me."

"Maybe that was a very strong word to use. It's just unbelievable how you have changed. When you dated Rome Franklin, you were a lot different than what you are now."

"I felt different at that time than what I feel now," Courtney commented.

"I can recall how much easier you were to talk to."

"I'm not here for you to examine my attitude. I'm here to see Sabrina and would very much appreciate it if you would fetch her for me," Courtney said anxiously, slightly trembling because she needed another drink.

"Something is the matter with you, Courtney, how you are standing here trembling. I don't think you need to see my sister. I think you need to see a doctor," Starlet suggested.

Courtney wanted to yell in Starlet face and call her a few dreadful names. Plus, she was frustrated that Starlet wouldn't run and get Sabrina. Nevertheless, she held her anger, knowing Starlet wouldn't fetch Sabrina if she didn't try to tone it down and be nicer.

"Are you going to let Sabrina know I'm here or not?"

Starlet stared at Courtney observing her anxious behavior. "I'm not sure if I should. You seem troubled and uneasy. Plus, you're standing here talking to me rather rudely, but you still want me to do you a favor and go upstairs at this insanely hour and wake my sister just because you are here to see her."

"I'm sorry if I was rude, okay?" Courtney calmly apologized. "I know how early it is. But I told you how vitally important it is that I see Sabrina."

Starlet wasn't buying Courtney's story. "It might be important, but I seriously doubt it. Besides, you haven't answered my question."

"What question are you referring to?"

"I asked you how you and Sabrina become so close."

Courtney rolled her eyes toward the ceiling, shaking her head. Her patience was wearing thin with Starlet, but she knew she had to hold back her anger. She took a deep breath. "Why is that so important to you?" she asked.

"It's important to me because my sisters and I are very close, and we look out for each other. Besides, you must admit how unusual your friendship looks with Sabrina. You too are an unusual pairing. I'm sure you see my point."

Courtney turned her back to Starlet and looked toward the carpet. "I'm not sure if I can see your point."

"Okay, I can be more specific. It wasn't that long ago that you were absolutely crazy about Britain Franklin." Starlet held up one hand. "Before you try to deny it. I know all about the Christmas disaster at Franklin House. Besides, Courtney, I think everyone in this community pretty much knows how you had such a huge crush on Britain Franklin, who is now my sister's boyfriend," Starlet politely explained. "You may still have feelings for him."

Courtney turned around on the heels of her Sears's flats and held up both arms. "Starlet, you got to be kidding me," she laughed anxiously. "You are so off track with your remark if you think I still have feelings for Britain Franklin," she protested anxiously as she fiddled nervously with her hands. "The association that I had with Britain Franklin has long been over. It's ancient history now! Sabrina doesn't have to fear any competition from me as far as Britain is concerned."

Starlet nodded with curious eyes as she observed Courtney's manner and words. Courtney's fidgeted behavior and unpersuasive words didn't convince Starlet that she was over Britain. "So, you're saying you're completely over Britain and my sister doesn't have to worry about you still harboring feelings for him. Is that correct?"

"That is absolutely correct," Courtney snapped irritated.

"Courtney, I'm not purposely trying to call you a liar. However, rumor has it that you have completely changed and gone off the rails because of Britain Franklin," Starlet said softly. "I don't know how true that is, but seeing you now, I can easily see that you have changed. You're not the girl I recall at Franklin House when you were dating Rome."

Courtney laughed nervously and glanced at her watch. "Starlet, I woke you out of your sleep and I thought you were anxious to get back to bed."

"You did wake me, but I'm fully awake now and might as well stay awake. Besides, I wouldn't be able to fall back to sleep after this discussion."

"That's my point," Courtney grumbled. "I dropped by because I need to see Sabrina about something vitally urgent. But instead of allowing me to see Sabrina, you're standing here having a discussion with me about Britain and Rome Franklin?" Courtney held up both hands. "I thought you had better manners. Besides, somehow engaging in this conversation with you feels inappropriate," Courtney calmly said to her.

"Excuse me if it feels inappropriate to you for me to let you know I think you still have feelings for my sister's boyfriend. If I'm off the mark, then your conscience is clear. But, my instincts tell me differently," Starlet said politely.

Courtney waved her left hand feeling irritated with Starlet. "Well, I guess you're entitled to your opinion even if it's wrong. Besides, just for the record. Rome is married, and Britain is with Sabrina; and I don't mean to be rude, but your instincts are a lie!" Courtney sharply said. "Britain Franklin has no effect on me what so ever. Just for the record. I loathe the man anyway!"

"You can't convince me of that," Starlet shook her head. "I happen to think you still care very deeply for Britain. Besides, I know something that you don't know I know," Starlet admitted.

"What do you think you know?" Courtney nervously asked.

"It's not really what I know, it's what I can see. As much as you stand here and protest about not having feelings for my sister's boyfriend, I know your words are not true because I can see through your eyes into your soul and it's clear as day to me." Starlet held her chest with both hands. "You love Britain Franklin like no tomorrow, which means you are madly in love with the man." Starlet held up both hands. "I rest my case."

Courtney laughed off Starlet's instincts. "You don't expect anyone to believe your instincts about me, do you? What are you psychic now?"

"No, but I know what I know about your past with Britain Franklin and my instincts tells me that you are still very much in love with him. Besides, when you were with Rome Franklin, you admitted to Rome in front of his entire family that you still wanted Britain," Starlet softly explained. "Therefore, you can deny your feelings as much as you like. It should be obvious to you that we're all on to you, Courtney."

"What are you getting at Miss Starlet?" Courtney asked calmly.

"I'm getting at the fact that we have figured out that this whole friendship thing that you have going with my sister is all bogus on your part."

"I don't know what you mean."

"I think you do know what I mean, Courtney."

"I don't know what you mean. I think you've just decided to look down your nose at me, thinking you're better than I am," Courtney rudely snapped.

Starlet swallowed hard as she kept her composure. She hadn't expected Courtney to say what she had just said. The words stabbed at her feelings. She wasn't a bigoted and was bothered that Courtney had referred to her as such.

"Courtney that was a mean thing to say, but I think you already know that," Starlet firmly said to her. "However, it still doesn't erase the fact that I feel you are tricking and deceiving my sister. I'm not trying to be rude or unkind to you. I'm just standing up for Sabrina and being a good sister, the way families should stand up for each other. I have nothing against you other than the fact that I feel you're pretending to be Sabrina's friend. I'm sure of it.

You still have feelings for her boyfriend," Starlet said firmly. "You are probably trying to figure out a way to have Britain Franklin for yourself."

Courtney looked at Starlet stunned. She knew Starlet had figured her out, but she kept her composure, trying show Starlet words didn't affect her.

"That surprise look in your eyes tell me I'm right about you wanting Britain. How am I doing in figuring you out? Did I hit the nail on the head?"

"If you insist on discussing Britain Franklin," Courtney said frustrated. "So be it! But can I help it if Britain and I dated first before he met Sabrina?"

Their voices floated up the staircase in the big quiet house as Sabrina could hear vague chatter as she lied half-awake in her bed. She yawned and then rubbed her eyes. She turned on her side and glanced at the small silver clock that sat on her bedside table. It was only 7:15 in the morning. She pulled the covers up to her shoulders and closed her eyes to try to fall back to sleep. But just then she thought she heard more chatter coming from downstairs. The staff or their Cook didn't usually stir about so early. She glanced toward her bedroom window and could see it was starting out as a dreary morning as she heard vague voices again. This time, she sat straight up in bed, threw the covers back and rubbed both eyes as she yawned. She needed to get to the bottom of the voices she was hearing. Therefore, she got out of bed and threw on her long satin white robe. She slowly, half-awake walked over to her bedroom window, pulled the curtains apart and looked down at the driveway. She noticed Courtney's car parked there. Suddenly seeing her car alerted her wide awake as she rushed out of her room and sailed down the hallway toward the edge of the hallway. She wanted to see if Courtney was paying a visit to her house at such an unspeakable hour. She figured for Courtney to show up at her home at such an early hour, it meant something wasn't right. As she reached the end of the hallway she could tell Courtney were talking to Starlet and she could hear heavy breathing coming from Courtney as if Courtney was out of breath. She was stunned that Courtney had found a need to visit her home at such a disrespectful hour. Nevertheless, she turned around and headed back down the hallway to her room. Whatever business Courtney had with Starlet was their business and she would just hop back in bed and attempt to get another hour of sleep.

Courtney glanced toward the window and looked out at her car, noticing that she had left her lights on. "I see I left my lights on. Is it okay if I run outside and turn them off and come back in to see Sabrina?"

"Sure, come on and turn off your car lights," Starlet said as she walked Courtney to the front door and waited in the door as Courtney rushed outside and turned off the headlights of her car.

Courtney hurried back inside, and the front door slammed loudly as the heavy wind pushed against it before Courtney could close it softly.

"Please keep it down," Starlet said softly. "Just because you and I are both awake with the birds. Let's make sure we don't wake everyone else in the house?" Starlet said in a whisper as she and Courtney headed toward the staircase. "I hope you don't make me regret allowing you to stay and visit this time of morning. My father, Samantha and Sabrina are all still in bed asleep and not even our house staff is stirring this early," Starlet pointed out.

"Well, it's good for me that I caught you stirring," Courtney mumbled.

"That would be because I'm a light sleeper. I heard your car engine pull into the driveway. I couldn't imagine who would be pulling into our driveway at seven o'clock in the morning. But when you rang the doorbell and knocked on the door that's when I hopped out of bed and looked out and saw your car. After I saw it was you, I had to come down and answer the door."

"Why do you say you had to come down and answer the door? I'm glad you did, but you didn't have to. You could have easily stayed in bed and ignored the doorbell and my knocks, and I'd have driven away," Courtney said.

"Maybe you would have, but once I saw it was you. I had to come answer the door. It would have been rude not to. Especially since you are supposedly Sabrina's new-found friend. It wouldn't have felt right to tell her I saw you knocking outside and didn't answer the door to see what you wanted."

"Thank you for letting me in; and I'm sorry the door slammed when I stepped outside to turn off those lights. But what did you mean about I'm suddenly Sabrina's new-found friend?" Courtney asked.

"You know what I meant by that statement, Courtney. You're being civil with me because you're a guest in my home; and I'm being civil with you because you're a guest in my home. However, just as I said before. I'm not convinced that you're really my sister's friend," Starlet said as she stretched her hand toward the staircase. "I think you and I have talked enough. I can show you to Sabrina's room now if you like."

Courtney shook her head. "I think you and I need to hatch our conversation out before I see Sabrina. I need to change your view about me, especially since you seem to think I'm deceiving Sabrina and I'm not really her friend," Courtney stated strongly.

"I don't think you'll have much luck with changing my view about you," Starlet said firmly. "Besides, it's not just my view. It's many others view as well. There's plenty talk around town that you're not really Sabrina's friend."

Courtney smiled. "But you still let me in."

"Yes, I let you in because I have no proof that you're tricking my sister. Therefore, until your actions prove otherwise, that you're not a friend to my sister, I guess I'll have to consider you as her friend. But as I said, we all know your history with Britain and the talk in town has it that you have befriended Sabrina to get to Britain," Starlet firmly stated.

"I'm sure the Taylor girls don't listen to gossip," Courtney snapped.

"Not really, but that's what's being said," Starlet told her.

Courtney suddenly drew an attitude and took offense to Starlet's remarks. "Frankly, Starlet I could care less about what is being said about me and my friendship with Sabrina. My friendship with your sister is between me and your sister and as long as she doesn't have a problem with it, then everyone else needs to keep their noses out of it, including present company if the shoe fits," Courtney snapped angrily.

"Okay, excuse my manners, but what's the matter with you, Courtney?"

"I'm pissed at you and everyone else for looking down your noses at me! That's what the matter!" Courtney snapped again.

"No, it's not that. Something else is wrong," Starlet observed.

"Why do you think something is the matter?"

"I just get the sense that something is. You seem nervous, and you're acting kind of peculiar. You have seemed anxious since you arrived," Starlet said. "I noticed that about your behavior from the moment I opened the door."

Courtney inhaled sharply to pull herself together. She realized she didn't want to upset Starlet and lose her chance at visiting with Sabrina. "I apologize for snapping at you the way I did. I'm just fine. But I have a lot on my mind. Plus, I need to talk to Sabrina."

"Okay, if you say so, but you don't seem fine. Try explaining away why you have traces of tears dried on your face?"

"What you're talking about, Starlet? There's no dried tears on my face."

"I have eyes and can see you've been crying. So, I'm sure something is the matter but apparently you only want to share it with Sabrina."

"Starlet, thanks for your concern. But really, I'm okay. I haven't been crying. I hurt my eye when I walked into a branch," Courtney insisted.

"Okay, I see, nothing is the matter you just hurt your eye on a branch and you haven't been crying. If I continue to listen to you, you'll probably tell me that you weren't the one who knocked on our front door at seven this morning, when you know that I know you are the one," Starlet said frustrated with Courtney. "Therefore, our conversation is over. I think you should head on upstairs and see Sabrina." Starlet left Courtney at the foot of the staircase as she headed in the direction of the kitchen.

Chapter Fourteen

Starlet had walked halfway across the living room floor when Courtney softly called out to her. "Should I stand here and wait for you to show me up to Sabrina's room?" Courtney asked, suddenly feeling uneasy in their big house.

Starlet glanced around and said over her shoulder. "No, you don't have to wait for me. I'm headed to the kitchen for some juice. It's okay for you to head upstairs. You know the way to her room, up the staircase middleway the hallway. It's the first door on the left." Starlet glanced around and stopped in her tracks, pointing up the staircase. "Now, if you'll please excuse me I'm headed to the kitchen for a much-needed glass of orange juice?"

"You're headed to the kitchen for a glass of orange juice?"

"Yes, would you like a glass of juice as well?" Starlet offered.

Courtney shook her head. "No thank you. I just thought you would head upstairs with me and knock on Sabrina's door to let her know I'm here."

Starlet smiled toward Courtney. "I'll let you in on a little secret. Sabrina doesn't like to be disturbed from her sleep. Therefore, I think I'll allow you the honors, since it's your idea to wake her at the crack of dawn," Starlet said, smiling; raised both hands and then turned on the heels of her white Bloomingdale's house slippers and headed toward the hallway in route to the kitchen. But stopped and stood still, looking toward Courtney when she noticed in the corner of her eye that Courtney hadn't headed up the staircase.

Courtney stood at the bottom of the staircase as if she was frozen in that spot. She had expected Starlet to escort her to Sabrina's room. Suddenly she felt nervous to head upstairs and knock on Sabrina's bedroom door. She felt anxious to confront her with the news she had to deliver. She glanced over her shoulder in the direction that Starlet went and noticed that Starlet was still standing there.

"I thought you headed to the kitchen for juice?" Courtney said.

"I thought you headed up to Sabrina's room," Starlet said.

"I was wondering if I should wait for you to fetch your juice. It feels uneasy stirring around in this big house so early in the morning without an escort." Courtney glanced at her watch and smiled. "It's seven thirty. There's a better chance she could be awake now."

Starlet nodded. "Yes, you're right. There is a better chance that she could be awake, especially with all the racket we have made talking and shutting the door loudly. However, I'm willing to bet that Sabrina is still asleep at this unearthly hour in the morning." Starlet waved her hand toward Courtney. "But please feel free to go knock on her door. She can yell at you," Starlet smiled, turned on the heels again and headed toward the kitchen.

On her own, Courtney slowly begun her way up the long staircase. Halfway up, she looked down into the enormous elegant living room but didn't see Starlet. She headed softly up the staircase and when she reached the top of the staircase she stood at the edge of the hallway for a moment before she began her journey down the long hallway. Her heart skipped a beat when she realized the enormous size of the Taylor home. Suddenly her heart raced, and she felt out of her element and more uneasy than she had imagined. She noticed all the large paintings on either side of the hallway and the hallway seemed endless as she put one foot before the other one in awe of the place and in her mind's eye she wondered what the other Taylors would say if they happened into the hallway to see her roaming their hallway. But just as her nerves got the better of her, still standing at the edge of the hallway, she glanced over her shoulders once more and spotted Starlet headed across the living room floor coming toward the staircase. She waited for Starlet to meet up where she stood, a couple doors away from Sabrina's bedroom door.

"Did you knock on Sabrina's door yet?" Starlet asked in a whisper.

Courtney shook her head and for someone who was filled with bitterness and anger, she suddenly behaved frightened. "I didn't knock yet. I don't know if I should," she said nervously, visibly trembling.

"Again, Courtney, I'm not trying to be rude to you. But just look at yourself. You clearly have some kind of an issue."

"I don't have an issue. I'm just thinking twice about being here."

"Well, you're here just a few feet from Sabrina's door. You might as well go ahead and knock and see if she'll let you come in," Starlet suggested.

"I'm having second thoughts about being here so early in the morning. I don't want to wake your father or anyone else," Courtney said in a timid voice.

Starlet was uneasy by Courtney's sudden timid behavior. She was acting completely different from her strong rude behavior when she was standing in the living room with her arms across her chest. "I'm not sure why you are not sure whether you should knock on Sabrina's door. You told me it was vitally important for you to see her. That's why I allowed you in the house at this hour. Therefore, just strolled down the hall to her door and knock," Starlet suggested, pointing toward Sabrina's room.

"What if I knock too hard and wake up your father. I don't want to get in trouble by being here in your home at this hour," Courtney said nervously. "Your father is a powerful person and he might take issue with me visiting Sabrina at this hour."

"Courtney don't worry about it. I'm sure you won't wake my father. Besides, if you do, I can assure you that Father will not say anything to you about being here as long as I'm standing here with you," Starlet assured her.

"Okay, I want you to stand right here by my side until Sabrina open her door and let me in. If she doesn't let me, I want you to escort me back out of this gigantic castle of a house," Courtney muttered in a low voice.

"That's fine," Starlet covered her mouth and yawned. "But go ahead and knock. I'd like to try for at least another hour of sleep before I face the day."

Courtney pointed toward Sabrina's door and Starlet nodded. "Yes, that's her room."

"Okay, I'll knock now," Courtney said as she slowly walked over to Sabrina's door. She went to knock but pulled her hand back. "I can't knock on her door at this hour."

"Courtney, what's with you? You knocked on our front door earlier than this. You said it was vital for you to see Sabrina, but you bothered to chat with me for a half an hour. Now you're acting timid as if your urgent reason to see Sabrina is no longer urgent."

"Maybe I have sobered up a bit from when I first arrived. I haven't taken one sip from the bottle in my purse since I arrived here," Courtney mumbled, nodding while looking at Starlet. "So, I'll say I have sobered up a lot. I arrived here from an all-night party where I had more than my share of drinks."

Starlet was surprised by her information. "I didn't need to know all of that. Your business before you arrived here is your business and not mine." Starlet raised both hands. "But suit yourself. I have done my good deed for the day. But you can suit yourself if you no longer want to knock on her door. However, I'll point out that you had no hesitation about the timing when you showed up here and woke me out of my sleep to open the front door for you," Starlet said in a whisper. "I can't get over your peculiar behavior. You say you were mostly drunk when you arrived and now you are supposedly sober. But if you ask me, you don't seem sober. You're carrying on like a frightened child. I really don't understand you, Courtney. You said it was urgent and earlier you seemed pushy. Now, you're at Sabrina's door and you have a completely different attitude," Starlet observed.

"Starlet, I seem odd to you because we're from two different worlds. So please stop trying to figure me out," she slightly snapped. "You never will. So just do me a favor and knock on Sabrina's door. If you knock and wake your father, he won't say anything to me for being here in your home."

"Okay, sure, I'll knock, and I hope she answers for your sake and mine. I need to get back under the covers and try to fall back to sleep. I have a busy schedule a head of me today," Starlet said as she stepped over to Sabrina's bedroom door and knocked softly two times, and on the second knock, the door flew open. It wasn't completely close. "It's already open," Starlet said as she stood sandwiched between the door and the doorframe. She held the doorknob and peeped in across the room at Sabrina.

Starlet was surprised to see Sabrina was wide awake, lying there under the covers with her head propped on two pillows. "Good morning," Starlet greeted her with a smile. "I was just checking to see if you were awake."

Sabrina nodded. "Yes, I'm wide awake and I know I have a visitor."

"Yes, Courtney is here to see you. I let her in the house. She said it's urgent that she talks to you. So, I hope its okay that I allowed her inside to pay you a visit so early."

"It is quite early," Sabrina agreed as she glanced at the clock on her bedside table. "But you let her in, so it's okay. Tell her to come on in."

Starlet waved her hand and beckoned for Courtney to step into Sabrina's room. Courtney stepped inside of Sabrina's room, walking slowly still displaying a timid behavior. She had obvious traces of tears on her cheeks and she was visibly trembling. She stepped across the room and took a seat on Sabrina's settee, looking down toward the carpet at first, and then her eyes started glancing about the large bedroom.

Sabrina and Starlet noticed how Courtney sat there glancing about the room as if she was in a wonderland. But Sabrina and Starlet didn't exchange looks with each other as Starlet turned to leave. "Okay, I'm heading to my room now," Starlet said, pulling Sabrina's bedroom door closed behind her.

Sabrina looked toward her bedroom door as Starlet walked out and closed it, then she glanced back over at Courtney for a moment before glancing at her bedside clock again. She shook her head against the pillow. However, Courtney didn't look toward Sabina since she was in awe of the eloquent room. Courtney eyes widened with admiration as she focused on the brilliantly decorated soft pink room that stood out from the refined design of the floral pink wallpaper and plush pink carpet. The room was three times the size of her own bedroom. It displayed graceful long flowing pink curtains at all four expressive tall windows. The spacious room showcased an eight-piece set of priceless feminine ancient white oak bedroom furniture.

"Courtney, I'm listening. I can't wait to hear your vital news," Sabrina said teasingly to make light of Courtney's rude timing.

However, Courtney didn't comment since she was still lost in the beauty of Sabrina's elegant room. It always made Courtney feel envy for those things and suddenly, hostility and anger flooded Courtney as she threw her head in the air and sailed over to Sabrina's bedside. For a moment, Sabrina laid motionless and speechless, looking up at her, and then she sat up and pulled her white robe tightly around her, and then threw the covers back. She was not pleased with Courtney for showing up at her home at such an early hour. Besides, she had told Courtney to stay away from her home but was willing to overlook it at the moment and hear Courtney out. But her willingness to hear Courtney out, quickly faded when Courtney drew a cold attitude.

"This is a very large room, but it's not that nice!" Courtney rudely stated. "Actually, it's not that nice at all. Besides, I'll have a room like this one day for myself! You'll all see!"

Instantly after Courtney's rude remark, Sabrina was furious with Courtney and her emotions overwhelmed her to the point that she had to calm herself to keep her composure and not speak too loudly. She realized it was quite early and the house was quiet, and voices could float. She didn't want to disturb or wake anyone else in the house.

"Courtney, when you walked in my room you seemed humble and almost frightened. Now you have the gall to stand here and say unkind rude things to me. However, I'm sure that's not why you showed up here at this insane time to visit me," Sabrina sharply stated. "You don't think my room is nice at all. But on the other hand, someday you plan to have a room just like it," Sabrina firmly remarked, shaking her head.

"Yes, just because I can. I do plan to have a room like yours even though I think this room is a heinous affair that fits you perfectly." She raised both arms toward the ceiling.

"That's it, Courtney. I'm not going to stomach your rudeness, for the sake of being rude! Just please leave my room and get out of my house, now!" Sabrina pointed toward the door. "I keep giving you the benefit of the doubt, allowing myself to feel sorry for you. But I'm not doing you or myself any favors by overlooking the obvious. You're seriously messed up in the head; and you're still filled with bitterness and jealously! It's obvious that you had nothing better to do than to show up over here at the break of dawn just to be nasty to me and try to break my spirits. That's been your game ever since I have tried to bend over backward and be your friend. But I'm done putting up with your petty rudeness and I want you to leave!"

Courtney shook her head and laughed. "Don't you know by now that I don't listen to a word you say? You might want me to leave, but I'm staying put. So, it would be a good idea to forget about me leaving your room for now! Since I'm not going anywhere yet! I just got here. Besides, you are ranting and raving, but you don't know why I'm here do you?" Courtney coldly fussed.

"No, I don't know why you're here. But whatever the reason it can't be any good. Not with the rude hostile attitude you're displaying right now. I'm sure you displayed nicer manners with Starlet. Otherwise, you wouldn't be standing here because she would not have welcomed you inside."

Courtney nodded. "I'll hand it to you. You're right about your baby sister. She's not the pushover you are, not by a long shot. But she still doesn't know jack if she thinks she can figure me out. That one can talk and ask questions like no tomorrow. But, I still played her like a fiddle. You Taylor girls need to be schooled in backbone and foresight. You're missing both, of course. Because as sharp as Starlet thought she was, I got just what I wanted from her, all while she thought she knew where I was coming from. Sydney Franklin definitely has a handful with that one. I'll see if their little affair last. I'm sure their relationship will crash and burn just like you and Britain."

"Britain and I are back together, engaged and happier than ever. If you'll spare me your nasty tongue I would greatly appreciate it. Afterall, Starlet was nice enough to let you in. And since you insist on hanging around, you better have a good reason to have shown up here this time of morning. I want you to say what you came to say so you can leave."

Courtney strolled over to one of the bedroom windows and pulled the curtains apart. She was in deep thought and boiled inside with animosity for Sabrina. Seeing Sabrina lying in her big fancy bed somehow made Courtney feel Sabrina had stolen her life. She begrudged Sabrina and felt that Sabrina had destroyed her life and was now living the life that she should be living.

After Courtney stood there in the window for a couple minutes, Sabrina nerves were wearing thin. "Courtney, my sister was decent enough to let you in at this hour, but was she wrong to trust you in our home?"

Courtney glanced around and stared at Sabrina with cold eyes. "No, she wasn't wrong to let me in. I'm not here to goof off. I have big news for you."

"Okay, big news, is that right?" Sabrina said annoyed with Courtney's behavior. "You have been here all of five minutes and you haven't given me a hint of any news! All you have done is shown me how much you are the same. You haven't changed at all and I think you're playing games again! I want no part of your schemes and deception again. Besides, I have asked you nicely to just stay away from me." Sabrina held up both hands. "You're telling everyone that we're good friends, but I know better. Therefore, get to the point of your big news and the reason you're here in my home waking me and my family up at this time of morning?" Sabrina stressed sharply, keeping her voice low. "You have some gall to drive over here and knock on my door and behavior so rude and oddly," Sabrina said quite irritated. "Who in the heck do you think you are, Courtney Ross?"

"Why don't you know? I'm your new friend, remember?"

"No, I don't remember! You have never been my friend."

"I thought we were friends," Courtney sniped.

"Well, you thought wrong! Besides, I'm sure you remember what I told you yesterday. I made it crystal clear that I wanted nothing else to do with your kind of friendship! So, there you have it, we are not friends!"

"So, I guess the real problem is not my attitude this morning. You're still upset about that lie they told on me?" Courtney snapped.

"Yes, I'm upset because it wasn't a lie! I know for a fact that you started that vicious spiteful rumor about me at Franklin Gas," Sabrina said firmly. "You have nerve to even show your face over here!"

"Sabrina, I didn't start that rumor," Courtney grumbled. "Do you want me to write my innocence in blood?"

"Please Courtney Ross; do not insult me by telling me you didn't start that rumor when I know you started it? I heard you do it."

"What do you mean you heard me do it?" Courtney asked.

"I was standing in the doorway of the cafeteria when you were running your mouth, telling those lies about me a couple days ago."

"It's not a big deal."

"Maybe it's not a big deal to you, but it's a big deal to me when someone spread an untrue rumor on purpose. Plus, you just stood here and tried to deny that you started the rumor!" Sabrina fussed. "I was standing there and heard every single word you said."

Courtney shook her head and threw up both hands. "Okay, so what if you were standing there and heard every single word I said; I wasn't the only one in the cafeteria discussing you that day."

"Maybe not, but you were the only one saying what I heard!"

"Okay, Sabrina. Believe what you please!"

"No, it's not believe what I please! You know, and I know that you started the rumor, so why can't you just admit it?"

"Forget it already! I said I'm sorry, Sabrina. What more do you want?"

"I'll tell you what I want. I want you to leave my house and leave me alone! I'm fed up with your games!"

"What games?" Courtney sniped.

"Just like now. What you are doing right now is a game," Sabrina said softly. "You are a grown woman, but you act irresponsible like a child. I have learned the hard way that you have zero respect or consideration for others," Sabrina said angrily in a low voice.

Courtney nodded. "But on the other hand, Sabrina Taylor is polite and proper." Courtney laughed. "But the way you are speaking to me right now is anything but respectful. Do Britain know you can have such a sharp tongue!"

"No, I'm not being respectful; and if I have a sharp tongue it's because you made it that way. I'm just dishing out to you what you dish out to me. Do you honestly think you deserve my respect when you have zero respect for me?" Sabrina angrily asked.

Courtney waved her hand. "Go on and get it out and say whatever makes you feel better. You would think I just asked you to jump off a cliff."

"No, you didn't ask me to jump off a cliff, but from past experiences I'm sure you are up to no good. Does tricking me to a cemetery and into a deep hole ring a bell? If not, it should. Plus, you're here way too early in the morning while my family and I are still in bed. It doesn't look pretty. So, what gives, Courtney? What's your problem and this big news you have to share?"

Sabrina was going on and on, and then suddenly Courtney froze up. She paced about and flopped down on the carpet in the corner of Sabrina's room. Her head was lowered as she sniffed. Then five minutes later, Sabrina noticed that Courtney had fallen asleep on the floor in the corner of her room. Agitated with Courtney she decided to give her ten minutes to nap and then would wake her. But as Sabrina laid back with her head propped on two comfortable pillows, her eyes became heavy and soon she had also fallen back to sleep.

Chapter Fifteen

One hour went by before Sabrina rolled over on her side and woke herself. Her eyes blinked open with a clear view of the bedside clock. She jerked in surprise when she noticed that an hour had gone by while she slept with Courtney lying asleep on the floor in her room. She hopped out of bed looking toward the carpet where Courtney sat with her back propped against the wall with both knees up. She had her head lying face down against her knees with both arms wrapped around her knees. Sabrina walked across the room to her closet where she pulled a long satin blue robe off a hanger. She threw it on over the long very sheer white one she was already wearing and then stepped into her connecting bathroom to wash her face. After washing her face, she walked across the room and stood before Courtney. She looked down at Courtney, but Courtney didn't look up.

"Look, Courtney! You need to wake up and get up off of my floor! Your behavior is freaking me out! If you came over here to fall asleep on the carpet, you need to leave!"

Courtney looked up at Sabrina and covered her mouth yawning. "Don't bitch at me about falling to sleep." Courtney glanced at her watch. "You fell asleep too." She laughed.

"Look, Courtney, you either tell me what's going on or I'm kicking you out of my room right now. You shouldn't even be here in the first place," Sabrina fussed.

"But I am here," Courtney snapped. "So just give me the benefit of listening to what I have to say, and I'll be out of your hair very soon!"

"That's one of the problems I have with you Courtney, there's really nothing you can say that I want to hear. At this point you have zero credibility with me. Besides, how many times do I have to tell you that I'm done with you? You won't listen, and you won't leave me alone. I'm trying to stay civil and not involve my family. But you need to lay off of me and stay away as I have asked you too! What part of, we are no longer friends and I don't want to be your friend, you don't understand? I have tried to be your friend over and over, but each time you stab me in the back! And I have been stabbed enough. It took me long enough to wake up, but my eyes are open now! So, will you please leave before I go down the hallway to my father's room and tell him you're distressing me?"

"No, Sabrina, hear me out. Just hear me out. What harm can come to you just to hear me out?" She pleaded, jumped off the floor, drying her tears with the sleeve of her sweater.

Sabrina shook her head no, as she headed toward her bedroom door. "No, Courtney! I'm done giving you chances and hearing you out. I always end up with the short end of the stick. So, please, just get out!" Sabrina pointed toward the door. "You have absolutely nothing I want to hear! Start stepping and leave now!"

"But Sabrina, before you kick me out so quickly, I think you'll want to hear what I have to tell you about Britain!"

"I dare you mention Britain. Just leave his name out of this conversation," Sabrina snapped and grabbed both cheeks. "Can you please just spare me your lies? Your heart is missing or frozen in your chest! You are the rudest and inconsideration person I know! Not only do you come over here at an insane hour, you come over here to purposely say things to stress me out; and they are all lies. This is just another stunt to get under my skin and break me emotionally. But I'm on to you, Miss Ross, so please take your filthy lies and the venom you are trying to spread and get out of my room and out of my house! I'm not interested!" Sabrina said firmly.

"Oh, but you should be! You were curious about my behavior and why I dropped over so early? That's what I'm trying to tell you. Where do you think I just came from? Why do you think I'm over here so early? Why do you think I was crying? It all has to do with your perfect fiancé Mr. Britain Franklin."

Sabrina was stunned and speechless for a moment and then she thought better of it and figured Courtney were trying to get to her with made up lies. "If it has to do with Britain, just keep it to yourself. I don't care! I just want you out of my room and out of my house!" Sabrina calmly held up both arms. "I asked you politely, so are you leaving, or should I go wake my father who will have our security staff escort you out."

Courtney stood there and acted indifferent as if she wasn't shaken by the thought of Mr. Taylor having her thrown out of the Taylors' mansion. "Sabrina, I'm not convinced."

"You're not convinced about what?"

"I'm not convinced you want me to leave," Courtney solemnly mumbled.

"Please be convinced! I want you to leave my house," Sabrina stressed."

"You say you want me to leave, and you probably do, but you also want to know what I have to say about Britain," Courtney uttered seriously as she stared in Sabrina's eyes. "You say you don't care about what I have to tell you, but the look in your eyes tell me otherwise. So, all you have to do is just calm down and give me a few minutes of your precious time, and I'll tell you everything. Then once I tell you what I came to say, then I'll leave, and you'll never have to bother with me again. So, Sabrina, it's your call. Are you really going to cut off your nose to spite your face? I have the goods on the guy, but you really want me to walk out of here without spilling? Like I said, it's your call. So, last chance, do you want to know what's going on with Britain or not? I can walk out of that door and you'll never know what I came here to tell you?" She pointed toward the door.

"Okay, okay," Sabrina nodded and politely said pointing toward a chair. "Have a seat over there in that chair near the window."

"Why do I need to sit there? I'll stand here and say what I came to say."

"If it's okay with you, I would prefer for you to have a seat over there, so I can see your face and look in your eyes as you talk! If anything, you say starts to sound fishy or off the wall, that's it! You hear me, Courtney? I will very politely ask you to leave; and if you refuse to do so, I will calmly march down the hallway and alert my father to your resistance to leave here. Have I made myself clear?" Sabrina politely asked.

Courtney nodded. "Yes, you have made yourself crystal clear! I guess you have a bit more backbone than I gave you credit for," Courtney raised one finger. "Nevertheless, you made the right decision," Courtney said as she slowly walked across the large room to take a seat in the small comfortable white chair near the window; and for a moment she just stared at the long lacy pink curtains as if she was miles away lost in thought. Then she glanced around and looked at Sabrina and what appeared to be a frown on Courtney's face seemed more like a smirk to Sabrina.

"Courtney, I'm not a complete fool, you know. How many times do you have to bump my head against the wall before I wise up to you?"

"Sabrina, you've every right to be leery of me, but I'm on the level."

"I see. Start explaining yourself," Sabrina said, taking a seat at the foot of the bed. "Don't beat around the bush. Tell me what you have to say about Britain. That's all I want to hear. I'm not really interested in hearing anything else: like your crack of dawn schedule or your tears! I just care about Britain. Say what you have to say so you can leave," Sabrina said calmly, looking her straight in the face.

Courtney's eyes widened, and a smile spread across her face, as if she found amusement in Sabrina's rudeness. She gripped the arms of the chair and leaned forward.

"Well, Sabrina, I guess I can't call you a sucker anymore."

"I guess not, Courtney. After run-ins with those like you, you learn quickly to toughen up. My eyes are wide open to schemers. Thanks to you," Sabrina calmly stated.

"Okay! Sabrina, I'll cut straight to the bone. I just came from Franklin House. I was there with Britain last night and I just thought you should know since you are engaged to the man. If the marriage will ever take place is another matter. But at least for now, you are engaged. Therefore, I felt you had a right to know."

"Courtney, you are not going to make me combative, belligerent or argumentative with you. I'm on to you and I'm aware of how you lie to try to get under my skin."

"Suit yourself, Sabrina. But what I just said is true."

"You expect me to get upset and believe you were at Franklin House with Britain last night?" Sabrina calmly asked. "I'm sorry, but I just don't believe you. I know you are playing games and I'm not having it," Sabrina calmly said and raised both hands. "However, I'm sure you remember that I explained to you that if you sounded off the wall that I would ask you politely to leave. That's what I'm doing, asking you politely to leave." Sabrina nodded with solemn eyes and pointed toward the door.

"Don't you want to know why I was at Franklin House?" She stood and nodded at Sabrina with a wicked look in her eyes.

Sabrina searched Courtney's face and eyes very closely and there was no doubt in Sabrina's mind that Courtney Ross had suffered a mental breakdown and needed professional help. She was different as day and night from her former self.

Courtney walked across the room toward the door, grabbed the gold-plated doorknob and leaned her back against it. "It gets better, Miss Sabrina!"

Sabrina stood up and pointed toward the door. "You need to leave! I know you're lying! You were not with Britain last night! He would never spend time with you under any circumstances! That's not who he is!"

"You're living in a dream world if you think Britain Franklin is above being a dog like the rest of these doggish men out here! He got you fooled!"

"If you don't leave, I'll do as I said and march down that hallway to fetch my father and see how much resistance you'll give him," Sabrina warned, pointing toward the door.

Nevertheless, with an anxious look in her eyes, hoping Sabrina wouldn't march down the hallway and wake her father, Courtney called her bluff and made no attempts to head out of her room. She just continued to talk. "I know you don't want to believe me, but I'm being truthful about this information I'm giving you. I was with Britain last night and as much as I love him, he always kicks me out of his bed at the crack of dawn. He always gives me the same song, that I'm just a meaningless warm body filling in for you! The nerve of him to say that to me! It always makes me cry. That's why Starlet found me at your door at the break of dawn with tears in my eyes. This is no game. This is the real thing and if you don't wise up to Britain's lies. You're going to be the laughing stock of this town. You say we are not friends but I'm doing you a big favor right now. But I should admit you're not alone in being a fool in love." Courtney grabbed her chest with both hands. "Look at me, I'm a bigger fool than you. I keep going back to his bed night after night, allowing him to use me as his plaything. He seems to need me around at night a lot. I wonder why that is? I could guess and would most likely be right. You're probably not keeping Mr. Franklin satisfied. Otherwise, why would he need me in his bed at all?"

Sabrina was so stunned at Courtney lies until she couldn't fight back anymore. Courtney's out and out lies had drained her of all her strength. She knew her words were lies to hurt her and she knew not to listen and take any of Courtney's word to heart. However, as Courtney went on and on about staying overnight with Britain, somehow the filthy lies penetrated Sabrina's heart and ripped at her soul. She was ready to take Courtney on and ready for anything Courtney had to dish out, but not what she had just said. Sabrina dropped breathless like dead weight down on the edge of her queen size bed and covered her face with both hands. Soon tears dripped through her fingers.

Courtney Ross, the twenty-four-year-old devil in disguise had hurt Sabrina once more as Sabrina sat powerless in tears. Courtney stepped to her bedside, dropped down to her knees in front of Sabrina and proceeded to torture her.

"You left me no choice. I had to tell you this, Sabrina. I couldn't keep it to myself any longer. Well, I guess I should probably tell you how long it's been going on. Well, let me see, we started fooling around with each other right after I tricked you into that hole and then allowed you to shower at my house. Britain saw you that evening for dinner and he saw me in his elegant white room on his elegant white sheets," Courtney said in a low voice. "And wouldn't you agree that his bedroom is one elegant retreat."

Courtney touched Sabrina's shoulder and Sabrina didn't blink. Sabrina was numb from her lies. "Save your tears. They don't help. I've been crying all morning too. We hung out in his bed making passionate love, and when he was finished he said I needed to leave his house. Men can be such bastards! Did you think Britain Franklin was any different from the rest of the male population?" She glanced at her watch. "Well, I'm here to tell you, he's no different. He's a two-legged dog just like the rest of them. But don't get me wrong, I'm not complaining. His behavior is fine by me because I love the guy with my whole soul."

Courtney paused when she vaguely heard someone open and close a door down the hallway. She stepped across the room and placed her ear against the door and listened for a moment; and then after all seemed quiet and still; she looked at Sabrina and laughed as she continued. "It's funny when you think about it. But the only way I was able to get close to Britain was through you. That's right; I never could stand the sight of you! From the first day I saw you walk into that cafeteria with Britain I knew I hated you. I knew you would be the one to bring great misery to my life and I wanted you gone." Courtney gritted her teeth in disgust of Sabrina.

Courtney stared into space for a moment, then continued. "Yes, Miss do-gooder! From that day on, it's been a game of pretending to be your friend, so I could get next to Mr. Britain Franklin." Courtney placed both hands on her hips as she kept talking. "Maybe you did wise up. But you wised up too late. You were your own worst enemy. You buried yourself when you had that old man from the cemetery drop you off at my house. But leave it to Miss Sabrina Taylor. You had to be a big person and play a saint to the troubled poor girl." Courtney shook her head, laughing but kept her voice low. "You had to forgive me for tricking you over into that deep hole. But I got news for you, doing that didn't make you a big person; it only made you a big fool. You should have left well enough alone and cut all ties with me right then and there on the spot! You say I'm nuts, but who in their right mind try to befriend someone who do something that awful to them?" Courtney laughed. "But there was no pushing you away. You had to be the bighearted bitch that you are! Well, your big heart just cost you Britain! He's mine now!"

Sabrina sat there frozen with contempt for Courtney, but from her behavior and the sound of her voice, Courtney had flipped off her rocker. Five weeks earlier when she tricked Sabrina into going with her to the old graveyard, Sabrina wish she had told someone about Courtney and Courtney could have gotten some professional help. But Sabrina reflected back on what Courtney had said that day after she tricked her into the deep hole. Courtney had apologized and told Sabrina that she had learned her lesson and wouldn't do something like that again to anyone. Sabrina believed her and accepted her phony friendship since she couldn't see through Courtney's lies and deception.

"Sabrina, what's the matter with you now?" Courtney asked in a low voice. "You had an awful lot to say a few minutes ago. You said you were on to me and you were letting me have it left and right. But I like you better with your mouth glued shut the way it is now. Besides, I have told you all of this, but you still don't have to worry. Britain Franklin made it painfully clear that he still plans to marry you."

Sabrina head popped up and she glared at Courtney with contempt, but she still felt drained with repulsion and couldn't say a word.

"But he also made it crystal clear that he still wants the two of us to get it on whenever or wherever we can." She stepped over to one of the four bedrooms windows, pulled the long lacy sheer pink curtains apart and stared out across their huge backyard for a moment; and her heart skipped a beat when she spotted Franklin House just across the next lot. Her love was so deep and dark for Britain until just seeing his home overwhelmed her in a deep emotional way. But, after a few moments, she collected herself, turned and stared across the room at Sabrina and blurted out in an upbeat manner.

"Before I forget to mention it, I think you should know that Britain and I have plans to make out later today. I figured one way to make a believer out of you would be to invite you to watch. So, here's the plan. Drive over to my house before one o'clock this afternoon. And you don't have to worry about any of my family being around." She waved her hand. "They'll all be out of the house. My mother has lunch plans with a friend and Trina is scheduled to work at Taylor Gowns. Kenny might be around, but he won't get in the way. But just for your information, Britain is coming over to my house today at 1:00 o'clock. What I'll do is hide you in the closet or under the bed, so he won't know you're here. Then when it's all over and he leaves, you can come out of hiding; and you'll be a believer. That's the only way you'll buy that Britain is cheating on you, is if you catch him redhanded. Otherwise, you're going to keep living in your fantasy world thinking he's faultless. But after today, you'll most likely dump him. But I'll be so kind to inform you of my intentions. After you dump him, I plan to stay his plaything." Courtney smiled and raised both hands. "Okay, that's it. So, do we have a deal or not?" Courtney casually asked.

Courtney last words seemed to echo in the room, but the echo was just a product of Sabrina's imagination saturated with the lies Courtney had filled in her head. Instantly, all Sabrina's strength came flooding back as she hopped off the bed and strutted across the room to her bedroom door. She snatched the door open and stared crossly at Courtney.

"Could you please leave now?" Sabrina asked firmly. "You know, Courtney, against my better judgement, with much torture to deal with I allowed you to say what you came to say. Now I just want you out of my house and I would greatly appreciate you staying out of my life! I also want you to be clear about something. Although, I heard you out, I'm not buying any of that filth you just rolled off of your tongue! Do I make myself clear?"

Courtney stared Sabrina in the eyes and smiled as if she found Sabrina's irritation amusing. Then she reached into her purse that hung on her left shoulder and pulled out a pint bottle of vodka. She calmly took her time and twisted the cap off and then turned the bottle up to her mouth and finished a fourth of the liquor before lowing the bottle.

"Sabrina, I'll leave because you're right. I've said what I came to say; and no matter what you say. I know you bought every word. I saw the torture on your face and the hurt in your eyes. It wouldn't have affected you so deeply if you didn't believe me." Courtney turned the bottle up to her mouth and took another swallow. "I know it's quite early to drink alcohol, but alcohol is my best friend since you sailed into town and crushed my world. Put this in your high-class pipe and smoke it. I can't seem to cope much without my booze," Courtney sadly admitted. "Besides, I needed extra courage to rat out Britain!"

"Courtney Ross, please take a look in my face," Sabrina asked politely.

"Why do I need to look in your face?" Courtney grumbled.

"Because I asked you nicely to just take a look at me."

"Okay, I'm looking straight in your eyes, now what?"

"I want you to tell me something," Sabrina calmly said.

"Tell you what? I thought you wanted me to leave?" Courtney grumbled with a smirk on her face as she stared at Sabrina.

"I do want you to leave but answer this question honestly." Sabrina pointed to her forehead. "Do I have writing across my forehead that reads sucker?" She calmly asked.

Courtney was lost for words and didn't reply as she stared glumly at Sabrina. She hadn't expected Sabrina to ask her such a question.

"Since you have no comment. I can assume you do not see a sign written across my forehead that says that. So, since the sign isn't there, that's your clue to get a clue and leave my room and this house," Sabrina firmly suggested.

"I promise I'll leave. Just give me a minute," Courtney said as she started pacing back and forth in front of the fireplace. It didn't help her emotional state that Sabrina had a 8x10 picture of Britain sitting on her fireplace mantel.

"What's the matter now? You said what you came to say, and you need to leave, now. We have said everything there is to be said. I know where you stand, and you know where I stand. You have given me fabrication information that you tried to push as the truth. But we both know I don't believe any of it," Sabrina stressed.

"Suit yourself. However, I'm not lying to you. But the first opportunity I try to prove I'm telling the truth, you don't buy it. Sort of like the little boy who cried wolf. You better listen to this, Miss Sabrina Taylor," she grabbed her mouth and laughed, keeping her voice low as she strutted over to the opened door. "If you continue to doubt what I have told you, the only winner here is going to be Britain Franklin. He'll get you as his bride. He'll keep bedding me down and, of course, keep using us both. Come to think of it, I don't mind being used by Britain. He can use me in that way anytime, day or night. I figured I would enlighten you as a favor. I know you're the type who doesn't like sharing. But get ready. That's what you'll be doing when you marry Mr. Franklin. You'll be sharing him with me." She laughed with both hands on her hips, propped against the frame of the opened door.

Sabrina bit down on her bottom lip and swallowed hard. Her stomach was twisted in knots from listening to Courtney gruesome nauseating lies. "Thank you for finally leaving, Courtney?" Sabrina said softly as she kept her composure feeling contempt for Courtney. "You might as well accept the fact that you wasted your time coming here spilling all those falsehoods. I told you I'm not buying any of what you said. So, do us both a favor and just walk out the door and be done," Sabrina said firmly. "You're standing at the door but you're still here and it's hard to look at you right now. Besides, how many times do I have to ask you to leave my house?"

"Okay, Okay, I'm on my way out, but just answer one question before I leave. Why did you allow me to go on and on? Why did you listen if you weren't buying? I think you did buy it, Sabrina. I think you bought it hook, line and sinker. And I think you know that deep down I'm not lying this time, but you're just too afraid to face it so you're going to pretend it's just another lie.

But think about it, Sabrina, I would have to be the biggest nut case or the best actress in Illinois to pull off one like this."

Courtney turned her back to Sabrina, stepped across the threshold out of Sabrina's room and into the hallway as Sabrina stood there in her room trembling with contempt. Yet she kept her composure and didn't allow Courtney foolishness to get too deep under her skin. Courtney glanced over her shoulder and winked at Sabrina.

"You know the way to my house. Therefore, if you change your mind and decide you would like to find out for yourself and catch your Mr. Franklin redhanded with me, just show up a half an hour before he is supposed to."

It was exactly 9:00 a.m. when Courtney finally left Sabrina's doorway and hurried down the long hallway and down the staircase, and across the living room floor to the front door to rush out of the Taylor mansion. Exhausted from Courtney's early morning visit, Sabrina pulled back the covers and hopped back in bed. Her heart was heavy and crushed from Courtney's unkind words that lingered in her room saturating her thoughts. All the offensive hurtful things Courtney said kept ringing in Sabrina's head. She hoped for more sleep as she buried her head under the covers, but all she found was tears. She was mostly upset with herself for listening to Courtney. She knew she shouldn't have listened, but as Courtney's cruel words rolled out, Sabrina felt vulnerable and helpless against the evil tongue that Courtney had showered her with.

Chapter Sixteen

The bright sun beamed through Sabrina's bedroom window and the thin white blanket covering her head could not keep out the light. She threw the covers back, only to pull them over her face again and cry in silence. As she lay there under the covers, she heard a dog barking in the distance, cars in a distance passing along the main road at the end of their long driveway; as well as the vague sound of a car horn. All these simple, familiar sounds just made her tears flow more. Sounds of everyday life going on, but Courtney Ross had just paid a crack of dawn visit to squash Sabrina's happiness in the palm of her mischievous hands. Courtney had dared Sabrina to face a lie: a lie that beyond a shadow of a doubt, in Sabrina's mind, could not be true. But as usual, Courtney lies were so smooth that Sabrina had fallen prey once more. Courtney had stacked the deck and played her hand well, and she knew Sabrina couldn't fold and that she would call her bluff.

Sabrina was in deep thought as she laid on her pillow looking up at the ceiling. But Courtney's words kept echoing in her mind and made her cringe with disgust. Courtney had promised to prove to Sabrina that she wasn't lying. Sabrina was disgusted with Courtney and didn't want to bother giving credence's to her lies. However, she was determined to see it through, and afterwards, she would look Courtney in the face to see her embarrassment of being proven a liar.

Sabrina was distraught by Courtney's rude and very harsh behavior, but she hoped seeing Courtney's scheme to the end would shame a large amount of the deception out of Courtney's system. In the meantime, Sabrina had to somehow digest Courtney's lies and erase them from her mind. She tried not to focus on them as she lied in bed exceedingly upset from Courtney's uninvited visit. She knew she needed to drag herself out of bed to join the family for breakfast, but she was still too visibly shaken by Courtney's visit.

Therefore, she was still lying in bed when Starlet, Samantha and Charles gathered around the breakfast table. It was 9:15, over two hours since Courtney had first stormed in but just fifteen minutes since she had stormed out of their home. Therefore, in Sabrina's mind, the visit with Courtney was still fresh in her head.

"Where's Sabrina?" Samantha asked, as she lifted the silver teapot and poured hot tea into her cup.

"She probably left with that weird Courtney Ross, who was over here this morning at the crack of dawn," Starlet softly said as she glanced toward the exit of the dining room. "If Carrie comes back in before we finish breakfast we can ask her if Sabrina left with Courtney. She would probably know."

Charles glanced at Starlet as he lifted his cup to his mouth and took a sip of coffee. "What is this about a crack of dawn visit?" he curiously asked. "You're referring to Mildred Ross's daughter, the young lady who used to date Veronica's son, Rome. Is that correct?"

"Father, that's correct but Courtney Ross isn't the same person she was when she dated Rome."

"I guess not if she thought it was decent to pay a visit at the crack of dawn," Charles said. "What happened to the young lady?" Charles asked.

"We don't really know what happened to Courtney. We just know she's not the same," Starlet politely uttered, exchanging looks with Samantha.

Charles nodded toward Starlet. "So, I guess you were up stirring at the crack of day?"

"No, Father. I was asleep but the sound of the doorbell and knocking broke through my sleep. Besides, you know I'm a light sleeper. I hopped out of bed and peeped out of the window and saw Courtney's car. I was anxious by the time and thought her early morning visit could have been urgent. Therefore, I decided to head downstairs to answer the door to see what she needed. Now, I know answering the door for Courtney Ross was one big mistake. She was rude, disrespectful and in some cases, downright unpleasant," Starlet softly uttered as she dropped two cubes of sugar into her hot tea. "Although, the more I think about it, Sabrina's so call friend or not, I should not have answered the door and let her in. Something was seriously not right with her earlier," Starlet said with concern.

"Gosh, it's barely after nine o'clock now," Samantha looked at Starlet curiously. "Courtney Ross was here earlier?" Samantha said, spreading butter on a piece of toast.

"That's right, she was here, and her behavior was more than just a bit strange," Starlet lifted her teacup with both hands and sipped her hot tea.

"And at the crack of dawn, did you say?" Samantha asked, biting into a piece of toast.

"That's right. It was around seven when I let her in. I opened the door after she kept ringing the doorbell and knocking on the front door," Starlet shook her head and stared down in her teacup for a moment. "It was so peculiar the way she made me feel when she was here. It was kind of an eerily feeling from the moment I opened the door for her. First of all, my heart skipped a beat when I noticed she had been crying. I had no idea what was going on with her and I was on edge to find out why she was at our door so early at the break of day with tears in her eyes."

"She was crying when you let her inside?" Samantha concerned asked.

"Yes, she was crying."

"That does sound strange. Did you ask or find out what was going on with her?" Samantha asked, lifted her orange juice glass and took a swallow.

Starlet shook her head. "She just wanted to talk to Sabrina. She said it was vital that she speak to her. She didn't tell me anything about what was going on with her. But, there's one thing I picked up just from her presence."

"What was that?" Samantha asked.

"Something is not right about Courtney," Starlet said with a worried look in her eyes. "She's more than just deceitful and dishonest, which is the straits she has displayed with Sabrina. She's also odd as if she's mentally unbalanced," Starlet said and looked toward her father. "Father, I'm sorry to say these things about Courtney Ross but I'm trying to describe her character; and I'm trying to be as honest as possible."

Charles nodded but he didn't comment as he lifted the silver coffee pot and poured more hot coffee into his cup. Then Samantha looked toward Starlet and asked. "Did you find out why she was crying?"

Starlet shook her head. "I mentioned it and she denied the traces of tears on her face. So, I dropped it, but I don't think she even knew why she was crying," Starlet placed a forkful of hash browns into her mouth. "Although, she wasn't sharing. I did inquire and tried to get her to open up about what was going on with her, and I also put her on the spot about her bogus friendship with Sabrina."

"What did she say?" Samantha asked.

"She denied that it was bogus," Starlet said. "But I told her I believed she was just pretending to be Sabrina's friend."

Samantha exchanged looks with Charles. "Of course, she would deny it's not sincere. You didn't expect her to admit her association with Sabrina was bogus. She's too clever to get caught at her own games," Samantha forked eggs into her mouth, chewed her food and continued. "However, something had to be amiss if she was in tears," Samantha wondered.

"You could be right," Starlet agreed. "Although, I'm convinced that she was just being a pest, coming here to see Sabrina at that time of morning. Her visit felt weird. I just felt something was off about her. I can't put my finger on it. But just being around Courtney sort of gave me the creeps. Something about her was obviously off."

"Well, you told us that, dear," Charles commented.

"I know I mentioned it. I just can't get it out of my head how she was crying and acting really peculiar," Starlet lifted the orange juice pitcher and poured more juice into her juice glass; and then poured more juice into Charles and Samantha's glasses.

After a moment of silence, Starlet continued. "I'm curious to know why Sabrina is still associating with Courtney Ross. I seriously believe she needs to stay away from Courtney Ross and she needs to make Courtney stay away from here," Starlet seriously stated. "Since we all know Courtney is not her friend and up to no good," Starlet explained. "Besides, I think Courtney is more than just a heavy drinker. I think she's on drugs or something. What else can explain her off the wall behavior?" Starlet stressed.

"I think you're right," Samantha agreed. "According to something Kenny told me back in college, Courtney has been on this slow track to destruction a long time. He shared with me that his sister drinking problem was more severe than his; and although, I didn't know Courtney was his sister at the time, I do recall him telling me about her major drinking problem and he also mentioned that she was also abusing subscription drugs at that time," Samantha shared with them.

"Heavy drinking and subscription drugs, that's not a good combination," Charles lifted his coffee cup and took a sip. "I hope Sabrina can branch away from that troubled young woman," he said seriously.

"No, Father. You have Courtney Ross figured out all wrong. She's not a troubled young woman who has lost her way," Starlet softly uttered, looking toward her father. "Courtney Ross is just a lot of trouble and most of her problems are manufactured by her."

Charles Taylor glanced at Starlet and nodded as he took his knife and fork and cut the country fried steak on his plate into bite size pieces. "I'm sure you know the young woman better than I. Therefore, if you say she's trouble then most likely she is."

Samantha shook her head. "It's a pity that Courtney has chosen the route she has taken. Once upon a time she was a smart young lady. She has a teaching degree; and her brother, Kenny, told me that she achieved a 4.00 in her college studies," Samantha said looking toward her father. "Plus, she's also very pretty and she had everything going for her, Father." Samantha raised both hands. "Yet, she still chose to turn to alcohol and drugs," Samantha caringly acknowledged.

"I don't think we should say she's on drugs," Starlet politely voiced her objection. "We know she's different and odd acting of late." Starlet glanced at her father and then back to Samantha. "We don't actually know for sure about the drugs. I know you said Kenny mentioned that she was into subscription drugs back in college, and there's a possibility that she could still be into abusing subscription medicine." Starlet forked hash browns into her mouth, held up one finger, chewed her food and swallowed. "The only thing we know for sure is that she's abusing alcohol," Starlet nodded. "Besides, I know she seemed out of sorts earlier. But I don't think drugs had anything to do with it. I'm starting to believe more and more that her problem is more mental."

Samantha nodded. "You could be right about the mental issue. That assumption is not far-fetched of her behavior since her breakup months ago with Rome."

"Sounds like this young lady has a lot on her plate," Charles commented, lifted his coffee cup and took a sip of coffee. "It's seriously unhealthy if she's poisoning her system with alcohol?" Charles glanced across the table at Starlet. "What's really going on with her? Is she in some kind of trouble?"

"Father, she's not in trouble with the law. She's in trouble with her life," Starlet said. "I guess she's dealing with a lot of issues. Sabrina mentioned, since their newfound short-lived friendship that Courtney has built up a lot of resentment inside of her. She resents and is very bitter toward her parents for hitting the news and highlighting their family in such a negative outrageous way. She also revealed to Sabrina that she's always on edge, living in constant agony about the possibility of hearing that her father has been hung or killed in prison while serving his sentence," Starlet explained. "Apparently when they were young, it was a lot of chaos in their home."

Samantha bit into a piece of toast. "I'm sorry about what happened at her home and how her father flipped out."

"I'll say he did more than flip out. What Mr. Ross did was insane how he shot up their home and almost killed his wife and another man." Starlet lifted her orange juice glass to her mouth and took a swallow.

Samantha nodded. "Yes, you're right. It was rumored that Mr. Ross killed the man, but at least he was cleared of that. I know he isn't completely innocent in all of this considering the crime he was charged with. But being charged with murder is a lot to deal with for anyone."

"It is a lot to deal with, but I would like to think if I was in Courtney's shoes, huge life changes wouldn't change my behavior. Afterall, we did lose Mother and managed to keep our sanity," Starlet commented. "Can't imagine anything hurting me more."

Samantha looked at Starlet with serious humble eyes. "I know Courtney isn't our favorite person. But we must admit that she's going through a rough patch right now. Although, it doesn't give her the license to be unkind to Sabrina. Plus, I agree with you that there's no excuse for her ill conduct against others. Although, she tries to hide behind the event that happened with her folks and how they ended up spotlighted in outrageous news, as an excuse for being rude and displaying such ill conduct and idiotic behavior?"

Starlet nodded and glanced at her father. "But she can't really use that excuse. She started spinning out of control long before that took place. That's why I seriously think it's all mental with her; and I also think it's very serious. I don't think she's just acting out. I think she's in serious mental trouble. Because awful things happen in everybody's life."

Charles nodded. "That's true and everyone has their own breaking point of how much they can bear or cope with; and if they cannot cope it's wise to seek professional help to ward off a breakdown." Charles reached out and lifted the silver coffee pot and poured more coffee into his cup. "Just like the situation with your sister. She couldn't cope on her own with the loss of your mother." He lifted the lid off the sugar bowl and dropped two cubes of sugar into his coffee. "There are usually warning signs in every case and we noticed your sister signs loud and clear." Charles lifted his coffee cup to his mouth and took a sip. "Starlet, if you have noticed warning signs in regard to this young lady, you need to contact someone in her family to make them aware of what you have noticed. They may have noticed the same signs and in the progress of seeking help for her. If not, it's your civic duty to contact someone in her family and relay your concerns."

Starlet nodded. "Okay, Father. I'll call Courtney's mother before we leave for the fundraiser. I'll let her know about Courtney's visit this morning and her erratic behavior."

Charles nodded. "Good. Make sure you make that call. Just listening to you two, I have a strong suspicious that the young lady is headed for a breakdown, considering all she's dealing with. She needs help before her condition becomes a real hazard to her or someone else."

"Also, Father, according to Kenny," Samantha said softly as she spread butter on her dry piece of toast. "Apparently while they were growing up, their parents fought constantly. He said the fights made their father stay away from home a lot and their mother would pack up and move back home a lot, leaving the three of them in the family home to fend for themselves a lot," Samantha solemnly shared.

"I'm not a shrink but being left home alone is probably not the source of this young lady's mental issues," Charles commented. "Sounds like they started with the breakup from Veronica's son, Rome."

Samantha and Starlet smiled at their father's comment. "Father, I guess you have been listening. We are all on accord with the same assumption about Courtney and when her behavior became so extreme," Samantha smiled. "At one point, we thought she was just acting out to be difficult. But we're pretty sure, she's not acting out."

Starlet held up one finger as she took a bite of toast. "She's not entirely over the edge and she could be acting out just a little. But she has a serious mental problem that needs to be addressed," Starlet compassionately said.

"I know she's troubled and have caused Sabrina a lot of heartaches," Samantha softly said. "Nevertheless, I feel for her family situation and my heart goes out for her. She seems to be really lost right now. The news that came out about her mother's affair and her father shooting up their home and her father almost killing her mother, had to be humiliating on so many levels. Add on top of that, her father that she loves dearly is sitting in a prison cell serving a five-year sentence for attempted murder."

"Since this young lady sounds so complicated and quite out of sorts and in need of profession help for her own sanity," Charles said with concern in his voice. "It would be in Sabrina's best interest to just cut ties with the young lady and keep her distant until the young lady receive some kind of treatment," Charles seriously uttered. "Based on what you two have said, no good can come from the association. Because even without the young lady having a possible mental issue to content with, if she's just pretending to be a friend to your sister while all Sabrina best efforts go to the wayside. That's no good," Charles shook his head. "A friendship of that magnitude based on deception cannot end well."

"Father, we're in accord with you on that decision one hundred percent," Samantha nodded and exchanged looks with Starlet. "We both feel that Sabrina should cut all ties and stay far away from Courtney Ross," Samantha agreed.

"That's true, Father. We do not support Sabrina's friendship with Courtney. All because we both know how Courtney have purposely deceived and hurt Sabrina. Sabrina has told us about some of the awful ways she has been treated by Courtney."

"Why would your smart sister attach herself with someone who's out to deceive her?" Charles curiously asked.

"Courtney tricked her into a friendship," Starlet told her father.

"Your sister is too smart to allow herself to be tricked into being someone's friend," Charles casually stated as he glanced at the newspaper that laid on the table to the right of his plate.

"I know she is, but in the beginning of their friendship, Sabrina felt sorry for Courtney and thought Courtney was sincere about being friends," Samantha added.

Charles nodded. "Your sister feeling sorry for the young lady is something I can believe. Sabrina has a soft spot for the world. You all do, but Sabrina even more so."

Starlet nodded. "You're absolutely correct Father about Sabrina's soft spot for Courtney. That's why she kept giving Courtney chances with trying to maintain their friendship," Starlet said solemnly. "But since that time, Courtney has caused Sabrina so many heartaches. I seriously think Sabrina might be wise to Courtney and ready to stop feeling sorry for her," Starlet hoped. "That's why it's strange that she left home with Courtney earlier," Starlet looked toward Samantha with worried eyes.

Samantha lifted her orange juice glass to her mouth but lowered the glass back to the table without taking a sip as she looked toward Starlet. "Why would you say it's strange for Sabrina to have left here with Courtney?" Samantha curiously asked. "I know we would all like for her to cut ties with Courtney Ross, but until she does I don't see anything strange about Sabrina leaving here with Courtney. Why did you call it strange?" Samantha asked.

"I think it's strange because of what Sabrina said to me and Father last night," Starlet looked toward Charles.

"What did she say to you and Father last night?" Samantha asked.

Starlet held up one finger toward Samantha as she continued looking toward Charles. "Remember, Father? Sabrina sat right there in her seat at the dinner table last night and told you and I that she wanted nothing more to do with Courtney. Can you remember Father?" Starlet looked toward her father, who nodded toward him as she continued talking. "Sabrina seriously explained to us that it had to do with something Courtney did to upset her at Franklin Gas," Starlet explained.

Charles nodded. "I remember the conversation. But dear, I'm sorry to tell you that I was only half listening when she was discussing the matter. Besides, during dinner last night while your sister was speaking of that, I wasn't sure who she was referring to." Charles looked toward Samantha. "Nevertheless, Sabrina did share with us last night during dinner while you were out having dinner with Paris, that she and some young lady at Franklin Gas had a falling out," Charles recalled and then glanced toward Starlet. "She mentioned that it was about some issue dealing with a rumor. Isn't that what she said, dear?" Charles asked, looking toward Starlet.

Starlet nodded. "That's correct, Father. She told us it had to do with an awful rumor that Courtney ignited at Franklin Gas about her. "Yes, Father; that's what she told us last night," Starlet answered.

"So much for cutting ties," Charles commented. "If Sabrina left with the Ross young lady. It would be just like Sabrina to forgive the young lady and be friends with her again. I guess she's giving the young lady another chance once again. Is that what the two of you are saying?" Charles lifted his coffee cup to his mouth and took a sip of coffee.

Samantha nodded as she lifted her orange juice glass to her mouth and took the last sip of juice. "You're right, Father; and it's what I'm saying since it appears that way. Sabrina may have mentioned cutting ties with Courtney during dinner last night but apparently she changed her mind."

"We don't know if she changed her mind," Starlet mumbled.

"You're right, we don't know for certain. But if Sabrina left here with her. It seems likely that they must have patched up things between each other during Courtney's visit earlier," Samantha softly suggested as she exchanged looks with her father and sister. "That disassociation did not last long. But I guess we shouldn't be surprised." Samantha placed her fork on the table and then lifted her napkin and patted her mouth a couple times while looking toward Starlet. "We all know how Sabrina is. She's too good for her own good. She's just like Mother. She sees the silver lining in everything. She knows Courtney is trouble, but of course, she feels she can help her."

Starlet nodded. "That's true about Sabrina, but in this case, I have a hunch that Sabrina did not patch things up with Courtney," Starlet seriously supposed. "I recall the way Sabrina felt last night. She was deeply hurt, and I could sense her deep heartbreak. Therefore, I feel there's too much animosity between them since Courtney started that rumor. Sabrina was genuinely crushed by Courtney's mean behavior. I'm sure she hasn't gotten over what Courtney done to her," Starlet assuredly explained.

"It would be ideal if Sabrina cut all ties with Courtney. Nevertheless, I don't mean to be a damper, but they must have made up in order for Courtney to show up over here so early to pay her visit. She must have figured Sabrina would let her in," Samantha softly assumed. "Otherwise, it would have been irrational to arrive at the crack of dawn on the doorsteps of someone who had asked you to stay away."

Starlet nodded. "I agree. Irrational is how we know her mind is functioning of late. Otherwise, there's no explaining her strange, hostile, outlandish behavior and actions. It's just what we discussed earlier that she's displaying warning signs that she's mentally ill," Starlet stressed seriously. "Nevertheless, I'm still quite convinced that Sabrina has wised up to Courtney. I do not believe those two have buried the hatchet."

Samantha had great concern in her eyes. "I hope you're right, since we all want Sabrina clear of Courtney," Samantha said.

Charles exchanged an indifferent look with Starlet and Samantha as he took his napkin and wiped his hands. He placed the napkin across the top of his place and then pushed the plate aside as he placed both arms on the table and leaned in toward his daughters who both sat on the opposite side of the table across from him. "Listen, you two. We all would like for Sabrina to cut ties with Miss Courtney Ross who appears to be the worst kind of friend, being hurtful toward your sister. Nevertheless, we have to keep in mind that it's Sabrina's choice. Sabrina is an adult and we cannot handpick her friends," Charles firmly stated. "I know you two do not have a bias bone in you. Your concerns and wishes for Sabrina to sever ties with Miss Courtney Ross has to do with Sabrina's wellbeing and peace of mind," Charles caringly uttered as he exchanged supportive exchanges with his daughters.

After a moment of silent, Charles continued. "We may not get it, considering how spiteful and unkind Miss Courtney Ross appears. But on the other hand, for some reason, your sister allowed this young woman into her life," Charles solemnly admitted.

"She probably pushed herself into Sabrina's life," Starlet said.

Charles nodded. "That could be true or not. Nevertheless, Sabrina allowed the friendship. Therefore, this is what I want you two to bear in mind," Charles exchanged looks with both of them.

Samantha and Starlet waited to hear what their father was about to say as they both looked toward him. They sensed it was some suggestion that he expected them to abide by.

"I can see you're both waiting for my suggestion, and this is it. If by some chance Sabrina has forgiven this young lady and has given her another chance at being her friend, then we have to respect her decision and let your sister find a way to deal with the young lady," Charles firmly said and then held up one finger. "Besides, it just crossed my mind. Sabrina may still be home. Just because she didn't make it downstairs for breakfast doesn't mean she's out of the house. Did either of you check her room before you came down for breakfast?" Charles asked.

"It crossed our mind." Starlet glanced at Samantha and she nodded. "But ever since Mother passed, we have all made sure to have breakfast together every morning. None of us have missed showing up for breakfast since we made that pact," Starlet reminded him. "Therefore, we just assumed she must be out of the house since she isn't here at breakfast."

"Yes, we made that pact. However, your sister could still be upstairs for any number of reasons, including sleeping in or not feeling well," Charles said.

Starlet exchanged looks with Samantha. "Father is right. She could be upstairs in her room. If so, that means she's not out with Courtney Ross," Starlet pleasingly said.

"It would be great if Sabrina is still upstairs, but she probably isn't," Samantha mumbled as she lifted her iced water to her mouth and took the last sip. "Nevertheless, whether Sabrina left with Courtney Ross or not, Courtney was still here to see her at the break of dawn," Samantha glumly reminded them. "Therefore, we have to keep in mind as much as it bothers me to say, Sabrina and Courtney may very well be friends once again."

Starlet looked toward Samantha. "It's funny that you mentioned the word friend in connection with Courtney and Sabrina. We both know Courtney is not a real friend to Sabrina. It was so cruel and vindictive of Courtney to start an awful rumor about Sabrina at Franklin Gas."

"What was the rumor?" Samantha asked.

"Sabrina didn't tell us the rumor," Starlet shook her head.

"That's right," Charles nodded. "She didn't feel comfortable sharing it."

"That's true, Sabrina didn't feel comfortable at all about telling us what had been said about her. The only thing Father and I could manage from her is how awful the rumor was and how it was just too awful to repeat." Starlet glanced down and lifted her napkin from her lap and then glanced to her left side at Samantha.

"What I can tell you is what I observed about Sabrina last night during dinner when she shared all of this with me and Father. She seemed shaken over the ordeal and completely adamant about cutting ties with Courtney," Starlet explained as she took her napkin and wiped her mouth and hands.

Charles glanced at his white gold Rolex watch as he stood up from the breakfast table. "The one thing I noticed about Sabrina last night during dinner, she seemed quite unyielding about cutting ties and not associating with Miss Courtney Ross," Charles said as he headed out of the dining room. "Therefore, I'm in agreement with Starlet. I'm relatively sure based on Sabrina's determination last night that she has not made up with Miss Courtney Ross."

Chapter Seventeen

Fred anxiously and nervously arrived on the front doorsteps of Franklin House at 9:45 that Saturday morning. He was dropped off by a limousine service at the request of Veronica. He had passed the evaluation and Shady Grove had faxed the complete report to Franklin House to the attention of Veronica. Nevertheless, Fred found no comfort in knowing he had passed the evaluation. His main focus was winning back the confidence of the Franklins and securing his job. He had a lot of time to think while committed at Shady Grove and realized the huge mistakes he had made toward the Franklin family. He was distraught at the idea of ending up off the Franklin House payroll. However, a subdued smile danced at the corner of his month when he thought of the words Veronica uttered during the meeting before he was signed into Shady Grove. She had promised to give his job back if he was sent home with a clean bill of mental health. Therefore, he stood at the front door cautiously optimistic waiting to be let in. He was leaning on the hope that Veronica would stick to her word and keep him on.

Fred had been given instructions by the limousine driver to meet Veronica and her sons in the library upon his arrival at Franklin House. He was let in the front door by Leola Bradley who also informed him that the Franklins were waiting for him in the library. When Fred reached the library before he reached for the doorknob of the double French doors, he swallowed hard when he noticed Natalie was gathered in the library along with the Franklins. His heart raced at the sight of seeing his wife sitting among them. He wondered what her appearance meant. He could only hope she wasn't aware of the whole story as she sat there motionless in a side chair with a distraught look on her face.

"Come in Fred and have a seat," Veronica beckoned him into the library and pointed toward the side chair near Natalie.

Fred slowly walked over to the chair with very little help of his crutches. He placed the crutches aside, pulled off his black jacket and hung it on the back of the chair, then removed a bottle of water from his jacket pocket. He placed the bottle of water on the side table next to his chair and then took a seat. He was anxious as he glanced at Natalie, but she kept her head down looking toward the floor. His heart pounded in his chest with anxiety. He was no longer worried about whether or not he still had a job. He was concerned about Natalie's cold unwelcoming attitude. He had been away for days, but she never visited him at Shady Grove; and he was quite disappointed that she didn't seem pleased to see him back at home. He was also anxious and bothered by her standoffish demeanor and bitter look on her face.

"Fred, we are pleased you're back," Rome warmly greeted him. "And it's good to see you're getting around so much better." Rome smiled.

Fred nodded as he anxiously rubbed his hands together. "In a few days, by Monday, I'm looking to be in tip top shape." He grinned and glanced toward his wife who still didn't look his way. By now he was afraid to open his mouth. He figured Natalie knew what he had done or the Franklins had told her they wouldn't be keeping him on. Either one would crush him. Therefore, he sat anxiously waiting to hear what was going on and why he had been called to the meeting.

"Fred, please help yourself to the coffee." Paris pointed to the coffee pot on the coffee table as they all sat sipping cups of coffee. Natalie also held a cup of coffee in her hand.

Veronica held up a sheet of paper and then passed it to Fred by means of Sydney who sat closest to Fred.

"Fred, this is the report we received from Shady Grove regarding your stay there. I'm not sure what they told you before your release. But in this report, the doctor who treated you feels you are quite stable minded. I want you to know I'm pleased to receive this report and it puts my concerns about your behavior at ease. You have been here at Franklin House with us long before any of my sons were born," Veronica stated appreciatively and stood from her seat.

Fred swallowed hard as his heartbeat eased at the approval in Veronica's voice about the favorable Shady Grove report on him. Her welcoming tone took away much tension as he sat waiting to hear what else she would say to him.

"Fred, I won't keep you in suspense." Veronica stepped over to his chair. "You passed the test and I'm pleased to give you back these."

They all looked toward Fred as he stared humbly at Veronica who stood before him. She had a serious professional expression on her face as she said, "Hold out your hands."

Fred smiled and held out both hands as Veronica reached into her suit pocket and pulled out four sets of keys to Franklin House and dropped them into his hands, giving him back possession of the twenty-five keys he had carried around for the past thirty years.

For the first time since Fred walked into the room, Natalie loosen up and released the frown from her face. She looked toward him and watched with a slight smile on her face as Veronica gave him back the keys to the estate.

"Welcome back onboard, Fred." Britain smiled.

"Yes, welcome home," Paris smiled.

Britain nodded, smiling toward Fred. "You didn't doubt getting your job back, did you? I hope you know how much you are appreciated. We would be pretty up in arms and lost without you." Britain leaned forward and grabbed his coffee cup from the coffee table, lifted it to his mouth and took a sip and then placed the cup back on the coffee table. He looked at Fred and nodded. "I'm glad it all worked out."

"We're all very pleased it worked out," Paris agreed. "You checked into Shady Grove and that made Mother happy. Now, you're back home with a clean bill of mental health and we're all happy," Paris said, smiling.

Fred placed his bottle of water on the side table next to his chair and stood at his seat. "Thank you, Miss Veronica, for allowing me to keep my job. I'm deeply grateful." He held out both arms. "This job means the world to me; and I don't take this chance lightly. I know I could have easily gotten a different result and would have found myself unemployed from the best bunch of folks I know," he stated sincerely as he looked seriously at Veronica. "You have my word I won't screw-up and let this family down again," Fred strongly stated as he sat back down.

Veronica nodded looking toward Fred. "Thank you for that heartfelt thank you. We are all pleased it worked out."

Fred held up one finger as he lifted his water bottle from the side table. "I'm not done with my thanks," he said as he exchanged looks with the four brothers. "You fellows are the best! Mr. Rome, Mr. Britain, Mr. Paris and you, Mr. Sydney. I appreciate your efforts in flying out to Vegas to fetch me. I know all of you quite well; and neither of you would ever breathe a word of what I'm about to say. But I know I had too much to drink on the train back to Chicago. Although, I don't recall what I said or done. I do remember having more bottles of beer than I can count." Fred glanced at Natalie and smiled. "Natalie is sitting here, and she can tell you'all that I'm not prone to heavy drinking," he honestly shared. "Nevertheless, every blue moon when I do over indulge, I'm told by family and friends that I can be an obnoxious drunk!" He held out both hands as he exchanged looks with the four brothers. "The four of you are too polite to tell me, but if I got too out of hands or said things that were disrespectful or inappropriate, I want to thank you for putting up with me inspite of my drunken behavior," Fred humbly stated.

"Fred, you're a good man and an excellent worker," Sydney smiled and exchanged looks with his brothers. "We thought it was only fair to put up with you for one night on a train. You have put up with us since we were born," Sydney said jokingly, and they all smiled and nodded in agreement.

"But seriously, Fred. One thing I know for sure," Sydney continued. "You are the most courtesy efficient driver I've met. Sam Westwood come in a close second. But I cannot stress strongly enough how good you are at your job."

Rome smiled, nodding. "Yes, Fred. We all can agree on that."

Fred was smiling and feeling better to the point that he had forgotten how Natalie was sitting there with them who appeared distraught, displaying such standoffish behavior toward him.

"I think I'll have that cup of coffee now," Fred said, feeling empowered and surer of himself now that he was back in the bosom of the Franklins. He stood from his seat and stepped over to the coffee table without using his crutches. He lifted the silver coffee pot and poured coffee into one of the empty cups on the sparkling silver serving tray. "I have to admit, they served some good coffee earlier with breakfast at the facility. But that was at seven o'clock this morning," he said, smiling as he lifted the lid from the sugar bowl and dropped two cubes of sugar into his coffee; and with his cup in hand, he took a seat smiling.

"So, Fred, what did you think of Shady Grove?" Rome asked. "How did you cope through each day? We're sort of curious to know, especially since you were dead set against the place. We hope being there didn't make you too uncomfortable." Rome exchanged looks with his mother. But Veronica was looking toward Natalie, who sat motionless, looking down in her coffee cup.

"It was not uncomfortable at all, Mr. Rome," Fred quickly said, smiling. "What makes you think it was uncomfortable for me? I know I put up a fuss and protested against going there but you guys did me a favor by pushing me through the door at Shady Grove. By being there I had a lot of quiet time to think and concentrate. I won't lie, the days felt twice as long. But I took assisted walks on those immaculate grounds. I participated in the game room and enjoyed their movie nights; and to be analyzed by a psychotherapist allowed me to free my conscience of a lot of stuff I have held inside for years. I forgave my father for being a workaholic. I no longer blame him for not giving up his job to spend more time with my Mom while she was alive," Fred humbly explained. "Yes, being at Shady Grove did me a lot of good." He nodded. "I also watched a lot of TV in my room and ate as much of that good food as I could. The food is unbelievable delicious. It's worth being mental just for the incredible food," Fred said jokingly.

Veronica nodded with serious look on her face. "I'm pleased to hear and I'm sure the boys are as well that you made the best of your stay at Shady Grove. But I'm also sure you see Natalie is here in the room with us." Veronica glanced toward Natalie and they nodded at each other. "If you're curious to why she was included in the meeting pertaining to you. She's here because she requested to be here for your acceptance back on staff," Veronica told him.

"That's fine with me. We were both highly concerned about the possibility of me losing my job here." Fred turned his coffee cup to his mouth and took the last sip and then placed the empty cup and saucer on the side table near his chair. "That's behind us now and all is good in the world again." Fred smiled, looking toward Veronica. Then he turned to his side and looked toward Natalie and she looked toward him and slightly smiled.

"Congrats! I'm glad you have been reinstated," Natalie softly congratulated him. "I know how much this job means to you. I'm thankful you have it back." She stared hard at him. "I hope you realize the break you have been given," Natalie said with subdued animosity.

Fred smiled at Natalie. "Of course, I realize it. I feel on top of the world like a new man. I have my job back. My foot injury has finally healed and I'm back with you and Helen. What more could I ask for?"

Dead silence fell over the room and they all were quiet for a moment as Fred instincts told him something wasn't quite right. "What's going on?" He looked toward Rome. He knew if he asked a Franklin guy, he would get an honest answer. "I'm asking that question because when I said what I said, I noticed how the room fell quiet. Is there something else you guys haven't informed me of? You gave me the keys to the whole estate, so I'm sure I have my job back. But I sense something isn't quite right," Fred insisted.

Rome nodded. "Fred, you are correct in your assumption. There is something you haven't been informed of. However, Mother will do the honors and fill you in," Rome politely told him.

Fred stood out of his seat and looked toward Natalie. Then Veronica looked toward Fred with compassionate eyes. "Fred, please be seated." Veronica held up both hands.

Fred slowly dropped back into his seat anxious to hear Veronica information.

"Listen, Fred. There's no need to get too overwhelmed. First of all, just as you figured. Your job is secure. Plus, there are no other conditions. You have been reinstated as if you never left. All your benefits, sick and vacation days are the same. You will be paid next Friday for all the days you have been off since your foot injury," Veronica explained and then exchanged looks with Natalie. "However, as Rome mentioned, there is something extremely important that you haven't been informed of. Natalie is here because it has to do with the both of you. She has informed us that she no longer wants you living under the same roof with her and your daughter," Veronica sadly regretfully informed him.

Fred jaw dropped as he stared at Natalie in shock.

"Fred, I know this is unexpected news of the worse kind; and it doesn't please me to share this news on top of your reinstatement. Nevertheless, I ask that you please keep your composure for the time being," Veronica said. "I'm sure you and Natalie will have a lot to discuss. But please do so in privacy after we have wrapped up this meeting."

Fred nodded toward Veronica as his heart raced with anxiety. He was blindsided by Natalie's news. But assumed she wanted out of the marriage because she had discovered his failed attempt on Antonio Armani's life.

"There's just one more piece of business to this meeting and then we'll exit the room, so you and Natalie can talk. We're giving you the one bedroom living quarters in the east wing on the lower level down the hallway from Leola and Dillion. It's fully furnished and here's the key." Veronica stood from her seat and the four brothers stood from their seats. She stepped near Fred and passed him the little gold key. "Just let us know if you take residence in those quarters. Hopefully, you and Natalie can come to terms and the new quarters won't be needed for usage. However, it's your business and if you cannot settle your differences and find it necessary to separate, you're welcome here in separate housing," Veronica assured Fred and Natalie as she and her sons headed out of the room.

Natalie and Fred looked at the five of them in silence and waited until they were completely out of their view, then Fred looked toward Natalie with an angry disappointed look on his face as he held up the key to the separate quarters and swung it back and forth near Natalie's face. He was boiling inside that she had blindsided him in front of the Franklins.

"Natalie, what has gotten into you? Why did you disrupt the Franklins lives by bringing them into our personal business? Why did you find it necessary to request separate living quarters for me? Those good people were considerate enough to give me my job back, but you spoiled it by your sour request," Fred angrily fussed.

Natalie stared bitterly at Fred and shouted angrily. "Man, you are lucky this is all I'm doing just putting your lying ass out! After you left for Shady Grove it dawned on me that we no longer have much of a marriage!"

"You decided all of this but didn't feel I deserved to know what you had decided!" Fred shook his head. "The gall of you to go and share our private business with your boss before you shared it with me. Why didn't you call me and we could have discussed this and shared our decision with the Franklins together? How do you think it felt to hear Miss Veronica tell me our marriage is over? She knew before I did since you chose to leave me out of the loop about my own marriage!"

"Now you know how I felt when you left that damn inconsiderate note declaring our marriage was over!" Natalie hopped out of her seat and paced back and forth.

"So, we're back to that?" Fred angrily asked, but relieved that she didn't seem aware of his failed attempt on Antonio Armani's life.

"Yes, Fred Madden, we are back to that! While you were lying up receiving royal treatment at that very exclusive Shady Grove facility, it dawned on me more and more what you did and why," Natalie angrily stated, shaking her finger in his face. "How ignorance do you think I am?"

"I don't think you're ignorance at all," Fred quickly grumbled.

"That's a stinking lie! You do think I'm ignorance. Otherwise, why would you expect for me to buy the lame story you have given me about why you left that note and left these premises! The lie you told me doesn't add up and it doesn't hold water! After thirty years of faithful loyal service, you expect me to believe at the spur of the moment you just decided to abandon this family and leave this great paying job for no significance reason?"

Fred sat there with his mouth open. He tried to appear sincere, but Natalie could see through his phony sincerity and her instincts told her he was keeping something from her. He wanted to come clean but deep down he knew he had to shield the truth from Natalie and Helen for the rest of his life. He felt the truth would change the landscape of his life and cause major changes to the relationships he shared with his wife and daughter. Therefore, he had to stick with his deception no matter how Natalie fussed and preached at him about not being on the level.

"Fred, here's my take on your deception. I believe you straight out lied to me about why you left these premises. I also believe you did something major that the Franklins didn't approve of; and since you knew you had majorly messed up with the Franklins, you ran scare and that's why you tried to skip town." Natalie placed both hands on her hips and stared Fred down with a disgusted look in her eyes. "Feel free to agree anytime you like! You can deny all you want. But it's the only thing that makes sense. You ended up in trouble with the Franklins and that's why you left here!" Natalie argued angrily. "Besides, that's the only sensible reason that would make them drop everything and hop a plane to track you down to deliver you back here."

"I guess you have all the answers so what are you hounding me for?"

"Thanks for nothing, Fred. After years of marriage you are showing me just how little you feel for me. You are willing to sit there and continue lying to me when we both know you are holding something back; and it's what I have said. You got in trouble with the Franklins. So much trouble until they thought you could be out of your mind. Why else would they track you down and ship you off to Shady Grove the instant you set foot in this house?" Natalie fussed, hoping for some answers.

"Well, I guess they can scratch insane off their list," Fred snapped. "Shady Grove gave me a clean bill of mental health. So, I guess my head is on straight."

"It might be on straight but you're still a messed-up individual!" Natalie sniped. "For one, you're a big liar and untrustworthy as a husband. I'm not going to put up with it anymore. Whatever took place the Franklins know? But they are not at liberty to share your personal work conduct with me. Therefore, I'm left in the dark and they probably know I'm left in the dark. They can see the louse you are for a husband. But you're lucky that your bad traits as a husband has no bearings on your performances as a good employee!" Natalie strongly pointed out.

"Natalie, I still believe we can come to some kind of compromise," Fred stumbled with his words.

"Fred, are you dense? Do you think I'm talking just to hear myself? All I want from you is the truth," she said in a trembling voice as she looked toward the floor shaking her head. "I believe what you wrote in that note was the truth. You no longer want this marriage."

"Natalie, that makes no sense. If I didn't want this marriage I wouldn't be back here in your face trying to save it."

"That's just it, Fred. You didn't expect the Franklins to drop everything and fly across country to track you down. You thought you were out of our lives for good. But after they dragged you back here, you figured it would be best to make light of the note, so you could keep a roof over your head. But that's not necessary. The Franklins are giving you your own separate living quarters. The sooner you pack your things and move out, the better! This way, whatever lie you're hiding, you won't have to worry about me finding out about it. At this point, I don't care anymore! You are one messed up fellow!"

"I'm no more messed up than the rest of you." He held up both hands. "Just get off my damn back, Natalie. If you want me out, I can pack up and leave! But I'm tired of you beating a dead horse! I have told you all there is to tell you!" Fred stood up and threw the crutches aside. "I'm done with these damn things." He watched as the crutches hit the floor. Then he looked at Natalie with disappointed eyes. "I can't believe you, Natalie. My life is in shambles and now you kick me out on top of it!"

"I disagree. Your life is not in shambles. You're riding high right back in the bosom of the Franklins. Therefore, whichever way you crossed the line with them. I'm assuming it wasn't too extreme since they're allowing you to keep your job," Natalie wondered.

"You're right, so this far-fetched idea of yours that I have done something majorly wrong to these people is off the mark," Fred stressed.

"I'm not off the mark. You are lying to me about something, Fred. I'll never buy you just up and sneaked out in the night to take a train to Las Vegas just for the hell of it or whatever lame reason you gave." Natalie headed across the library floor toward the door to leave the room. She looked over her shoulder and he had both hands on the fireplace mantle with his back to her.

"I expect you to have all your things out of my living quarters before noon," Natalie said as she continued toward the door. When she reached the French doors, she didn't step out of the room. She paused at the door, but didn't look toward Fred. "I'm guessing you were not informed yet, but everyone in the household, including staff is invited to the WJJ Theater this afternoon to hear Miss Starlet sing at the Disadvantage Children Fundraiser," Natalie informed him.

Fred didn't comment as Natalie slowly made her way out of the library and headed down the hallway toward the kitchen area. He then stepped over to the coffee table with his cup in his hand. He glanced at his watch and then reached down and lifted the coffee pot and poured more coffee in his cup. He was basically still on sick leave until Monday and didn't have to do any work. He took the cup of coffee and took a seat back in the side chair. He sipped and sipped half of the coffee before he lowered the cup. His mind was free and content after the Franklins reinstated him. But the joy only lasted a short time to be overshadowed by Natalie's news of kicking him out of their three bedroom living quarters. He felt like a louse because he knew Natalie was right. He no longer was in love with his wife, but he knew he had a zero chance with Catherine the woman he did love. Knowing he had no chance with Catherine, he wanted to stay with Natalie for the companionship. Nevertheless, Natalie knew he was holding something back and could sense no warmth from him toward her. He wanted to come clean with Natalie but decided it was best to take his secret to his grave. Although, he was no longer in love with Natalie, he still cared and wanted her happiness. It was vital to him to maintain some kind of relationship with his wife and daughter. He knew in the depth of his soul that the information about his feelings for Catherine and his failed attempted murder attempt against Antonio Armani which was all done out of his love for Catherine, would crush Natalie and Helen. He wanted to spare them that hurt at all cost. Living in separate quarters and having Natalie and his daughter disappointed in him because of an assumed secret was the better of two evils.

He finished the coffee and got out of the chair. He rubbed his hand down his slightly grayish blond hair and then bend down and grabbed his crutches from the floor and carried them in his hand as he slowly walked out of the library and headed to his three bedroom living quarters to pack. Although, he dreaded leaving to set up residence in the one bedroom living quarters across the hall from Dillion and Leola Bradley.

During the ten days of Fred's healing from his foot injury, he had lost about ten pounds and his weight was down to just above 155 pounds for a 5'10 male. He had average looks and had never been the type of man that women flocked to. Seriously in his mind as he headed down the hallway toward his lower level living quarters, he was almost beside himself focusing on the possibility of Natalie asking for a divorce. He didn't want to be alone at this stage in his life. He cringed at the possibility since he knew a romantic future had come to an end for him. Especially since Catherine was in a serious relationship; and even if she wasn't, she made it clear that there could never be anything between them.

Chapter Eighteen

Veronica and her sons lingered in the living room for only a few minutes before they all scattered in other directions. Britain left the premises as Paris and Rome headed toward the staircase. Sydney stayed in the living room with his mother. She took a seat and he continued to stand. He seemed a million miles away as he stared above the fireplace mantle at his father's portrait.

Veronica glanced at him as she leaned forward and lifted her phone from the coffee table and buzzed for Leola Bradley. "I was dreading this day. But I guess you're probably heading to the lake house this morning. Did you call Starlet? Does she know you're back home?"

"I haven't had an opportunity to give her a call yet. But I plan to just as soon as I'm sure," Sydney answered still facing the portrait.

"Sure, about what? Are you thinking about maybe heading to the lake house tomorrow instead of today? She's giving a performance for the Disadvantage Children Fundraiser at the WJJ Theater, you know. I'm sure it would brighten her day to see you in attendant. We have all decided to attend including the staff. Although, I think Britain may have other plans. He didn't confirm that he was attending. He and Sabrina are still busy with some of their wedding details. Your brother is a happy fellow. Being engaged looks good on him," Veronica said, smiling. But she noticed how Sydney appeared preoccupied still looking at his father's portrait.

"So, Sweetheart, what are you going to do? Would you like to wait and drive up to the lake house tomorrow? This will give you a chance to attend the fundraiser and hear Starlet sing."

"Mother, I'm wondering what Father would do and how would he handle my situation if he had gone through what I have gone through, the kidnapping and all of that." He looked around at his mother. "Can you tell me to the best of your ability how Father might would have handled a similar predicament?"

Veronica held her hands together and stared out into spare for a moment. "Sydney, dear. It's hard to say. Your father was fortunate enough to have never experienced a trace of the kind of hardship you have faced." She grabbed her face for a moment choked up. "The fact that you have, make me feel as if I have failed you in some way," she said sadly, shaking her head.

Sydney stepped over to his mother and patted her shoulder. "Mother, please. Don't go there again trying to blame yourself for the horror Jack Coleman put us all through. You are the best mother in the world. There's nothing more you can do for us than what you are already doing. We love you dearly and I don't blame you for one single thing and neither do anyone else," Sydney stressed. "So, please, Mother. Let's stay focused. I would like you to concentrate and try to answer the question I asked you about Father. It's quite important to me to know the answer."

"Okay, but it's hard to give you a genuine answer since I can only think of a few disappointing times in your father's life. But I guess I can tell you how he handled those events. One of those times were when his folks cut your Aunt Catherine out of the will and left everything to him."

Sydney nodded as he took a seat on the sofa next to his mother. "Okay, that was a huge occurrence. Can you recall how Father handled something like that happening to his sister by his own parents?"

"He didn't fret or lose any sleep over it."

"Okay, but did he share his objections with parents?"

Veronica shook her head. "No, your father didn't have a sit-down conversation with his parents about how he felt about their decision to cut Catherine out of the will. But he made a few polite remarks to his folks that clearly stated his objections. Then your father went on with life as usual showing his folks as much love and warmth as ever. He was not happy with their decision, but he knew their one poor inconsiderate decision did not define who they were. He loved his folks but hated the choice they had made toward his sister. Yet, he also knew they were stubborn and set in their ways and once they made a decision they stuck with it to their own detriment. He knew there were nothing he could say that would change his folks mind about reconsidering their decision to disinherit Catherine," Veronica softly very seriously explained. "Therefore, he didn't try to change what he couldn't. To keep the peace and move forward, he changed what he could. They had made him sole heir to their estate, so he just took it upon himself to share with

Catherine his money, so she could stay accustomed to the lifestyle she had always known."

"That was very generous and considerate of Father. He sounds almost unreal and I feel I struggle to live up to his standards," Sydney solemnly said.

"Sydney, dear. You don't have to struggle to live up to your father's standards. You are a fine young man just the way you are. You have to do what you think is best for you," Veronica caringly said to him. "That's what your father would want."

Sydney nodded. "I'm sure you are right, Mother. It just seems Father had it so together until everyday life and decisions came quite easy for him."

"Believe me, that's not true. Your father was not perfect. He made his share of bad decisions and mistakes just like the rest of us. He just made fewer," she said lighthearted. "Anyway, he had a heart of gold and when your grandparents blew Catherine out of the water with their earthshaking bad news, he just countered it with his good news. He got Catherine alone and told her that as long as she lived she would never have to want for anything. He cut her an enormous check every week," Veronica caringly shared. "Your father was the type of man who never allowed a problem to consume him. He always tried to find a solution to fit whatever seemed broken with much success. Ryan never gave in to defeat," Veronica said with conviction.

"Mother, do you think that's what I'm doing regarding Starlet?"

"Well, of course, Sweetheart. If you are entertaining the thought of walking away from the young lady. Nevertheless, I feel it's not you or in you to do something as bold and without real cause as that. I know how much you adore that young lady. The two of you are perfect for each other. Your father would say, walking away from something is not an answer. It's usually an excuse not to face it."

"I read that statement by Father."

"Yes, that's how your father felt about walking away from problems. Therefore, according to your father's standards, it would be a huge error in judgement to walk away from Starlet just because you feel you can't give her what she needs."

"Mother, I know she needs me, but I don't feel like myself. I feel consumed with my grief of what I have been through. I don't want to be consumed with these unpleasant images in my head. Yet they are there. They take up a lot of my time," he admitted solemnly. "Maybe I'm the weak link in the family and not as strong as Father. He would have pushed these images out of his mind. He would stand strong and go on with his life."

"Sydney, you can't beat yourself up over the way you feel. We are all different and we all handle and cope with situations that happen to us in our own way," Veronica compassionately explained. "You have to do what you think is best for you. No matter what I want or what anyone else wants of you, you have to do what you think is best."

"Mother, I'm at a crossroads for the first time in my life and I'm not sure what I think is best in terms of spending time alone at the lake house without any communication with anyone for a while or staying put right where I am."

"I thought your mind was quite set about spending time at the lake house. You gave me no indication otherwise. You were quite sure that spending time there alone would help you put some things in perspective."

Sydney nodded. "Yes, Mother, you're right. I was quite sure of spending time there alone," Sydney said as Leola Bradley strolled across the room to stand facing Veronica.

"Thanks for coming, Leola. Natalie is tied up at the moment. Could you be so kind to bring in a serving of tea for two?"

Leola nodded. "Of course, Miss Veronica. It's coming up right away," she said and turned to leave the room.

After Leola left the room, Veronica looked at Sydney and grabbed his hand. "Okay, you were sure, but now you're having second thoughts?"

"Mother, I was flat out convinced that spending time alone at the lake house would somewhat help me sort some things out in my mind. However, after our flight out to Las Vegas to fetch Fred, I see things differently."

"Differently how? What made you unsure about sticking with the plan at the lake house?" Veronica was curious to know. "I'm pleased you are thinking of not going, but I would like to know what changed your mind."

"I guess all the chaos surrounding the predicament with Fred. I thought about how close he came to destroying his life and spending the rest of his life behind bars. If he had actually committed the crime that he thought he had, that would have been cold blooded murder without a real motive." He rubbed both hands across the back of his neck and stared across the room toward the fireplace for a moment. "Then I think of the heartbreak Natalie is going through breaking up with him. They have lost that special connection and apparently no longer have true love for each other," he said compassionately. "One thing I know for sure, Mother, is that true love doesn't just die on its own. It has to be destroyed."

"I agree and understand how you don't want to destroy what you have with Starlet. You're having second thoughts because you feel staying away from her for two weeks without any communication just might hurt your relationship," Veronica said.

Sydney nodded. "I have thought of that possibility because something for sure weighed on Fred and Natalie's marriage to break them apart. I don't know what other problems they faced, but I believe his sudden trip out to Nevada is what pushed her over the edge to break up and end their marriage. She feels she cannot depend on or trust her own husband," Sydney softly explained. "I'm quite disturbed over their plight. Natalie has always felt like a second mother to me."

"We all feel just awful for Natalie and Fred and hope they can compromise or find a solution to their problem, so they can remain together."

"That would be great if they could work things out. Fred is a good man and I want him to find the peace he's looking for. But without a doubt, Natalie deserves to be happy," Sydney seriously stated. "She's a deeply kind person who gives her all to make others happy. Plus, you know how she feels like family to me. Ever since I was old enough to remember, she was always there for me. I was too young to go to some of the events. She would babysit and play with me. On any given day, she always had a new toy or candy for me."

Veronica smiled. "Natalie always gravitated toward you from the time your father and I brought you home from the hospital. It's quite obvious she has a special place in her heart for you. But as for her giving you toys and candy, she did that because you were the baby in the house."

"Mother, the point I'm trying to make is we only know what today holds. I'm sure Natalie and Fred didn't expect to be separated at this time in their marriage. Therefore, I have decided to embrace what I have with Starlet instead of pushing it aside. I refuse to allow my insecurities to dictate my life. I'm amazed by her and love her too deeply to take a ridiculous chance as Fred did and possibly lose her," Sydney seriously explained.

"I will not deny its music to my ears to hear you say that you have considered not isolating yourself up at the lake house. Besides, you know I have never been onboard about your plans; and I haven't been silent. I told you my views about what you had decided. But, it is you who are going through what you are going through. Therefore, it had to be your decision whether or not you retreated to the lake house to cut off communication with all of us. I'm just so pleased you have changed your mind."

"Yes, I have changed my mind. After great consideration, I don't think I need to distant myself from my family and friends in such a dramatic way to achieve my goal. Plus, most importantly, I don't want to be away from Starlet. I don't want her to think she's not a priority in my life."

"Sweetheart, I'm glad to hear you talk this way. Starlet is precious, and she loves you for you. I know there are a lot of nice young women out there, but my greatest fear was to have one of you get hooked up with someone who didn't truly love you for yourself. Money is a major motivator and can easily sway someone to pursue a person for financial reasons," Veronica softly said.

Sydney nodded. "No truer words have been spoken. But Mother, when you met Father, his family had money, but yours did not? Is that correct?"

"Yes and no. Your father family was rich, and my family was well-off. But in the eyes of a rich man, well-off is at the bottom. But, I fell for your father for himself. His family wealth never dawned on me. I just loved and wanted to be with your father. And although, my folks didn't have the kind of money to stack up against the Franklins. We were not dirt poor as a church mouse. We did better than okay with a few servants. Plus, they sent me to one of the best universities; and I was able to wear nice clothes all throughout high school and college. But as I said, compared to the rich, my folks were just considered well-off. Their financial worth didn't put them on the Franklins social list."

Sydney nodded. "I see. So, when you and Father dated, how did his family feel about you as a possible wife for him? Can you recall if they accepted you with open arms?"

Veronica smiled. "At that time, we were all connected in a close-knit community. The famous Franklins family lived here in this house, of course. The Coleman's and the Sterlings lived on opposite sides of the Franklins. And on the next block also lived Antonio Armani family. Then three blocks down from my family, the Parkers, lived Mildred Ross family, the Latham's, and one block from Mildred lived Raymond Ross family and at the end of Mildred's block lived Fred Madden and his family. We all sort of grew up together; and all the kids in the community were fortunate to make Catherine and Ryan's acquaintance since their parents sent them to public school. When your father and I discussed schooling for the four of you, he was adamant that we send the four of you to public schools. But I have never claimed to share all your father's views. Therefore, being true to my own wishes, I persuaded him against his wishes to send you all to private schools. However, on the flipside, if your father had attended a private school, he and I probably wouldn't have ended up together," Veronica softly admitted and shivered at the thought. "Nevertheless, same community or not. Your father was destined for greatness. He shot to the stars with his movie career. His fame sort of pushed him in a whole different circle from the rest of us," Veronica said, smiling from the memories. "But I have gotten off track because you wanted to know did your father's parents accept me with open arms. My answer is absolutely.

They loved me. And it could be that they knew all the kids in the area since we all knew each other and went to school together. Besides, your father folks knew me quite well since Catherine and I was good friends before your father and I started dating. Yes, dear. Your grandparents had seen me many times in and out of Franklin House before I became your father's girlfriend."

"The fact that they accepted you, I'm sure that helped you and Father in your relationship."

Veronica nodded. "It did help. But they were quite protective of Ryan and Catherine; and was pleased with their friends if they sensed genuine care. They could obviously tell how much I loved your father."

"I'm glad they didn't cause a conflict between the two of you or try to keep you and Father apart," Sydney seriously said.

"Dear, why would you say something like that? Grandpa Samuel and Grandma Ellen always treated me like a second daughter," Veronica said.

"I guess I'm thinking how they were just the opposite with Aunt Catherine. They disowned her because of who she chose to marry. Antonio grew up in the community, but they didn't like him and banded Aunt Catherine from home for being with him," Sydney reminded his mother.

"You're right. But that was a long time ago and your grandparents are both deceased and cannot defend their reasons and I'm sure they had their reasons," Veronica caringly stated.

Sydney nodded. "Yes, I'm sure they did have their reasons."

"Of course, they had their reasons and they're the only ones who knew what those reasons were," Veronica thoughtfully said. "Nevertheless, I'll have you know that I never agreed with how Grandpa Samuel and Grandma Ellen handled that situation."

Sydney eyes lit up and showed approval of his mother's statement. But he stayed mute and continued to listen.

"Your Grandpa Samuel and Grandma Ellen disapproved of Antonio because it was obvious to them and everyone else that his relationship with Catherine was a completely one-sided affair." Veronica stared into space as she reflected on the past for a moment. Then she looked at Sydney with sad eyes. "Your Catherine loved Antonio Armani with all her heart and soul and then some." Veronica sadly nodded. "Listen, sweetheart. I guess I'll tell you, I have never known anyone to love a boy so desperately the way Catherine loved Antonio," Veronica said with conviction. "It broke my heart, your father's heart and your grandparent's heart. Because it was crystal clear that he didn't love her."

"Mother, surely he cared something for her," Sydney commented.

"Maybe he cared something," Veronica agreed. "But it was nothing close to love. He showed her no respect and based on his ill treatment of her and his constant talk of getting a hold of her inheritance. Her parents were trying to protect her from Antonio Armani. They felt if they cut Catherine out of the will that he would show his true colors and take off. That's exactly what he did," Veronica said and swallowed hard from the memory. "But after he left everyone was stunned when they didn't draw up a new will, so she could be slated to receive her inheritance. But make no doubt, we realize that one mistake doesn't define who they were. They were good people who made a bad mistake for good reasons, so they thought. But the fallout outweighed any amount of damage that they were trying to prevent," Veronica solemnly explained as the memories tore at her feelings. "I cannot tell you how it tore me apart to see your Aunt Catherine suffer from the aftermath of being disinherited. Nevertheless, I honestly believe they didn't want Catherine with Antonio because they honestly didn't believe he wanted Catherine for herself. And as I said, it turned out they were right. Antonio boldly mistreated Catherine and made it appear quite obvious that he only wanted her for what he could get from her."

"Mother, that's true and it's pretty much all over the community's newspapers how Mr. Armani used Aunt Catherine all down through the years while he carried a torch for Courtney' mother's, Mrs. Mildred Ross."

"Sydney, my darling, are you saying you feel Grandpa Samuel and Grandma Ellen did the right thing by Catherine to cut her out of the will because she was hooked up with Antonio Armani?"

Sydney shook his head. "Mother, that's exactly what I'm not saying. It doesn't matter how awful Antonio Armani was. He's not the point. Therefore, whether they thought he was the right person or not. In my opinion, they didn't hold up their part of the bargain by being the best parent possible to their child. When they cut her out of the will on the condition that she married someone they didn't approve of, what kind of love is that to show your child?" Sydney asked. "I have to admit that it does bother me some that my grandparents could hurt Aunt Catherine in such a significant way."

"It bothered me and your Father when it happened. But your grandparents were living in different times. They honestly thought they were doing the right thing by Catherine. They thought they were saving her from herself. And although, Ryan and I did not agree with their decision we understood how they thought they were doing the best thing for their child."

"Mother, what bothers us the most about the situation that happened to Aunt Catherine concerning the will, is how Grandpa Samuel and Grandma

Ellen did not draw up a new document to place her back in their will after Mr. Armani left town," Sydney softly said. "We do get the point of how they decided to cut her out of the will in order to protect her inheritance from someone who was only interested in swindling her out of her money. However, after Mr. Armani left town they should have done right by Aunt Catherine and given her what was rightfully hers. But they allowed her to continue suffering."

"Your grandparents always felt Antonio Armani was your Aunt Catherine's Achilles' heel and I must agree with them on that. Therefore, even though they knew Antonio had left town, it gave them no peace of mind as far as Catherine was concern. They felt if he ever showed his face in these parts no matter how badly he had treated Catherine, that he would be able to swindle her out of her money. I heard them in conversation once discussing among themselves how they didn't want to see chunks of the family fortune swindled and pulled out of Catherine's bank account by Catherine's treacherous husband."

Sydney grabbed his face and paused looking toward the fireplace for a moment. "Mother, I'm sure Grandpa Samuel and Grandma Ellen felt they were doing the right thing, otherwise they wouldn't have done that to Aunt Catherine. However, we all feel just horrible about their decision and do not feel they did the right thing to continue to keep Aunt Catherine out of the will. The pain they conflicted on her is far greater than anything Mr. Antonio Armani could have done to her. She has gone through life feeling unloved by her parents. I can't even begin to imagine that kind of heartbreak. Therefore, we see them for who they were. They did some great things and they produced two great kids. But they made one huge mistake. But with that said, we love our grandparents with all our hearts. We do not love what they did to Aunt Catherine, but we love who they were. Because as you said, Mother. One bad mistake does not define who they were."

Veronica smiled and tapped Sydney's arm. "Loving who they were is loving what they did?"

Sydney nodded. "That's true. We loved who they were for us. They were the people who brought Father and Aunt Catherine into the world. They were our grandparents. They were the people who did a lot of good and helped a lot of underprivileged people. They were good people who made one bad mistake, and nobody is perfect."

"That's true. That's how your father and I saw it."

"Besides, Mother. When we all discussed this incident among us, Rome mentioned to the three of us that he was certain the mistake of cutting Aunt

157

Catherine out of the will was a gamble on our grandparent's part," Sydney seriously relayed. "He explained his theory to us how he felt they rolled the dice hoping for the best. However, hindsight shows they won in one way, and lost in another. They won by protecting Aunt Catherine's inheritance. But it ended up being protected so well that she couldn't even touch it. Therefore, there was no victory in that win. Then on the other hand, they lost when Aunt Catherine mistook their tough love for less love," Sydney said and then stretched both arms back behind his head and leaned back on the sofa. He looked up at the ceiling in silence.

In a few moments, Sydney glanced over at his mother who was just reaching for a copy of Fortune Magazine from the coffee table.

"Mother, I didn't stay behind to discuss Grandpa Samuel and Grandma Ellen. How did we ever get on the subject of discussing them? I basically wanted you to know that I have decided to throw the lake house out of the window. I have decided to take a page from Father's book. He wouldn't let anything beat or control him. The event that took place with Jack Coleman will not make or break me. In time it will all roll off my back. I will cope and deal until it does. Starlet is the love of my life and I want it to remain that way."

Chapter Nineteen

It was 10:30 that morning when Catherine softly knocked on Julian's front door. Earlier that morning, not long after breakfast, she had looked out the living room window and noticed his black Mercedes in his driveway. She felt uneasy about showing up on his doorstep unannounced, but she convinced herself it was time to do so. Not long after she knocked, Julian answered the door smiling. He was dressed neatly in jeans and a red shirt. Catherine smiled and glanced down at his feet, noticing his red socks with no shoes, holding a cup of coffee in his hand. His eyes showed surprise as he waved Catherine inside.

"It's great to see you. What a nice surprise. Please come in. How are you?" he asked as he closed the door and then gave Catherine a slight hug careful not to spill his coffee.

"Please come and have a seat." He pointed toward the sofa as Catherine followed him across the room toward the sofa.

They took a seat on his long black leather sofa as he placed his cup on the coffee table and looked at Catherine, smiling. "Can I get you a cup of coffee or some breakfast? I don't think you have ever visited at such an early hour. But I'm glad to see you," he assured her. "Let me look at you. I feel as if it's been ages since I looked in your nice eyes." He held up both hands. "So, what can I get you? Breakfast, coffee, tea?"

His compliment about her eyes warmed her. But Catherine shook her head feeling somewhat apprehensive. She hadn't seen or spoken to Julian in so long until she wasn't sure where she stood or how he currently felt about her. She looked in his face. "I'm fine. I have had breakfast and also a few cups of coffee. But I'll take another cup." She smiled.

"Sure, wait here." He hopped off the sofa and headed out of room.

Catherine sat there nervous wondering what she would say to Julian. She still cared about him but the past few weeks she hadn't shown that she cared. Therefore, five minutes later when he returned to the living room with a cup of coffee in his hand. She looked at him and knew she had to beg his pardon about her inconsiderate behavior toward him.

He passed her the cup of coffee and then he took a seat beside her on the sofa. "I put sugar and cream in your coffee. That's how you liked it during the times we went out.

Catherine slowly lifted the cup to her mouth and took a sip. Suddenly she seemed two quiet. Julian looked at her and wondered. "Catherine, is anything the matter? You seem a bit uneasy."

She nodded. "That's because I am. I'm mostly just so sorry about how I didn't take your calls over the past few weeks," she regretfully explained.

Julian nodded. "I was quite concerned about you. Is everything okay? Did something happen?" he curiously asked.

Catherine nodded with the cup to her mouth while looking at Julian. "Yes, something did happen. But over the past couple weeks, it smoothed itself out. Before now I was in no condition to spend any time with you or anyone else. I have been stressed and out of sorts until just recently. But now with all that chaos behind me, I wanted to drop by and say how deeply sorry I am about my rude behavior toward you," she kindly apologized.

"I was bewildered to say the least to be blown off by you like that," Julian said. "The time we spent together getting to know each other had meant so much to me and I was under the impression that you felt the same. Therefore, after enjoying some of the best days of my life with you. I was completely blown away and beyond stunned when you rejected all my calls and ignored my text messages. Frankly, Catherine, I have to be on the level with you and tell you how disappointed and bothered I was that you felt I didn't even warrant a call or any explanation for your silence and absence."

"I realize how awful it was of me to be so inconsiderate of your feelings. But as I said something took place in my life that overwhelmed me and turned my life upside down. I wasn't thinking straight for a while," she strongly said.

"Catherine, from the sound of your voice. It sounds as if you faced something quite disturbing. I'm not trying to pry, but is it possible to share with me the life altering situation that took place in your life that caused you much distress?" Julian caringly asked.

Catherine looked at him with humble eyes. She knew she couldn't reveal to him about how she thought she had killed a man; and all the other stuff that was involved along with it, like Fred's role. Therefore, she looked at Julian and shook her head. "I'm sorry but I can't share what happened. It was a private family matter," she kindly explained, looking at him. "I hope you understand."

Julian nodded. "Yes, I understand family privacy, Catherine. I'm not offended at all. I'm just mostly disappointed that I didn't receive a call or a message from you before now. I understand it was a chaotic time, but it would have only taken a second of your time to call or send a text message. Afterall, I was under the impression that we were seriously dating. We hit it off surprisingly well and went out three nights in a row. Then after that everything started to cool. But I can't recall the last time I had so much fun."

Catherine smiled. "You were under the right impression. It's the same impression I was under. We were seriously dating, and I had a lot of fun as well," Catherine softly uttered as her hand slightly shook as she lifted the coffee cup to her mouth to take a sip.

Julian cell phone rang, and he stood from the sofa and stepped across the room to retrieve the phone from the shelf of the stereo stand. "Excuse me, Catherine. I need to take this call," he said, and walked near the stereo stand. "Okay, I haven't forgotten. I'll see you in a couple hours and I also haven't forgotten about our plans for tonight," he said and then ended his call.

Julian walked over and took his seat next to Catherine and she was just finishing the last sip of coffee. She looked at him and smiled. "I know I disappointed you while I had so much chaos going on in my life. But all the chaos and sleepless nights are over for me. That's why I drove over here to see if we are still good to pick up where we left things."

Julian looked at Catherine for a while before he shook his head and said sincerely. "I'm sorry, but we are not still good. I didn't want this to happen that we wouldn't make it. But when I didn't hear from you after all that time, I had no other choice but to move on. I thought you were no longer interested in going out with me. I didn't throw in the towel lightly. I gave it much effort, calling and leaving numerous messages. But it comes a times when a man has to have some kind of pride and dignity. Therefore, after many attempts to no avail, I think anyone would have thought as I did," he regretfully uttered.

Catherine nodded as she placed the empty coffee cup on the coffee table. "I can understand how you gave up waiting around. But would you like to try again?" she swallowed her pride and boldly asked him.

Julian felt awkward that she had asked him that question after he had just told her that he had moved on. "Catherine, didn't you hear me say, I have moved on? I'm afraid it's too late for us. I'm dating someone else now."

Catherine eyes widened with surprise. "Is it anyone I know?"

"I'm not sure if you know her personally. But she knows you. She told me that the two of you went to the same high school."

"In that case, I guess my name came up," Catherine solemnly mumbled.

"Yes, your name came up. When I met Mildred and asked her out, I told her about my hopeful romance with you that went downhill without an explanation from you. We met through her youngest daughter, Trina, who is dating Oliver. I bumped into Trina at the grocery store. She introduced me to her mother, Mildred, who was shopping with her. Mildred and I hit it off so well until I asked her to a movie five minutes after meeting her," Julian expressed with warmth. "It was something kind and inviting about her," Julian caringly said as Catherine sat there with a fake smile on her face.

Catherine felt so small sitting next to him. She just wanted to leave his premises and stay out of his sight. He had moved on and she knew it would bother her to see him around, knowing she messed up what she could have had with him.

Julian touched Catherine's arm. "I don't mean to be inconsiderate of your feelings if it bothers you to hear me speak of Mildred. But I figured if nothing else, you would be happy I found someone since you and I couldn't make it."

"Julian, of course, I'm happy for you that you found someone. But it seems abrupt. Plus, I did go to school with Mildred and she was a nice girl. It's just her chaos life now that you should steer clear of," Catherine warned him.

"If you're speaking of the shootout in her home by her soon to be ex-husband, Raymond Ross, she told me all about it. Oliver also voiced his concerns that Raymond Ross could be friends with people on the wrong side of the law. But that didn't scare me away from Mildred. I'm not concerned about that. Mildred is a good woman who is very easy on the eyes and I feel lucky that I even met her. But between the two of you, it's a tie in terms of who suffered and faced more heartbreak at the hands of a man. She had a sad, battered unhappy marriage in the household with an alcoholic. Then you on the other hand, faced a lifetime of heartbreak from your ex-husband. On top of that, you also said you suffered from actions of your parents. My heart goes out for you both and you both just need the love of a good man. I wanted to be that man for you, Catherine. But you didn't give me the chance. Now, I have a second chance to make another precious woman happy."

Catherine wiped a tear from her right eye. She was deeply hurt and upset with herself that she had unintentionally pushed Julian out of her life. She knew deep down that he was probably it for her. She had been foolish and unwise to allow him to slip between her fingers. Veronica had warned her that she would lose him if she wasn't careful to give him more attention. But of all the women in Barrington Hills, she was crushed that Julian had chosen the same woman that Antonio had left her for.

Julian walked Catherine to the door and gave her a tight hug. "It was good sees you again. Take care of yourself. Next time we run into each other, you'll probably be telling me about your new man. You're a good woman, Catherine and there's a good man waiting around the corner for you." He watched at the front door as she hurried across the front yard to the driveway, entered her car and drove away.

Catherine didn't exit her car right away when she pulled into Franklin House driveway. She felt extensive heartbreak. But she realized she couldn't sit there and display too much emotion in front of possible watchful eyes. She glanced at her watch and knew she needed to head inside and take care of some personal things. But she hoped not to bump into Veronica. Nevertheless, when Catherine stepped through the front door, Veronica was waiting in the foyer with a smile on her face. Catherine closed the door and headed into the living room. Veronica noticed how quiet she seemed. They both took a seat on the sofa and Veronica snapped getting out of her seat to leave the room. "I have other things I could be doing other than waiting around to hear your sad story. When I noticed you had driven over to see Julian Bartlett, it lifted my spirits and I couldn't wait for you to get back, so I could hear your good news. But from the look on your face, what I told you would happen, did happen," Veronica said as she slowly headed out of the room.

"Could you please wait a minute? You are right. Julian broke up with me. He's seeing someone else now," Catherine sadly admitted.

"Don't tell me, you are surprised. What did you expect? He definitely didn't know you wanted a relationship with him. A fine decent guy like Julian Bartlett out of your sights forever, all due to you," Veronica fussed.

"I know it's all my fault, but I was so distraught and wrapped so tight in everything before until it was impossible to have a relationship with anyone. You know I was a basketcase in no shape to talk or spend time with Julian."

"You were at your worst," Veronica agreed. "It's just rotten luck on your part that he met someone else so soon. Otherwise, you two might could have started back up. Did he mention who he's dating now?"

Catherine nodded. "Yes, he did and you're not going to like it."

"What you mean I'm not going to like it. I wish he was dating you, but I have no beef with whoever that man dates," Veronica seriously said.

"He's dating Mildred Ross."

"What did you say?"

"I said, Julian is now dating Mildred Ross."

Veronica jaw dropped as she grabbed her face with both hands. She hadn't expected Catherine to announce that Julian Bartlett was now dating Mildred Ross. "You're telling me Julian is now dating the woman that Antonio left you for?" She shook her head. "Catherine, I tell you. You can't seem to escape bad luck. It seems to find you no matter what. Of all the women in this town, the man you're interested in breaks off with you for Mildred Ross," Veronica sighed. "Anyway, Catherine, I'm sorry. I know it was hard enough but to be passed over again for Mildred Ross. I'm sure it hurts a lot."

"It does hurt a lot. But I can't blame Mildred. She has been through a lot of misery herself. Maybe even more than I have. She had to endure abuse constantly for over twenty years. I suffered while Antonio was around. But we both know, he wasn't around long."

"Why are you feeling sorry for Mildred Ross? She has the man and you don't!" Veronica fussed.

"I know but as you told me long before now. You said I would lose Julian if I didn't give him more time and my attention," Catherine reminded her.

"That's the truth! Thanks for reminding me! I had amnesiac there for a moment. But, Catherine, as much as I hate to kick you while you're down. It's actually all your fault. You singlehanded sabotaged every chance you had with Julian," Veronica sadly admitted.

Catherine grabbed her face. "You are absolutely right. What's wrong with me to allow Julian to slip between my fingers as I did? Besides, I had and still do have feelings for the man. But yet, I ignored him while in cahoots with Fred thinking I had murdered Antonio," Catherine sadly cried, wiping her tears with the back of her palms. "I wouldn't listen to you. You tried to reason with me and pleaded to me. You told me to look ahead and not back. You were never convinced that I had harmed Antonio. If I had just listened maybe Julian and I would still be together, and I wouldn't be sitting here feeling like a fool with this crushing agony flooding through me," Catherine admitted. "Can you tell me, how and why I turned my back on Julian and allowed him to slip away?" she seriously asked.

"Catherine, I can see you're hurting but you brought this heartbreak on yourself. You just seem prone for misery," Veronica compassionately uttered.

"You didn't answer my question," Catherine said, wiping another tear.

"Maybe I didn't answer your question because I don't have the answers. I cannot tell you why you do the imprudent things you do. All I know is that when you're doing them, you're usually dead set on course, not wanting to back down or listen to reason. That's how you were about wanting to admit to the police that you murdered Antonio. That's how you were about believing you had killed the man. You wouldn't accept any other possibility of his demise. You were convinced it was you and no one else. I couldn't convince you otherwise," Veronica firmly reminded her. "You're stubborn and set in your ways to your own defeat."

Catherine didn't like being criticized by Veronica. "So, you're saying I lost Julian because I'm too damn stubborn and won't listen."

"Yes, Catherine. You threw that good man away because of your one-track mind! You were consumed with the aftermath of Antonio Armani's death, and everything else around you fell by the wayside. You were too absorbed in the mess of that loser who ruined your life to open your eyes to see the wonderful man that was right in front of you!" Veronica firmly stated.

"I guess you're right," Catherine sadly mumbled.

"You know I'm right. Besides, although you are still fairly young. Considering your shut-in ways and nonsocial lifestyle, your chances of meeting a good man are slim. I hope you realize that Julian Bartlett was probably the end of the romantic line for you!" Veronica stared at Catherine.

Catherine stared at Veronica but didn't comment since she felt Veronica statement was uncalled for during her moment of such enormous heartbreak.

"Catherine, I'm not trying to be insensitive or hurtful right now. I'm being realistic as far as your romance life is concerned. For the past twenty years, you pretty much carried a torch for Antonio Armani and didn't seem that interested in meeting anyone else. Suddenly, after the untimely demise of Antonio, you met Julian who took a liking to you. It was a rare chance that a decent, established man as Julian Bartlett would fall for you."

"Why do you say it like that?" Catherine asked.

"Catherine don't get me wrong. I'm trying to be on the level with you. I know you are an attractive woman. It would be impossible for you not to be attractive coming from the good-looking parents that you and Ryan had. However, you don't have that confident and you don't think you are attractive. You have always believed your brother was the good looking one. Although, Ryan looks were flawless. You are also a beautiful woman. What I'm trying to say Catherine is complicated. But the bottomline is you. You don't seem to have any confident in yourself and that's a big turn off for men. On top of that, you tend to stick inside of this house as if you're afraid to branch out into the world," Veronica caringly explained. "I'm not a shrink, but maybe you're afraid with such low self-esteem because of what you have been through. That's why I said Julian Bartlett was probably the end of the romantic line for you. Antonio Armani has always been your Achilles' heel and even in death he has managed to put his final nail in your coffin!" Veronica loudly fussed.

"Veronica, can you be any more hostile? You're speaking above your voice as if I'm sitting in the next room."

"Catherine, I'm not being hostile. I'm being sympathetic and what I'm trying to say is unless you change in a big way, I cannot see you meeting anyone new down the road."

"I'm very distraught over losing Julian. But we can't know what the future holds for me. Only God knows that," Catherine sadly grumbled.

"Catherine, you are missing my point. This isn't just about meeting someone new, it's about meeting someone that's worthy of you. Someone established with a good life who won't be after what you have. Your track record proves that your money is what Antonio Armani wanted from you," Veronica sighed in frustration and disappointment of how badly Catherine had messed up what she had with Julian. "Catherine, what you had with Julian Bartlett was the likelihood of a bright future with each other. He and I talked in-depth after the two of you started dating each other."

The fact that Veronica and Julian had communicated without her acknowledge seemed to irritate Catherine. "Why did you feel the need to discuss me with Julian? You always want to be in the middle of my business."

"Yes, want to be, but you always resist and maybe that's why you fall flat on your face each time. But that's neither here or there. Just listen, Catherine. Based on my conversations with Julian. He was sincerely excited about the two of you. It was all good until you kicked him to the curb by not answering his calls and messages," Veronica firmly stated. "Cruel outlandish behavior displayed like that against another party when two people are just starting out, cannot be expected without repercussions."

"You don't have to remind me of my foolish mistake. I know all too well the mess I have made, and I have to live with my mistake," Catherine acknowledged. "Also, I have listened to you and I have no illusions of thinking there's another Prince Charming waiting for me around the next corner. Julian was my chance at happiness and I blew it. Now I have to lie in my bed of despair of my own doing," she sadly admitted.

Chapter Twenty

Sabrina managed to drag herself out of her room by 11:00 that morning. She hadn't slept as late or stayed tucked in her room so late in the day since adulthood. Courtney's horrifying visit broke her sleep and her spirits, and she just wanted to stay tucked away in her room and pretend Courtney had never showed up at her home. But the bright sun of reality hit her in the face and she had to face reality and move forward with her new heartbreaking information. Therefore, she needed much pampering and lingered in a warm shower for twice the time that she would usual take to shower.

She looked the picture of refinement, dressed in a pair of Oscar de La Renta sapphire slacks and a Saint Laurent blue pullover top. But, she noticed she was still tired and not actually ready to face the morning as she slowly headed down the hallway toward the staircase; and with each step she took she could hear the echo in the hallway from her flat navy Givenchy heels as a roaring storm brewed inside of her making water well up in her eyes.

Yet, she continued down the long hallway. But as she fussed with the sleeve of her pullover top, she noticed how quiet and still the house seemed. She couldn't hear anyone stirring inside of the house. But as she made her way into the dining room she walked over to the back wall that was eighty percent windows and pulled the white curtains apart. She spotted Sam and Larry Westwood carrying two small white stones a piece heading toward the small duck pond. From a distant, she could see that they were encircling the little pond with the white stones. She could vaguely hear Sam and Larry's voices as they were doing their work on the back grounds. She dropped the curtains and walked slowly down a short hallway into the kitchen. She was headed to the refrigerator for a glass of orange juice, but the moment she stepped into the kitchen she noticed a plate sitting on the kitchen counter covered with plastic wrap. She smiled at the thought, but she didn't have the stomach to eat a thing. Apparently, Carrie had left a plate of breakfast for her and she felt that was thoughtful as usual of Carrie. However, as she stood there eyeing the covered breakfast plate, she grabbed her cheeks and shook her head. She wasn't pleased that she had missed a family breakfast, which she hadn't done so since her mother passed away.

Sabrina had stayed in bed since she didn't want to face anyone after her dreadful time spent with Courtney. But with her back propped against the kitchen counter, she turned around to the vague sound of voices. She stepped over to the kitchen window, pulled the white curtains apart and looked out and spotted Sam and Larry at the patio walkway taking a few white stones from that section to carry to the little pond. This time she noticed that Carrie Westwood was now standing outside holding a conversation with Sam and Larry. Sabrina dropped the curtains, stepped over to the counter and uncovered the plate. She looked at the breakfast plate and took a piece of bacon from it and ate half of it; and then placed the other half back on the plate. She then slowly headed out of the kitchen and back up the staircase toward her room to fetch her purse. She felt mentally drained and exhausted and in a sour mood from Courtney's visit.

Britain would pick her up at 11:30 for lunch; and at 11:30 on the nose, Britain pulled into her driveway and blew his car horn. She heard his horn, but she just sat there on the sofa with her face in her hands. Then Carrie appeared in the living room and noticed Sabrina sitting with her face covered, appearing to be in a disheartened mood. Carrie curiously stepped over to the living room window, pulled the long yellow lacy curtains apart and glanced out. She could see it was Britain, and now she was confused as to why Sabrina was just sitting there as if she didn't hear his car horn.

She glanced over her shoulder at Sabrina. "Miss Sabrina, that's Britain outside blowing his horn. Should I tell him you'll be right out?" Carrie asked, confused. "He doesn't appear to be getting out of his car to head inside. I wonder if everything is okay. I can't recall ever seeing Mr. Britain pull up in the driveway and blow his horn."

Sabrina broke out of her emotional daze and shook her head at Carrie. "Thanks Carrie. Everything is fine; and you're right. He would never drive up and blow his horn. But I asked him to blow when he got here," Sabrina said as she stood from the sofa and grabbed her black Christian Dior Vintage purse from the coffee table. "I'm headed outside now." Sabrina hurried toward the door as Carrie stepped away from the window and headed out of the room.

Sabrina stepped outside and walked slowly across the front porch and down the steps. By now, Britain was leaning up against his car with his arms folded. She could see that he was smiling with a cheerful look on his face as she headed down the walkway toward him. She didn't look toward his face too long. She pretended to be looking for something in her purse as she headed toward him. He had no idea she was deeply distraught over Courtney's rude treatment toward her as he stood there with his arms folded looking as immaculate and fashionable as usual, dressed neatly in Givenchy clothing. A neat blue shirt and a pair of black slacks, sporting a trendy brown leather jacket that matched his Fendi brown leather shoes. However, his presence didn't lift her spirits as she had hoped, it just brought Courtney's malicious, spiteful words louder and louder echoing in her mind. She didn't want to concentrate on Courtney or her cruel words, but she couldn't seem to shake the mountain of fabrications from her thoughts. Therefore, with each step her nerves tightened. She felt uneasy, sensing Britain would be able to detect a chilly attitude from her; and she felt awful having a displeasing attitude toward him. But Courtney's mean-spirited visit was controlling her thoughts.

Her long waist length French curls flowed down her back like robes of black silk as she walked toward his car with her head slightly lowered, purposely not looking in his face. When she approached the car, she still didn't look him in the face as he gallantly as usual pulled open the passenger's door for her to be seated. She flopped on the front seat and he leaned down giving her a kiss on the forehead before closing the door. She slightly stiffened as he kissed her, but she hoped he hadn't noticed.

"You look sensational. But just how are you this sunny day?" He grinned.

"I'm fine," Sabrina mumbled in a low voice.

He gracefully slid into the car and started the engine. He threw the car in gear and drove slowly to the end of the driveway. Then he eased his foot on the brakes and looked at Sabrina and smiled. "Is everything okay? You seem sort of quiet," he casually noticed and then glanced at his gold Rolex watch and tapped twice on the face of his watch.

"That reminds me, my darling." He placed the car in park and rested both arms on the steering wheel as he looked at Sabrina. "I have another appointment this afternoon. It was last minute, but I want to keep it." He held up one finger. "However, we can still have lunch, but we'll have to cut it short if that's okay."

Sabrina shook her head, smiling at him. "Please, go to your appointment. We can see each other later," Sabrina suggested.

He nodded. "I really don't like cancelling our plans. I figured we could still grab a quick lunch? I do have some time before the appointment," he tried to persuade her.

"I don't want to make you late for your appointment," she said as she pondered whether to have a quick lunch with him. "What time is your appointment for?" she asked.

"It's at one o'clock, so I do have a small window of time. But, I do need to keep it," he softly said. "I'm sorry about this last-minute appointment. I could have texted and told you, but this appointment completely slipped my mind."

Sabrina grabbed her chest and almost choked when he said one o'clock, which was the same time Courtney told her that she was expecting him.

He patted her back. "Sweetie, are you okay? Don't tell me you're getting choked off of air?" he said teased. "Are you okay now?" He held her left hand.

"Of course, I'm fine; and I'm also fine with waiting until later. You have an appointment and honestly, I don't care for the idea of squeezing in time for lunch," she told him. "I think it's best if we just wait until later to get together."

Britain narrowed his eyes and smiled. He wasn't sure how she really felt about postponing their lunch. He sensed vague irritation in her voice.

He nodded. "Okay, if you're fine with waiting until later." He softly touched the side of her face as she was purposely trying not to look him in the eyes. "I can detect a tad of irritation. I'm sorry if you're disappointment. Look, if you like, we can still drive over to the Upscale Café and have a quick lunch." He glanced at his watch again. "Besides, we do have some time to kill, just not a lot if I want to make the appointment on time."

Sabrina didn't want to give him the wrong impression that she was irritated with him since she was really irritated with Courtney. Therefore, she forced a smile and looked at him gracefully shaking her head. "No, I'm okay with not during lunch." She touched his arm and smiled. "Really, I'm not disappointed in the lease. Besides, we have dinner plans later. So, let's just do that? That way we don't have to hurry through lunch to keep your appointment," she softly suggested.

Britain noticed that she was smiling and didn't comment about being a tad irritated about something. So, he didn't mention it again. But he could see it in her eyes as he continued to smile and touched the side of her face. "Okay, most beautiful. Good idea. I'll pick you up later at 6:00." He nodded, threw his car in reverse and backed back into her driveway.

Sabrina quickly pushed open the passenger's door and stepped out of the car. She was preoccupied with the nonsense Courtney had said to her. She didn't look toward Britain as she closed the car door and headed up the walkway without saying a word.

He felt a slight chill coming from her and could now more than before detected her irritation, but he didn't know why. He stuck his head out of the car window and called out to her as she headed up the walkway. "I don't get a wave or one of your kisses in the wind?" he asked teasingly. "You say you're okay with canceling lunch? Maybe it's just me, but I get the feeling that you're sore at me," he said, smiling.

Sabrina glanced over her shoulder and forced a smile. "No. Don't be silly. I'm okay. I'll see you later, okay?" She threw him a kiss in the wind.

He smiled at her and nodded, threw the car in gear and slowly drove away. She stood there and kept her composure as she watched his car fade out of view. Then she stood in the driveway trembling with agitation as she grabbed her face and cried silent tears. She was frustrated and confused and wasn't sure what to do about the uneasy feeling stirring in her. She thought to herself. "Of all his appointments in a given day, why did this appointment have to be at one o'clock, the same time Courtney bragged about seeing him."

Sabrina didn't bother going back inside, standing in the driveway she turned on her low Givenchy black heels with her Christian Dior Vintage shoulder bag swinging on her shoulder, and hurried across the driveway toward their four-car garage for her car. She was troubled by the far-out things that Courtney had filled her mind with. Things she didn't want to think of. But she knew exactly where she was headed when she punched in the code number to raise the garage door. She stood at the back end of her car and hesitated for a moment. But she couldn't shake the nagging feeling in the back of her mind to call Courtney's bluff. Therefore, she slowly and reluctantly stepped around the car to the driver's side and swung open the door. She begrudgingly hopped in her car, started the engine, and slowly backed out of the garage. Afterward, she hit the garage button on her car dashboard to lower the garage door. She watched the garage door go down as she sat there anxiously in the driveway with the motor running. She had decided that her mind wasn't going to rest until she proved to herself that Courtney had lied to her. Therefore, she glanced at her watch and realized she had an hour and fifteen minutes to kill before one o'clock. But she didn't want to go back inside and pace the floor thinking about Courtney's words. So, she slowly backed out of the driveway and headed to Starbucks in town. When she arrived at Starbucks, she walked up to the counter and ordered one regular coffee with cream and sugar. After she was served, she took her cup of coffee and took a seat at a small round black wooden table that seated two. She sipped her coffee slowly as she tried to fade out the noise of Courtney's incredible tales. She tried to think clearly and told herself that Britain most definitely had a one o'clock appointment somewhere other than at Courtney's house. Nevertheless, after she finished one cup of coffee and one cup of latte, she hurried out of Starbucks and headed straight to Courtney's house. But with thirty minutes to spare, she detoured and drove around town for a while before convincing herself to show up at Courtney's front door.

It was a quarter to one when Sabrina killed the engine of her S-Class Coupe Red Mercedes right dab in the middle of Courtney's driveway. She felt out of place just being parked there as the bright sun beamed down through the windshield on her. She glanced at the house and then noticed Courtney's green 2008 Ford Fiesta that was parked directly in front of her car. Suddenly everything seemed too quiet as Sabrina tapped her well-manicured soft pink fingernails anxiously on the dashboard. She wasn't pleased with herself as she thought to herself: "My word. I shouldn't be here at Courtney's house. What I'm doing is completely ridiculous. I have more smarts than this – allowing myself to fall into Courtney's trap."

Nevertheless, against Sabrina's better judgment, she sat there trying to decide whether to drive away or get out of the car and go inside. She looked up at the house and noticed Courtney standing in the living room window with the curtains pulled back, looking out, staring at her. Then moment Sabrina and Courtney made eye contact and Courtney realized it was Sabrina parked in her driveway, she dropped the curtains and rushed to the front door. She swung open the front door and stepped out on the porch wearing a short black dress and beige high heels with her hair sweeping across her shoulders. Sabrina swallowed hard to see that she was dressed as if she really did have a date, but Sabrina believed Courtney was lying about having a date with Britain.

Courtney stood there on the front porch smiling as she beckoned to Sabrina to drive her car around to their back driveway.

"Please park your car around back," she hollered off the porch.

Sabrina nodded, started her engine and drove her car around back and parked. She killed the motor and dropped her head on the steering wheel. She counted to ten and then pushed open the door and stepped out of the car. She felt uneasy as if she had hidden within herself and that someone else was controlling her actions. She couldn't believe she had fallen for Courtney's trick. Here she was heading inside of Courtney's house, when deep down inside, she knew Britain would not be showing up.

Courtney was standing on the front porch smiling when Sabrina walked around from the back. She stood there nodding and smiling, holding the front door open as Sabrina headed up the front steps.

"Come on in. I've been waiting for you. I knew you would show up at my front door. You would have been a bigger fool than I thought you were if you hadn't! I didn't figure you wanted to miss this perfect opportunity of catching your Mr. Perfect in the act of not being so perfect!" Courtney sharply said.

Sabrina knew she had to keep her composure and call her bluff. She walked across the small living room floor and tried to tune her out. She took a seat in the old maple rocker and focused her eyes on the design of the orange floral design curtains at the window.

"Well, Sabrina. You can ignore me if you want, but you are sitting here in my living room, and that tells me one thing. You don't trust Mr. Franklin. Therefore, no matter what you think of me, the way I see it, I'm doing your thin butt a favor! What do you think?"

"Do you really want to know what I think?" Sabrina asked politely.

Courtney nodded, feeling assured that she had Sabrina right where she wanted her. "Yes, just what do you think?"

"I think I'm losing my mind to fall for your tricks," Sabrina said irritated.

"This is not a damn trick!" Courtney snapped. "You're just so full of yourself and can't see what's staring you right in the face." She waved her hand. "You're definitely not losing your mind. You're being wise to show up here and see this through. Besides, I'm the mental case, remember?"

Sabrina held up both hands and spoke politely, "Courtney, I don't plan to allow you to get under my skin. I'm here to prove a point."

"What point is that?"

"The point that you have been completely untruthful about all those things you told me about Britain this morning. Plus, you know, and I know that Britain Franklin, my fiancé is not coming to your house at one o'clock or any other time," Sabrina politely stated as she maintained her frustration and irritation of dealing with Courtney's devious behavior.

"You can keep your head in the clouds and believe what you will. But Britain will be here shortly, and you can eat your words at that time." Courtney threw both hands on her hips. "I feel sorry for you in a way. But at least this will save you the trouble of catching Britain naked in bed with another woman and then having to dump him after the wedding. Yes! Sabrina Taylor, coming over here was very wise and smart on your part." She laughed!

Sabrina looked at Courtney and politely uttered. "Please don't talk to me, Courtney. I'm not here to hear your rude mouth! I'm just here to prove to you that you are a liar! Because just as soon as one o'clock ticks around, I'll have the last laugh," Sabrina said firmly, folded her arms and sank back in the rocker. "There's no way Britain will be paying you a visit."

Courtney rolled her eyes at Sabrina. She wanted to keep talking to upset Sabrina as much as possible. But Sabrina had asked her nicely not to converse with her. Therefore, Courtney didn't want to push her luck with too much negative exchange that would cause Sabrina to leave her house. She knew if Sabrina left that would spoil her plan. Therefore, she kept quiet and grabbed a small clock from the fireplace mantel. She held the little black clock in both hands as she took a seat on the beige sofa near the double window; and for a few minutes the room was filled with silence as Courtney sat there staring at the clock and bumping her knees together.

Sabrina glanced about at the living room and noticed their modest surroundings. The living room was neat and clean and decorated nicely. Seeing the neatly orderly room, Sabrina thought of Courtney's mother and how she had only heard decent kind things about Mildred Ross, other than the sensational news of when her husband, Raymond Ross, shot up their own home after learning the information that she was having an affair and about to flee town with that person. Then she recalled all the hostile unpleasant things she read about Raymond Ross and instantly sympathized with Mildred Ross and why she may have wanted to flee her home with another man.

From the corner of Sabrina's eyes, she saw Courtney glance toward her and look away as Sabrina's eyes shifted to the assortment of portraits above the sofa and noticed college graduation pictures of Courtney, Trina and Kenny. She thought how Trina and Kenny were decent working-class people. Then she recalled the time that Courtney had displayed the same decent traits in the beginning. Then suddenly she trembled with Raymond Ross and Courtney in the same thought. She hoped Courtney wasn't headed down the same path as her father. Then she reflected back during the time when Courtney dated Rome. She recalled how completely different Courtney behaved during her courtship with Rome. The difference overwhelmed Sabrina and struck her as unbelievable. Nevertheless, it was clear to her that Courtney had changed and seemed unwell as if she wasn't completely in touch with all reality. Sabrina had an uneasy feeling in the pit of her stomach regarding Courtney mental state as she sat there in Courtney's living room.

She felt restlessly in the comfortable maple rocker, as she slightly jerked when she glanced at her watch. It was 12:50. Only five minutes had passed since she arrived at Courtney's house. Sitting there counting the minutes before one o'clock, Sabrina heart skipped a beat when she heard a car engine pull up into the driveway and kill the motor. Courtney was already standing at the window with the long orange curtains pulled aside; looking out. But when she spotted the car, she quickly tore out of the front door and ran outside to greet her visitor.

Sabrina shifted in her seat and grabbed her stomach with both hands. She was on edge with wonder as she waited to find out the identity of the visitor. But after sitting and waiting for a couple minutes, curiosity got the best of her as she sprung from her seat and quickly strolled over to the living room window. She pulled the curtains aside and looked out at a 2009 black Ford Focus. Courtney stood at the front of the car as a tall, slender man stepped out of the car. He faced the house and Sabrina could clearly see it was Courtney's brother, Kenny. He was dressed neat in blue jeans, black gym shoes and a black pullover top. He closed the car door and Courtney stepped over to him and whispered in his ear. But Kenny was suspicious of what she had whispered in his ear as he took his left hand and pushed her away, shaking his head. Then Courtney put both hands on her hips and stood facing him as they became heavy in discussion.

Sabrina kept curiously looking out of the window at them, but she couldn't make out what they were saying. Then she quickly dropped the curtains and stepped away from the window when Courtney and Kenny both headed toward the front door. When they stepped inside, Sabrina had returned to her seat in the rocker, and she wondered, "Why had Kenny come back home to hang around when Courtney was supposedly expecting a date?"

Kenny stepped inside and walked across the floor where Sabrina was seated and smiled at her. "Hi, Sabrina," he said with a surprise look on his face. "I would say I'm surprised to see you here. But Courtney mentioned a few times that the two of you are fairly close friends now." Kenny exchanged looks with Courtney. "Who would have guessed? Although, lately we have to take what Courtney says with a grain of salt."

Sabrina nodded hello to Kenny and didn't confirm or deny friendship with Courtney as she hopped out of the rocking chair and stood there anxious, counting the minutes until she could call Courtney a liar.

"Wonders will never cease if you and Courtney are good friends. So, are you and Courtney good friends now?"

Sabrina looked at Kenny with friendly eyes. "We used to be somewhat friends. But we're not friends now."

Kenny nodded. "Okay, but you have paid her a visit anyway?" Kenny stared and narrowed his eyes at Sabrina.

Then he suspiciously glanced toward his sister. "Something doesn't add up, starting with the lie you whispered in my ear outside." Kenny shook his head, raising both hands.

"What lie?" Courtney asked.

"You know what lie!" He pointed to Sabrina.

"That's Sabrina Taylor and not Samantha Taylor." Kenny stared at Courtney with confusion on his face. "You just told me outside that Samantha was in here?"

Courtney stood there staring at Kenny as if she was lost for words. But he continued to inquire about her being blatantly untruthful.

"So, what's going on with you Courtney? Why did you straight out just lie to me? You said Samantha was inside when you knew she wasn't? You clearly know Sabrina from Samantha, so what gives? Why did you tell me that lie?" Kenny shook his head. "You have gone from bad to worse. There's no doubt you're drinking again! You probably never stopped." He grabbed the back of his neck with both hands and shook his head toward the ceiling, and then narrowed his eyes toward Courtney. "However, lately, drinking or not, your mind is somewhere out in left field," Kenny fussed, irritated that his sister had purposely tricked him to come inside. "Right now, I don't like what I have walked in on. Therefore, I'm leaving. I'll be home later as Mom asked. But right now, I'm out of here!" He threw up both arms.

"Wait a minute, Kenny and listen," Courtney urged.

"Wait a minute and listen to what?" he asked. "Something feels off with you! And whatever is going on in this house right now, I don't want no part of it! I don't know why Sabrina is here, but she doesn't look happy. Besides, she just announced you two are no longer friends." He glanced toward Sabrina who was looking down in her lap. "You are most likely up to something that you have pulled Sabrina in the middle of," Kenny suspiciously grumbled. "It's obvious you're drinking and high as a kite. I can see it in your eyes."

"Kenny, just shut up. If anybody is drinking again, it's you! Dad isn't around but all the booze is gone just the same!" Courtney snapped.

"Who cares, maybe he took it with him," Kenny snapped.

"How crazy does that sound? Dad was on the run from the law for a while, and now he's in prison. You think he took the time to take bottles of vodka with him?"

"It doesn't sound any crazier than him trying to kill Mom, now does it?"

"He wasn't trying to kill her! He aimed at her legs. If he had been trying to kill her – she would be dead!" Courtney snapped.

"He's our father, but I can't believe you're finding excuses for his crime. He never should have pulled a gun on Mom! He damn sure shouldn't have pulled the trigger! What he did was heartless; and the fact that my own father shot my mother rips at me so deep until I guess you wouldn't understand," Kenny firmly stated.

"Kenny, you don't think Dad had a right to be upset with Mom for being unfaithful, fooling around on him?" she angrily shouted.

"Absolutely, he had a right to be upset. Everybody gets upset from one time or another! But being upset didn't give Dad the right to take the law into his own hands."

"Well, I can understand how upset Dad was about being deceived and pushed aside as if he didn't matter!" Courtney agitatedly fussed.

"You really are sick in the head if you think just because Dad was upset, he had a right to behave as he did. You feel his anger and disappointment justifies his cruel, criminal actions toward our mother? There is no excuse good enough for almost taking Mom's and that man's life! How would you feel if Mom hadn't made it?" Kenny firmly asked.

"That's a stupid question since she did make it. Besides, you already know he wasn't trying to kill her. Mom told us herself what he said his intentions were."

"Courtney Ross, what happened to your brain?" Kenny angrily asked. "You're not making any sense. Basically, what you just said, the face that he wasn't trying to kill Mom, makes it okay that he shot Mom as long as he didn't kill her?" Kenny angrily roared.

Courtney threw up both arms. "I don't have time to stand here and fuss with you. But I'll tell you this much! I don't care what Dad did. I'm worried about him and you should be too. He's locked up behind bars and we don't know how he is." Courtney cried.

"I care about Dad just as much as you do! And of course, I hope he's okay! But he brought this on himself. He made a choice to do what he did. I know it's painful to think about, but there's a price to pay for attempted murder and even a bigger price to pay for killing someone," Kenny sadly stated. "Nothing Mom did to Dad warranted him trying to take her life!"

"Whatever, we see things differently. You have no compassion for our father. But I do. I know how it feels to get kicked in the teeth. So, until you walk down that road, you should stop pointing fingers at Dad's actions!"

"I'm not pointing fingers at his actions. I'm just facing them. Something your brain doesn't currently seem to be cable of. Anyway, he missed the bullet of being charged with murder. Since at least, it turned out that he didn't kill an innocent man who was still asleep in his hospital bed. That would have been cold-blooded, murder one!"

"That's right. He didn't kill that man. But what's the difference? They still sent him to the big house!"

"Yes, they did because he shot two people. That's called attempted murder! You didn't expect him to get off scot-free for putting bullet holes in two people, did you? So please cry and feel sorry for Dad as much as you like, but where was his pity for Mom and that man when he pulled his gun and used them for target practice?" Kenny sadly fussed.

"Shut up, Kenny." Courtney covered her ears with both hands. "I don't want to hear it! Dad was driven to do what he did," she shouted. "Take it from someone who knows, a person can be perfectly okay, and someone can drive them to do crazy stuff! It's called temporary insanity."

"Are you talking from experience, because what you are doing right now is crazy stuff? Are you temporary insane?" he seriously asked.

Stared mute for a moment before she spoke. "Maybe we all are insane and none of us really know what sane is," she laughed.

He narrowed his eyes at her. "Speak for yourself." He pointed to his head. "I think all my screws are in place."

"Whatever, just come with me." She grabbed him by the arm.

He jerked his arm away. "What are you doing? Let go of my arm. I'm taking off. I don't want to hang around for any of your craziness. You're acting weird and talking stupidly. Plus, I don't need your attitude!" Kenny snapped. "Besides, I'm still waiting to hear your explanation for the lie about Samantha. Spill or I'm out of here right now!" Kenny held out both arms.

"Okay, I'll tell you why," Courtney said in a low voice and waved her right hand. "When you drove up I told you Samantha was inside, so you would come inside and stay," Courtney confessed.

"Why did you want me to stay? I'll be back later for the get together Mom mentioned at breakfast."

"What's the big deal? You're back now."

"Yes, but I have other plans. I only came back because I thought I left my wallet in my room. But it just so happened, I noticed it on the passenger side floor just as I killed the engine. By then you had sailed out to the car with your lie! So, tell me what's up with you, and why did you so desperately want me to come inside and stay?"

"I have my reasons and knew you would if I mentioned Samantha."

"I'm sure you have your reasons and I just asked you what they are," Kenny said firmly. "You are jumpy and acting odd and I want to know what's up with you," he said, looking her in the eyes as he held up one finger. "Please think before you speak, and make sure not to give me some lame story that your jumpy odd behavior is connected to our family life!" He held up both hands. "No more trumped-up excuses that your bizarre behavior is because of what Dad did to Mom and what she did to him."

"Kenny, calm down already," she snapped. "Don't get so bent out of shape. I wasn't going to blame it on any of that. I'm just a little on edge." Courtney strolled over to look out of the window.

"On edge about what?" he asked.

Courtney was almost trembling. "I'm on edge because since you're here as well, I'll have to put you both in my closet."

"What the hell are you talking about; putting us both in your closet? You won't be putting me in your closet because I'm getting the hell out of here. You must be stone out of your mind to say something like that. Sabrina needs to get out of here if she knows what's good for her!" he strongly suggested. "I'm sure she doesn't know how you are when you're smashed out of your mind with booze!"

"I'm not wasted, you jerk! I just need to hide you both. Britain just turned off the street and pulling into the driveway," she fanatically announced, walking quickly away from the window to the center of the room to stand near Kenny and Sabrina.

"Did you say Britain Franklin?" Kenny curiously asked, looking at Courtney. "What the heck is Britain Franklin doing here?" Kenny exchanged looks with Sabrina. "Is he here for you?"

Sabrina grabbed her face with both hands and shook her head in astonishment. "No, Kenny, he's not here for me. Because I'm sure Britain didn't just pull into your driveway out there." She pointed toward the front door. "I'm sorry to say this, but your sister is just doing what she does so well and that's lie!" Sabrina angrily relayed.

Standing there anxiously looking from Kenny to Sabrina, Courtney kept her voice low. "It's Britain alright, but if you don't calm down and just keep quiet, you're going to blow it!" she said with a smile dancing at the corner of her mouth as she pointed toward the short stairs. "Now, will you two please cooperate and head upstairs to my room. He's going to knock on the door at any second now. So please run upstairs and hide in my room so he won't know you're here?"

Kenny held up both arms, shaking his head. "Why shouldn't he know we're here? I live here, remember?" Kenny argued.

"You used to live here, but he knows you moved out."

"This is still my home. I'm here more than my own place. What different does it make? Besides, why are we having this silly conversation? If he's outside, then he's outside. He's dating Sabrina, is he not? I thought maybe she was the reason he had dropped by. Nevertheless, I don't know what you're up to, Courtney. But I have no intentions of getting in your closet and neither will Sabrina. Britain will just have to see us both. I don't know why you feel he shouldn't see us here." Kenny raised both hands. "You just need your head examined and I'm sure it's all that Vodka. You smell like you took a bath in it! It's pouring from your pores. Look at you. You can hardly keep your balance. You are falling down drunk. Why didn't I notice that before? I'm leaving," Kenny snapped as he headed toward the front door.

Courtney nerves tightened as she stared at Sabrina. "Here's your chance to catch Britain in the act! I'm warning you to stop Kenny from leaving here. Make him cooperate and head upstairs to my room closet with you. If you don't, you won't catch Britain."

Kenny stopped in his tracks after Courtney warned Sabrina. He was curious and suspicious of what Courtney was trying to rope Sabrina into. He stood at the door holding the doorknob as Courtney continued pressuring Sabrina into stopping him from leaving.

"Listen to me Miss Sabrina Taylor, I'm sure you're frowning on the idea. But you need to suck it up and do it anyway! Otherwise, you can kiss this eye-opener goodbye! It's not going to work if Britain sees you two here!" Courtney firmly urged her.

Sabrina stared at Courtney with her mouth open as if she was frozen and couldn't concentrate or think.

Courtney was anxious and peeved with them both as she slightly raised her voice. "Earth to Miss Sabrina Taylor! You need to get a grip and make up your mind fast if you want to get the goods on Mr. Franklin or not! If you do, you need to stop my brother from walking out of that door!" She pointed toward the door. "And the two of you need to head upstairs to my room and hide in my closet and be quiet until Britain leaves."

Sabrina swallowed hard and looked at Kenny with solemn eyes. She was reluctant to do as Courtney had suggested. But she wanted to see it through to get to the bottom of what Courtney was up to. Therefore, she knew she had to somehow persuade Kenny to go along with his sister's craziness. She stepped across the room where he stood near the door and tapped him on the shoulder. But he was preoccupied staring at Courtney with disbelief in his eyes of her behavior.

She tapped him on the shoulder again and he looked down at her and shook his head. "You're not going to ask me to stay and put up with this craziness, are you?"

Sabrina nodded. "Yes, Kenny I'm asking you to stay. Although, I know what Courtney is asking us to do makes no sense and it's actually downright disgusting. I'm trying to follow through on a hunch to catch Courtney in the biggest fib of all time," she explained nearly out of breath from all the tension. "Therefore, could you please do as she has asked and accompany me upstairs to her room?" Sabrina politely asked. "This shouldn't take long. Plus, you were right when you said she had pulled me in the middle of something. That's why I'm here. This is not a social call. Nevertheless, I can't believe I'm here in the middle of this foolishness and I can't believe I'm asking you to go along with it. But please do. In the end, Courtney will be the liar. I'm absolutely positive of that. So, if you don't mind seeing this crazy thing through. Let's go upstairs to her room and hide in her closet until Britain leaves," Sabrina kindly urged him.

Kenny nodded and scratched his head in confusion as he stared at Sabrina. "Okay, if that's what you think we should do to bring a head to this madness. But I'm really lost now," Kenny calmly said, looking toward Courtney. "The fact that Sabrina is in on this, whatever this is, has me baffled." He held up both arms. "I wish someone would fill me in."

"Kenny, it's a long story and I promise to fill you in later. But I don't have time to fill you in right now," Courtney anxiously fussed. "So, can you please run upstairs with Sabrina and hide in my closet before Britain knocks on the door. He's heading up the walkway now. He's going to knock on the door at any minute," Courtney urged strongly as she took both hands and literally shoved Sabrina and Kenny toward the stairs. "Please hurry to my room quickly. He's coming up the steps now," she demanded.

Courtney kept her eyes upstairs and when she heard her bedroom door open and shut, her quick breathing calmed. But when Britain didn't knock on the door, she looked out of the window and noticed that he was back at his car standing with the door open while talking on his cell phone. She figured he got a business call and went back to his car to take it. Seeing him talking on his phone, gave her time to run upstairs to her room where she found Kenny and Sabrina just standing about. Courtney looked irritated at them both.

"What are you two doing? I said hide in the closet," Courtney insisted as she pulled open the closet door and waved them into the small quarters.

Sabrina swallowed hard at her unbelievable actions. Nevertheless, she stepped right into the closet without hesitation. Kenny was not a willing candidate since he had no idea what Courtney was up to. Therefore, he shook his head, determined not to hide in his sister's closet. But when Britain rang the doorbell and knocked on the front door, Courtney took both hands and shoveled Kenny into her bedroom closet with Sabrina and quickly shut the closet door, flipping the lock.

Kenny was suspicious and felt Courtney was acting stranger than usual. He had heard that Courtney and Sabrina were supposedly new friends. But Sabrina had just told him that their friendship was over. He wondered what was going on with Sabrina and Courtney regarding Britain. Plus, he could tell from the animosity in Sabrina's voice toward Courtney that their new friendship was definitely over or seriously on the rocks. He had moved away from home into his own apartment but hadn't had the opportunity to enjoy his new place since he was staying at the main house more than he was staying at his apartment. But yet, he wasn't aware how emotionally unstable and how much of a mental wreck Courtney really was. He could detect that something was more disturbed and odder about her behavior. He had always chalked it up to too much alcohol in her system, but now he noticed that her behavior seemed more sinister, creepy and eerie than drunken.

Kenny tumbled inside the dark closet, almost falling as he grabbed a hold of hanging clothes. When he caught his balance, he looked to the right and Sabrina's dark shadow stood in the corner of the closet shaking her head, holding her face with both hands.

"Courtney, what's the hell into you, shoveling me into your closet! The way you are behaving, I'm sure you are drinking straight Vodka again. That's the only explanation that I can think of that would make you come up with some absurd idea to stick us in your closet! You're going to kill yourself if you keep hitting that damn bottle!" Kenny sharply fussed.

"Quiet please! No talking until Britain leaves," she whispered. "I'm bringing him upstairs to my room. So, no matter what, do not make a sound while he's in here. But Kenny, I'm not letting your Vodka remark slide. Besides, who are you to talk? You're the poster boy for Vodka drinkers on this street! You drink Vodka like a fish drinks water!"

"Not anymore since Samantha made me see it was destroying my life."

"You're telling me, you have given it completely up?" Courtney suspiciously asked.

"No, I haven't given it completely up. But I'm drinking less, and you can find me sober more than wasted. Like today for instance, I haven't had a drop," he proudly shared.

"Well, today is still young," Courtney grumbled.

"I have cut down and it's all because of the generous effort Samantha put in trying to help me."

"You may think I'm loony, but I know this much. Cutting down for an alcoholic doesn't count. You have to give it completely up for it to count," Courtney snapped.

"Well, thank you for that negative comment. But, at least I'm heading in that direction whether you give me credit or not."

"Whatever, I'm sure I don't care. I just want you to shut your mouth and be quiet until Britain leaves!" Courtney sharply stated in a low voice. "I'm headed downstairs to answer the door and let him in now."

Standing in the dark closet, Sabrina thought she would throw up from disgust with herself. She wondered how she had allowed herself to be a pawn in Courtney's game. But she listened closely as the front door squeaked open and closed. Then what she thought wouldn't occur, occurred when she heard Britain's voice.

"So, what's up, Courtney?" He asked. "I guess you'll tell me the details of the party and what kind of help you need from me," he inquired.

"This way, Britain," she laughed loudly as if she forced the laugh. "I have something I would like to show you. This way please, right up these stairs," she said as she led Britain upstairs toward the open bedroom door.

Sabrina nerves tightened as she heard Britain and Courtney's footsteps on the hardwood floor as they stepped into Courtney's bedroom. Sabrina grabbed her mouth to keep from screaming. She thought her heart was going to burst with disillusionment.

Courtney continued to laugh in a forced manner. "Britain, this isn't a good time for me. Let's make it another time if that's okay with you."

He glanced at his watch and narrowed his eyes at her. "Are you kidding around or something, Courtney? You seem a bit anxious. Besides, I actually cancelled plans to meet you at this time," he seriously informed her. "So, if possible, since I'm here I would prefer to have the discussion and mark it off my list," Britain seriously suggested.

Courtney realized that if she didn't get Britain out of her room quick enough, Sabrina would figure out he wasn't there to romance her. She realized with Sabrina in the closet, she needed to make it appear that Britain had dropped over to see her in a romantic way. Therefore, she quickly snapped.

"Britain, I'm sorry but you'll have to leave. Right now, is not good," Courtney said.

Britain held up both hands. "Okay, I get it. It's not a good time. So, I guess I'll just see myself back out," he said looking suspiciously at Courtney. She was pacing the floor and that made him skeptical of her behavior, but he decided not to question her. He could see she was acting peculiar and figured it would be best for him to just leave her house.

She stopped pacing and looked at him. "I apologize if I took you from an appointment. But I hope you understand how this isn't a good time," she said rather loudly.

Britain nodded. "Yes, I understand. If it's not a good time, it's not a good time. I'll take off and we can talk later." He held up one hand. "However, Courtney, I will say this. It would have been considerate to have given me a call and saved me a trip here," Britain said, headed toward the bedroom door.

Courtney stood there staring at Britain and admiring his Bloomingdale's attire. She still loved him deeply and couldn't think clearly in his presence. As he headed toward the bedroom door to leave, for a while she was so lost in his stunning appearance and the whole essence of him and how much she wanted to be near him, it slipped her mind that she wanted him to see Sabrina and Kenny tucked away in her bedroom closet. But just as he twisted the doorknob and squeaked opened the door to head out of the room, she blinked out of the daze and rushed toward the door, heavily pushing her hand against it, shutting it closed. She threw her back against the door and smiled at him.

By now, Britain was more than just a little suspicious of her odd behavior and at this time, due to their close proximity he caught the scent of Vodka pouring from her pores. Now he was uneasy about being in her house and in her bedroom in her obvious intoxicated state. She was standing against the door smiling and his imagination was running wild reflecting on her past misconduct. But he kept calm.

"Courtney, what are you doing? No scratch that, don't tell me what you're doing." He glanced at his watch again. "I need to leave, now," he looked in her eyes and firmly said. "You said this wasn't a good time to discuss what I came here to discuss. So, could you please step aside so I can be on my way?"

"I thought you wanted to know what I'm doing?" she asked.

He shook his head. "I said scratch that. Since I seriously do not have the time to hang around and find out about what you're up to. Listen, Courtney," he said kindly but losing his patience. "I don't mean to be rude but it's obvious you have been drinking and my instincts are screaming to me right now."

"What are your instincts screaming about?" she blinked to stay alert.

"They are telling me, I need to leave your room now."

"In that case, just don't listen to your instincts. Because you can't leave now," she said, smiling as if she became more alert.

He stared at her as he stood there with an uneasy feeling in the pit of his stomach. "Okay, Courtney, you seem to be playing some kind of game. So, I guess I'll play along and ask you why I can't leave?"

"You can't leave because I told you I had something to show you."

"You told me that?" he asked, not recalling what she said that to him.

"Yes, I told you when we first headed to my room," she laughed loudly.

"Okay, Courtney, what do you want to show me?" he asked with his arms folded. "Is it very important or can it wait? I really need to be somewhere else as we speak," he stated.

Courtney drew an attitude as she stepped away from the door and walked toward her closet. "I'll say it's very important," she said in a low solemn voice as if a switch clicked inside of her and her eyes turned stone cold as she laughed. "But it's nothing to smile about that's for sure! Your bride to be as well as my brother is hiding from you in my closet!" She laughed out and then unlocked the closet door and pulled it open.

Sabrina stared at Britain, stunned and speechless. He looked at her with surprise in his eyes and before he could say a word, she ripped out of the closet and ran out of the small crowded bedroom, racing down stairs and out of Courtney's front door. She was crushed and felt no explanations were needed. The simple fact that he was at Courtney's house at the time Courtney said he would be spoke volumes as far as she was concerned.

She ran around to the back driveway, snatched open her car door and flopped inside drained with despair. She had been so stressed when she arrived at Courtney's house until she didn't even remember to lock the doors of her highly expensive car. She couldn't focus for a moment as she sat there staring through the windshield. She felt like she was having an outer body experience. She knew she wasn't dreaming but it all seemed like an awful nightmare that she was living wide awake.

What had just happened inside of Courtney's house didn't seem real to her. Britain had just showed up at Courtney's house and in real time, Sabrina was convinced Britain wouldn't have visited Courtney. Sitting there glancing through the windshield looking at the surrounding, she took a deep breath and laid her head back on the headrest for a moment. She was confused and deeply disappointed in Britain. But she was absolutely sure she wasn't having a horrible nightmare. She realized she was actually sitting in her car after running out of Courtney's house after witnessing Britain showing up there. Then suddenly reality had hit her in the face at full force. Then it dawned on her she needed to get away from Britain and Courtney. She searched through her purse for her car keys and when she located the keys at the bottom of her purse, her right hand trembled as she turned the key in the ignition. She started the engine and quickly backed out of Courtney's driveway and headed for home. She was crying so hard until she could hardly see the road.

"How could anything out of Courtney's mouth be the truth? What I just witness can't be true. But he was there. Why was he there?" Sabrina cried as she headed home.

Chapter Twenty-One

It was 1:05 uptown, Julian and Mildred were together sitting in Olive Garden restaurant enjoying a bowl of Minestrone soup and bread sticks. Mildred had decided she would explain to Julian why Raymond had such a jealous nature and was never trusting of her during their marriage. She picked up a bread stick and broke it in half, and then dipped it into the small clear bowl of marinara sauce.

"Julian, you have asked me a few times about why Raymond had no trust in me. I didn't feel comfortable discussing it before. But now I feel I can, and I'd like to answer you." Mildred took a small bite from the bread stick.

Julian smiled and shook his head. "It's no big deal and I hope you don't feel pressured to share your past. I don't really need to know all about your past history unless it's something you would like to share. I was basically asking for conversation in trying to get to know you better."

"I thought about it and I really don't mind sharing it now," Mildred said.

"Okay, but I hope you don't feel like it's something you need to share. Mildred, you don't have to tell me anything. But on the evening, I asked you about Raymond, I admit I was quite curious." He lifted his glass of ice water and took a sip. "I was just wondering if he had always been that way and if so, why did you marry the guy?"

"It's a long story. But I sort of pushed Raymond away in the beginning. It was because of my love for another boy, Raymond lost trust in me. You see, years ago when Raymond and I were dating, he knew I really liked Antonio Armani." She lifted her glass of Coke and took a sip. "If you have time, I'll tell you all about Raymond, Antonio and me. It was the best and worst time of my life during our triangle years ago when we were teenagers during our senior year in high school."

Julian smiled as he lifted his glass of Coke and took a sip. "Sure, if you want to share it with me. I'm happy to hear about your life. I want to know as much as possible about you Mildred. You are an extraordinarily beautiful fascinating woman that I'm dying to know more and more about. I feel privileged to have you in my life," Julian seriously stated.

"Okay, it started out like this. Raymond and I were walking down the street from school one Friday afternoon when he picked a fight with me. It was late April, but the weather was cool enough for a light jacket. Raymond and I were holding hands, heading home from school. Raymond seemed anxious and he wasn't saying anything. It dawned on me that he hadn't spoken from the moment school let out. I sensed a cold shoulder, but I didn't say anything since I wasn't sure what his beef was about. But as we continued to walk down the sidewalk a couple blocks from the school grounds, he stopped and released my hand in a jerking like manner. He stood there and stared at me with angry eyes."

Just then Julian phone rang in the middle of Mildred starting to tell him a little about her life with Raymond and Antonio. It was a business call that Julian had to take.

"Excuse me, Mildred. I really need to take this call." Julian got up from the table and stepped outside of the restaurant.

He wasn't on the call long before he stepped back into the restaurant and shook his head. "I'm sorry, but this is a possible million-dollar customer that I need to get to and drop off some documents," he said as he stood at his chair without being seated. Then he reached into his back pocket and pulled out his wallet and gave Mildred a hundred-dollar bill. "Here, take this and continue to enjoy your lunch. I'll probably be wrapped up for maybe an hour or less and then I'll drop by your house if you like. I can't apologize enough for leaving you like this."

Mildred gave him the money back. "No, just pay for what we just ate. I won't stay." Then she looked across the restaurant to her left at the cozy lounge section. She smiled. "On second thought. Maybe I will stay and wait for you to return and when you return we can start over with a meal or drinks at that time." She pointed toward the lounge section. "I'll wait over there and relax in the lounge section until you return," she suggested.

Julian stared at Mildred and didn't answer her right away as he gave thought to what she was suggesting. He wasn't keen on leaving her sitting in the lounge section alone, but it was a nice place and others were relaxing in the lounge section, reading and enjoying drinks. He looked at her and nodded. "Okay, if that's what you want to do." He glanced at his Movado watch and smiled. "It's 1:10 now. I should see you back here in about twenty minutes or so," he said as they stepped to the counter and he paid the check.

He walked her over to the lounge area and watched as she made herself comfortable on one of the lounge sofas. He didn't take a seat as he waited for the waiter to deliver Mildred a glass of wine. The waiter placed the glass on the coffee table in front of Mildred and asked. "Are you running a tab?"

Julian answered. "Yes, place it on a tab and give this lady whatever she wants. I have to leave for a while, but I'll return to take care of the check."

"Yes, sir," the waiter said and then turned and walked away.

Julian leaned down and kissed Mildred on side of face and then left the restaurant. And while relaxing on the comfortable lounge chair, Mildred laid her head to the side focusing on the green flowery pattern of the lounge sofa as her mind went back in thought about what she was about to tell Julian about her teenage years with Raymond and Antonio. Then suddenly she was sitting there daydreaming about the past: "Mildred, I heard something today at school and it's bothering me!" Raymond said.

"What are you trying to say? Is it something I should care about?"

"I guess you should care about it, since it was most definitely about you. And for the record, it really ticked me off! Plus, I'm still pissed!"

"Raymond, you know you can't believe everything you hear. Especially at this school. So, what in the world did you hear that got you in such a knot?"

"If you must know, Mildred. I keep hearing unfavorable things about you. It's mostly the same stuff I have heard before about you!" He said.

"Okay, can you tell me what?"

"Rumors about you and Antonio Armani!"

"What kind of rumors about me and Antonio?" Mildred edgily asked.

"Just what I said, Mildred. Rumors about you two!"

"Well, you need to make yourself clear, because right now I haven't a clue to what you are trying to point out," Mildred forced her words out calmly.

"Mildred, I'm not going to beat around the bush. I'm quite pissed with you since I'm positive you know what I'm referring to!" He angrily snapped.

"Raymond, I'm not a mindreader. Just tell me what you heard!"

"Okay, I will," he loudly replied. "I overheard one of your classmates gossiping about you and Antonio Armani."

"Okay, what were they saying and who were saying it?" Mildred asked.

"I shouldn't say I overheard it. They were speaking loudly and anyone passing by their lunch table could hear what was being said about you two!"

"Are you going to tell me what was said and who said it?" Mildred asked, instantly upset that she had been talked about. She became more tensed. She swallowed hard feeling guilty, hoping he couldn't read her mind. She actually had a huge crush on Antonio Armani. So, she lowered her eyes toward the sidewalk to the guilt in them. But hearing she had been talked about didn't surprise her. Gossip was constant at the high school. Most students were friendly face to face, but many talked about others behind their backs.

"I'm sure you didn't hear anyone chatting and spreading rumors, except that stuck-up society snob Catherine Franklin," Mildred snapped, feeling his eyes glued on her like he was trying to see inside of her head. "Catherine wants Antonio herself, you know? But I don't see him going out of his way to chase her." Mildred rolled her eyes, now looking straight ahead and not at him, feeling a pinch of jealousy about Catherine Franklin, who was best friends with the very popular, homecoming queen two years straight, Veronica Parker. Veronica was slender at 5'4, one hundred and eight pounds. She could usually bat her big brown eyes that complimented her tan honey complexion and get any boy at school at the drop of a hat.

Defensive Mildred asked. "What did Catherine say about me anyway?"

Raymond spoke in a loud, sulky tone as his words rolled out sharp as nails. "What do you think she said, Mildred? She was telling her best friend, Veronica, how you're making a fool of yourself for Antonio Armani!"

"How would she know that?"

"She knows because Antonio is into her and not you!"

"Catherine would say that," Mildred sadly mumbled.

"Well, that's not all Catherine Franklin had to say about you."

"I'm sure it's not all! They both hate me! Her friend, Veronica, hates me as much as she does. I think I told you that!"

"I know no such thing! But I know what I heard!"

"Believe what you want, Raymond! You always do! Once you get your mind set on something, there's no changing it."

"I don't know what to believe. But I think I have a right to be upset with you! And you can bet I'm ticked as hell about what I heard. Especially the part about you throwing yourself at Antonio Armani." He shook his head. "You are driving me to drink."

"I'm not driving you to drink, Raymond. You may only be nineteen. But you're already a big drinker. I know you sneak liquor in your water bottle."

"So, what if I do? I'm not the only one doing it," Raymond roared.

"Maybe you're not the only one doing it," Mildred softly uttered. "But Raymond, it still doesn't make it right. That stuff isn't healthy, and you could get hooked on booze. That's how people become alcoholics. Don't you listen to

190

any of the stuff they try to instill in us in class about alcohol, drugs and cigarettes? They are all bad for us."

"I have heard everything the teachers have to say, but I still like my Vodka. I need it to get through the hell I have to go through," he snapped.

"What are you talking about now? What hell are you going through?"

"Don't worry about that. Just worry about the issue at hand with me hearing all this shit about you," he roared.

"Whatever, but if you keep sneaking alcohol into class, you'll get caught and kicked out of school. You're not worried about that?" Mildred asked.

"No, I'm not. Besides, if I can drink and not get caught by my folks, I'm not worried about damn spaced out teachers."

"Okay, Raymond. But back to what we're discussing. I'm sorry you had to hear all that gossip about me and Antonio. But you realize, that's all it is!"

"Mildred are you sure about that?" he asked.

"Yes, I'm sure; and I'm sure I don't want to hear what Catherine Franklin had to say about me! Anything she says about me is bias."

"Mildred, I'll just tell you what she said. It doesn't make it true. But I would just like for you to know what was said so you can give me your side," he said calmly. "Besides, you need to hear how she bad mouthed you, almost shouting that you're crazy for the guy!" He kept shaking his head. "But at the same time, she made it quite clear that Antonio doesn't have feelings for you! That you are doing all you can to get his attention, Mildred," Raymond told her, disappointedly as they both continued walking down the sidewalk.

"Whatever? I'm sure I don't care what they were saying."

"You should care. They were making fun of you. I guess you know?"

Suddenly it dawned on Mildred how upset she was about the conversation about her. But she didn't say anything as she walked, holding her textbooks tightly against her chest. But after a few minutes had passed and Raymond was still silent, Mildred hoped he was going to drop the subject that had gotten them both upset. But when she glanced at him, his sad eyes were sparkling with anger and filled with resentment.

Seconds later, he stopped in his tracks again, grabbed her arm, stopping her in a sudden jerk motion. He looked down at her with heavy watery eyes that seemed ready to pour. Yet the water stayed in the corner of his eyes.

"Mildred, I want you to tell me right here and now what's going on with you and that boy. Maybe it's not what I think it is. But I know it's something; and I would like to know what that something is!" he demanded.

"Raymond, it's nothing and I wish you would drop this conversation."

"Don't tell me it's nothing, Mildred!" We both know something is up!"

"It's nothing, I'm telling you. You're just upset and thinking something is up because of those rumors you heard today," Mildred softly said.

"Is that so?" He mumbled.

"Yes, Raymond. I think that's why you think something is up?"

"Well, maybe I asked the wrong question. Let me put it this way." He glanced down toward the sidewalk and then looked at her. "How do you feel about him?" He asked, motionless on the sidewalk staring her in the face, not making a single frown from the bright sun beaming down against his face.

Mildred stood there looking him straight in the face, frowning from the sun in her eyes as tears rolled down her face. One of his textbooks fell and he bent over and picked it up and she started shaking, wondering how she could answer his question. Looking down toward the sidewalk, she quickly said. "How do I feel about him?"

"Yes? Do you have feelings for him or what? How do you feel, Mildred? Just tell me the truth!

"I feel about him the way I feel about any student," Mildred mumbled.

"That's bull and we both know it!" He shouted. "I want the truth, okay? How do you feel about Antonio Armani?"

"I think he's alright! A nice guy! How do you think I feel?"

"Do you really want me to answer that?"

"Raymond, what are you trying to imply? I just think Antonio is a nice guy. And I think he's a lot friendlier than many students. Take Jack Coleman for instance. Everybody knows he's on the stuck-up side."

Calling Jack Coleman stuck-up didn't seem to help Raymond's mood. He gave Mildred a cold stare. But she continued before he could say anything.

"I meant to say that Jack isn't all the way stuck-up, but sort of." She threw him a quick glance. He still had fire in his eyes, staring her down.

"Raymond, why are you looking at me like that? You, yourself know how stuck up Jack Coleman can be. Well, don't you? He's in your class, isn't he?"

"So, what if Jack Coleman is stuck up? What does that have to do with Antonio who is worse than stuck up? That guy is a user!"

"That's pretty bold of you to call Antonio a user!" Mildred said offended.

"Everyone at school knows it and would say I'm not lying."

"You may call him a user, for whatever reason you want to think that about him. But like I was saying, I think he's nice and friendly."

"That's what he wants you to think."

"It's not what he wants me to think. That's how he is."

Raymond looked up at the sunny sky for a moment as the sun beamed on his face. He inhaled sharply as he planted his eyes back on Mildred and didn't seem uncomfortable from the bright sun in his face. He looked neat in his new burgundy suit. It was the only new outfit he had ever worn to school.

"Grow up, Mildred. That's not what you call friendly, it's called a user."

It was like Mildred didn't even hear Raymond as she kept talking of Antonio. "Come to think of it, he is kind of quiet when he wants to be," Mildred said, getting a personal kick out of talking about Antonio Armani. "Often he'll sit right next to me in class, and never say a word to me or anybody else." She held up one finger. "Don't get me wrong, that's just sometime. Most of the time, he's talkative and quite friendly." She glanced at Raymond and noticed even more irritation in his eyes.

"You think I give a hoot about hearing what you think of Antonio Armani's moods in the classroom? To chat with you or not to chat with you?"

"Well, no. I'm just letting you know that sometimes he can be quiet."

"And I just told you I don't give a damn about that. Plus, have you ever stopped to think, Mildred, that maybe he just doesn't have anything to say to you?" He fussed. "Does it bother you that much that he doesn't always chat with you?" He glanced at his watch, then looked at her. "It sounds like you're dying for his attention," he snapped. "Like he is some God or the answer to all your prayers." He looked down at the ground and rubbed his hand down his face, then looked at her. "So, are you hoping he'll talk with you all the time?"

"Raymond don't put words in my mouth. I did not say that," Mildred answered. "Plus, I thought you didn't want to hear about it."

"Mildred, just answer the question. I just want to know if you're hoping Antonio will start talking to you more." He inquired.

Mildred was silent and didn't comment.

Then he touched her arm. "Answer me, Mildred. Are you hoping Antonio will start talking to you more? Well, are you?"

"Okay, since you keep pressuring me, Raymond. Yes!" Mildred admitted. "Maybe he would make for good conversations! It wouldn't be the worst thing in the world if he and I held a conversation with each other. Just as I said before, I think Antonio is a nice guy."

"By whose standards?" Raymond asked.

"By my standards, who else? He's friendly and funny, and above all else, he seems to be completely in charge of his life." Mildred placed her books under her arms and pulled a Kleenex tissue out of her purse.

"What life is that? Chasing skirts?"

"No, I honestly think he has it together."

"Oh, he does? Does he?" Raymond yelled. "If using girls like they're pieces of furniture means he has it together, then I guess he does!"

"Raymond why are you so against Antonio?" Mildred curiously asked. "You hang with guys just like Antonio. So, if you can be that tight with guys just like Antonio. What in the world do you have against Antonio?"

Raymond stared into space like someone had just stabbed him in the chest. "I know his type all too well. He's like a damn thirsty sponge. He soaks up all he can get out of a girl, but once he gets it, he throws it away."

"What are you talking about? You don't even know Antonio that well."

"I know his type well enough to know what he's up to."

"That's a lame justification of a putdown to say you know his type!"

"It's not a justification! It's the way I see it!" Raymond nodded with a look of deep frustration and sadness in his eyes as if mentioning Antonio brought him discomfort.

"You know, Raymond, we need to change the subject."

"No, Mildred. We won't be changing the subject," he said sharply. "Since we're in the middle of you beating around the bush!"

"What is that supposed to mean?"

"You know what it means. You're beating around the bush about how you feel about Antonio Armani. I don't buy what you're saying. Telling me he's a nice guy. If the truth be told you're his biggest fan," Raymond said boiling.

"I don't know what else you want me to say or tell you regarding Antonio Armani. I think I have opened up quite a bit. Besides, why should I be so quick to open up with you about anything, Raymond? Do you open up with me about anything? Why can't you tell me a little more about your folks and why you felt you needed to run away from home? I think that's a big deal that you ran away from home and now sleeping on a relative's couch!"

He stared into space and didn't answer.

"Raymond, you make me think bizarre thoughts about your folks!"

"No odder than what I think of yours!" He snapped right back.

"Are you sure about that? Do you ever think my folks beat me? Those are the thoughts I have of your folks!" Mildred stared straight in his eyes.

"Beat me, you're not even close?" He blurted staring back at Mildred.

"No even close? What is that supposed to mean? Why did you leave home? I know you mentioned once how your father has a drinking problem and you told me he's a mean person. It would reason that he could beat you."

Raymond didn't comment as he stared with irritated eyes into space.

Mildred held up both hands, holding her text books under her arm. "So, I guess what I just said doesn't warrant a comment?" She kept her eyes on his.

"Get real, Mildred! Do you really expect a comment? What kind of comment do you expect from an off the wall remark like that?"

"It wasn't off the wall to think a drunk, mean person could beat you! But if I offended you, I'm sorry. It just came out," she apologized.

"You're sorry? It just came out!" He shouted. "But you were thinking it!"

"I know I was thinking it. But I said I'm sorry," she thought for a second and then blurted out. "If it's not true, why are you so upset that I said it?"

"Mildred! Stop it! Just cut it out, okay?" He seemed anxious.

"Okay, I'm sorry again. "But I'm just trying to figure you out. You never want to talk about your folks."

"Stop trying to figure me out. I told you I'm at odds with my folks."

"At odds?"

"Yes! I'm at odds! Distant! Whatever you want to call it. So, please! If you don't mind, I would rather not talk about them." He threw up both arms.

"You never want to talk about them. That's what I'm getting at."

"Mildred is it so hard to understand that I'm not interested in discussing my folks with you?" He asked. "Please stop trying to pry information out of me, okay?" He said sharply. "You need to stop being so nosey."

"It's not about being nosey. It's about trying to get to know you better."

"I think you know me well enough," Raymond snapped. "Besides, you do this every time we're discussing you. The conversation gets turned around to end up about me. So, do you mind if we get back to the matter at hand?"

"Sure! Go on! What do you want from me, Raymond?"

"I want the truth of course, and an answer to what I asked you."

"Okay, whatever?" Mildred waved her hand exhaustedly.

"Whatever?"

"Yes! Whatever? I'm so frustrated with you Raymond."

"That makes both of us! I'm peeved with all your talk about Antonio."

"I'm frustrated with you because I can't understand why you have to be so private about your folks! It always ends up like this. I ask you about your folks. You get on the offensive. You get upset. You don't want to talk about them. I end up not knowing anymore about them than I did at first."

"Mildred Latham, back to the point, please!"

"Okay, to answer your question. I only said, I think Antonio Armani is a nice guy. What's the problem with me saying that about the boy?"

"What's the problem with that?" He repeated, gently grabbed her arm. "The problem with this mess is I don't know what you are getting at, Mildred!"

"You don't know what I'm getting at?"

"That's right. I don't know what you are getting at." Sheer disappointment poured from his eyes. "Therefore, could you please enlighten me? Just tell me what you're trying to tell me, Mildred?" He angrily. His eyes were still watery with a deep frown stretched across his forehead.

"I'm not trying to tell you anything!"

"That's the problem. I need you to be up front with me about this dude."

"I'm being up front with you."

"No, I don't feel you're being on the level. I get the sense that you're holding something back," he firmly stated. "So, do me a favor right now and let's stop beating around the bush. I wasn't born yesterday, Mildred. It's obvious you want Antonio Armani in your face chatting. You all but said so."

"Don't go putting words in my mouth."

"I'm not putting words in your mouth. You just said, you think he's a nice guy! So, what it boils down to is what you're up to!"

"Since you're trying to read my mind. What do you think I'm up to?"

"You want Antonio Armani to ask you out?" He stared at her

Mildred looked deep into Raymond's eyes. But she couldn't answer him.

"Can you please just answer me, Mildred? I want to know once and for all. Do you want Antonio Armani to ask you out? Do you want to ride in his old yellow Chevy and invite him over to visit you? Well, do you?" He asked angrily with deep sadness in his eyes.

They stood and looked at each other awhile, and then Mildred glanced down toward the sidewalk to hide her obvious answer. She couldn't say a word. She knew he was right.

"I guess you're looking toward the sidewalk to keep from answering my question," he said angrily. "But, you know what, Mildred? After hearing the way you've praised that playboy, I have my answer loud and clear! So, I don't give a damn! I'm done with this bologna you're trying to feed me!"

"Who asked you to give a damn?" Mildred snapped.

"Not you, right? You know exactly what you're walking into! I heard how he uses girls," Raymond fussed. "You probably have too. The truth is, the way you're headed, you'll soon be one of his throw-a-ways! But go on! See if I care!" Raymond threw up both arms as he broke away and started walking quickly, leaving her behind as he hurried down the sidewalk.

Mildred walked as fast as she could, not wanting the other students to see that Raymond had left her walking alone. But she wasn't successful. Other students noticed their fuss and how Raymond left her alone on the sidewalk.

Chapter Twenty-Two

Mildred was brought back to the present, reluctantly letting go of her daydream when a waiter walked over to where she was seated and removed a couple glasses from the coffee table in front of her. He noticed that her wine glass was half full. "Would you like another glass of wine?" he asked.

"No, thanks. I'm fine," she said and watched as the waiter walked away. She leaned forward and lifted her wine glass from the coffee table. She took a long sip, holding the glass to her mouth as she sat there and focused back on her daydream about the past:

The morning after Mildred and Raymond quarreled, Mildred felt drained after a restless night of lying wide-awake most of the evening daydreaming about Antonio Armani. Her feelings surprised her from the moment she got out of bed and started to dress for school. She wasn't focused on making up with Raymond. She was completely focused on trying to figure something out that would make Antonio Armani notice her. She decided that her blue high heels hopefully would get his attention. So as soon as she got to school, Mildred hurried down the hallway with her textbooks in one arm and a small overnight case in the other. She rushed in the girl's restroom and quickly changed out of her regular shoes into the high heels. The stylish shoes matched the blue knit dress she had on. Dressed in the knit dress and nice shoes made Mildred feel more assured that she would get Antonio's attention. Therefore, with more assurance about herself, she placed her other shoes in the overnight case and stepped out of the restroom with confident written on her face as she headed down the hallway toward her locker to put away the overnight case.

The second period was English, and Mildred had waited anxiously to walk into class. Antonio's reaction or none reaction to her attire and high heels would give her some kind of clue of his possible attraction toward her. However, when Mildred stepped into class and smiled toward him, he glanced at her and smiled with no more interest on his face than usual. She waved as she took her seat at her desk. He waved back and then looked down toward the papers on his desk, doing what he was doing, stacking them in two stacks. Mildred's attire didn't seem to get the response she had hoped for. She had set her heart on an interesting stare from him. But after a short moment of what felt like a knife turning inside of her, Mildred didn't feel too set aside. Her instincts told her that Antonio liked her as much as she liked him. She felt maybe he was shy about showing his feelings for her.

Not pulling Antonio's attention in class made Mildred feel down in the dumps by lunch time. Therefore, while sitting in the crowded, noisy cafeteria she felt hungry enough to eat a bear, but yet with a tray of chopped steak, yellow squash and green beans sitting on the food tray in front of her, Mildred couldn't stomach one single bite of food. She was thinking about Antonio while tapping her nails on the table. She had no time to relax and eat. She was much too upset and too busy thinking about Antonio. The fact that he had out and out ignored her in her only designer outfit had crushed her and made her feel more strongly about getting his attention. The more he seemed disinterested in asking her out, the more she had the need to win him over. She was pleased that he interacted with her and appeared nice and friendly toward her, but she wanted to be more than his friend.

Halfway through lunch period while gathered at the cafeteria table with other students, Mildred grabbed her chest and stared hard as Antonio and Jack Coleman walked into the cafeteria. Antonio had a sturdy build and was the best-looking boy at school in Mildred's eyes. She felt he looked especially handsome dressed in an all-black blue jean outfit. He walked across the floor to the pop machine and got a bottle of Pepsi from the machine. He twisted the cap off his drink and then glanced over at Mildred's table with the bottle up to his lips. He winked and smiled at Mildred as he and Jack Coleman walked toward the rear of the cafeteria and took a seat at Antonio's usual table.

The seniors at Mildred's table were mute with their eyes on Antonio Armani and Jack Coleman. The moment they took their seats, the seniors at Mildred's table all started chatting and whispering to each other about Antonio and Jack. Both boys were popular with the female seniors. Therefore, sitting at the table listening to the other girls chatting excited about how fine Antonio and Jack were, Mildred noticed that Jack had just gotten up from their table to leave. In that instant, Mildred decided she would wear her heart on her sleeve and walk over to Antonio's table. She started walking toward his table, and the other students stop chatting and suddenly it was quiet enough to hear a pin drop. They all looked on as Mildred headed toward his table.

Mildred approached his table, looking straight in his eyes. "Hi, Antonio." She smiled and looked down at the table in front of him. She noticed he didn't have a tray of food. "I guess you don't like this cafeteria food?" she said.

He smiled at her. "I like it just fine. I just haven't gotten in line yet," he said, pointing to a chair at his table.

Mildred looked at the lunch line. "The line is short now."

Antonio nodded. "I know, but I'm not hungry. But it's good to see you for a change without Raymond Ross glued to your side." He grinned. "But didn't you just ask me if I liked the food here yesterday?"

Her heart sunk deep inside of her at the thought of repeating herself to him. But before she could comment on what he said, he spoke.

"What're you up to?" He glanced at his watch. "I know lunch is almost over, but would you like to join me? Can I get you a soda or juice?" He held out his bottle of coke and pointed to the vending machine against the wall.

Mildred felt butterflies in her stomach and thought she would stumble or appear anxious in his presence. The chemistry she felt was overwhelming.

"No thanks, I just finished my lunch," she nervously said as her heart raced and pounded in her chest. She could hear and feel the vibrations. But she was trying to keep her composure. He made her feel like a candle standing before a blazing fire. She was hoping he was genuine about wanting her company since he asked and also pointed to the chair. But just as she took a seat at his table, Jack Coleman stuck his head in the entrance door of the cafeteria, beckoned and called out to him.

"Antonio. Come here for a second." He beckoned for him. "Catherine Franklin drove her new car to school. You want to see it?"

Antonio held up one finger, turned his bottle of coke up to his mouth and drained it. "Hold up Jack. I'll be right there." He sat the empty bottle down on the table loudly. "Of course, I want to see Catherine's new car." He glanced at Mildred as he stood from his seat. "It must be nice to be 18 with a new set of wheels. Catherine and that brother of hers are the only two students at this school that drives brand new luxury cars," he said under his breath, getting up from the table. "That family is loaded but good."

Antonio headed toward Jack as Mildred watched him hurry across the floor. He looked stunning to her dressed in the black outfit that hugged his frame like it was tailor made for him. He glanced over his shoulder and waved at her. She sat there feeling awkward wondering what he felt or thought of her. He had given her mixed signals. Now sitting there feeling foolish that he had left her sitting there, she wanted to kick herself for being too nervous and not opening her mouth to say more than she said. Nevertheless, after a few seconds she collected her thoughts and felt more at ease. She figured she had another chance to talk to him when school let out. On that hopeful thought, she stood from the table to leave and only took a few steps when he rushed back over and tapped her shoulder. She stopped in her steps and turned around, almost brushing up against him.

"Mildred are you leaving?" he asked. "It was nice chatting with you." He looked toward the entrance as Catherine and Veronica walked passed the entrance way headed down the hall. "You want to hang out later?" He asked as he turned and looked in her face.

Mildred heart raced at the thought of Antonio asking her out. She couldn't seem to open her mouth to respond. He started backing away toward the exit. "What do you say?"

"Sure, I would love to," Mildred finally answered.

He nodded. "Okay, good. But I'm in a rush right now." He pulled a small note pad and a fancy Mount Blanc pen from his jacket pocket. "What's your address, I'll pick you up around five-thirty and take you to the show or we can do whatever you like, okay?"

"My address is 210 Sutton Rd," she gleefully replied.

"I'll see you later, gorgeous. You are by far, the prettiest girl at Barrington High," he said with warmth as he rushed out of the cafeteria.

Mildred stood stunned and feeling elated that Antonio had called her the prettiest girl at school. She had gotten her wish since she had secretly liked him for a while. She wanted him to ask her out and wanted to be his girlfriend.

Therefore, after she got home from school it seemed like the evening dragged on and five-thirty took forever to tick around. But when Antonio slowly pulled into her driveway in his old yellow Chevy, she was anxiously looking out of the window and quickly grabbed her purse from the coffee table and rushed out of the house before he had time to turn off his engine and step out of his car. She was consumed with excitement as she quickly hurried off the porch, pushed her hair off of her face and stepped across the yard, smiling. She was wearing her favorite red jeans and white blouse that reached middle-ways her hips. She had her fingers crossed that all the fussing she had just gone through with her make-up and curling irons, would meet with his approval, and apparently it did. His eyes lit up the closer she got to him. He was just stepping out of his car, dressed handsomely in a pair of black Levi's jeans and an olive-green shirt.

"Antonio, I need to tell you something before we go inside," Mildred softly said, smiling, looking in his eyes. "This is something that I should have mentioned to you when we were chatting in the lunchroom earlier." She lowered her head for a second, and then glanced over her shoulder toward the front door, then back at him. Now nervously twisting the gold-plated Avon ring on her pinkie finger. "I had planned to mention it, really I had, Antonio. But you had to rush off so abruptly, remember? It just slipped my mind," she said, stumbling with her words, trying to find the right words to say.

"Okay, what's going on?" He asked casually as he looked her up and down with pleasing approval. He seemed delighted with the way her outfit complimented her figure. He was looking at her as if she was a complete delight to his eyes. He grabbed his chin with his right hand and kept nodding. "Don't you look hot this evening? I never realized just how stunning you really are," he said sincerely.

"Stunning? That's quite the compliment," she said, smiling.

He nodded. "Yes! Mildred Latham, you are stunning and some." He gave her a sexy stare. "Now, what about what you were saying? Something you should have told me?"

"Okay, but I'm sort of embarrassed to tell you."

"Tell me what? Out with it already," he urged.

"I'm not allowed to go out on a date with a boy," Mildred blurted out.

"What? Are you joking around?" He asked before she finished talking.

"I'm not joking but let me finish. I know it sounds weird, but it's only if my parents haven't gotten acquainted with the boy," she quickly explained, biting down on her bottom lip, hoping he wouldn't be too disappointed and hop in his car and leave.

Her statement caught his attention as his eyebrows lifted and his mouth flew open. He placed his finger on his bottom lip and stared at her. "Mildred, why didn't you tell me this at school. This is a big deal. You got to be kidding, right?" He seriously asked.

She shook her head. "No, I told you I'm not joking or kidding around with you, Antonio. I'm serious." She held out both arms. "This is my life."

His smile faded as disappointment poured from his eyes. He turned his back to her and grabbed his head, staring up at the sky. He faced her, tapping his finger on his chin.

After a five-second stare, he threw up both arms. "This is unreal." He glanced toward their average, white frame, four-bedroom house that was in much need of painting. Then he had a flash of the mansion Catherine Franklin lived in. "I don't have time for this kind of situation. This is a deal breaker for me," he said, as he noticed lights inside of the house switched on. "Mildred, your folks are still treating you like a kid." He shook his head as he grabbed the door handle of his car.

Her heart was beating anxiously at the thought of him leaving. "But, Antonio. Wait a minute. What are you doing? You don't have to run off because of what I say."

He ignored her, waved a hand and pulled his car door open. "I think it's best if I just take off. I'll see you at school tomorrow."

"Antonio, you don't have to leave. It's okay for you to be here, really."

"It doesn't feel okay to me after what you just told me," he whispered.

"But I'm telling you it is. I'm sorry if I made it sound otherwise," she anxiously said, staring out at him with a silly nervous grin on her face. "I can have a boy over, but I'm just not allowed to go to their house," she explained, hoping he would stay awhile.

He held her stare as if he was hoping she would say something that would spark his interest and convince him to stay.

"I just can't leave home with a boy my parents haven't gotten to know. I would have told you earlier, but you were in a big rush."

What Mildred was saying didn't seem to be doing the trick to hold him there. He glanced away and grabbed the door handle again.

"Antonio," she said, swallowing her pride. "I really wanted you to come over, and I figured you wouldn't if I had mentioned what I just said."

Standing there at his car door, he rubbed his chin as a small smile came to his face. Her statement warmed him as he looked out into space for a second, in deep thought of what she had just said. He stared curiously at her. "Okay, Mildred. Let me get this straight. You can't go on dates?"

"I didn't say that."

"But you did say, you can't leave home with a boy. But you can have one over in your home under your parent's nose? Is that about the size of it?"

"That's about it, Antonio." She nodded, praying inside for him to stay.

"That's a bomber." He laughed and kept smiling.

His laugh and smiles instantly made her relax a bit, thinking that maybe they were going to spend the evening together, that he would stay after all.

"You said you're a senior, graduating this spring just like me, right? Are your folks a little nutty? This is 1974, who in their right mind would keep a high school senior under lock and key?" He asked smiling.

Mildred nodded. "Yes, I graduate this spring. But I do agree with you."

"Agree with what?" He asked.

"That my folks are a little nutty," she said and laughed. "But I have to admit that they really don't keep me under lock and key. I have my own car, even if it's not running at the moment. Plus, I can pretty much come and go as I please. I go to school dances, parties and ballgames whenever I want. They are only strict when it comes to going to a boy's house. You know what I mean, right? Or leaving here with one."

Antonio had a serious expression on his face and disappointment and half interest in his eyes. "It sounds weird to me. You can go and come as you please in your own car, but you can't leave home in somebody else's. For all they know, when you leave home you could be going to a guy's house."

"Yes, I know you are right." She laughed at what he said, and then continued. "But they are really not as strict as it sounds. They are pretty easy going; and understanding."

"Easygoing and understanding? It doesn't sound that way to me."

"But they are easygoing and understanding. Their beef is me leaving home with a boy they haven't met."

"I guess you're allowed to leave home with Raymond Ross?" he asked.

She nodded. "Yes, I can leave home with Raymond. We have been friends for a long while and my folks know him quite well."

He stood staring out into space as he rubbed his chin. But after two minutes of silence and he hadn't said anything, Mildred spoke.

"Antonio, when you think about it, I guess it makes sense."

"What makes sense?" He asked, staring into space rubbing his chin.

"My parents wanting to know the boy before I leave home in his car."

"Oh, that?" He looked at her and nodded.

"Yes, that. Isn't that why you are suddenly quiet?"

"Mildred, how old are you?" He leaned against his car with arms folded.

"I turned eighteen last month."

He shook his head as he walked toward her, looking in her eyes.

"You're 18, but you're still being treated like you're 12," he said, stared into space, then looked at her. "I'm sorry Mildred, but this set-up is a real drag." He glanced at his watch, then looked her in the eyes, reached out and wrapped one of her long, blonde curls around his finger. He pulled her face closer to his, and just as she thought he would kiss her, he released her hair.

"You are super pretty," he said honestly, glancing down at the ground, and then set his eyes on hers. "But as pretty as you are, I have to be on the level with you. I don't think we can be together." He rubbed his finger across his chin. "Our lifestyles are too different. I'm loose and free and my folks don't hold me back. But you're restricted; and I just can't see myself getting involved with some girl who can't leave home on a date."

He was cut off by the vague opening of the front door of Mildred's house. Her mother had just stepped outside onto the front porch. It startled Mildred because she thought her mother was in the basement doing laundry.

"I thought I heard a car pull up." She smiled. "Why are you kids talking outside in this cool breeze?" She asked, and then looked toward Antonio.

"Mildred is this your classmate you'll be studying with this evening?"

"Yes, Mom. This is Antonio Armani," Mildred anxiously replied.

"How are you this evening Mrs. Latham?"

"I'm just fine, young man, thanks for asking," Mrs. Latham smiled.

"Well, you two should come on inside soon, it's pretty cool out here," she said with her voice full of approval. Apparent approval of how attractive he was and neatly dressed.

"Okay, Mom, we'll be right in."

The moment Mrs. Latham stepped inside, he shook his head. "This isn't going to work out for us. I need to leave, Mildred." He headed toward his car.

"Antonio please," she said quickly and grabbed her mouth.

He stopped in his tracks and glanced over his shoulder. "Please what?"

"Please stay for just awhile. If you leave now, Mom is going to think we were up to no-good out here." She got a sniff of his enchanting cologne floating past her nose in the cool evening air.

He slammed his hand on the top of the car hood and shook his head. Then he rushed over to her and wrapped his finger around one of her long golden blond spiral curls again. This time he held her face, bringing his face down to hers. He covered her lips with demanding urgency in a passionate kiss, then slowly pulled away looking in her eyes. "This I can get used to," he softly whispered as he held her in his arms; and as he released her, she grabbed her stomach, amazed by the desire he stirred in her.

He looked at her and winked. "Okay, I'll stay for a while, as long as I can kiss you like this again?" He grinned as they headed inside.

After brief introductions, her parents left them alone in the living room. Her folks made their way to the den where they comfortably watched re-runs of Lassie as Mildred and Antonio sat on the sofa next to each other talking, getting to know each other better.

Chapter Twenty-Three

Mildred leaned forward and lifted her glass of wine from the coffee table, brought it to her mouth and took a small sip. She crossed her legs and comfortably leaned back on the firm cushions of the sofa. She glanced at her watch and noticed only ten minutes had passed since Julian left the restaurant. She looked about at all the customers having lunch and a couple sitting close on the next sofa, having wine and talking softly to each other. Seeing the couple took her mind back to Antonio and her thoughts of him:

Mildred had a sleepless night, tossing and turning in her sleep. She woke up several times during the night, going over and over in her mind wondering if Antonio had enjoyed his time with her. The next day in class, she was anxious about seeing him. Her mind was filled with hope and wonder just as the night before. She couldn't concentrate on any of her schoolwork and during her morning classes, she neglected studying her school assignment as the teacher had instructed. She was a devoted straight A student, but she didn't even open her History textbook. She sat at her desk and counted the minutes before the lunch hour. When the lunch bell sounded, she hurried out of her History class and rushed to the cafeteria where she was surely to spot Antonio at his regular table. But she was so focused on Antonio until she lost her appetite and didn't get in line to grab a tray of lunch. She walked straight over to Antonio's table. She was glad to see he was eating with some students she didn't know. Jack Coleman made her nervous how he always stared at her.

"Hi, Antonio. I had a nice time last night," she said, smiling.

Mildred stood nervously with her heart racing like a rushing freight train. She was praying he wasn't too upset over her folk's rules.

"Hi, Mildred. I had a nice time at your house. But your parents in the next room was a drag," he said seriously, looking her in the face. "An even bigger drag is the fact that you can't leave your house with me." He shook his head. "So, I don't know."

"You don't know what, Antonio?"

"I just don't know if we can be more than friends."

Mildred heart raced with excitement of what he had just said. "I guess you have thought of being more than friends with me?"

He smiled and nodded. "Of course, I have. But it wouldn't work out."

"How do you know it wouldn't work out?"

Antonio didn't answer, he just glanced at his Timex watch and smiled at her. "Okay, I have a question for you, Miss Mildred Latham."

"What's your question?"

"Do you want to go home with me after school? Folks are out of town."

"What about your sister?"

"Terrie is gone to."

"She's not gone. I just saw her in class earlier."

"I don't mean she's out of town with my folks. But she won't be home tonight. She's staying over at some classmate's house."

"I see." Mildred narrowed her eyes at him but didn't comment further.

"So, what's your answer?"

"I'm not sure I believe you, Antonio."

"I wouldn't lie to you about having the house to myself. It wouldn't be much good for you to come over and find everybody is home."

"So, let me get this straight. You're inviting me over and it just so happen that both of your parents, Mr. Peter and Miss Ellen are both out of town and your sister, Terrie, is staying over with a friend? Is that right?"

"That's right," he quickly replied.

"You'll be home alone all evening and all night?" Mildred asked.

"That's the truth and I cannot think of a better time for you to come home with me. We'll have the house to ourselves. So, what do you say?"

"I agree with your folks out of town and Terrie out of the house, it's a perfect setting to spend some time together," Mildred softly admitted.

He smiled, thinking she was on the verge on saying yes. "If you agree it's a perfect setting. Say yes," he urged her.

Mildred was thrilled as all kind of excitement dashed through her mind from the thought of being alone with him. She wanted to say yes so badly until it ached inside just thinking about it. However, a caution light went off in her brain. She knew if her parents found out, she would be in hot water because they would pitch a fit to no end. She went behind their backs once and was grounded for an entire month. She didn't want a repeat of that miserable predicament she found herself in; and just the thought of possibly being grounded by her parents made her too uneasy.

"Antonio, I'm sorry. But I can't say yes. I'm flattered that you asked, and I would love to say yes. But you already know my situation at home. My folks won't allow what you're asking. I explained this to you last night."

"Did you really?" he said disappointedly.

"What you mean, did I really?" Mildred nodded. "Yes, I told you and you know I told you. That's why we couldn't leave my house."

He stared at her but didn't comment.

"Antonio, I'm sure you haven't forgotten since the topic became a big deal to you," Mildred reminded him. You were turned off and quite thrown by the news," Mildred said irritated that he was pretending not to know her situation at home. "I know you remember and just pretending you don't. Maybe you only asked me to your house to see what I would say. Now I wonder if your folks are really out of town and if Terrie is really planning to stay overnight at a friend's house."

"It's all true what I told you about the folks and my sister," he sniped. "And damn right, I can remember."

Mildred shook her head. "Well, why were you trying to act as if you had no clue of what I was saying?"

"Just listen." Antonio shook his head disappointedly. "That's my point and the reason we can't be an item," he firmly stated.

Mildred swallowed hard at what he had just said but stay mute.

"That's a damn shame considering you're the prettiest girl at this school as far as I can see."

"Wow, that's a nice compliment considering I was under the impression that most of the students considered Veronica Parker the prettiest on the school grounds. They have selected her two years in a row as homecoming queen," Mildred reminded him.

Antonio nodded. "You're different from Veronica Parker."

"What you mean different?"

"You're so damn nice, and sweet to boot. And Veronica Parker isn't a girl I would call sweet," he said and paused. "However, I have to give credit where credit is due. She is also exceptionally good looking. But in my eyes, all I can see is you. And as far as I'm concerned, the rest of the female population at this school just don't stand a chance next to you, Miss Mildred Latham. Your eyes alone are enough to drive any boy at this school stone crazy." He pointed from her head to her feet. "Your long golden curls right down to your size six shoe. You're one perfect package." He held up both hands, shaking his head.

"But I still have to stay clear of you. Your situation at home cramps my style; and I just don't see you and me going anywhere." He touched his chest and then pointed to her as his smile faded.

"Why do you have to be such a pessimist? But, thanks for all those nice things you just said about me. I feel the same about you," Mildred admitted.

"What do you mean, you feel the same about me? I didn't mention any feelings. I just told you how incredibly gorgeous you are."

Mildred nodded. "I know, and I thank you. But I'm just trying to tell you I like you," she softly said and shyly glanced down and then back at him. "But I think you probably already know that."

He shook his head. "You're wrong. I don't already know that. How would I know? I can't even get you to come home with me!"

"Well, I do like you more than words can say! And I really want to go to your house, Antonio. But as I mentioned I could get into some serious trouble with my folks if they were to find out I went to your house after school, especially if your parents are out of town."

"Get real, Mildred. Stop being such a worry wart. How are your folks going to know if you leave school with me? Do they know everywhere you go? You go wherever else you want to go, right?"

"Well, yes. But what's your point, Antonio?"

"My point is, just tell your folks you went to a friend's house after school. Anything because they sure won't know the difference." He laughed. "Do you think they'll just somehow figure out where you went after school? I don't think so."

Mildred shook her head. "I'll know the difference and I don't make a habit of lying to my parents. I just cannot go to your house. I'm sorry, Antonio. Come visit me again," she softly suggested as she took a seat at his table.

He looked at her with solemn eyes and disappointment written all over his face, shaking his head. He didn't bother to reply. He pushed his half-eaten lunch tray aside and grabbed his math book and hopped up from the table. He walked away from the table and headed toward the exit. He looked over his shoulder and shook his head at her as he rudely walked out of the cafeteria.

Mildred sat there feeling silly with both hands holding up her face when she glanced across the lunchroom and spotted her class mate Belle Madden. Belle was walking toward the table with a lunch tray in her hands. Belle walked up and tapped Mildred on the shoulder, then placed her lunch tray on the table and took a seat.

"Hi, Mildred. What's the matter? Where's your lunch tray? You're sitting here looking sad like you just lost your best friend," Belle caringly asked.

Mildred shook her head. "You're wrong. I'm not sad."

"Well, you surely look sad," Belle said.

"But I just said I'm not sad."

"Okay, good. I'm glad you're not sad. But why are you looking so sad? Where's your food? You didn't get in line yet?" Belle asked.

"I'm not hungry," Mildred said looking down at the table in thought.

"Okay, because you sure don't have to diet," Belle said, laughingly.

Mildred looked across the table at Belle and spoke honestly. "Belle, I'm really glad you came to my table. You're just the person who can help me."

"Help you how?" Belle took her fork and put a piece of Salisbury steak in her mouth. "What's going on?"

Mildred eyed her Salisbury steak, mashed potatoes and butter beans and suddenly it dawned on her that she was hungry. She held up one finger. "Please excuse me. I just realized that I'm starving. I'll be right back. Let me go and grab myself a tray of lunch."

In a few minutes, Mildred was seated with a tray of food and a carton of chocolate milk. She opened the carton and took a sip of milk; and then took her fork and begin to enjoy her lunch. She forked a piece of steak in her mouth and some butter beans.

Belle wondered what help she needed from her as she ate her lunch and Mildred ate hers. Then halfway through their meal, Mildred held up one finger. "Oh, I almost forgot the help I need from you. But believe me when I tell you that I really need your help," Mildred stressed desperately, looking Belle in the eyes. "My stomach is rolling over with anxiousness and I'm so excited until I could scream!"

Belle smiled. "Wow, what's so exciting?"

"I'm going to Antonio Armani's house after school."

Belle grabbed her mouth with both hands. "I see why you're so excited. Now, that's something to be excited about. I knew he liked you. He finally asked you out."

Mildred smiled. "Not exactly in the way you think. But I'm going to his house after school just the same and I need you to cover for me."

"What do you mean, cover for you?" Belle asked.

"I need you to cover for me because I plan to tell my mother I'm going to your house after school."

Belle stared at Mildred as she raked one medium length brown curl out of her face, and then forked butter beans in her mouth. "But why are you telling your Mom you're visiting me? You haven't visited my house in the past." Belle stared somewhat confused.

Belle and Mildred were classmates, but they were not close friends. They socialized at school and shared their lunch and were friendly to each other. They were in the same economical circle; and were not part of Catherine and Veronica's circle.

"I know but Mom doesn't really know that." Mildred reached across the table and touched the top of Belle's hand. "Can you do me this favor? I'm begging you, please."

Belle laughed. "Okay, sure. You can tell your Mom you're visiting my house," Belle assured her. "But my goodness. I can see it in your eyes. You are crazy about Antonio Armani and that's for sure."

Mildred nodded. "I guess I am. So, you'll do it. You'll cover for me?"

Belle nodded. "Yes, I'll cover for you. But you need to clue me in on everything. Like do you plan to give my number to your Mom?"

Mildred smiled. "Yes, I plan to give your number to my parents."

"Okay, but what am I supposed to say if one of them decide to call my house looking for you? Plus, if my folks pick up the phone they'll tell them you're not at my house."

Mildred waved a hand. "I'm not worried about them calling your house. They don't have a reason to call as long as I get home on time, which I plan to do. So, don't worry about that happening." Mildred lifted her milk carton to her mouth and took a sip. "Just know you are doing me a big favor. Plus, I have gotten so excited about going to his house. I'll admit I was nervous and unsure about going at first."

Belle stared. "But now, you're not nervous?"

"I'm still nervous, but I'm going anyway. If I don't, I'm sure Antonio will have nothing more to do with me."

"Nothing more to do with you?" Belle asked with a surprised look on her face. "I think you're wrong. I have seen how Antonio Armani looks at you, Mildred. He doesn't look at any other girl the way he looks at you. I think he really likes you," Belle said assuredly. "What's make you think differently?"

"The fact that he walked away from me and left me sitting alone at his lunch table was a big red flag that he's not that into me." Mildred touched her chest. "If you ask me."

Belle grabbed her mouth with both hands. "He walked away from you and left you sitting at this lunch table alone? I guess that's why you looked so miserable when I walked over to the table."

"That's right. Soon after I said I couldn't go to his house with him. He stood up from the table without saying a word to me and he left the cafeteria," Mildred told her.

"I can see why you would think he's on the fence about you." Belle waved her hand. "But I'm convinced that boy really likes you. But no worries. I'll cover for you," she assured Mildred, and then forked a piece of steak into her mouth. She held up one finger as she chewed her food, then she said, smiling. "Who knows, I might need a favor myself one day." Belle continued to smile, sucking on her vanilla milkshake. "Besides, now that you and Antonio might be getting together. It gives me hope about Don."

"Wait a second," Mildred stared with surprise eyes. "Are you talking about that rich Taylor boy from downtown?" Mildred asked.

Belle smiled. "That's exactly who I'm talking about."

"But you only saw him once, is that correct?"

"I know I only saw him once. But once was all it took for me to fall head over heels in love with Don Taylor." She placed her fork on her tray and pushed the tray aside, placing both elbows on the table to hold up her face. "I can't stop thinking about that boy. I just hope his basketball team will eventually visit our school again, so he can ask me out."

"Belle, I don't know what to say. You are just as crazy about Don Taylor as I am about Antonio."

Belle laughed. "But there's a big different in the two boys."

"What do you mean?" Mildred curiously asked.

"You should know what I mean," Belle grinned. "Don Taylor folks are filthy rich, and Antonio Armani is as poor as the rest of us," Belle said.

"I know that, and it doesn't matter."

"It may not matter now since you're in high school. But my mother told me that when it's time to choose a husband I should marry into money. She has told me that since middle school. Therefore, she finally cemented it into my head. So, if I can't marry for love and money. I probably won't marry anyone," Belle seriously stated.

"Belle, you shouldn't think like that. We are both too young to know how we may think or feel when we decide to marry. I just know what I know right now." Mildred grabbed her chest with both hands. "Antonio Armani has put a spell on me and I like it."

"That's the same way I feel about Don Taylor and none of these boys at this school can compare to Don. Ryan Franklin is filthy rich, but he only has eyes for Veronica Parker."

"Belle are you just into Don Taylor because he's rich?"

Belle shook her head. "No, absolutely not. I'm crazy about that boy. But he just happens to be rich and his status just happens to coincide with my Mom's wishes for me pertaining to marrying into a rich family."

"But Belle, I know you're not holding out hope for Don Taylor, are you? I was at that game and I saw him leading his team to victory. But he was only here with his ball team and has no reason to return."

"Maybe not, but when his team played here and beat our school basketball team, Don and I did get an opportunity to talk to each other for a while. During which, he asked for my number. That's why I have some hope."

"Wow, I didn't know he asked for your phone number." Mildred excitedly grabbed her mouth with both hands. "Belle, you really might have a chance with high society," Mildred seriously acknowledged.

"I can hope, but I don't plan to lose a whole lot of sleep over it. Although, he stood in the hallway during their break and talked to me and asked for my number. It's been several months since that time and he hasn't called once." Belle waved her hand. "So, realistically I'm daydreaming a lot about the possibilities. But I'm not holding out a lot of hope for Don Taylor."

"Okay, but it sounds like he found you attractive. He did ask for your number," Mildred reminded her.

"Mildred, you need to get out more," Belle grinned.

"Why did you say that?" Mildred asked, smiling.

"What I'm trying to say is, what good it does me if he asked for my number if he's never going to dial it?" Belle sadly grumbled as she pulled through the straw of her milkshake. "Let's just get back to your situation since mine seem hopeless."

"Okay, sure. But I think we're good. You'll cover for me with my folks while I'm at Antonio's house."

"Mildred, I know you said I shouldn't worry about your folks calling my house. But after giving it some thought. I'm concerned. Maybe they won't call. But there's always a chance they could. So, if they do call, what should I say?"

"Belle, I don't want you to worry about my Mom calling your house. I don't want to put any stress on you for this favor you're doing me. But if you think about it for a moment, you'll realize that my Mom has no reason to call your house?" Mildred pointed out. "She has absolutely no reason to think I would have lied. So, why would she call to check up on me?"

"But you're leaving my phone number with your folks. That's why I feel they might call my house," Belle said.

"I will call home after school and give Mom your number when I say I'm going to your house instead of coming straight home. That's one of their rules. Whenever I'm going over a friend's house after school, they expect me to call home and let them know and of course, give them that friend's name and number. That's why I'm giving my Mom your number. My folks haven't called checking up on me in the past at a friend's house."

"Okay, good. I'm glad to hear that," Belle inhaled sharply. "Thanks for that explanation. It makes me feel a lot easier. But if you're not concerned I shouldn't be," Belle said and then glanced about the lunchroom to make sure they had privacy. She leaned in across the table closer to Mildred. "Do you plan to sleep with Antonio this evening?"

Mildred jaw dropped. "Why would you ask me that?" She narrowed her eyes, staring at Belle.

Belle smiled and felt embarrassed of what she had assumed about Mildred and Antonio. "I'm sorry I asked you that. But I was just wondering."

"But why were you wondering something so extreme?" Mildred asked.

"I don't think it's so extreme," Belle quickly offended herself. "But to answer your question. It was probably on my mind because of you."

"What do you mean by that?" Mildred asked.

Belle smiled. "You seem so anxious and I'm just trying to figure out what you two are up to."

"Why do you say it like that, Belle? We just want to get together and spend some time with each other," Mildred softly said. "We're not up to anything except trying to spend some time together."

"Well, it seems like you're up to something to me. Especially, since it's such a big secret from your folks. Otherwise, what's the big deal?"

Mildred widened her eyes at Belle. "What do you mean, what's the big deal? What are you talking about?"

"I'm talking about, what's the big deal with going to Antonio's house? Why can't you just invite Antonio over to your house?"

"I could. But this is a special occasion for us to be alone."

Belle nodded as she narrowed her eyes at Mildred. "That's your business whatever you and Antonio decide to do."

"I see that look on your face. But listen, Belle. I'm crazy about Antonio more than words could ever express. But I'm not sure if I'm ready for that step with him or any boy. I just want him to fall in love with me."

"I'm a little confused about your feelings for Antonio Armani. I was under the impression that you were dating Raymond Ross. So, what happened with you and Raymond? Everybody knows how crazy Raymond is about you."

"I know how Raymond feels about me and I like him too," Mildred humbly admitted.

"Okay, let me be clear on what you're saying. You like Raymond Ross, but you're crazy about Antonio Armani." Belle nodded. "In that case, what's going on with you and Raymond? Are you and Raymond still dating?" Belle narrowed her eyes toward Mildred.

Mildred nodded. "Yes, we sort of are," she said, looking Belle right in the face. "But being around Raymond doesn't excite me as much as I'm excited by being around Antonio."

Belle smiled caringly as she looked at Mildred. "I wonder why that might be; too much Antonio on your brains?"

"You're being funny, but that could be it," Mildred mumbled.

"I'm not being funny. I'm being very serious. You have fallen in love with Antonio Armani. You know, and I know. The only person who doesn't have a clue is Raymond!" Belle seriously stated.

"He does have a clue. Raymond backed me into a corner and demanded to know if I was interested in Antonio," Mildred shared with her.

"What did you tell him?"

"I told him the truth; and in so many words I told him I liked Antonio."

"How did Raymond react? I'm surprised he didn't break up with you right then and there. If you admitted to his face that you liked another boy," Belle seriously mumbled.

"Maybe you're right, Belle. Maybe Raymond have broken up with me. Nevertheless, I still like Raymond. I just like Antonio more."

Chapter Twenty-Four

Mildred paused from her past memories and reached down and lifted her wine glass from the coffee table. She took a small sip and then placed the glass back on the coffee table. She was smiling inside from the thoughts of the past as she rested her right elbow on the right arm of the sofa and faded back into her daydream:

Mildred was anxious and slightly nervous as her heart raced with excitement in her chest as she hurried down the hallway to catch Antonio at his locker. School had just let out and it was 3:00 o'clock on the nose when she softly stepped up behind him and tapped his shoulder.

"Hi Antonio, you'll never guess what news I have for you." She smiled.

"It must be good news. You seem in a really good mood," he observed.

She nodded, smiling. "Yes, I am, and I'll tell you why? You're going to have a visitor?"

"Who? You?" He pointed both hands at Mildred.

"Yes, me." Mildred glanced over her shoulder and back at him. She hoped Raymond wouldn't spot her with Antonio. She didn't want to hurt Raymond's feelings.

Antonio smiled, closed his locker and placed his back against it with both arms folded across his chest. "You are a little unpredictable, Miss Mildred Latham." He nodded. "I mean that in a good way. I'm glad you came around. We'll have fun. You'll see."

"I'm sure we'll have fun. Its fun just being with you," Mildred softly admitted and then turned to walk away. She glanced over her shoulder and he was still propped against his locker with both arms folded across his chest. "I'll follow you in my car," she told him.

"Just a minute," he said as he headed toward her.

She stood still and waited for him to reach her.

"There's no need for you to follow me home." He grabbed her hand and they walked down the hallway, out of the building.

When they reached the school parking lot, Antonio looked at her and smiled. "There's no need for you to follow me because I want you to ride with me. Just leave your car parked over in that stall," he suggested.

"Okay, I'm sure it's okay to leave my car here for a couple hours."

"Sure, it's fine. Some of the teachers stay here for hours after school let out. I have seen cars parked in this lot past ten at night," Antonio told her.

"That's fine. I'll leave it here and ride with you."

"I'm glad." He opened the passenger's door for Mildred. "I'll bring you back here to pick up your car after our visit together."

Mildred and Antonio didn't hold a conversation enroot to his house. Mildred wanted to talk to him, but the music volume on his car radio was turned up way too high. When they pulled into the driveway of Antonio folk's average looking lime green home, Mildred glanced at Antonio and he had a slight smile on his face as if he was having pleasant thoughts. Then he showed good manners when he exited the car and walked around to the passenger's side to open the door for Mildred. He then took Mildred's hand and escorted her inside of his home. Then left her standing in the middle of the living room floor as he rushed off to the kitchen to fetch them a bottle of Pepsi. They took a seat on a long navy-blue cloth sofa and he slipped out of his shiny black Sears loafers and threw his legs up on the matching navy-blue ottoman in front of the sofa. He took only two sips from his bottle of Pepsi before he threw his arms around Mildred and then started getting romantic. He didn't seem interested in holding a conversation and getting to know her better. It appeared to Mildred that he only seemed interested in getting her in bed. But Mildred was so strung out over him that she was extremely vulnerable.

"Are you glad you came?" He asked with a smile.

"I'm very glad I came," she said looking into his eyes.

He caressed her cheek and uttered in a low sexy voice as he kissed her neck. "I'm very glad, you're glad you came."

His touch made her feel like her strength was draining out of her and suddenly she felt light as a cotton ball. He slowly laid her back on the sofa and held her face gently with both hands and softly kissed her. They stayed on the living room sofa kissing with her keeping him under control for over two hours. But he got so excited until he suddenly grabbed her up and carried her down a short hallway into his room. He pushed the door open with his back and carried her across the room and placed her on his bed. Lying there on the bed holding each other and kissing, Mildred reached deep inside of herself and found the determination to stop him and rolled to the other side of the bed.

She spotted the tall grandfather clock in the corner of his room and could see it was already 5:05. She swallowed hard and felt a knot twisting in her stomach. Where had the time gone? It had ticked away too quickly.

"I better go Antonio," Mildred muttered in a low voice. "I told Mom I would be home in time for dinner. We usually eat around six-thirty."

He didn't reply, rolling to her side of the bed wrapping her back in his arms, more demanding. "I want you, Mildred," he whispered against her mouth as he kissed her urgently. "I know you want me too. We have the house all to ourselves, and knowing how your parents are, we may not get another chance like this for a really long time. What do you say?" He whispered.

"Antonio, I want to stay, but I can't."

"Yes, you can. Just do it. Relax and enjoy the moment."

"I do. I am," she said breathless. "Being with you like this is all I want. But I'm not ready to do this with you yet. I want to get to know you better."

"What's a more perfect way to get to know me?" He kissed her neck and face. "If you're worried about protection, don't. I have a condom that I plan to use." He pulled the condom out of his shirt pocket and showed it to her.

Seeing the condom made Mildred feel more at ease as if she had nothing to hold her back. Plus, the stereo in his room was blasting with her favorite song by Barry Manilow "Mandy," which was the number one song in the country and Barry Manilow first hit.

"Mildred, just when I thought I could only have thoughts of you in this way, now you're right here with me," he softly whispered against her lips.

Mildred turned to face him, and they looked in each other's eyes as he spoke with his hand caressing the side of her face. "Mildred, words can't even express what it means to me that you trust me to be with me like this. I'll remember this image of seeing you lying here in my bed next to me forever." He grabbed her face and kissed her passionately. Then he pulled away and looked down at her beneath him. "Being with you is amazing. I can't explain it, but I feel like I have been divided into millions of pieces and mended back together just as quick as they divided," he said kissing her neck.

After they made love, Antonio laid breathless on his back with his hands under his head, looking up at the ceiling as Mildred head laid against his chest. She snuggled next to him, savoring the loving feelings she had just experienced with him. But within seconds of snuggling next to him with her head on his chest, he glanced at his watch and hopped out of bed. It had just dawned on him that he had made movie plans with Catherine. He didn't want to miss his opportunity to take Catherine out. He had deep profound feelings for Mildred but dreamed of a privileged life at his disposal with Catherine.

"It's getting late," he said stepping into his blue jeans. He glanced at Mildred and beckoned her with both hands to get out of bed. "I'm sorry I'm rushing you. But it just dawned on me. I had made some plans and forgot."

"You have plans?" Mildred asked, wondering with whom.

He nodded. "Yes, I'm sorry. But being with you. It completely slipped my mind. Besides, I need to get you to your car anyway. I want you to get home in time, so your folks won't get suspicious," he said stiffly with warm eyes.

Mildred heart sunk inside of her as a sharp pain dashed through her stomach. She had just had the most wonderful time with him, experiencing the most wonderful feelings of her life. Now suddenly, his behavior seemed anxious to get rid of her.

"I understand if you already had plans," Mildred mumbled with no pep to her voice. "Afterall, I didn't give you any kind of heads up that I would be coming to your house. I just sprung it on you when school let out," she said, still lying there wrapped in the aftermath of the incredible, never before thrills that had ran through her.

"Don't get me wrong," Antonio said with deep warmth in his voice. "I'm glad as hell you decided to come home with me," he said, sitting in a nearby chair slipping on his socks. "And if I could break these plans I would. But this is something I have wanted for a while, so I need to keep them."

"No worries," Mildred smiled, looking at him as he slipped on his socks. She figured anything that made her feel as wonderful as she felt just being near Antonio had to be love.

He glanced at her while she sat on the edge of the bed. "I wish I could tell you to just stay in my bed until I get back. But I know you have to get home."

She nodded. "I do have to get home. But it's only 5:30. If you didn't have other plans we could stay here and hang out a little longer," Mildred suggested, sitting there smiling at him, holding one of his pillows next to her chest as her body still tingled from his passionate lovemaking.

He looked at her with serious eyes. "Look, Mildred, I hope you don't get the wrong impression and think I actually want you to leave my house. Because that couldn't be the furthest thing from the truth. I'm crazy as hell about you and if I could keep you here all night I would," he said warmly and held up both hands. "I just need to keep these plans I had already made for this evening," he said in a relaxed, sincere tone. "Otherwise, I would love to spend more time with you," he said, slipping into a fresh black shirt that he grabbed from the back of a nearby chair.

"Okay, sure. I said understand." Mildred quickly hopped off his bed.

Mildred told him she understood, but she was pouting with a strange feeling rushing through her stomach. Something didn't feel right to her. Although, he was being honest with her. She felt his attitude had changed and that he was giving her the brush off. Therefore, she slowly stepped into her skirt and threw on her blouse, not saying anything.

He noticed. "Hey, you. Why so quiet all of a sudden?" he asked.

"You're quiet too." Mildred smoothed her hair back with both hands.

"Your hair looks beautiful as ever," he quickly said, pointing toward the door. "But if you need to use the bathroom to freshener up before you head home, it's the second door to the left when you leave the room."

"Second door to the left when I leave this room?" Mildred asked.

He didn't reply to the question. But Mildred stood there and watched him for a second, as he seemed rushed to get himself together. He was standing at his dresser looking in the mirror brushing his hair. He noticed Mildred through the mirror just standing there watching him. He placed the hairbrush in the plastic holder that sat on the dresser and then turned around to face her. He folded his arms and narrowed his eyes. "What are you doing?" He grinned with a warm look in his eyes.

"Just watching you since I can't believe we're here in your home alone."

"Me too," he said as he picked up the brush and started brushing his hair some more. Then he looked toward her. "Do you need me to show you to the bathroom?"

"I'll find it," Mildred softly said as she turned her back to him and headed to the bathroom with her shoes in her hand.

Mildred was done in the bathroom within five minutes. But she heard Antonio's voice as she headed out of the bathroom back toward his room. She stood outside his bedroom door trembling with contempt as she listened for a second. He was talking to Catherine Franklin and seemed engrossed in their conversation.

"Catherine, I mentioned to you in class that I might end up coming over a tad later than I originally thought. But I promise I'll be over in the next ten minutes," he said and hung up the phone.

After Antonio ended his call, Mildred sneaked back to the bathroom. She didn't want him to know she had just eavesdropped on his conversation to Catherine Franklin. She placed her ear against the bathroom door and could hear his footsteps on the gray wooden floor. He was checking to see if Mildred was still tucked away in the bathroom. But a couple minutes later after Mildred had managed to pull herself together from feeling so used, after listening to him talk to Catherine Franklin over the phone, she stepped out of the bathroom again. Her eyes were dry and she could finally face him. But sharp rips of pain dashed through her stomach at the thought of Antonio being interested in Catherine Franklin and not her. Then as soon as she collected herself, her stomach balled right back in knots and she started crying again when she made it right outside of his bedroom door and heard him talking on the phone to another girl from school, Jessica Hanes.

"Jessica, I can't come over tonight. Can you believe my car is acting up again?" he said in a convincing voice. "I don't care if I did just get it fixed last week, I said it's acting up. We'll go out tomorrow. Don't be mad. Just make sure you use some makeup next time or maybe you could borrow an older friend I.D. I know you're 18 but you don't look your age; and I don't need you restricting my evening like before, when the doorman turned us away because you look too young," he said firmly. "You don't have to worry about me. I never get turned away. I guess it's my thick mustache that makes me older."

Quietly, Mildred sneaked back to the bathroom holding her face in tears. She took her fingers and dried her eyes, looking in the vanity mirror. Suddenly, she felt cheap and foolish. She had just been used by a smooth player. She cared more for Antonio than any other boy she had dated and hoped she was special to him and not just another disposal female to toy with and use. But in her mind, it seemed he was having a race against himself to see how many girls he could use.

Finally, sitting on the front seat of his car, while he drove down the street headed back to the school parking lot to get her car, Mildred felt crushed and suddenly she didn't want to be near him. She pushed herself against the passenger's door so hard as if she was trying to push through the metal. They didn't exchange many words between them. She felt his attitude and feelings for her had changed. But what she didn't know was that he had deep feelings for her and no feelings for the other girls.

He gently touched her arm and glanced at her with a big smile on his face. He felt happy and content in her presence. "How are you, beautiful?"

She glanced at him and forced a smiled. "I'm good."

"Are you sure you're good? You seem a little quiet and I have a hunch you're sore at me for cutting our time short," he said.

She crossed her fingers and mumbled. "I'm not sore at you, Antonio. I'm just wondering about something."

"What are you wondering about?"

She looked straight ahead through the windshield and swallowed hard to collect herself, then she softly asked. "Did you have a good time?"

"Don't be silly." He laughed and gently touched the side of her face. "What kind of question is that? Why would you wonder something like that? I can tell you without a shadow of a doubt that I immensely enjoyed myself."

It took all of Mildred's will power to hold back what she had overheard. She wanted desperately to tell him how she didn't want to talk about anything else except how she knew he had used her and that she had overheard him on his phone with the other girls. Mildred kept it all inside. She desperately cared deeply for him and didn't want to rock the boat. She was hopeful he would eventually care more for her than any of the other girls.

"There you have it! I had a better than a good time. Don't you know, being with you is out of this world? It's the closest I'll ever get to heaven here on this earth." He gave her a quick glance and winked at her. "Maybe we can do this again some time. What do you say? Think you'll be up for an afternoon at my house again one day after school?" he asked.

Mildred lips felt glued, as she threw him a smile. She didn't reply as she sat there boiling inside with contempt for him. She didn't know his true feelings for her and felt he wasn't sincere, since she had just discovered that he had interest in two other Barrington High students as well.

He was smiling but she wasn't. He was in the dark concerning her distress toward him, since she had chosen not to reveal how she felt and why. Therefore, he dropped her off at the school's parking lot and waited until she was in her car and had started up the motor before he drove away. Then after he drove away from the curb, his instinct told him to make sure she was okay. He quickly backed up, rolled down the window and asked. "I'm sorry, but I should've asked you if you want me to follow you home?"

Mildred looked toward him and forced a smile. "No thanks," she softly said as she waved good bye. "I can make it from here."

She knew he had another date waiting. Plus, she didn't want her parents to see a boy following her home after she had told them she would be at Belle's house.

He nodded. "Okay, I'll see you at school tomorrow." He threw his car in gear and speeded down the street from the school parking lot.

Mildred couldn't stop crying as she drove slowly down the street just a few blocks from home. She pulled into the driveway, turned off the motor and dropped her head on the steering wheel. She felt hurt and used, but still hoped he could love her. After a while she stepped out of the car and quietly made her way inside. Her heart raced in hope that her parents wouldn't spot her coming inside. She didn't want them to see the wreck she was in. Her legs felt like a mass of jelly as she walked through the front door, still crying. She closed the door softly and rested her back against it for a moment. She could hear voices coming from the kitchen. Dinner was about to be served. Nevertheless, she felt drained all of a sudden as she laid against the door holding her textbooks tightly against her chest. She loved Antonio desperately but felt he had no feelings for her. Knowing her parents could walk into the room didn't seem to faze her at the moment as she stood there crying and wiping her tears on the back of her hand. But when she heard her mother call from the kitchen, she rushed out of the living room and hurried down the short hallway to her room. She closed her bedroom door and took a deep breath trying to collect herself.

"Mildred, is that you, dear? Dinner will be ready shortly."

Mildred slowly opened her bedroom door and peeped out. She looked toward the kitchen. "Okay, Mom. I'm just putting my books away," she said, closed the door and placed her books on the dresser.

She stood looking in the mirror for a moment and couldn't believe how wonderful and yet so awful her afternoon had turned out. She couldn't find any hope in the situation as she turned away from the mirror and stepped over to her twin size bed and fell across it in tears. She rolled over and stared up at the ceiling. Her heart was beating fast with a sick sad feeling in the pit of her stomach. She realized she had to find the strength to pull herself together. She couldn't walk into the kitchen and face her parents in such a defeated gloomy state. They would take one look at her sad eyes and immediately know something was troubling her. Therefore, she pulled herself up and sat on the edge of the bed for a moment. She held her face with both hands and breathed slowly for a while. Then she dried her eyes, hopped off the bed and rushed to the bathroom and took a sponge bath. Then she threw on another skirt and top and while standing in the mirror combing her hair, she thought how foolish she was to chase after Antonio Armani. A boy who she felt only wanted to take her to bed. Their time had been so precious together. He was her first. But being with him had crushed her dreams. It seemed apparent that he wasn't serious about a serious relationship with her. Yet, as disappointed and upset as she was, all she could think of was being with him again.

Chapter Twenty-Five

Mildred blinked alert from her thoughts of the past when an elderly lady took a seat at the opposite end of the sofa where she was seated. She had a magazine in her hand and didn't look toward Mildred as Mildred faded back into her daydream:

Mildred couldn't wait to get to school the next day, hoping for an opportunity to spend some of her lunch hour with Antonio. However, during the lunch hour, she didn't find him at his usual table and she didn't see Catherine Franklin or Jessica Hanes sitting at any table. That made her wonder if Antonio was somewhere in the building talking to one of them. She finished her lunch and left the cafeteria feeling low. But her emotions jumped high, and her heart raced with excitement when she ran into him right outside the cafeteria. He was headed into the lunchroom. He looked warmly at Mildred and smiled. "What are you up to? Did you just finish lunch?" he asked.

She smiled excited. "Yes, I just finished. Are you just having lunch?"

"Yes, my math teacher held the class over for a pop quiz." He glanced at his watch. "But you want to hang out at my table with me for a while. We still have thirty minutes before the bell," he suggested.

Mildred followed him back into the cafeteria. "Sure, I'll sit with you."

"Good." He put his hand behind her waist as they walked toward his regular table. "Just wait here until I grab my tray," he said as he walked across the room to the serving counter.

In a few minutes, he stepped back over to the table and placed his food tray of Baked Chicken, Green Beans and Yellow Squash on the table and took his seat, smiling. "I'm glad I ran into you, Mildred. So, I can tell you once again how much I enjoyed you visiting my house yesterday. Plus, I want to give you a personal invitation to a small costume bash at my house tonight. But you don't have to wear a costume. Besides, I didn't encourage it and don't really think anyone will be in costume."

Mildred nodded. "Okay, a customer party without costumes?"

"That's right. My folks are back, and Terrie had planned the party a while ago. So, it's really just a gathering with food and punch," he explained. "I hope you can make it over."

Antonio's unexpected invitation kept Mildred excited and hopeful for the rest of the school day. When school let out, she rushed out the building and headed straight to the parking lot. She didn't linger in the parking lot talking to friends. She quickly hopped in her car and drove straight home to dress for Antonio's party. But before she had a chance to finish dressing, her mother hollered from the living room. Mildred glanced toward her open bedroom door while standing in the mirror brushing her hair.

"Mildred, Raymond is here."

"I'll be right there." She hollered back. But continued fussing with her hair. But before she could leave her room, she glanced around, and Raymond was standing at her bedroom door. She quickly picked up the hairbrush and started brushing her hair, so he could see she was busy getting ready.

"So, this is your private château?" He smiled.

She placed the brush on the dresser and held out both arms. "If you want to call this humble room a château, then be my guess." She smiled.

"I think it's cute how you have it decorated in orange and white. Normally, orange isn't my color. But it looks good in your room," Raymond complimented and as he started to say something else, she interrupted.

"Raymond, I don't mean to be rude. But could you please wait for me in the living room, I'll be done in a few minutes."

He nodded and saluted her, and then walked away from the door. She could hear his shoe heels on the old wooden floor as he headed down the hallway toward the living room. By the time Mildred finished dressing and stepped into the living room, Belle was still seated in the living room waiting for her. Belle had been waiting there for a while as Mildred dressed. She waited around to wish Mildred good luck with Antonio at his party.

Raymond stood in front of the fireplace, looking at pictures of Mildred on the mantle. He looked around and his jaw dropped at the sight of Mildred.

"My goodness, you look magnificent," Raymond said, smiling.

"Yeah, she does look magnificent," Belle agreed, hopping off the sofa. "But looks like it's not for your pleasure," Belle said in a low voice as she headed toward the front door to leave. "I'm taking off now. I'll see you at school tomorrow." Belle grabbed the doorknob and glanced over her shoulder, waving goodbye. "See you, Mildred; and you too, Raymond," she said laughingly, and then she was gone.

Raymond looked puzzled at Mildred. "What was Belle Madden trying to say? What did she mean when she said it's not for my benefit?"

Mildred crossed her fingers. "I don't know what she meant. She probably meant nothing," she softly mumbled.

"I think it has to do with how you're all dressed up." He was annoyed.

Mildred smiled at him but didn't reply. She felt awkward in his presence wearing a nice outfit for the benefit of another boy. The blue knee-length skirt and navy low cut top was way sensual than anything she normally wore. But since she was headed to Antonio's party, she wanted to outshine Catherine Franklin and Jessica Hanes +to get and keep Antonio's attention.

"Hello, I'm waiting Mildred!"

"You're waiting?" She stared.

"Yes, I'm waiting for your comment. Are you going to tell me what Belle Madden meant by what she said?"

"You don't get it Raymond. She didn't mean anything other than I'm dressed up for a party that you weren't invited to," Mildred say convincingly.

"Oh, I see." He nodded, giving her a long stare, and then changed the subject. "I know this is last minute, but I dropped by to see if you wanted to catch that movie you have talked so much about seeing."

"You mean, *The Exorcist?*" Mildred was excited by the offer.

Raymond nodded, smiling. "Yes, that scary ass movie all the students are raving about. You said you couldn't wait to see it," he reminded her.

"You're right. I can't wait to see it." She stared at him pondering for a second. Then the priority of Antonio's party hit her thoughts. "Raymond, you should have called first," Mildred sighed, not pleased to miss a chance at seeing, *The Exorcist.*

"I didn't think I needed to call. I don't usually call. I usually just drop over, and we spend time together. That's why I figured tonight would be a good night to catch that movie," Raymond humbly said.

"Raymond, I'm sorry because I know you came here in good faith. But what can I do? I'd love to see that movie, but it can't be tonight. I just told you I already have plans. I'm going to Antonio's party." She held out both arms. "Look at me. You think I would be dressed like this if I didn't have plans?"

"I know about the costume party, Mildred?" He admitted. "But it's going to be a damn drag for sure!" Raymond said coldly. "Besides, it's not really a costume party anyway. Nobody will be in a costume. It's just another opportunity for Antonio Armani to have some of his wild friends over to sneak in Vodka and beer. I know all about his parties. It's nothing new. He throws a party at his house every chance he can."

"Well, I don't know about all of that. But he said Terrie decided to have the party," Mildred informed him.

"It doesn't matter if his sister decided the party. It's still at his house."

"So, what, Raymond. Are you trying to put Antonio down because he drinks Vodka and beer?" Mildred asked. "No harm intended, but you drink like a fish. You're a closet drinker and probably drink more booze than any senior at Barrington High. Therefore, how can you make issue about how much booze is at Antonio's parties?"

"I'm just telling you because you think the dude is so perfect," Raymond snapped irritated that Mildred was so excited about going to Antonio's house.

"I know he's not perfect," she said. "He has flaws like the rest of us."

"We all have flaws but pretty soon you'll find out that Antonio Armani is a player and only after what he can get from a girl. Besides, you're not his type."

"What do you mean I'm not his type?"

"There's a rumor floating around school about Antonio. Apparently, he's only interested in filthy rich girls like Catherine Franklin and Jessica Hanes. He only wants them for their money," Raymond told her.

Mildred shook her head. "I don't believe those rumors. Antonio is not like that," she tried to convince Raymond as she had a flash in her mind of overhearing Antonio on the phone with Catherine Franklin and Jessica Hanes. But she would not allow her mind to believe Antonio was really that way.

"Believe what you want. Antonio makes no secret of chasing rich girls."

"So, I guess you shouldn't be jealous that I'm going to his party."

"What do you mean by that?"

"You just said he's into rich girls. I'm a poor one."

"Maybe, but he's an animal with no morals. He'll still use you if you let him. Therefore, if you ask me, I don't think you should go to his stinking party! You should come with me to see that movie you told me you wanted to see."

Mildred cut him off. "I know I told you I wanted to see, *The Exorcist*. But not tonight. We didn't have plans. You just figured you could pop over and interrupt my plans?"

"Yes! Mildred! That's it! I figured it was worth a shot."

"Well, Raymond. You can just forget it and stop trying to get me to go see that movie. I'm dying to see it, but not tonight! I'm going to the Antonio's."

"So, you rather go hang out at Antonio's house than change your plans and go out with me?" He pointed to his chest. "The guy you are supposed to be dating. I don't know about you anymore Mildred Latham," he snapped.

"What is that supposed to mean?" She anxiously asked.

"It means I can't figure you out anymore. I don't know if you're my girl or not. The word is all over school that you're chasing after Antonio Armani. But the other gossip is that he's chasing after Catherine Franklin. I don't want to believe what I hear. But now you're standing here, telling me you have no intentions of changing your plans because you're excited to go to his party."

"Look, Raymond, I'm not trying to be rude or ignore you. But I want to go to Antonio's party. He asked me, and I was given permission by my folks and I don't want to change my plans just because you don't like the boy. Besides, you dropped in at the last minute about that movie. She could have called or asked me at school before Antonio invited me to his house. Then you and I would have made plans ahead of time and I would have said no to Antonio when he asked me. But since you and I didn't have any plans. I said yes because I was free to go to this party."

Mildred words annoyed Raymond and he was extremely frustrated and disappointed with her decision to attend Antonio's party and not go out with him. He glanced down at the carpet with sad eyes and just stared at the designs in the brown rug for a few seconds before uttering another word.

"Mildred, if you're trying to think of an excuse not to go out with me." He raked his hand down his hair. "I think you should think of something I'll buy!"

Mildred turned her back to Raymond and walked over by the window and pulled the sheer brown curtains apart and while standing in the window looking out, her heart reached out and felt compassion for Raymond. She wasn't happy with his constant drinking and secrets about how he was treated at home. But otherwise, he treated her nice and liked her a lot. But she couldn't give her heart to him, because her heart also belonged to Antonio and she had deeper feelings for Antonio than what she felt for Raymond.

"Okay, if that's what you want." He rubbed both hands together. "Don't let me hold you up," he said, heading toward the door with a broken look in his eyes. He grabbed the doorknob, twisted it and pushed the door open.

Mildred heart screamed out to her to invite Raymond to come along to the party with her. "Would you like to come with me?" She asked just as he stepped out the door.

Standing at the edge of the porch. He glanced around at her and shook his head. "Thanks for asking, but I don't think so."

Mildred stepped out on the porch and couldn't believe she was trying to convince Raymond to attend a party where she really wanted to be alone with Antonio. Yet she was trying to convince him to attend. "Why not Raymond?

You may like Antonio, but as you said, his friends will sneak in Vodka and beer. I know you would love to have access to free drinks," she said teasingly.

Raymond nodded and sort of smiled but disappointment showed on his face. "What you just said might be true. But I just don't feel right about this. Maybe I am jealous and whether I have cause or not. I hate the idea of you spending any time in Antonio Armani's presence. So, thanks but no thanks."

Mildred held up both hands. "Well, I tried to include you."

"Yes, you tried to include me. But look, Mildred. Can you blame me if I don't want to hang around and watch you fall all over yourself for that boy," Raymond solemnly stated as he pulled a pint of Vodka out of his jacket pocket and turned it up to his mouth. "This is all the party I need." He held out his bottle for her to see as he headed across her driveway toward his car.

Guilt ripped through Mildred as she stood on the porch and watched him get into his car to leave. And when he drove away, she rushed down to the basement where her mother was doing laundry and her father was lying on the basement floor working on the dryer. She told them she was leaving for the party and then rushed back upstairs. She smiled as she threw on her jacket, grabbed her purse and rushed out the door. But when she hopped in her car and started the engine, it dawned on her, she was too excited and had pushed in the back of her mind how Antonio had taken her to bed and then talked to two other girls on the phone after being intimate with her. She wanted to be with him but wondered if he felt the same or was she chasing a dream that couldn't be. It dawned on her that she was rushing to get to his house when maybe he already had Catherine Franklin or Jessica Hanes as his guests. Then she thought of what Raymond said how others felt she was chasing after Antonio. She didn't want to appear desperate for Antonio if he wasn't interested in her. So, she thought of not going to his house. But just as she was about to get out of her car, her mother stuck her head out of the door.

Mildred rolled the driver's window down. "Mom, what is it?"

"I was just locking up and noticed you were still in the driveway," Mrs. Latham said. "I thought you had left for the party. Is anything the matter?"

"Nothing is the matter. I'm just leaving now," Mildred said.

"Okay, dear. Make sure you're home by midnight. I know we usually allow you to stay out at house parties until 12:30. But those parties usually take place on the weekend. Tomorrow is a school day," her mother said.

Chapter Twenty-Six

Mildred quickly zoned out of her daydream and snapped her head up from resting back against the sofa when the thin elderly lady called out to her. "Miss, I'm sorry," the 83-year-old high class dressed little lady said in a soft low voice. "It just dawned on me to ask if this seat belongs to anyone. Maybe you're waiting for someone?" she said friendly.

Mildred waved her hand and nodded toward the little lady. "I am waiting for someone. But it's okay. You don't have to move."

The little lady nodded toward Mildred as the waiter placed a glass of white wine on the coffee table in front of the little lady. Mildred smiled and glanced at her watch and faded back into memories of the past:

Mildred knocked on Antonio's door and she had subdued excitement when he answered the door and showed her inside to the living room where all his friends were gathered for the party. All the furniture was placed against the walls and a long table draped with a red table cloth stood against one wall with a few folding chairs sitting against the wall as well. He showed Mildred across the room to sit on the sofa that was pushed against the wall.

"When you're ready, you can help yourself to the food and punch on the table." He pointed toward the refreshment table. "I'm really glad you came," he said with warmth. "You look beautiful tonight." Then he shook his head standing before her. "I shouldn't say you look beautiful tonight. The truth is. You look beautiful anytime." He glanced over his shoulder when he heard someone call his name. "I don't mean to leave you alone. But I'm being beckoned, and I guess I have to mingle at my own party." He held up both hands. "But don't run off without letting me know you're leaving," he said and walked away from where she was seated on the sofa.

Two other students from Barrington Hills High were sitting on each opposite end of the sofa, but they were both talking to someone. Mildred felt left out and a bit awkward since she didn't have anyone to talk to and Antonio seemed too busy mingling with his other friends and didn't seem to have any time to sit and talk to her. Restless, she got up from the sofa and headed across the crowded floor toward the refreshment table. The music was slightly high, and the room was filled with chatter. But she was glancing about trying to spot Antonio. Finally, she spotted him behind a group of students over by the stereo stand. He was reading the label of an album in one hand, while passing an album to the DJ with his other hand.

Mildred stayed put where she was as she kept her eyes on him. She hoped he would look in her direction where she stood restlessly near the refreshment table. Irritated and frustrated, she stood in the same spot and watched as he picked up another album and read the label. He was about to pass it to the DJ when he looked across the room in Mildred's direction. A tall person who was standing directly behind Mildred had just called out Antonio's name. Antonio looked in the direction of the call and spotted Mildred leaning against the refreshment table.

He glanced down at the stack of albums he held with both hands as the DJ held the receiver of a ringing phone to Antonio's ear.

"You're welcomed to come to the party," he said. "Take care or maybe I'll see you later," he said and ended the call.

The DJ took the receiver and hung up the wall phone near the stereo stand. Antonio then placed the stack of albums that he had in his hand down on the stereo stand and headed in Mildred's direction.

His living room was crawling with students from the high school. Therefore, getting across the room wasn't an easy task. A few students were on the floor dancing, some were sitting in corners kissing, some were standing around talking, some standing around eating, some talking loudly, and some drinking heavily.

Someone pulled Antonio by the shirttail as he made it halfway across the living room floor. He jerked loose only to get grabbed by the arm by his sister. Mildred watched as his sister, Terrie, handed him a note and pointed to Catherine Franklin, who was now seated on the sofa where Mildred had sat. But after Terri pointed toward Catherine, Catherine grabbed her red Gucci shoulder bag, hopped off the sofa and hurried over to the stereo stand where Veronica stood mingling with other students. Catherine was dressed in a lilac dress with her hair hanging loosely on her shoulders. She seemed anxious as she scanned the room standing by the stereo with Veronica Parker. Veronica was dressed in a little black dress with her hair hanging loosely on her shoulders.

When Catherine spotted Antonio, he excitedly waved her note back and forth in the air to acknowledge he had gotten it. She smiled excitedly and waved back to him. Watching Catherine and Antonio exchange friendly exchanges, Mildred heart sunk deep inside of her with anxiety. She hoped Antonio wasn't getting ready to walk over and talk to Catherine without continuing his trip across the floor to see her. She and Antonio had not found a chance to spend any time with each other.

Mildred stood at the refreshment table with her heart in her throat, hoping Antonio was still interested in her. She was crying inside, hoping he wasn't going to give her the cold shoulder and give all his attention to Catherine Franklin. In the back of her mind, she kept thinking of what Raymond had told her about Antonio being interested in rich girls for their money. She knew Catherine Franklin was one of the richest girls in the whole community. Therefore, a nagging thought in the back of her mind kept telling her, he would lose interest and push her aside for the girl with the biggest bank account. Those thoughts were especially strong after overhearing him on the phone with other girls, realizing she wasn't the only girl at Barrington High who had caught his eye.

Finally, Antonio were just a few feet away from Mildred, but Mildred was annoyed with him as she took a deep breath to collect herself. She was irritated how he was discreetly sneaking warm looks at Catherine Franklin as he walked up to her. When he made it to the refreshment table where Mildred stood, he turned his back to her and started talking to one of his friends. He had a cup of red punch in his hand, lifted it to his mouth and took a swallow. The punch was spiked with Vodka.

Mildred tapped his shoulder to get his attention after he continued to stand at the refreshment table talking to his other friends, ignoring to acknowledge her.

He turned around on his shoe heels and smiled at her. "Hi, there you. I see you left the sofa," he said, laughing.

"Yes, I did."

"But I was going to make my way back over there," he said.

"I know. But it was too lonely over there." She pointed toward the sofa. "Besides, I kept waiting and it didn't seem you were coming back to join me."

He held out both arms. "You know I was going to make my way back over there to you." He held up both hands. "But what can I say? It's my party and everybody wants my attention it seems," he said and paused at her. "But look at how this sounds. My house is crawling with students – nearly all of our senior and junior classmates. But you're lonely?" he teased.

"I just mean. I didn't have anyone to talk to sitting all the way over there on that sofa. You know I came here to talk to you."

"I know, and I want to talk to you too. But it seems half of Barrington High School showed up here this evening. I hadn't expected so many guests when I invited you."

Mildred solemnly glanced at her watch. "Maybe I should just leave."

He touched her arm. "No, I don't want you to leave. I'm hoping we'll get a chance to spend some time alone away from all these students after the crowd thin out a bit. How does that sound to you?" He asked, still discreetly sneaking looks at Catherine Franklin.

Mildred liked the idea of spending some time alone with Antonio. Plus, she figured if she got Antonio away from the party, maybe he would keep his eyes off of Catherine Franklin and put them on her. "Sure, Antonio, you know that's why I came. I'd love to spend some time with you," Mildred assured him.

"Wonderful. That's good to know," he said, glancing toward the spot Catherine Franklin was standing, noticing she had her back to them.

Antonio turned to Mildred, lifted her face with both hands and gave her a quick passionate kiss on the lips. But just as quickly as he kissed her, he pulled away and smiled.

"How was that for starters? I have wanted to kiss you from the moment you walked through that door. You look so stunning in what you're wearing."

Mildred legs and stomach felt weak from his kiss. She could only look at him and smile. She was so overwhelmed that she couldn't respond verbally. He grabbed her hand and smiled. "I'll take that as a yes that you do approve," he said, leading her out of the living room, through the kitchen and then down a short hallway to his bedroom.

They sat on the edge of his full-size bed in silence. Then shortly, he stood up and pulled her up off the bed and they looked at each other in silence for a few minutes, standing only a couple feet from each other. Mildred was wearing a blouse that was being held together by six white buttons. She inhaled sharply as he reached out and unbuttoned the top button. By the time he unbuttoned the last button, she knew she wanted to give herself to him. She would not have the strength to say no. She loved and wanted to be with him more than anything else in the world. He slipped both hands inside of her blouse and caressed her and with a little bit of effort he helped her blouse slip off her shoulders. His hands felt like warm silk against her skin as he moved his hands over her bare shoulders. His touch reached the depth of her longing.

It felt so right being with him in that way. Sweet sensations just like the night before filled her entire body.

With one gentle swing, he had jerked her in his arms and wrapped her tightly against him. It was like they were the only two people alive. She could feel his heartbeat and noticed how his body temperature had made his shirt slightly damp with perspiration.

While in a firm embrace, he lifted her face toward his with one finger. They looked at each other and smiled. Mildred thought she was in heaven looking up in his dreamy eyes and while looking up at him he stroked her hair aside and anxiously pushed his lips against hers and kissed her passionately. His kiss took her breath away. She didn't want him to ever stop. They were so lost in passion, until she was in a daze as he was gently sliding both of his hands up her blouse. It felt right just like the night before and she wanted to be with him again. But she had to be strong and pull away to make sure he used a condom.

"No, Antonio, wait."

He stood, staring at her with a puzzled look on his face. "What are you trying to say? You have gotten me in the mood, now you're pushing me away."

Mildred nodded and took a seat on the bed. He took a seat beside her and put one arm around her back.

"What's wrong? If you don't want to do this, I guess we won't. But frankly, I thought you wanted to be with me like this again. Last night when we were together like this it was wonderful. Don't you think? So, what's the problem?" he softly whispered.

"Antonio, we need to discuss something first." She looked down at her hands, squeezing them tight as if she was holding on to a cliff.

"Well," he said, placing his hand over hers to relax the tight squeeze she had on them. "In case you're wondering about my feelings. I like you more than I thought possible."

After a slight silence, he cleared his throat and repeated. "I really do. I like you more than I thought possible; and I had a great time with you last night. I'm hoping moving forward that we can spend more time together."

"You mean, maybe we can become an item?" Mildred asked, wondering if he was going to choose her over the rich girls he was chasing.

"Hell, yes. We can become anything you want us too." He kissed the side of her neck and rubbed his hand down her arm.

Mildred's spirits lifted after his confession. All she wanted to hear was that he really wanted to be with her, and hearing those words was all it took to reinforce her decision to go all the way with him again.

"Antonio, I want you too. I just wanted to make sure you had a condom."

He nodded and smiled. "Yes, I do. And no need to worry." He assured her. "I'll be gentle with you. Just as gentle as I was last night. Just let yourself relax and don't worry about a thing?" He grabbed her face with both hands and kissed her hungrily, caressing her long golden curls with his fingers as he kissed her in a warm passionate manner.

Mildred was breathless as she threw her arms around his neck as he kissed her passionately. Being in his arms made her feel light enough to just float away as she gripped him as if her life depended on it.

"Antonio, I promise I'll love you always?" She softly whispered. "Can you promise me the same? I love you so much until a thousand years couldn't fade how I feel about you, Antonio," she lovingly whispered.

"Yes, I can promise you the same," he said sincerely with a voice filled with love and warmth for her. "And please believe me when I tell you, I make this promise from my heart and soul; and not because you have asked me to promise you. Mildred what you don't know is that I'm crazy about you. You are the only girl that I have feelings for. The only one and that's the way it will always be for me," he whispered in a sensuous voice as he tenderly kissed her. "There is something about you, Mildred that makes me incredibly happy to be near you. Being with you is unlike anything I have ever known. All I know is what I know, that you're damn awesomely difference and special beyond words. I think I love you, Miss Mildred Latham."

"Antonio, do you mean that?" she uttered breathless. "Your confession means everything to me. I know I love you and I'll feel this way forever."

"Forever is a long time," he teased.

"I know it's a long time. But no matter what happens between us. I know I will feel this way about you for as long as I live," she lovingly whispered.

They made love and forgot for a while that they had left a party going on in Antonio's living room. They laid inches apart, breathless on their backs, looking up at the ceiling in his bedroom, smiling and still lingering in the aftermath of their passionate time together. They both were startled at the loud ding-dong of the little clock above his bedroom door when it struck ten p.m. He reached and grabbed her hand and squeezed it.

"I know I keep repeating myself," he warmly said. "I just cannot stress enough how being with you is so precious. Somewhere so far out in another incredible dimension," he whispered next to her neck in a loving voice.

She snuggled next to him and threw her arms around him, placing her lips on his, and then he grabbed her in his arms once more and kissed her passionately. Then reluctantly, they hopped off his bed, quickly dressed and left Antonio's room. They were both surprised to see that the crowd of students attending his party had grew as he and Mildred made their way back into the living room. It was a weeknight, and many had midnight curfews, but cars of his senior classmates were still pulling into his driveway and students were still knocking on his door at 10:15 in the evening. But as crowded as the room were, Mildred stomach turned over in knots as she scanned the room and spotted Catherine Franklin and Veronica Parker still in attendance in the corner of the living room sitting on the sofa. They seemed preoccupied talking among themselves. Mildred paid close attention to Antonio, observing if he was paying close attention to Catherine. She was pleased to observe that he wasn't paying as much attention to Catherine as he had earlier in the evening.

While Mildred and Antonio stood at the refreshment table, Antonio helped himself to a cup of red spiked punch. Mildred noticed a smile on his face as he poured the punch into two cups. She smiled, hoping she was responsible for his smile.

He handed her a cup of punch, which she took and sipped immediately, but shook her head and made a big frown from the sting of the Vodka." She elbowed Antonio and said softly. "You're not afraid your folks might come in and sample this punch?"

He smiled and shook his head. "They never do that. They're both in bed down the hall. Trust me when I say, loud music, loud chatter or commotion would ever tear them from their beds."

Mildred nodded with a big smile on her face. "Wow, your folks are not that strict. They're just the opposite of my parents, who would definitely sample the punch and make sure the music was turned down low enough that they couldn't hear it in their room."

"What can I tell you? Maybe your folks care more deeply for you."

Mildred was surprised by Antonio statement. "Why would you say something like that, Antonio? I'm sure your parents do too."

"Well, sometimes I wonder."

"What is that supposed to mean?" she asked.

"Mildred, I never told you this, but I'm adopted."

Mildred was surprised to hear. "You are? I didn't know that. Not that it's something I needed to know. So, why didn't you tell me?"

"No reason, I guess. But on the other hand, being adopted sometimes I have crazy thoughts that I shouldn't," he admitted.

"What kind of crazy thoughts are you talking about?" Mildred wondered.

"Crazy thoughts like wondering if my adopted parents love me as much as they love my sister, who's not adopted."

"I'm sure your folks love the both of you the same," Mildred caringly encouraged him. "Besides, you shouldn't entertain thoughts like that until your parents have actually shown a difference between you and Terri," Mildred caringly stated. "So, have they ever shown a different that you can recall noticing?"

He stared at Mildred for a long while and shook his head. "No, I have to be truthfully; and as hard as I try to think of a time that they may have shown a different toward me, I cannot think of a single time. I have never noticed a difference in their treatment of us."

Mildred smiled. "Okay. There's your answer. So, please take my advice on this. Please end those wondering thoughts about whether your parents love you more or less because you're adopted. Because, if your parents do not treat you badly or make you feel unloved, you should never think such thoughts like that about them," Mildred told her. "It's really dishonoring them to think those thoughts when they have only shown you love," Mildred passionately stated with conviction.

He nodded and smiled. "You're right and I don't like having these thoughts from time to time. But I don't think I'm dishonoring them by having the thoughts. Being adopted, I suppose maybe every adopted child have the very same thoughts I'm having from time to time, once in a while." He waved his hand. "But I heard what you said, and I know you're right. Therefore, moving forward whenever you hear me talking that way, don't take me seriously or pay me any attention. I'm probably talking crazy because this red punch has gone to my head."

"I'm sure the red punch has gone to your head. Because not you too."

Antonio stared at Mildred with curious eyes. "What do you mean by that statement, not you too?" he asked.

"When you said that about your folks it just reminded me of Raymond. He has some strong issues at home with his parents."

"What do you mean he has some strong issues with his parents?"

"I don't know what's going on with him at home. I just know it's so awful that he had to move out and he's staying with a relative," Mildred explained.

Antonio laughed. "If you're still seeing him, you need to drop that loser like a hot potato. There's rumors around school that he's a lush and his father is a lush," Antonio blurted out with no compassion.

Mildred didn't like that Antonio had bad mouthed Raymond. She felt deep compassion and sorrow for Raymond because of the misery he seemed to be experiencing at home. And as much as she wanted to speak up for Raymond, she couldn't defend him because she knew Antonio had not lied in calling Raymond a lush. Although the word "lush" was an unkind word, she clearly knew Raymond was a heavy drinker, and she also knew Raymond had complained about his father being a big drinker. He had also made reference to his mother not standing up to his father in protection of him. However, Mildred quickly shook those thoughts from her mind as she wondered would Antonio spend the rest of the party keeping her company instead of mingling with other friends, especially Catherine Franklin.

He turned the punch cup up to his mouth and took the last swallow of punch. Then he looked at Mildred and grabbed her hand and squeezed it. "Do you need a ride home? Did you drive or come in a taxi?"

"I'm here in my car," she said, smiling."

"Mostly everyone else came in a taxi; and I do know why," he said, smiling. "They knew they would be hitting the punch bowl. Then there's those like you who drove, who took one sip of punch and couldn't stomach another drop," he teased.

Mildred laughed at his comment as she thought to herself how much she didn't want to leave his house while Catherine Franklin was still in attendance. But she didn't want to get home too late and end up feeling too drained to get up for school. She glanced at her watch. "I think I should get home. It's almost eleven and as much as I would love to stay with you a little longer," she paused as she covered her mouth and yawned. "I must admit I'm getting quite tired."

She grabbed her jacket from the back of a folding chair and threw it on. Then Antonio walked her outside where her car was parked in the driveway. She got inside and started the engine as he stood at her driver's door with his arms folded on her lowered window.

"I'll see you in class tomorrow and if I live to be hundred years old, I'll never forget what it felt like having you in my bed next to me tonight," Antonio said in a sensual whisper.

Unfortunately, just as he softly spoke those words, Raymond had just stepped up to Mildred's car on the opposite side. He was close enough that he had heard Antonio's words. And those words were like a hard punch in the stomach that cut deep into his soul. He immediately turned his back, so they wouldn't see him standing there. But just as Antonio walked away from the car and headed across the porch to step inside, Mildred glanced to her right and spotted Raymond standing there in the dark looking toward her car. He had a broken, disappointed look in his eyes. Her heart sunk deep inside of her at the thought that he had apparently overheard Antonio whisper to her and most likely knew she and Antonio had just had sex in his room.

During her short ride home, she kept thinking about the disappointment she saw in Raymond's eyes. She was deeply sorry that he was hurting over what he overheard. Yet, she felt on top of the world, knowing Antonio loved her. He had confessed his love to her and that meant more to her than anything else in the world.

Chapter Twenty-Seven

Mildred blinked her eyes, as she tore away from her daydream. She glanced at her watch and glanced about the lounge area where she was seated. She noticed only fifteen minutes had gone by since Julian left, and she noticed the 83-year-old high class dressed little lady was still seated at the opposite end of the lounge sofa, engrossed in a magazine. Finding all well with Julian still at his appointment, Mildred pleasingly laid her head back to indulge in the past about the man she loved and lost.

Two weeks later, after Mildred and Antonio's time together at his house party, Mildred sat in her history class trying to concentrate on her upcoming history exam as a disturbing anxious feeling consumed her. A couple weeks after the party she and Antonio had gotten off to a smooth start. Like clockwork she could expect calls from him every evening before bedtime. He also pursued her at school and spent time with her during the lunch hour and their study period. She had two solid weeks of pure bliss dating Antonio. But on Easter Sunday, April 14, 1974, Mildred waited at home after church for Antonio, but he never showed up at her house. Antonio cooled his contact and communication with her starting on that Sunday. Then mid-week at school, rumors were floating heavily at the high school that he had stop talking to Mildred and was now dating Catherine Franklin. Mildred overheard some students discussing how he had joined Catherine and her family for Easter dinner. Therefore, the moment school let out, Mildred rushed out of her history class before anyone else had a chance to leave their desk. She tore out of the classroom and hurried down the hallway directly to Antonio's locker. She could see him standing at his locker from a distance and the sight of him made her heart beat fast with anxiety as she approached him. She smiled and tried to appear at ease.

His back was to her, but he glanced around when he heard her footsteps approach. "Hi beautiful," he said friendly as he looked at her with a warm stare longer than she expected. It was a loving look that didn't fit the way he had recently ignored her.

"Antonio are you mad at me?" she asked.

He shook his head. "Why would I be mad at you?" He closed his locker and laid his back against it as he lovingly looked her in the eyes. "I have no reason to be mad at you, Mildred. Besides, you're the last person I would ever be mad at." He held up both arms. "Why in the world would you think that?"

"I guess I'm just confused," she admitted.

"What are you confused about?"

"I'm confused about us. I thought we were fine, but lately I'm not sure. You seem preoccupied around me lately," she softly mumbled, holding her hands looking down.

He reached out and lifted her face and looked at her with serious eyes. "I'm not preoccupied."

"Maybe not, but something is the matter. You just seem distant and distracted whenever I'm around you lately."

"Well, if you remember nothing else, remember that you are the angel of my heart," Antonio seriously said to her.

"Why do I have to remember anything? Are you leaving town or something?" Mildred asked, not feeling assured by his words. "Plus, I think I should tell you that I heard you spent Easter at Catherine Franklin's house. Is that true? I waited and waited for you on Sunday, but you never showed up and you didn't call. Did you forget you promised to take me to see, *The Exorcist*? Everyone in class has gone to see it but us."

"I know you want to see that movie. But it sounds too weird for me."

"It's fine if you're not interested in seeing, *The Exorcist*. We could have gone to see *The Sting*, starring Robert Redford and Paul Newman. You said you wanted to see it," Mildred softly chastised him for standing her up. "But I'm sure you didn't stand me up because you didn't want to see, *The Exorcist*."

He looked seriously in her eyes and nodded. "You're right. It's not about the movie. I have been distant since Easter Sunday," he solemnly admitted. "Let's go out to the parking lot.

When they made it to the school parking lot, Antonio stood against his car with his arms folded. From the sad look in his eyes, Mildred started shaking with nerves. She sensed he was about to tell her something that wouldn't make her happy. She stood there with one textbook under her arm and her hands squeezed together as she looked at him, anxiously awaiting his explanation. Sharp heartbreak pains dashed through her stomach.

"Antonio, tell me what you asked me out here for," she mumbled sadly.

"I'm getting to that," he said, looking at her with warm eyes trying to think of a caring way to tell her what he knew he had to tell her.

"I guess you're trying to think of a way to explain your distant behavior toward me for the past week?" she softly mumbled.

He nodded and placed both hands in the pockets of his short black thin leather jacket. "There's no good way to tell you this. But I promised myself that I would always be on the level with you. You deserve nothing but honestly from me," he humbly said, looking in her eyes as if he wanted to tell her he loved her.

"I'm glad you want to be honest. But what's the big mystery? Was that rumor right and you actually had dinner at Catherine's house. If you did, I'm not happy about it, but I can forgive you and we can move on from that," Mildred quickly assured him.

"That's proves to me that you are too good for me," he told her.

"Antonio, why would you say something like I'm too good for you? Are you breaking up with me?" Mildred jaw dropped. "Is that why you asked me to the parking lot, so you could end things between us?"

He folded his lips and took a deep breath as if his heart was being ripped apart to say what he had to say to Mildred. He looked at her and nodded. "Mildred, you are too beautiful for words and what I'm about to say is not personal. But I have to be straight with you at this point." He looked over his shoulder and glanced about the parking lot as other students were rushing out of the building, heading toward their cars.

Mildred visibly shook as he spoke. "How can I take what you say any other way but personal. You're not making any sense to me."

"I may not be making any sense to you. But in my heart, I know this is what I have to do," he strongly stated.

"Not seeing me anymore and breaking up with me is something you have to do?" Mildred raised both hands. "That really doesn't make any sense to me. You don't have to do anything. If you want to see me, you can. If you stop seeing me it's because you want to and not because you have to," Mildred snapped. "So, stop making it sound as if you have no other choice but to give me this bad news."

"Mildred, please make no mistake, doing this is hard as hell on me," he said as water formed in the corner of his eyes. "What I allowed to happen between us was a mistake," he said and looked down toward the pavement.

Mildred grabbed her face with bath hands as she stood there before him with her mouth open. Then she took the back of both hands and wiped the tears that quickly rolled down her face. "Antonio Armani, please look at me and tell me what you just said."

He looked solemnly straight at her, holding out both arms. "Mildred, my heart is broken as well. I can't tell you how sorry I am."

"I'm sorry too because I was a big fool to believe you loved me!"

"Believe it or not, Mildred Latham. But I do love you."

"Okay, you love me so much until you don't want to be with me!"

"It won't work. I can't be with you; and as I said, being intimate the way we were was a big mistake," he gently stressed. "I never should have approach you in that way since I knew this day would come. I just couldn't help myself in your incredible presence."

"You knew you would stop talking to me when you were saying all that stuff to me?" Mildred snapped, too choked up with heartbreak to get her words out. "I guess you're the player everyone says you are!"

He shook his head with sad eyes. "It's not about that. Just believe me, this is for your own good."

"I'm sorry, but you'll never convince me that breaking up with you is for my own good," she said with conviction. "And you'll never convince me that being together with you were a mistake."

"I wish I could convince you. Because it was a mistake."

"If it was a mistake, who mistake was it, yours or mine?"

"Mildred, it was my mistake. I knew better because when I first started pursuing you I knew what I was really after," he gently admitted.

"I guess you're talking about to get me in bed," she sadly said. "Is that what you were really after?"

His eyes were sad. "Not even close." He shook his head. "I didn't think of you in that way." He stared in space for a moment before he sadly looked at Mildred. "Just forget me. Things have not worked out for us!"

"Things were working out. But you stop calling me and stop talking to me at school. I thought you were mad at me or something," she cried. "But now you're saying things didn't work out. But why are you saying that? Things can't work out on their own! It takes two people to make a relationship work out. You stop trying."

He sadly nodded. "You're right. I did stop trying and now I'm trying to be on the level with you about why I stop trying. I know you think I'm the biggest jerk ever. Nevertheless, this conversation we're having couldn't be avoided. Soon or later, it had to happen."

"Maybe it couldn't be avoided. But I don't plan to stand here and keep listening to your excuses for thinking our being together was a big mistake!" Mildred turned her back to Antonio and started walking toward her car.

"Mildred wait up. I'm not finished explaining myself," he sadly mumbled.

She glanced over her shoulder as she kept walking. "You may not be finished. But I'm finished! I don't want to have a conversation where you're looking me in my eyes telling me what we feel for each other is a mistake."

"Mildred, you are putting words in my mouth. I didn't tell you what we feel for each other is a mistake. I said being intimate together was a mistake."

"What's the difference? You're saying the two of us together is a mistake." She stopped at her car and stood next to the driver's door. "Therefore, I'm going home. You have made yourself crystal clear and there's nothing else left to say?"

Antonio wanted to tell Mildred he loved her but forced himself to be strong willed to break off with her. Catherine had agreed to date him, and he had decided that he would sacrifice love and everything to be with Catherine since he dreamed of one day being in control of Catherine's inheritance. After a moment of looking at Antonio and he wasn't saying anything, Mildred pulled her car door open. But Antonio rushed over to her car.

"Don't leave until you hear me out. This is very important," he urged her.

She closed the car door and shook her head with tears in her eyes. "It's not important to me to hear you break up with me," she tearfully told him. "It's stunning and doesn't make any sense because your eyes don't tell me you think we're a mistake. Your eyes make me think you love me. Your actions and words are saying something else."

"In that case, you should go by my actions and listen to my words." He held up one finger. "Now, I need to tell you it's best if you don't call anymore."

"Antonio, you'll telling me not to call you anymore." Mildred grabbed her mouth with both hands. She was in shock of his request. "Don't you think you're going a bit extreme with that request? We see each other at school and we're still friends."

He shook his head. In his mind he had promised Catherine that he would break off with Mildred and he and Mildred wouldn't be associating with each other at school anymore. Plus, he promised Catherine that Mildred wouldn't call him at home. "You heard me, Mildred. It's best if you don't call me anymore. I want this to be a clean break," he seriously insisted.

Mildred was stunned as she uncovered her mouth and grabbed her stomach in agonizing pain. She hadn't experienced anything so hurtful in all her life. The boy she loved was telling her he didn't want to be with her and she couldn't even call him anymore.

"Antonio, Raymond was right about you. He said you were heartless!"

"Think whatever you like, but there's nothing left for us but to cut ties!"

"I hear you talking but you don't even sound like the same Antonio that I dated for two weeks. What happened to you?" Mildred sadly cried.

Antonio was deeply saddened by Mildred's pain. He thought of telling her the truth. Then he had a flash of what Catherine told him that she doesn't believe he's done with Mildred, since it's all over the school how he's into Mildred. Catherine warned him that she would break off with him if she found out he was seeing Mildred again.

"So, can you answer my question?" Mildred asked.

"What question, Mildred?"

"I asked you what happened to you between now and two weeks ago?"

"Nothing happened to me. I'm the same. I just need you to listen to me and do as I'm asking you, Mildred. No good can come from you holding on to a dying thing. In my mind's eye. I see absolutely no hope for us," he stressed seriously. "Besides, it doesn't help when you're spreading news all over school that we're together."

"What's the big deal? So, what if I told some friends," Mildred admitted.

"I don't want to send mix signals that you and I are together!"

"Why not?"

"Because we're not together, Mildred."

"Is that for your benefit or Catherine Franklin's," Mildred snapped.

"It's not for anyone's benefit. Besides, I thought I made myself quite clear." He raised both arms to the sky and shook his head. "I just don't want these nosy students getting the wrong idea about us when I know what we shared has ended." He pointed to her and then himself. "So, before you take off. Have I made myself clear?"

"Yes, Antonio. You have made yourself crystal clear. I get it. You are no longer interested in me and you probably never were." Mildred stepped closer to him and pointed her finger in his face. "I'm so disappointed and angry at you until I could scream. Because what I remember is how you made yourself crystal clear two weeks ago when you told me all those wonderful things that I wanted to hear. I guess that was for your benefit, to talk me out of my clothes and into your bed! On not one, but two occasions!"

"Look, Mildred," he said calmly. "I know all the things I said and believe it or not. I meant every single word I said to you."

"I'm supposed to believe you meant all those wonderful things you said, while you are standing here kicking me in the teeth right now? You're telling me we were a mistake and you don't even want me to call your house anymore." She wiped a tear. "But yet, you want me to believe you care for me in the way you told me at your party."

He nodded with love pouring from his eyes. "I did mean it and I still feel the same about you, Mildred." He touched his chest with one finger. "The way I feel about you will never change."

"Antonio, I wasn't born last night. I'm not buying your bologna. I'm supposed to believe you love me, but you just don't want to be with me!" Mildred angrily shouted.

"Look, Mildred. I can't tell you not to leave this parking lot upset because I know you are upset and deeply disappointed. But I honestly thought about the two of us being together in the way that you want. I actually gave it some serious thought that maybe we could develop a lasting relationship," he said sincerely, looking in her eyes. "And if you think about it, we worked out for a while. But the change you noticed took place after Easter," he told her.

Mildred eyes widened as it dawned on her. "Yes! Right after you had dinner at Catherine's house?"

He nodded. "Yes, I did have Easter dinner at Catherine's house and she and I talked and came to an understanding," he painstakingly explained.

"What kind of an understanding?" Mildred curiously inquired.

Antonio looked at her with sad eyes for a moment before he spoke. "Catherine and I decided to date each other exclusively; and she made it clear that she didn't want to see me around school talking to you," he sadly explained. "I intend to honor her wishes."

Mildred was looking down toward the parking lot pavement, so Antonio couldn't see the deep hurt in her eyes as she tried to collect herself. After a moment, she looked at him and held her head up high. "So, in other words, you just used me?" She said sadly with a broken voice and a broken spirit. "I thought you had some feelings for me and cared for me. You promised to always love me, but I guess that was a lie," Mildred placed her purse on the hood of the car and searched in it for a facial tissue. She pulled out a facial tissue and wiped her tears that wouldn't stop rolling down her face.

Standing there looking at Antonio as a cool April breeze swept across her faces. She was waiting for his reply as she watched him pull the collar of his short black leather jacket up around his neck. The cool breeze was blowing harder and getting colder and was making them both impatient as they stood there looking at each other.

"Mildred, what can I say? I feel like the biggest jackass that ever lived, but I'm being straight up with you." He pulled a tube of lip balm from his jacket pocket, pulled off the cap and rubbed it across his lips. "I think you know as well as I do," he said, putting the cap back on the lip balm, placing it back in his coat pocket. "That when it comes to a relationship there's no guarantee. It works out or it doesn't work out. In our case, it didn't work out," he caringly explained, glancing across the parking at Catherine's friend Veronica as she entered her car and drove off the parking lot without noticing him talking to Mildred.

He kept his eyes on Veronica's car until she was completely out of view. He felt standing there talking to Mildred was a close call and he definitely didn't want any information getting back to Catherine about him spending time in Mildred's presence. Therefore, after Veronica drove out of the parking lot, Antonio seemed more anxious, glancing back and forth at his watch.

"I see how you eyed Veronica Parker. Are you worried she'll run back and tell Catherine she saw you talking to me?"

He shook his head. "No, I'm not worried about Veronica saying anything to Catherine. I doubt very seriously if she even saw us. She didn't even look in our direction," Antonio said assured. "But back to our discussion. I feel breaking up is the best for both of us."

"So, you know what's best for both of us?" Mildred sadly asked.

"In this case I do. I know I'm not the best for you. My God, Mildred. You're beyond beautiful and can do a thousand times better than me!" he held up both arms. "We're about to graduate from high school and make our mark on the world. I have nothing to offer you. My folks are just getting by and probably won't be able to send me or Terrie to college," he seriously shared. "I'm not doing this because I want you out of my life. I'm doing this because you need to be out of my life. You're so smart and have often talked about being a teacher; and I'm sure you'll be a great teacher one day." He reached out and touched the side of her face." I know you can't see it right now and you're mad as hell with me. But seriously, Mildred. You need to be with someone who has something to offer you."

Mildred wasn't moved by his words. She felt he was just giving her the brush off. "I guess you mean like Catherine Franklin has something to offer you, her family wealth?" she angrily snapped.

Antonio didn't comment as he just stared at her with sad eyes.

"I guess you're telling me all of this to get me out of your hair, so you can be with that rich girl you have wanted to be with all along," Mildred sadly said, as she wiped her falling tears with her fingers.

He shook his head, grabbed his face with both hands and stared up at the sky for a moment. He looked at Mildred with water in the corner of his eyes. "I need to leave now. Besides, we can talk about this for another hour and you'll still believe what you want to believe. You feel I betrayed you and used you. You also feel I have no feelings for you; and there's nothing I can do to make you believe otherwise."

"I guess not, when you're standing here telling me to get lost because you want to date someone else!" she sadly uttered. "Why can't you just admit the truth and be done with it. Instead of standing here trying to make me think you're breaking up with me for my own good. If the truth be told, it's for your own good. Just like Raymond told me, which I didn't believe at the time. You are only interested in rich girls."

"If that's how you feel, I'm sure I can't change your mind. So, I guess this is where we say good-bye." He held up both hands, backing away from her.

His words of good-bye sounded so final until they made Mildred tremble with nerves and too choked up to speak for a moment. He stood there and watched since it appeared hard for her to catch her breath as she bent over holding her stomach with both hands.

"Mildred are you okay?" He asked with concern.

She caught her breath and stood up straight. "Of course, I'm okay. But why should you care? I mean nothing to you. After I thought you cared so much for me. How could I have been so wrong? You used me and now you want to stroll into greener pastures with your rich girlfriend," Mildred grabbed her face and cried.

"Don't cry, please. You have nothing to cry about. Believe me, I'm not worth your tears." He squeezed both hands together. "I wish things could be different, but they can't. You deserve my honesty and nothing less. That's why I'm standing here and pouring my heart out to you being on the level. I just can't see you anymore."

"It's not that you can't see me anymore. You just don't want to see me anymore." Mildred opened her car door and hopped inside.

"Okay, Mildred. The hard-cold truth is. I can't see you anymore because I don't want to risk messing things up with Catherine!" He looked Mildred in the face. "As I mentioned, Catherine has made it quite clear to me that she will not tolerate me spending anytime in your presence. She feels like that because she knows there's something in here for you," he lovingly said as he touched the middle of his chest with one finger.

"Don't give me that lie!" Mildred cried. "There's nothing in your heart for me but a bunch of lies."

Antonio swallowed hard and kept his composure. "Okay, Mildred. Believe what you want to believe. But do you at least get what I said about Catherine? I'm sure you should be able to see that I'm trying to be candid and as forthright as I can with you."

Mildred slammed her car door but rolled down the window. She looked at Antonio with teary eyes and nodded. "Of course, I get it all right."

He nodded. "I'm glad you do. It's nothing personal. I just don't want to mess up what I have with Catherine?"

Mildred nodded. "I understand exactly what you're saying to me. You don't want to mess up what you have with Catherine Franklin, the way I messed up what I had with Raymond! Does that size up what you're trying to say?" Mildred sadly mumbled, shaking her head as she looked him in the eyes. "Antonio, where were all this honesty and concern for me when you were using me and sweet talking me into your bed? If you had been on the level with me at that time, you could have spared me all this heartbreak of being kicked in the teeth by you! Besides, Raymond was my boyfriend and I stopped seeing him because I thought you and I were together."

"I'm sorry, Mildred, that things didn't work out for us. But either way. You need to stay away from Raymond Ross. That boy is worst for you than I am. He's an accident waiting to happen if you ask me or any other student at school," he warned her. "You're too good for Raymond Ross."

"You have made your choice, Antonio. You have no right to voice in on who I see or don't see. Besides, there's nothing wrong with Raymond."

"Except all the things that are not right about the guy," Antonio firmly urgently stressed.

"Well, Antonio. Raymond thinks the same about you. He thinks you're the worst boy in the world just like you think he's the worst. So, I guess that makes you two pretty much even in each other's eyes. But as far as I can see. There's a big difference in you two."

"What's that?" Antonio curiously asked.

"Raymond loves me, and he has never used me or tried to get me in his bed. Plus, not in a million years would he ever dump me for some rich girl like Catherine Franklin," she sadly said, quickly rolling up her car window, not giving him a chance to reply.

Mildred started up her engine and drove away leaving Antonio in the school parking lot walking toward his car. She drove slowly to be careful on the road since she couldn't see that clearly between driving with one hand and wiping her tears with the other one. She had talked in the school parking lot for a long time with Antonio. Therefore, when she pulled into the driveway she noticed her mother and father's car were both in the driveway which meant they were both home from work. She killed the engine and sat in the car wiping her tears with the back of her hands. She was so crushed over her breakup with Antonio. It was like a nightmare that she couldn't awaken from. In her reflections over the past two weeks, she and Antonio were so happy spending time with each other. It just didn't make sense that he had broken off with her. He was the only boy she really wanted to be with and she didn't know how she would move on without him in her life. But he had made it clear to her that he wanted to be with Catherine Franklin and not her.

Mildred looked through her purse and pulled out her Cover Girl compact powder, took the sponge and powdered her face and then pulled out her lipstick tube and put some on. She needed to look representable and not like she had been crying just in case she bumped into her mother or father while headed to her room. However, luckily when she unlocked the front door and stepped inside into the Living room, the house was quiet. She slipped out of her jacket and pulled open the coat closet and hung it up. She glanced about the room and was glad the living room was empty as she headed down the short hallway toward her room. She figured her parents were probably down in the basement since she didn't hear anyone stirring in the kitchen. Plus, if they had been in the kitchen they would have called out and spoken to her as she came through the front door.

Downhearted beyond words, she changed out of her school clothes and threw on a pair of blue jeans and a cedar green pull over top and as she stood in the mirror brushing her hair, thoughts of Antonio flooded her mind. All the good times they shared would not leave her mind. She was so heartbroken until she knew she would never get over losing Antonio. She placed the brush on the vanity tray and noticed the school day picture that Raymond had given her. It was sitting at the left end of her dresser. She stepped toward the picture and picked it up. Then she took a seat on her bed while still looking at Raymond's picture. She thought of how she had broken things off and stop going out with Raymond, so she could date Antonio. She fell over on the bed looking up at the ceiling with Raymond's picture held tightly against her chest. She felt sorry for hurting Raymond, but she knew she only liked Raymond, but she deeply loved Antonio.

She was still lying back on her bed thinking of how she had hurt Raymond and how Antonio had hurt her when she was startled out of her daydreaming from the sound of her mother's voice calling from the kitchen. "Mildred dinner is ready, dear."

She hopped off the bed and stepped over to her dresser to look at herself. She wanted to be sure there were no traces of tears on her face. But she still felt uneasy since her parents knew she had broken up with Raymond and they were still under the impression that she and Antonio were still dating. She hoped they didn't ask any questions about how she and Antonio were getting along.

Fortunate for Mildred, when she took her seat at the dinner table, her folks jumped right into a discussion about making their small vegetable garden to the left of the house into another flower garden to match the flower garden to the right of the house. Her parents were excited since the Latham household had been written up in the local newspaper three years in a row in regard to the beautiful outstanding flowers they grew.

"I don't think we'll miss having that section to grow vegetables. Besides, we only use it to grow tomatoes and onions," Margaret Latham said and glanced toward Mildred. "What do you think, dear? Do you think we'll miss the fresh tomatoes and onions?"

Mildred solemnly mumbled, poking in her salad, but not eating. "Mom are you talking to me?"

Margaret nodded. "Yes, I'm talking to you. Eric and I have decided to turn that section of the yard where we used to grow veggies into another flower garden. We were just wondering your thoughts? We know how much you love the fresh tomatoes."

Mildred shook her head and lifted her glass of ice water to her mouth and took a sip. She lowered the glass back to the table and nodded. "Yes, I love the fresh tomatoes, but I'll love another flower garden even more."

"That's good to know that we're all onboard with the new flower garden," Margaret said, noticing Mildred wasn't eating much. "I guess you're not that hungry. Is Antonio coming over to study with you this evening?"

Mildred shook her head as she became instantly tensed up from her mother's question. She discreetly took a deep breath, looking toward her mother. "I'm not sure," she said casually as she pushed her salad aside, lifted her soup spoon and started eating her beef stew as if she was hungry. Her heart was beating fast with nerves as she hoped her mother wouldn't ask another question about Antonio.

They managed to finish dinner without Mildred's parents asking her any more questions. And right after dinner her parents left the kitchen while Mildred stayed seated in her chair full of heartbreak. She pushed her soup bowl aside and put both elbows on the table holding up her face. She knew it would take time to get over Antonio and, in the meantime, she had to suffer through each minute feeling more like an eternity. Sitting there alone at the kitchen table thinking about Antonio she could feel water building in the corner of her eyes. She didn't want her parents to figure out that she was heartbroken. She needed to get busy and stay busy to keep Antonio off of her mind. Therefore, she quickly hopped out of her chair and started gathering the dirty dishes from the table and placed them in the sink. She wiped off the kitchen table and stove and also wiped the outside and inside of the refrigerator and then stood at the sink and washed the dinner dishes.

It was around seven when Mildred finished cleaning the kitchen. She stepped out of the kitchen, walked through the living room, headed straight to her room. Her folks were sitting in the living room watching a movie. They didn't say anything to her as they were engrossed into the movie.

Once in her room, Mildred closed the door and dropped down on her bed and grabbed her face. She was so sad and lonely for Antonio. She uncovered her face and glanced over at the phone on her bedside table. It had become routine that every evening around seven she could expect a call from Antonio. She stared at the phone hoping it would ring. Then a sharp pain ripped through her stomach as it dawned on her, as if for the first time, that he wouldn't be calling her anymore. She fell over on her back staring up at the ceiling with a river of tears falling from her eyes. She was so heartbroken it made her feel nauseated in the pit of her stomach that made her rushed out of her room to the bathroom.

An hour later into the evening, while her parents were still in the living room watching a movie, Mildred was still tucked away in her room sitting in the big rocker in the corner, reading her history book and taking notes for her history class. She was fully concentrated on her studies when the phone rang. She glanced up at the phone and put her eyes right back into her text book. She figured it wasn't ringing for her and was startled when shortly after it rung, her mother called her name, then knocked on her bedroom door.

"Mildred, dear. The phone is for you."

"It's for me?" Mildred said to herself as she hopped out of the rocker stepped over to her bedroom door and quickly opened it. She stuck her head out of the door and looked down the hall in time to see her mother headed back toward the living room. "Mom, did I hear you correctly? Is the phone for me?" Mildred asked, with surprise in her voice.

Margaret Latham glanced over her shoulder. "Yes, dear. It's for you. I don't think it's your new friend, Antonio. It sounded like Raymond Ross."

Mildred was stunned to hear that Raymond could possibly be waiting on the line for her. She had hurt him deeply and wondered why he would call her. "Mom are you sure it's Raymond. I think he's pretty mad at me."

"Well, it sounded like Raymond. Please, get the phone. Whoever it is, you shouldn't keep them waiting on the line," Margaret insisted as she headed back to living room.

Mildred closed her bedroom door and rushed over to her bedside table and grabbed the receiver without lifting it to her ear. Her heart was beating fast with nerves as she held the receiver against her chest for a few seconds before she lifted the receiver to her ear. Although, her mother was quite sure the caller wasn't Antonio. Mildred silently prayed it was Antonio as she placed the receiver against her ear.

"Hello," Mildred softly said, not letting on how sad she really was.

"Hi, Mildred. What are you doing?" Raymond asked kindly.

"I'm not doing anything right now. It's a dull Wednesday night for me. I just finished up studying for my history test for tomorrow," she politely said.

"I know I haven't called in a while. But you're dating Antonio Armani and I didn't want to bother you too much. But decided to give you a call tonight regardless," he said and paused for a moment. "If nothing else, I was hoping we're still friends," he humbly said to her.

"Absolutely, Raymond. We'll always be friends."

"I'm glad you said that. I was hoping to drop by for a visit. I miss talking the way we used to talk to each other," he laughed friendly over the phone.

But after a moment of silence and she didn't reply, he quickly said, "I understand if it's not okay for me to drop by."

"Yes, it will be okay. You can come over for a while," Mildred told him.

Chapter Twenty-Eight

Julian hurried inside the restaurant and spotted Mildred sitting in the lounge section where he had left her thirty minutes earlier. The little old lady who were sitting on the opposite end of the lounge sofa with Mildred had just left the restaurant five minutes before Julian arrived. He glanced at his watch as he walked toward the lounge section. He wasn't pleased that he had left her alone for all that time. But when he walked over to the lounge section where she was seated, he noticed that she appeared to have fallen asleep with her head tilted to the side with her eyes closed. He softly tapped her on the shoulder and she quickly opened her eyes and smiled at him.

"I wasn't asleep. I was just daydreaming about the past," Mildred said.

"I apologize for taking so long and leaving you here," Julian caringly said.

"No apology needed. I wanted to stay. Remember?" she reminded him.

"Yes, I remember," he said as he took a seat on the lounge sofa beside her, leaned in and kissed the side of her face as he passed her a spring assortment bouquet of flowers.

"Someone was selling these on the street. I couldn't resist buying you a bunch," he said cheerfully, smiling at her.

"Julian, you are so thoughtful and sweet. You're a good man and any woman would be blessed to have you in her life," she softly stated.

"Well, thank you. I'm certainly glad that woman is you," he quickly replied. "I see you have finished your wine. Would you like another or you prefer to move to a table for the meal we didn't have?" he eagerly asked her.

Mildred didn't comment. She was feeling awkward and uneasy because she knew they needed to have an important conversation that would put a damper on his good mood.

Julian touched the side of her face. "You seem a little down," I apologize again for making you wait here in this restaurant alone for nearly thirty minutes. I didn't expect it to take as long as it did. I just had to drop off some documents to a possible million-dollar buyer." He smiled. "But this couple never stops talking. Anyway, I rushed back just as soon as I could."

Mildred shook her head. "I said there's no need for you to apologize for how long it took you to get back. It's not your fault that I waited here. I insisted on staying here and waiting for you. I'm not bothered by the time you stayed away."

"That's good. But you're clearly bothered by something," he said in a concerned voice. "Did something take place while I was out on my appointment?"

Mildred nodded. "Yes, something took place."

He grabbed her hands with both hands with great concern. "What happened?" He glanced about the restaurant, wondering what could have happened to upset her in an Olive Garden restaurant.

She gently pulled her hands from his in a non-offensive way. "Julian, it's not what you think. Nothing actually happened here in this restaurant. I was physically fine while you were away. What happened, occurred in my head."

His eyes widened with confusion as he slightly smiled. "I'm afraid you have me at a lost. I'm not really following you, Mildred."

"I can understand that you would be at a lost because I'm at a lost in how to approach what I need to say to you."

"I'm really curious now," he said feeling slightly alarmed. "I leave you for thirty minutes and I get back and you don't know how to approach something that you need to say to me? Mildred, please tell me what you need to say. You should know by now that you can tell me anything. I'm sure whatever you haven't shared with me, I have probably heard it all, if it has to do with what was printed in the paper. The unfortunate, incredible incident that happened at your home that caused your ex-husband to be imprisoned. I have already made it clear to you that none of that matters."

"Julian, just listen. It actually has to do with the comment that I made when you first arrived back at the restaurant."

"I'm afraid I don't remember what comment you are referring to." He smiled. "Stop being so evasive and just tell me what's going on," he insisted.

"Remember the comment I made about any woman would be blessed to have you in her life," she asked humbly looking in his eyes.

He was silent before he answered. It dawned on him what she was probably getting at. "Any woman except you. Is that what you're trying to tell me?" he said confused.

Mildred nodded. "Yes, Julian. You're correct. No matter how I try to convince myself that I would be better off with you than living in the past thinking of a dead man, it won't stick in my brain. My heart isn't in it," she honestly stated.

Julian stared at her in silence. He was stunned at her declaration which had left him momentarily lost for words.

"You were gone for half an hour and it felt like five minutes since the whole time you were gone, I was daydreaming about the past and my life and time with Antonio. I'm not over Antonio and it's not fair to you to say I am."

Julian held his hands tightly together and glanced down at the floor and then looked in her eyes. "Well, you have stunned me, and I don't know what all this means for us. But I thank you for being on the level, sharing your true feelings. But I have to be straight as well. Your news has ripped the rug from under me," he said seriously. "I consider myself a very good judge of people and can read situations quite well. And I tell you, I was completely under the impression that we had something special." He took a deep breath and paused in her eyes. "I didn't imagine it, and you won't convince me that I was that far off course with you and me."

Mildred looked down and spoke softly. "Julian, I'm deeply sorry and I don't know what else to say. But you were off course about us."

Julian felt his chest tighten with disbelief of the conversation they were having. Mildred's news to end their relationship had highly disappointed and shook him up. He had no inkling that she was considering ending their affair. And just then, a waiter walked over to them and looked at Mildred.

"Can I get you another glass of wine?" he said and then looked at Julian. "And can I get you something, sir?"

Julian held up one finger to the waiter and looked at Mildred. "Would you like to remain here in the lounge section or would you like a table?"

"I think we should get a table," she said softly.

Julian looked at the waiter. "The tab she accumulated, can you please just add it to this bill?" Julian asked.

The waiter nodded. "I sure can. Please follow me."

Mildred grabbed the flower bouquet from the coffee table as Julian grabbed their jackets. Then they followed the short waiter to the rear of the restaurant as he showed them to a cozy out of the way corner table as if he knew they wanted lots of privacy. Mildred placed the flowers across the edge of the small round wooden green table as Julian hung their jackets on the back of the green wooden chairs. But as they took their seats at the little table, the waiter glanced over his shoulder and then hurried over to another waiter that had beckoned for him. The two waiters spoke briefly and then the waiter returned to their table with his pad in hand.

Julian glanced at Mildred. "Would you like the same?"

Mildred nodded. "That will be fine."

Julian looked at the waiter. "You can bring us both a glass of your Sutton Home Red Moscato," Julian said to the waiter.

"Two glasses of Sutton Home Red Moscato coming up," the clean shaven, blond hair waiter said. "Would you like to see a menu?" the waiter asked.

Julian looked at Mildred. "Are we staying for a meal?"

Mildred nodded. "I could eat a little something."

Julian looked at the waiter and nodded. "Yes, please. We'll take a menu."

The waiter nodded and then stepped away from their table. He arrived a few minutes later with a tray holding two glasses of red wine and two menus under his left arm. He placed a glass of Sutton Home Red Moscato in front of them both and then handed them each a menu. "I'll give you a few minutes to decide what you're having, and then I'll return to take your orders," the 25-year-old waiter said, and then stepped away from their table. He returned three minutes later with his pad.

Mildred looked up at him and said. "I'll have the Eggplant Parmigiana."

"Would you like a salad and bread sticks with your order?" he asked her.

Mildred shook her head. "No thanks."

The waiter looked at Julian. "And you sir?"

"I'll have your Shrimp Primavera and I'd like the salad and bread sticks."

"Thank you," the waiter said and walked away from their table.

Julian noticed that Mildred seemed quiet and preoccupied. It ripped at his heart every time he thought about what she had said to him. He looked across the table at her and smiled. "Well, I feel like this is my last supper with you," he said jokingly.

Mildred smiled at him. "You're a good man and I wish things could have worked out differently for us," she said sincerely as she lifted her glass of wine to her mouth and took a sip as she continued to hold the glass in her hand. She took another small sip before she placed the glass back on the table.

He lifted his glass up to his mouth and finished half of his wine before he lowered his glass and placed it back on the table. He shook his head in confusion as he looked across the table at Mildred with humble eyes. "You are so sweet and kind and nice beyond words. I guess I took your kindness for love. But I couldn't have misread you that much." He rubbed the back of his neck for a moment as if to loosen his tension. "In the beginning, you really appeared to genuinely want the relationship," Julian said sincerely. "I leave you at this restaurant and return a short time later to find everything between us has changed.

Mildred looked at him with solemn eyes. "You are right, and I'll admit to what you just said." She placed her hand against her chest. "I definitely wanted the relationship with you and I welcomed it wholeheartedly."

Julian felt blindsided by her announcement. "Okay, what happened that made you want to end things?" he asked confused. "It's almost like your mind changed from the time I left and returned."

"Julian, that's only half right. I knew from the start deep down in my heart that our togetherness would not last. Yet, I was excited about the possibility of exploring a loving relationship with you. I allowed myself to dream a little. Yet, all along I knew it would come crushing down around us," Mildred admitted.

"Mildred, I don't follow you not even a little. The only thing I'm clear about is the fact that you want and intent to end this relationship. I'm totally in the dark to why and would very much appreciate an explanation."

Mildred reached over and patted the yellow, pink and white flowers and then placed her hand on top of Julian's hand. "Thank you again for those beautiful flowers. You really are such a nice guy and I want to be completely clear with you that none of this is your fault. Here is my explanation. When you left the restaurant for your appointment, my thoughts went back in the past. Far into the past to my high school senior year of 1974."

Julian looked at her with gripping anticipation of what she would tell him. He desperately wanted to know why she had decided to break off their relationship that was developing so nicely between them.

"My senior year in high school is the time Antonio and I fell in love with each other. I loved him deeply beyond words or explanation. I can tell you the number one movie and the number one song of 1974. It's glued in my brain, since it's the only time in my life that I was ever totally and completely happy. For two whole weeks my life was pure bliss," Mildred softly admitted.

"So, the information in the papers were true. You and Antonio Armani had actually planned to leave town together?" Julian asked.

Mildred nodded. "I didn't really read any of the material that was printed about us. But everything printed was most likely true."

"Well, it stated that you and Antonio Armani were having an affair and planned to leave town together, but Raymond Ross spoiled your plans when he caught you two off guard in your home," Julian said awkwardly. "That's what I read as well as more graphic material that I won't elaborate on."

"Whatever you read probably didn't sound pretty, but it was most likely accurate. We loved each other. It was just that simple. This was going to be our chance for happiness. We had both lived without happiness all our lives. Those moments with him and believing we would somehow end up together were the happiest times and thoughts that I have ever known," Mildred held up one finger. "I know I have gotten off track. But while you were away from the restaurant, I went into deep thought about my life and time with Antonio. When we fell in love back then I made him a promise that I would love him always. That's why I can't be with you, Julian. I still love Antonio deeply."

Just then, the waiter rolled his serving cart up to their table. He placed the Shrimp Primavera, a salad and bread sticks in front of Julian. Then he placed a dish of Eggplant Parmigiana in front of Mildred. Then he left their table and rolled his cart over to another table a few tables away from where they were seated.

They started to eat their meal and as Julian took both hands and broke a bread stick, he looked across the table at Mildred. "The incident that took place with Antonio and your ex-husband. It all happened not that long ago. I understand how you're still wrapped up in it all. And I can only imagine your grief and pain and the disappointment of losing someone you loved so deeply and expected to spend your life with," Julian said with heartfelt compassion. "I'm assuming unfortunate circumstances didn't allow you two to end up together when you were younger."

Mildred sadly nodded with distant eyes thinking of 1974 when she was blissfully happy with Antonio. But she blinked the thoughts out of her mind to give Julian her attention and answer his question. "I'm sorry, could you please repeat what you just asked me?"

"I just figured unfortunate circumstances didn't allow you and Antonio to end up together when you were younger."

"You're absolutely correct. We had the worst luck in that department. And of course, Antonio blamed himself for the choices I made."

"What do you mean?" Julian asked as he took a bite from his bread stick.

"I mean he felt guilty for how my life turned out with Raymond. He feels I only married Raymond because he didn't ask me," she forked a piece of eggplant into her mouth.

"If he thought that, was he right?" Julian curiously asked as he forked salad into his mouth. He chewed his food and continued. "Were you not in love with Raymond Ross when you married him?"

Mildred looked at him with sincere eyes. "I did love Raymond. I just loved Antonio more in a deeply more special way. But if Raymond hadn't been so unkind to me so often, I think I probably could have been happy with him. But from the moment we said I do, he was always irritated and upset about how I had stop dating him to date Antonio. Every little quarrel we had drove him to drink more and more. Then his drinking became constant until it was a permanent part of his daily routine. It held him back and he couldn't move up in his jobs because of his drinking. He also lost many jobs do to his drinking."

"So, in other words, Antonio Armani felt you married Raymond, ending up in an unhappy marriage, because he didn't ask you to marry him?"

Mildred nodded. "That part is absolutely true. I definitely accepted Raymond's proposal after I read about Antonio's upcoming marriage to Catherine Franklin. But I don't want you to think I didn't also love Raymond when I married him. I did love him."

"But you just told me you loved Antonio more," Julian reminded her.

"I know I told you that and that's true. But I also loved Raymond. He's the father of my children. I'm sure I would have grown to love him deeper and stayed in the marriage if he had showed me and the children one iota of real love and warmth," Mildred solemnly stressed. "It was like he didn't know how to show love or be warm. He made it easy for me to throw in the towel."

"I wouldn't call sticking with the man for over twenty-five years throwing in the towel. Based on my assumptions of what I think you faced at the hands of Raymond Ross, I would call it courageous that you stuck it out as long as you did."

At that moment, Julian phone rang. He pulled it from his jacket pocket and glanced at the call coming through. He held up one finger and stood from the table. "Excuse me, Mildred. I need to take this call. Its business," he said and stepped away from the table and headed out of the restaurant to take his call-in privacy.

Julian's business call lasted only a couple minutes before he headed back into the restaurant toward their table. Mildred could see him heading toward the table and she could see that he didn't have the same cheerful look on his face as he displayed when he first returned from his appointment with the bouquet of flowers for her. He noticed her looking toward him and he smiled, but he felt out of sorts as if the wind had been knocked out of him. The unexpected decision Mildred made to end their relationship came as a complete shock to him. It crushed his former good mood.

"I'm sorry, but I had to take that call," Julian said as he stepped over to the table to take his seat.

"That's fine I understand. You're a real-estate agent and your work is never done," she said. "You could get a call anytime of the day or night."

Julian nodded. "You're right at that," he commented dryly and raised his finger. "Where were we? I think we were discussing why you stayed married to Raymond."

"That is what we were discussing; and I was explaining to you how I would have stayed in the marriage if Raymond hadn't been so filled with bitterness and anger toward me."

"That's ashamed because he lost a good woman," Julian praised her.

"Thank you for saying that. But it is true, I would have stayed in the marriage if Raymond had shown anything that resembled compassion and care," she strongly explained, and then stopped herself and paused for a moment. Then she looked at Julian with serious eyes. "I won't go into any particular details, but Raymond treated me quite appallingly over the course of the years we were together."

Julian felt sad to listen to her tell him she was treated badly by Raymond. He wanted to encourage her as he nodded. "I get that, but now you're free of Raymond. You have a chance to be happy."

Mildred shook her head. "I want to be happy and at one time I believed I could be happy," she said choked up with the pain of what could have been. Then she collected herself and continued. "But my reason for happiness died when Antonio passed away. He wasn't a perfect man and he did some things I'm ashamed of. But he was perfect for me and the only man I have ever felt completely alive and happy with."

"It's a shame that he didn't ask you to marry him when he had a chance instead of wrecking three lives by marrying a woman he wasn't in love with," Julian strongly stressed. "And yes, I know the whole story surrounding why he asked Catherine to marry him," Julian admitted.

Mildred eyes widened with surprise. "You did date Catherine briefly. So, I guess she filled you in on all the details."

Julian nodded. "That's why I'm not with Catherine. She was obsessed with including Antonio Armani in all of our conversations when we were seeing each other. She shared with me how he married her just for her money when they were young. She also shared with me how he abandoned her and walked away from their marriage as soon as he learned she had been left out of her parent's will. But I guess at that point, after Antonio left Catherine, you were too upset with him to get back with him."

"No, Julian. It wasn't like that. The way I felt about Antonio never left my heart. On my wedding day to Raymond, I still loved Antonio as much then as I do now. The love I feel for him will never die!"

"You're making that abundantly clear. But I assume Antonio didn't contact you after he ended his marriage to Catherine?"

"Why do you assume he didn't contact me?" Mildred asked as she lifted her wine glass to her mouth and took a sip.

"I just assumed he didn't contact you. Otherwise, you would have married Antonio instead of Raymond," Julian pushed his half-eaten salad aside and pulled his plate of Shrimp Primavera in front of him and then forked a shrimp into his mouth.

"You are right, Julian. But by the time Antonio left Catherine, I was already married to Raymond. Just the marriage license wouldn't have kept me with Raymond. But when Antonio contacted me on that rainy afternoon in the middle of the day while Raymond was at work, I thought my heart would burst with happiness just to hear his voice. But I was already seven months pregnant with my first child," Mildred sadly recalled. "Now, I realize I should have divorced Raymond and married Antonio when he begged me to at that time. But I was young and unsure and felt being pregnant with Raymond's child glued me to him. Not leaving Raymond to marry Antonio condemned me to a life of unhappiness and pure misery. I never experienced one single happy day being married to Raymond. All my happiness and joy came from within me for the love of my children."

"I get it. You married the wrong guy after the one you loved got away," Julian said, nodding with compassion in his eyes.

"Yes, I absolutely married the wrong guy," Mildred agreed.

Julian lifted his wine glass to his mouth and took a sip and then slowly placed the glass back on the table. "You know, Mildred. You may have married the wrong guy, but all that happened so many years ago."

Mildred nodded with sad eyes. "Yes, it happened many years ago, but it feels like yesterday?"

Julian held up with hands. "I know I said it happened many years ago, but I don't want you to think I'm overlooking how you and Antonio had reconnected and were planning a life together. Nevertheless, that part of your life is over," Julian tried to plead his case.

"I know that part of my life is over." Mildred took one finger and touched her chest. "But inside of me, it doesn't feel over."

"Mildred, I don't mean any disrespect to Mr. Armani and what he meant and still means to you. Yet, you need to accept that Antonio is dead and buried," he said humbly.

Mildred stared at Julian and didn't comment. She was offended and displeased by his statement.

"Mildred, please listen to me when I say, now is your time to love and live." He reached across the table and placed his hand on hers. "I see that unhappy look you're giving me. But I'm trying to open your eyes to the facts."

"To what facts?" she asked.

"The facts that your divorce is almost final from Raymond," Julian stressed seriously. "Don't you agree that this is your time to love and live? Whether you do or not. Please, drop the notion of breaking off what we have. Give me a chance to make you happy. You feel you made a big mistake by not following your heart and giving Antonio a chance when he contacted you all those years ago after he left Catherine. I know you deeply regret your decision. He was your happiness that you didn't give a chance when he asked. Don't make the same mistake twice. I'm asking you to give us a chance. I don't want to lose you and this special connection we have developed between us."

"You'll get over me and find someone that can give you what you need. Besides, we haven't been seeing each other long," Mildred encouraged him.

"I know we haven't been seeing each other that long. But it's something about you that makes me feel alive in your presence," Julian confessed.

"You told me when we met that you had had high hopes for you and Catherine. You shared that you cared a great deal for Catherine at that time. It's probably not too late to call on Catherine again," Mildred encouraged.

Julian took a bite of his food and then took his fork and placed it face down on his dish. He pushed his plate aside and put both elbows on the table holding up his chin as he leaned in toward Mildred. "When I was looking forward to a solid relationship with Catherine, I didn't know you then. Now, that I have met you and spent time with you. You are by far an unforgettable person. I can easily see why Antonio Armani never forgot you."

"Julian, I'm asking you to forget me. I can't make you happy. I'm being on the level because I owe you that much. I have enjoyed myself extremely the times we have shared. But I know I'll love Antonio forever and any love for any other man will be second best. I don't want to live that way again. I know Antonio is not alive, but he's very much alive in my heart. You deserve to be with someone who can let you into her heart where only love for you will live and you won't have to compete with another man," Mildred said.

Julian inhaled, shaking his head. "What a small world we live in."

"Why do you say that?"

"It's quite simple why I say it." He smiled. "I'm crazy as hell about you. But you can't be with me because you're still in love with your first love. Nevermind that he's deceased."

"I still don't get the connection of that and the world being small," Mildred said.

"Well, I wasn't finished. I was also about to say to you how Catherine was in the same boat as you. She was still very much into her first love, who was also Antonio Armani, while she and I were seeing each other," Julian admitted.

"Is that what broke you two apart?"

Julian shook his head. "No, I can't say that it did, not directly. However, indirectly I'm sure that's what it boiled down too," he lifted his wine glass up to his mouth and drained the last sip, shaking his head all while placing the glass on the table. "You see, Catherine stop taking my calls. She didn't give me the respect of an explanation as you are doing right now. She just wouldn't take my calls or answer any of my text messages."

"I'm surprised to hear that. Never figured Catherine Franklin could be purposely rude to someone. I'm sure there has to be a good explanation behind that."

Julian nodded. "Well, she was quite rude. And I'm certain the explanation had to do with her grieving for Mr. Armani."

Mildred nodded. "I'm sure that's it. She did care deeply for Antonio."

Julian was irritated that Mildred was breaking up with him and their whole talk was centered on Antonio Armani. "Listen Mildred. Do you get my point? Catherine and I couldn't make it because of Antonio Armani, and now you're breaking off with me for almost the same reason. She couldn't forget the man and you refuse to forget him!" Julian held up both hands. "Do I have to leave this town to run into a woman not wrapped up into Antonio Armani?"

"Julian, that's not funny."

"I know it's not funny. But you have to admit it's pretty lousy for me. The two women in this town that I wanted to get to know. They are both off limits because of some Casanova that's not even alive."

"Julian, that's not entirely correct. I'm off limits, but Catherine isn't."

"And how would you know that?" Julian asked.

"Well, according to you, she dropped over to see you this morning. I'm sure she didn't just drop by to say hello."

Julian nodded. "You're right. She made it clear that she hoped we could pick up where we had left off, but that's when I told her that you and I were seeing each other."

"If she said that, it's crystal clear she's still interested in you," Mildred paused. "I don't assume to know how you feel about Catherine, but if you care anything for her, the two of you shouldn't have anything standing in your way. Besides, Catherine is your best choice. Including my never-ending love for Antonio, you shouldn't want to get saddled with me to endure all the bad press out there about me," Mildred pointed out.

"I think I can decide what I want to deal with and endure," he said.

"Julian, you see it one way and I see it another. But I'm sure you read in the papers how nearly everyone in this community feels I brought the tragic on myself. Most of the readers who read about how Raymond shot up the house after catching me in the process of about to leave town with Antonio, felt sympathy and compassionate for Raymond. They felt Antonio and I brought that destruction on ourselves. Now Raymond is in prison and many people feel he got a raw deal. They feel his five years, slap on the wrist, prison term should have been overturned due to temporary insanity of what Antonio and I drove him to do. All the public know is what they have read." Mildred lifted her glass to her mouth and took the last sip of wine. She lowered the glass to the table and stared at the empty glass as she collected herself. "They were not in the house with me and Raymond. Therefore, they don't know how terrible Raymond treated me verbally and physically. But even if they knew that, it'd all still be my fault and they would be right," Mildred sadly admitted.

Julian eyes widened as he looked across the table at Mildred. "I don't know where you're going with this trip down a sad memory lane. But I don't like the sound of it. Admitting your ex-husband was in the right to abuse you. Besides, who cares what others may think of you. But why would you assume others would be right to blame you for Raymond's crime against you?"

"I said that because if the public knew of his abuse, I would be blamed for staying with him to put up with that abuse. And I have no excuse to have stayed with Raymond. I could have divorced him after Kenny, Courtney and Trina finished college, but I did not."

Just then the waiter arrived at their table removing their dishes. "Can I get you both another glass of wine?" he asked as he placed all the dirty dishes on the serving cart.

Julian glanced at his watch and then looked at Mildred and she nodded okay. Then he looked at the waiter and nodded. "Yes, we'll take another glass each of the Sutton Home Red Moscato."

After the waiter stepped away from their table, Julian looked across the table at Mildred. "Have you thought of why you stayed with Raymond to endure such abuse?"

"Yes, I have thought of it; and it's just like his mother told me. I stayed because I was too afraid of what Raymond would do to me, and what would happen to him if I left him alone. I was afraid he would drink himself to death. He's my children's father and although, I'm not in love with him I do care about what happens to him."

"I'm sort of lost in this conversation, Mildred. I don't see the point of discussing and rehashing all of these sad memories of your past. Is there a reason why you're sharing all of this with me during this breakup?"

Just then the waiter arrived back at their table and placed fresh glasses of Sutton Home Red Moscato in front of them both and then stepped away from the table.

Julian looked seriously across the table at Mildred as he continued. "If you're sharing these things in an effort that they will make me think twice about wanting to be with you. I can tell you right now that you are wasting your time. I have already crossed that line from care into real feelings for you and couldn't care less about what people think about why your marriage fell apart. All I care about is being with you." He held out both hands. "But I really don't want to pressure you. I realize you are still trying to deal with everything that happened. And although, I'm not a shrink, it would make sense if you feel it's too soon for you to jump right into a relationship with someone else," he said and was silent for a moment before he continued. "I really feel that's what's going on. Because frankly, I don't buy that you'll stick with the thought of never being with another man."

"Julian, you should buy it. Its how I feel."

"I'm sure that's how you feel right now. And I have no other choice but to accept this parting of ways. Nevertheless, I still want you to know that this isn't goodbye for me."

"But Julian, it should be goodbye," Mildred strongly suggested. "You can't put your life on hold in hope that I will one day wake up and no longer feel this hold that Antonio has on me. Besides, you can't will or wish me into feeling something I do not," Mildred firmly uttered as she grabbed her chest with both hands. "I know how deep I love Antonio. Nothing and no one can fade this love I feel for him. All the years after high school didn't fade it. How can you bank on a few weeks or a few months to do what over twenty-five years couldn't do? I'm pleading with you to forget me and turn your thoughts and efforts toward Catherine. She's a good woman and she deserves some happiness."

"You don't have to convince me that Catherine is a good woman. I know she's a good woman and once upon a time I wanted to explore the possibilities of a possible future with her. But that was then, and this is now." He lifted his glass and took a sip of wine. "And now, I want to explore possibilities with you. I know Catherine deserves some happiness. But I'm afraid I'm not the man who can make her happy at this point when the only woman I want to make happy is you, my dear."

"I know you feel that way about me right now, Julian. And I understand how my decision is a blow to you. But in time you'll get over me. And the easiest way to help yourself get over me is for you to try to find a way to reconnect with Catherine. You were just telling me last week that you are struggling to meet your mortgage on your home," Mildred hesitantly mentioned to him.

He looked at her with a curious expression. "What does telling you about struggling with my mortgage payments have to do with Catherine?" Julian lifted an eyebrow.

"It just dawned on me while we were talking that if you and Catherine get together, she would be financially situated to help you keep your home. She could help you with your mortgage payments."

Julian stared with surprised eyes. "I'm not sure if I appreciate what you are suggesting," he calmly commented.

"Julian, I'm not saying get with her for her money. I'm just stating a fact that would be beneficial to you if you and Catherine reconnected and ended up with a future together."

"No disrespect intended but I do think you're confusing me with your deceased friend," Julian calmly commented.

Mildred shook her head. "Julian, how could you think that?"

"I can think it if you think I would ever get together with someone for their networth," Julian firmly stated.

"You misunderstood me. I'm not suggesting that you would get together with Catherine for her money. I'm only saying, if you and Catherine reconnect and start a future together, she'll be able to help you keep the mansion. I'm sure she would love the idea of living next door to Veronica and her nephews," Mildred politely commented.

"Okay, I see your point. But right now, it's moot. I'm so crazy about you until I can't even think of Catherine or any other female for that matter."

"That's understandable. But Julian, this is my life and I'm being one hundred percent on the level with you. You are a good man. And if I wanted to start a life with another man, I think I could be happy with you. But it's not what I want, and I can tell you with one hundred percent certainty that it's something I'll never want for the rest of my life. I had my chance at love two times: once in high school and again this year. But I missed my chances and now Antonio is dead. His death means there will never be another chance for love for me. And I'm okay with that. Antonio and I loved each other so deeply. We talked about our future together and how it would be. I have those memories to hold on to, and that's more than enough for me. Nothing anyone could say or do would ever change my mind. That's why I beg of you to forget me and try to pick up the pieces of where you left off with Catherine. If it seems like I'm trying very hard to push you toward Catherine, you are right. I'm doing it because I care about you and want you to be happy. I feel Catherine could make you happy. Besides, unlike me, Catherine really wants to be in a relationship with you. I refuse to do to another man what I did to Raymond."

"You're a mighty beautiful woman to give up on love," Julian told her.

"I didn't give up on love. My chances died with Antonio and I accept that. Besides, if I can't give my complete heart to someone, it's best I don't get involve in a relationship at all." She sat her wine glass at the edge of the table.

Julian watched how she sat her wine glass at the edge of the table. "You don't want the rest of your wine?" he asked.

She shook her head. "I think I have had enough. Remember, I had a couple glasses while you were on your appointment."

He nodded. "If you don't want it. That's fine," he said frustrated. "I know you have a lot going on in your head. The love of your life was murdered and taken away from you. Then on top of that. I know you feel just awful that you married Raymond knowing you didn't love him as much as you loved the other guy. It all turned out so wrong and brought so much heartache. Raymond ended up being a lousy husband who treated you badly. However, you shouldn't allow what happened with Raymond to dictate your future."

"Raymond wasn't just an awful father to his kids and a lousy husband to me. He was simply bitter toward humanity. He found fault with everyone," Mildred sadly admitted.

"I guess he was quite troubled. Not a good way to live," Julian said.

"No, it wasn't a good way to live, but it's how Raymond lived. I refuse to take the blame for his hatred of humanity."

"You shouldn't take the blame for any of your ex-husband craziness. He and he alone is to blame for the choices he made in life. Maybe he did feel unloved by you. But it didn't give him a right to take the law into his own hands. It didn't give him a right to be mad at the world as if he was the only person to be unloved by a significant other."

Mildred stared into spare sadly. "Raymond wasn't just mad at the world. He simply hated most people it seemed."

"That's a pretty strong statement to say he hated most people."

"I know. But Raymond and I was married for over twenty-five years and that's the attitude and behavior that he displayed toward others."

"That's messed up," Julian shook his head. "I'm assuming he mostly behaved this way toward others when he was hitting the bottle."

"Raymond was angry all the time even when he was sober. Drinking just intensified his anger and bitterness."

"Since for some reason, we seem to be discussing your ex-husband's anger and ill behavior toward others. I'm curious to know was he always hard to take, rude grouchy toward others throughout your marriage?"

Mildred stared into space for a moment and then looked at Julian. "I must admit, Raymond and I had a few good years when he wasn't drinking as much. He didn't strike me or treat me as badly during my pregnancies or when the children were small. But as the years went by, he grew bitterer and became more addicted to Vodka. That's when he became physical toward me and started finding fault in everyone. He complained about the kids on the block that lived two houses down. Whenever they played basketball outside he said they were too noisy. He fussed and grumbled the whole time they played. He also complained about our neighbor's dog. He didn't think the dog should ever bark," Mildred softly explained. "It breaks my heart to say I was married to Raymond for all those years and I never once heard him say a kind word about another human being other than his mother. But in a drunken state, he sometime disrespected her as well."

"Mildred, I'm sorry you had to endure the manners and traits of such a bitter man who also disrespected his own mother. From what you have told me, Raymond Ross was a piece of work and some," Julian strongly stated. "Did he physically abuse your children?"

Mildred shook her head. "No, he never laid a hand on them," she said with conviction. "But he was verbally abusive to them at times. But not much. He saved all his energy to bicker and quarrel with me. Not even his own mother could talk sense into him."

"Usually that person's mother is the only one that can usual get through to a bitter person like your ex-husband," Julian caringly stated.

"In most cases that's probably true. But in Raymond's case, he has geared his anger toward the whole world for his lousy childhood. He blames me for condemning him to a loveless marriage and he blames his mother for his father's abuse toward him."

"So, Raymond Ross was physically abused as a child?"

Mildred hesitated for a moment and then reluctantly answered. "Yes, Julian, I might as well share that part of the puzzle as well. Raymond was brutally abused as a child."

Julian nodded. "Hearing that sheds more light on your ex-husband's vehemence bitterness. It explains some of his rage. But in his case, he didn't open his eyes to pledge to never be abusive toward his own family."

"In his own mind, since he never laid a hand on any of the kids, he feels he has been a better man than his father, who basically beat Raymond every single day from the time he can remember until he ran away from home to live with a relative during high school."

"I guess his own father was a bigger damn louse than him. I'm sure Raymond didn't have a whipping coming to him every single day. His father was apparently mental with diminished capacity. Are his parents still alive?"

"His father, Ray Ross is deceased, but his mother, Emma Ross, is still alive. She lives in Chicago. She swore me to secrecy years ago that it would be in the children's best interest if we never breathed a word about Raymond's abuse as a child. It wouldn't undo the damage and it would most likely make the children hate her for allowing the abuse."

"Do you think she could have prevented the brutal abuse Raymond faced at the hands of his father?" Julian asked. "Afterall, a mother is supposed to protect her child at all cost. She could have called in the authorities or pursued efforts to get herself and child away from the harm of such a dangerous man," Julian stressed.

"Grandma Emma hands were tied at that time. Ray Ross abused her even worse than the abuse I received over the years from Raymond," Mildred sadly mumbled.

"I disagree that her hands were tied. I feel the reason your ex-mother-in-law doesn't want Raymond's abuse mentioned to your children is because she knows she failed her son," Julian said with conviction. "I have a son and I would move mountains to protect him from harm's way. I'm sure you would do the same for your children. So, I don't buy the lame excuse that your ex-mother-in-law is selling," Julian seemed bothered. "No decent parent would allow their child to suffer like that under no circumstances. End of story!"

"I'm inclined to agree with you," Mildred solemnly uttered.

"You should agree with me. I'm not sure of your relationship with Emma Ross, but the old lady is dealing with her own demons to allow such horrific abuse to her own child. I'm no shrink, but it sounds like Ray Ross was using his own child as a whipping boy for penned up anger most likely related to Emma Ross other than your soon to be ex-husband," Julian theorized.

"I'm not sure what Grandma Emma's state of mind was at that time. I just know she has been good to me and the kids over the years. But when Raymond was old enough he tried to protect himself and his mother from Ray. But Raymond was no match for big, tall, strong angry Ray. That's when he ran away from home to live with his Uncle George, Ray's brother, after Ray Ross tried to choke him to death. This tragic occurrence happened one afternoon after school, during our senior year, when Raymond tried to stop his father from beating his mother. Raymond confessed to me that if he hadn't broken away from his drunken father's grip he believed Ray Ross would have choked him to death. At that point, Raymond was too afraid to stay under the same roof with his father and that's why he ran away from home to live with his Uncle George and never returned."

Chapter Twenty-Nine

After Mildred and Julian left the restaurant, they were mostly quiet enroot to Mildred's house. Julian heart was broken, and he couldn't believe what they had shared was now over without any sign beforehand that things between them might not work out. He glanced over at her slender figure and her long golden hair as she sat silently looking out of the passenger window. He didn't want to give up on the connection they had built between them, but something inside of him strongly told him that his best efforts would not make a difference. His instincts strongly told him that his chances with Mildred were completely over. She had been adamant that he should start over with someone new. As much as he hated to admit it to himself, he knew she meant what she had said.

Julian nerves tightened as he pulled into her driveway. Their time together flashed before his eyes. Every meal, every moonlit walk, every dance, every smile, every movie and every phone call. It all flashed in his head in overwhelming beautiful memories. He had enjoyed his time with her immensely. He swallowed hard as it dawned on him that when she stepped out of his car, she would be walking out of his life forever. Suddenly he felt choked up as he threw the gear in park. He didn't kill the engine as he looked at her with warm eyes. "Mildred, take care of yourself," he solemnly said.

She leaned over and kissed the side of his face and then patted the top of his right hand as she looked at him for a moment before she spoke. "Julian, you do the same," she softly said as she let herself out of his car.

Mildred stood on the walkway and waved at him as he slowly backed out of her driveway and then headed down the street. She slowly made her way up the walkway in deep thought about her past memories of Antonio. She stepped across the porch and searched at the bottom of her purse for her door key. She located the door key after a little bit of effort to find it. But as she removed her key from her purse to unlock the front door, the door was pulled opened by Trina who was about to head out of the door.

"Hi, Mom. I'm headed to drop off and pick up some dry-cleaning," Trina said as she stepped outside. "I'm not sure where Kenny and Courtney are. They were both gone when I got home a few minutes ago from Taylor Gowns. Although, Courtney's car is still parked in the driveway. She's not home."

"I told all of you at breakfast this morning, that I wanted us to do something as a family this evening. I thought maybe we could all go see a movie together."

Trina nodded. "I remember you said that, and maybe they do to. It's only one-forty-five in the afternoon. You wanted us all to do something together much later this evening, right?"

"That is correct. So, I hope you all are around later," Mildred said glumly as she stood in the front door.

"Mom, is everything okay? You seem sort of sad," Trina said, standing with her right elbow propped against the house.

"I'm fine, Sweetheart."

Trina searched her mother's face with concern. "Mom, I'm sorry to say. But you don't really look that fine," Trina said respectfully with two dresses for the drycleaners draped across her arm.

"I just have a few things on my mind," Mildred admitted.

"You had lunch with Julian, didn't you?"

"Yes, he just dropped me off."

Trina smiled. "Mom, he's a really nice man just like his wonderful son," Trina said laughingly. "After my disappointment and awful breakup with Wally. I'm so happy I was lucky enough to meet someone like Oliver," Trina excitedly said, smiling at her mother. "We both got lucky. I'm really glad you met a nice man like Mr. Bartlett."

Mildred swallowed hard as she solemnly looked at Trina. She knew she had to inform her that she would no longer be dating Julian. "Trina, you might as well know, Sweetheart. I won't be seeing Oliver's father any more after today," Mildred told her.

Trina smile faded as her eyes widened with surprise. "But I thought you two got along well? He's a really nice man, Mom. Did something happen?"

"Nothing happened and of course, you are right. Julian is a really nice man. But I explained to him as well as I could, that I'm just not interested in getting involved in a relationship with anyone at this time in my life or ever, for that matter," Mildred softly stated.

"Mom, you told Mr. Bartlett that?"

Mildred nodded. "Yes, Sweetheart. I was truthful with Julian. I didn't want him to invest any more time with me when he could be investing his time with someone who's interested in a possible future with him. I know that person could never be me."

"I guess I'm just a little confused that you broke off with Oliver's Dad. I thought you sort of liked Julian; and liked spending time with him."

"Spending time with Julian was swell. But as I told him I'm just not interested in a relationship with anyone. Plus, if you don't mind, Sweetheart, I would rather not talk about this right now," Mildred waved her hand. "Go on and run your errands. Maybe we can talk further about this some other time when I don't feel quite so glum."

"Okay, Mom. I'm just going to the cleaners and right back." Trina turned and headed off the porch but stopped at the edge of the porch and looked around before her mother closed the door. "The mail carrier dropped you off a small package by priority mail. I placed it on the coffee table," Trina said and then she headed down the front steps toward the old car that Mildred drove back and forth to work.

"Thanks, Sweetheart. I see it," Mildred said as she closed the front door.

Mildred pulled off her jacket and placed it across the back of the sofa as she placed her purse on the coffee table. She picked up the manila envelope and noticed it was addressed from some attorney's office in Chicago. She was curious as to what it could be. She took a seat on the sofa and slowly opened the small package. Inside was a letter and a check made out in her name for $50,000. It was from Antonio Armani. His last will and testament.

Dear Mildred,

You were always the most beautiful woman I had ever laid eyes on. But I never felt good enough or worthy of you. Yet, someone as precious as you saw something special in me that caused you to love me with all your heart. But if you are reading this letter, it means I have passed on. The money is what I earned when I was in my thirties and missing you like crazy. I put it in a safe deposit box and never thought of it as my own. I wanted you to have it in case of my death whether we were together or not. This letter is being written in the year of 1990. I hope by the time you read this letter that you and I would have found our way back to each other and had our chance for some happiness down through the years before my death.

It was always you, my sweet, darling Mildred. I was such a fool back in high school to push you away in pursue of Catherine's wealth. At that time, I had it all orchestrated in my mind that I would marry the riches girl in town to try to live and imitate the life apparently my birth parents lived. I was told my biological parents had everything on a silver platter. I don't know if this information was true or false. I never found out that much about my biological parents. All I know is what I have been told and things I have heard. Apparently, they were both United States citizens, but their folks were born in Liverpool, England. They were newly married, in their thirties and quite wealthy when they were both killed in their three-bedroom home in a violent rain storm. The house fell in on them. Their bodies were discovered in the debris along with their seven-month-old infant, which was me. What puzzled me for a while, I wondered about my biological folk's money. It should have transferred to their only child, which was me. But of course, somehow, their family took whatever wealth they had accumulated; but couldn't bother with an infant. So, they left me in an orphanage to be adopted to never know my real roots. I guess it was a blind adoption, so no one could locate my biological parent's relatives. But with all that said, I'm thankful for my parents who always showed me love. I was rebellious toward them and resented them for the mere fact that they were dirt poor and not my biological parents. But in all fairness, they were good to me. It still didn't stop me from leaving home after high school as if they were not.

With all that was going on with me as a teenager, searching for riches and turning my back on true love, there were no doubt in my mind that I loved you beyond words or description, so very deeply. You were my angel on earth. Nevertheless, I was a fool with my priorities geared in the wrong direction. I failed you and I failed myself by walking out of your life making you feel second best to Catherine Franklin. Although, I will admit the truth about Catherine. She was a good woman who would give anyone the shirt off her back. But I just didn't love her. I cared about her as a person but was never in love with her. But she loved me with all her heart. Why? I'll never know. It's not like I gave her a reason to love or trust me. Yet, she turned against her own family for me. She came from a good, decent family but they hated me like I was a deadly disease. But I'll admit in this letter that her parents had a right to hate me and I'll admit that they did the right thing to cut her out of the will. Because if they had not, and I had had my way, I know for a fact I would have drained her bank account dry of all those billions or whatever her portion would have been, and I still would have left her. I'm not proud of the way I treated Catherine but it's a fact of my life. She was my opportunity for the fortune that I felt was stolen from me as a baby. In the process, I'm the reason she lost her fortune. Yet, all the things I sought after regarding Catherine and her family fortune, none of it ever came to past. But I felt I should tell you this, so you could know why I chased after money when I was a teenager and a young man. I fantasized about the life that I thought was meant for me that I didn't get to have.

I was simply a dumb fool chasing after Catherine when you were the woman I loved and the only person I wanted to marry and build a life with. Yet, I destroyed your youth and my own by chasing the skirt tail of wealth. My thoughtless actions ignited your reaction to give up on true love. It breaks my heart to know you condemned yourself to a life with a man that you knew, going into the marriage, wasn't good enough for you. I have cursed myself many nights over the rumors of how awful Raymond Ross treats you. I don't believe everything I hear, but surely half of it is most likely true. Plus, I have read between the lines of your letters enough to know his treatment of you leaves a lot to be desired. Yet, somehow, you have remained with him and you have taken his abuse. That extremely boggles my mind. My darling, Mildred, surely you don't feel that you are deserving of his hateful treatment. If you do, please bear in mind that your feelings are misguided to believe just because he ended up in a loveless marriage that you are deserving of even one ounce of his wrath.

You are the love of my life, and if I could go back in time to the day that you first came home with me, I would treasure that day and I would never let you go. The day I broke up with you is the day I destroyed my own happiness and self-worth. I have felt worthless and unhappy from that day on. I was in search of power and wealth at such a young age because I thought those things could make me happy and make me feel like the man I thought I was born to be. But if I died without finding you again, I died a very sad and lonely man. I love you so deeply until I know death could never erase the love I feel deep down in the pit of my being for you. Some people live their whole life and never know true love. It's the epitome of joy. Everything else pale in comparison.

Please take this money and free yourself from Raymond's abuse. I'm so hurt that I allowed you to be treated so cruelly. But the truth is, I left you vulnerable, standing alone to be grabbed up by Raymond Ross. You always wondered what his troubles at home with his folks added up to. I knew then and I know now. Yet, I chose to never tell you. But the truth is, when we were seniors in high school, I overheard my folks discussing Raymond's father. They mentioned that he was an abusive heavy drinker and that he constantly used to beat Raymond. I also overheard my folks say Raymond was actually brutally injured by his father once when he tried to keep his father from beating his mother. Plus, I overheard them say how Raymond's father used to force him to sit at the kitchen table and drink Vodka with him from the time Raymond was twelve years old. His father's excuse was that he needed Raymond to act like a man since he was trying to be a man by standing up to him when he tried to strike his mother. That's why Raymond left home and was staying with a relative during high school. I'm telling you this now because I think you should know why Raymond was so bitter and cruel. I know you have written and said you feel Raymond is hostile because he sensed you never loved him. All that is probably so. But before he even met and married you, he was dealing with some huge abusive issues at home. I didn't mention this in high school when I first overheard my parents talking about it because I was jealous of Raymond and I didn't want you to feel sorry for him and get with him out of pity. Plus, if the truth be told, I was full of myself and felt no compassion for Raymond when we were young. I knew at that time that the abuse from his father was extreme and criminal. But I just wanted Raymond out of your face. Nevertheless, I pushed you right in his arms.

Miss Mildred Latham is who I fell in love with and I will love you for all eternity. When you read this letter I'm not sure if you will still be married to Raymond or maybe you will have found happiness with someone else, or hopefully you and I were finally together. But I remember one day many years ago when you made me a promise that no matter what happened between us, you would love me forever! I have carried those beautiful words with me through life. I hope your heart still loves me; and if you love me with just a faction of my love for you. It's enough to make the whole world move. Goodbye most beautiful woman in the world, until we meet again in heaven. I will always love you.

Antonio Armani, written Summer of 1990

Mildred sat and cried after reading Antonio's letter. She knew then that she would never be able to love another man the way she loved him; and she knew then that she had done the right thing by ending things with Julian. She didn't want to go through the motions of pretending to be happy with another man as she had done with Raymond. She owed it to herself and Antonio's memory to be completely honest about her feelings. Therefore, she knew in her heart that she had done the right thing by breaking things off with Julian. It was as clear as day to her that she would never love another man other than Antonio Armani, who was now dead. She didn't want to kid herself about a happy ever after with anyone else. She had enjoyed Julian's company as a friend. She had no romantic notions toward him. She was pleased that she had found the courage to be on the level with him before he fell too deep for her. Antonio's death erased every daydream and fantasy that had crossed her mind about a happy ever after, since all her daydreams and fantasies had been about a happy ever after with him. She loved Antonio more than anything and now that he was deceased she knew she couldn't love anyone else the way she had and still loved him.

Chapter Thirty

Sydney found his way back stage at the WJJ Theater. He was in search of Starlet and spotted her standing in front of a dressing mirror. She was standing with her back to him and didn't glance in his direction as he walked over to her. She was looking down buttoning the sleeve of her stage attire. She was beautifully dressed in a long cotton and satin teal blue eighteen century dress. She was listed in the Fundraiser Program Book to sing: America.

Sydney softly tapped her on the shoulder and she looked up and noticed his reflection in the mirror as she excitedly turned to him smiling.

He placed his hands in the pockets of his sapphire blue suit blazer as he whispered in a low voice. "I hope it's okay that I stepped back here," he said softly as he leaned down and kissed the side of her face.

"Sure, it's okay. I'm not scheduled to sing for another thirty minutes. We came early because of a mixed up with the program. I was originally scheduled to sing at eleven o'clock this morning. But the schedule was adjusted at the last minute and now I'm scheduled to sing at 2:15; and after I sing, Father, Samantha and I plan to stay for the rest of the fundraiser that ends around thirty minutes after I do my song." She grabbed his hand. "Let's have a seat in there." She pointed to a closed door that read: Dressing Room.

The fundraiser was hosted and sponsored by the City of Barrington Hills twice a year. The Disadvantage Children Fundraiser would provide clothing, coats, shoes, toys and school supplies for disadvantage children throughout Cook, Kane, Lake and McHenry counties. Charles Taylor is a faithful committee member of the semi-annual fundraisers, hosting and raising money for a different charity each event. He persuaded and passionately pushed the committee to spearhead a fundraiser for disadvantage children after it was suggested to him by Samantha.

Starlet looked out the door to her left and then to her right before she locked the dressing room door behind them. The small room housed two racks of men and women clothing, four-floor to ceiling mirrors, a makeup table with a large round mirror displayed with lights circled all around the edge of the mirror, one chair at the makeup table and three comfortable beige leather chairs.

Sydney took a seat in one of the chairs and pulled Starlet down in his lap and held her hand as she laid her head on his shoulder.

"I'm really glad you could make it," she softly uttered.

"We all made it and I think all the staff from Franklin House and your home is in attendance as well. Everybody wants to hear you sing. You do have a beautiful voice," he complimented her.

"But you haven't heard me sing."

"That's absolutely true. I haven't heard you sing, but I know you have a beautiful voice from just listening to you."

She slightly elbowed him in a playful way. "You are being funny of course. You know it doesn't work that way. You can't tell if a people can sing from the way they talk."

"I'm holding firm. Your voice is beautiful to me," he teased.

"You mean my speaking voice?"

Just then someone knocked on the dressing room door. Starlet hopped off Sydney's lap and stepped to the door. She turned the doorknob and pulled it open. It was Samantha smiling face and Paris was standing there at her side.

"Paris wondered where Sydney had disappeared to when he didn't see him mingling with any of the other guest," Samantha smiled. "But we both came to the conclusion that he was most likely backstage visiting with you."

"Come in if you like. I still have 20 minutes before I go on stage to sing."

Paris and Samantha exchanged smiles with each other and shook their heads. "No, we'll leave the two of you in privacy as you were. We'll go back out and mingle with all the town executives who showed up to give their support and donations toward this worthy cause. Father and Uncle Don are both on the committee and quite pleased with the donations that have piled in so far."

Paris raised one finger. "I don't know what the total tally is right now, but I heard Mother mention to Aunt Catherine that it's approximately $200,000 over last year's pledges," Paris shared.

Starlet grabbed her face with both hands and looked at Sydney. "That's incredible news. It will help so many unprivileged children." Starlet looked at Samantha. "Thanks for suggesting I sing. The turnout this year is impressive."

Samantha smiled. "It's very impressive. But it's not over yet. The crowd is anxiously awaiting Tyjuan Peoples-Jones, the thirteen-year-old talented kid from Detroit, Michigan. He's performing next, dancing to his own song titled: "Juju on the Beat." According to all the write-ups, young Tyjuan is the greatest sensation since Michael Jackson."

"That's incredible. So, he's performing next?" Starlet asked.

"That's what the program says, so we're going to head back to our seats." Samantha nodded.

"Okay, but thanks again, especially for making the suggestion to Father to host the fundraiser for unprivileged children." Starlet threw her a kiss.

"You're welcomed. But all the thanks I need is that the fundraiser has turned out so well." Samantha smiled.

Paris leaned down and kissed the side of Samantha's face. "There are so many reasons why I adore you. Your big caring heart is just one."

Samantha slightly elbowed Paris in a playful way. "That means a lot coming from you," Samantha softly said as she exchanged looks with Paris and then looked over at Sydney. "Especially, since you two and your brothers are the biggest hearts we know. If my family and I could do half as much for the community and others as the four of you, I would feel we're doing our share."

Starlet looked at Sydney and smiled. "She's right. You and your brothers are the most generous men in this town," Starlet sincerely agreed.

"We can't take all the credit. Many others, including the two of you and your family helps the community plenty," Sydney reminded her.

"That's true. But you guys do more than just the routine donations to different charities. Your generosity is incredible. You made the Ross's mortgage on their home for six months last Christmas," Starlet caringly reminded them.

Paris and Sydney exchanged looks and discreetly nodded. They didn't like to be praised for their generosity. It didn't feel natural to be praised for doing something that they felt was just a part of their makeup inherited from their father. Plus, deep down no matter how much they reached out and helped others, they always felt they fell short to what their father stood for when he was alive. Nevertheless, they always thrive to do their upmost to help the community and others just as their father before them.

After Samantha and Paris walked away from the dressing room door, Starlet glanced at her solid white gold watch. It was fifteen minutes before her curtain call. Still standing she glanced around at Sydney.

"The time is ticking away fast. It's almost time for me to go on stage. How do I look?" She held out both arms.

"You look beautiful, of course."

"Thank you for coming. I wasn't sure if you would get a chance since you're still preparing for your get away at the lake house. Are you heading up there tomorrow or Monday?" she reluctantly asked.

Sydney shook his head and smiled. "My answer is no and no."

"I got your text this morning that you were back home from the emergency business trip that you had taken at the last-minute yesterday morning. I just figured since your trip didn't take longer than you expected, you were back on schedule to head to the lake house."

Sydney stood up from the chair and reached for her hands. "I know we can't really talk that much right now since you need to head toward the stage. But just know this: I have decided not to spend any time at the lake house or anywhere else to clear my head. I thought about it long and hard and what I need most, I already have. The love and support of the most beautiful girl that I'm looking at; and of course, my family. I don't need to go away to find myself. I'm doing what my father would do in this situation. I read in some of his papers where he said: Live with your struggles and accept that bad things sometime happen to good people. And when it does, don't fall apart. Let it make you stronger. Those were my father's words."

Starlet smiled with excitement bubbling up inside of her as she threw both arms around Sydney's waist and held him tight. "I'm so happy to hear you say that."

Sydney smiled. "Well, I'm happy that you're happy."

"Of course, I'm very happy." She smiled. "The fact that you have changed your mind and you won't be going away to isolate yourself from me and your family is incredibly wonderful news to my ears. But I will admit. Although, with much heaviness and sadness." She placed both hands on her chest. "I had accepted your decision that you had to do what you felt was best for you. But now that you have decided not to go, I must be honest and tell you, I wasn't able to make peace with your decision within my heart."

"At the time I thought it was the right decision for me," he said.

"I know you thought that; and I guess I was too afraid of what your going away would mean to our relationship and how it would affect us. I was mapping out many scenarios and none of them was good. I was convinced it would impact our relationship in a negative way. Now, to hear you say you're not going away is so unexpected and the best news you could have given me," she inhaled deeply, taking in the joy of his news. "I was so afraid for us and what would happen to us while you were away clearing your head." She put both hands on her face and looked at him humbly. "Sydney, I'm so happy you changed your mind," she said almost feeling choked up with happiness as she glanced at her watch and looked at him and uttered slowly. "I guess I need to head toward the stage. But I just want to ask you, how do you feel about us?"

Sydney stared at her a bit too long without answering, which made her feel she needed to explain. "I'm asking because you felt strongly that you needed to clear your head to even be sure about the strength and future of our relationship. I haven't been able to think of anything else since we had that talk," she softly reminded him.

Sydney grabbed the back of his neck with both hands and stared up at the ceiling for a moment. Then he looked at Starlet with apologetic eyes and grabbed both of her hands into his. "Please forgive me for my pessimistic thoughts during that conversation. My only excuse is that I wasn't fully thinking at my one hundred percent capacity. However, I'm crystal clear in my thoughts at this moment. So, to answer your question. We are better than okay. I'm madly in love with you, Miss Starlet Taylor, now and forever as life goes on. When I look ahead in the future, I can't imagine it without you by my side. It's all so incredible what got us to this point where we are. How I feel and what I'm saying to you right now, is exactly how I felt from the moment we sneaked away into your dining room at your Halloween party and kissed each other for the first time," he lovingly told her. "It was a surreal moment. Like a glimpse of utopia and that's the way you make me feel whenever we're together," he softly whispered.

Starlet heart skipped a beat from his heartfelt confession, as her eyes glowed with love as she stared in his eyes. "Meeting you at my family party last year was the highlight of my life. I thought I was happy and content with life until you walked into my life and made me realize I had never known real happiness before we met. It's hard to explain, but after you came into my life, you filled a void in me that I didn't even know I had," Starlet softly admitted.

Sydney smiled at her. "On that very special evening, I seemed quite poised, but deep down I knew I had found my fair lady. Our meeting was like fate in my mind, since I only attended the party to humor my mother. Then, on the other side of that door stood you, my whole future right in front of me," he whispered near her ear as he pulled her in his arms and tenderly kissed her.

During their kiss, Samantha knocked on the dressing room door again. "The music is about to begin for you to be announced," Samantha anxiously informed her.

Sydney and Starlet quickly ended their kiss as Starlet swiftly grabbed a facial tissue from the makeup table, patted her lips a couple times with the tissue and then opened the door and rushed out pass Samantha. Luckily their kiss did not spear her makeup or mess up her hair style. In passing she said, "Thank you," to Samantha as she turned and threw Sydney a kiss with her right hand as she gracefully hurried to stand behind the stage floor curtain. Samantha and Sydney hurried out to the audience to be seated.

Chapter Thirty-One

Time hadn't softened Sabina's misery as an entire hour had gone by since Sabrina confronted Britain at Courtney's house. She painfully cried silently in her room and realized she was home alone when she noticed the entire family and all the staff were off the premises. She was filled with too much anguish, shock and disappointment to think clear to remember that the family and staff were all out of the mansion at the fundraiser where Starlet was scheduled to sing, America.

Sabrina felt hopeless as she paced back and forth in front of her bedroom fireplace, then it startled her when she heard the doorbell. She grabbed her face with both hands and shook her head in anguish and disappointment. It dawned on her that if she didn't answer the door there were no staff around to answer it. She had second thoughts about leaving her room and heading downstairs to answer the door. She was in no condition to face anyone. Plus, she figured it would be Britain showing up to try to explain himself. She was too disappointed and upset with him to confront him. Therefore, she made no attempts to head downstairs to answer the door. She continued to pace back and forth in front of the fireplace until soft knocks begin at the front door. Standing in the middle of her bedroom floor, she placed her hands over her ears and closed her eyes. She was wishing the knocking away, when suddenly the knocks stopped but the doorbell sounded repeatedly. Sabrina tried to fade out the ding-dong as she continuously held both hands over her ears. Nothing mattered, she was numb with anguish.

Moments later, the ringing of the doorbell and the knocks at the front door ceased. Sabrina swallowed hard and took a deep breath and stood still in the middle of her bedroom floor hoping to hear the sound of a car engine starting up and leaving her driveway. But as she stood there in tears, she didn't hear the start of a car engine leaving the driveway. She wondered if Britain had given up on trying to get her to answer the door. Crushed with heartbreak, she dropped down on the side of her queen size bed and grabbed her face in her hands. She felt drained and exhausted as she fell over on her back and stared up at the pink ceiling. She couldn't shed anymore tears as her eyes were red and felt sore from her flow of tears. She was lying there trying to make sense of what had just happened nearly an hour ago at Courtney's house. But suddenly, she sat straight up in full alert from the sound of footsteps headed down the long marble hallway toward her room. She sat there on the side of her bed motionless looking toward her open door when suddenly to her surprise, Britain walked up and stood in the doorway. He had a confused sad look on his face.

"Sabrina, I know you're upset about something based on the way you tore out of Courtney's house. But please, we need to have a discussion. We both need to find out what just happened at Courtney's," he frustratedly said.

"Britain, please leave. I can't talk to you right now," she sadly mumbled, pointing toward the door. "Besides, there's nothing you can discuss that I want to hear," she sadly uttered, looking in his eyes. Then it dawned on her, he had gotten inside without her answering the door.

"Sabrina, I will leave after you hear me out," he firmly stated.

"I'm not interested in hearing you out. You need to leave now," she strongly urged him. "I wasn't going to let you in. So, how did you get in?" she curiously asked. "There's no one else here that could have let you in."

"The front door wasn't locked. I rang the doorbell a few times and knocked and when you didn't answer, I grabbed the doorknob and turned the knob and the door opened. I guess you forgot to lock it when you got here."

"Maybe I did. You have me out of my mind with your sneaking around," she tearfully fussed.

"What do you mean by that statement?" he asked confused.

"You know what I mean," she glumly mumbled.

Somehow just seeing his face choked her up and brought forth overwhelming irritation and disappointment. She hopped off the bed and threw up both arms. "Britain why are you standing there staring at me as if you have no clue why I'm so upset with you?"

"Maybe, because I have no clue what's going on in this house or Courtney's?" He pointed toward the window.

Sabrina shook her head. "You know plenty. I'm the one who's in the dark. So, please don't insult my intelligence by standing there looking innocent. Besides, I'm really disappointed in you and I have asked you to leave, but you're being rude by ignoring my wishes," Sabrina sadly stated, looking toward him.

"Listen, Sabrina," Britain said frustrated. "You're not listening to me it seems. I'm trying to tell you that I have no idea what you're distressed about. I know you asked me to leave, and I'm not purposely trying to be rude, but we're both adults and we need to get to the bottom of why you're peeved at me and why you think I also know why you're peeved."

"I don't want to talk about it," Sabrina said looking toward the floor.

"Maybe you don't want to talk about it; and I still don't know what you don't want to talk about. Nevertheless, we seriously need to have a discussion before I leave. We can't just leave things up in the air," he calmly suggested.

Sabrina didn't comment as she continued to look toward the floor with her arms folded around her chest.

"I'm confused and I'm sure you are too. We need to talk about it. Is it okay if I come inside your room?" he softly asked.

Sabrina looked toward Britain and shook her head. Looking in his face irritated her more and made her relive the image of seeing him in Courtney's bedroom. That image was carved in her brain as the shock of her life. She was beside herself with heartbreak of him visiting Courtney's house and ending up in Courtney's bedroom. It made Courtney's words about going with him appear true in her mind.

"I don't want to talk right now. I just want you to leave," Sabrina said in a choked-up voice. "Why did you bother coming over? You didn't have time to spend with me earlier! So, I don't have time to spend with you now."

Britain propped an elbow on the doorframe. "Maybe I should leave because you're just not listening to me; and right now, we're getting nowhere with a lack of much needed communication. Plus, you have me at a disadvantage since I'm in the dark about whatever it is that you're supposedly irritated with me about," Britain calmly said as he slowly walked across the room and grabbed both of her hands in his. He looked at her with serious eyes. "We need to talk and get to the bottom of what put you in this mood."

"Britain Franklin, don't you pretend you don't know what I'm upset with you about! I'm sure you know what I'm talking about?" She pulled her hands from his and turned her back to him.

"Please turn around and look at me, Sabrina," he asked with confusion in his eyes. He was in complete wonder about her upset behavior.

She turned around and looked at him with solemn eyes. "Britain, you're acting oblivious to all of this." She held up one finger. "But allow me to refresh your memory. Does a one o'clock appointment ring a bell?"

He stood there bewildered by her anguish and was too disturbed by her touchiness with him to put the dots together that she was upset about his visit to Courtney's house.

"Sabrina, in order for me to properly offend myself, you need to explain the issue you're upset with me about," he very calmly and politely suggested.

"I think you already know my issue with you; and if you don't, you should," she softly mumbled, grabbed her face with both hands and cried.

"I'm on the level. I don't know what you're getting at. Just tell me already," he strongly suggested. "I'm confused but mostly I'm concerned about you and how whatever this is have gotten you in such an emotional state. So, what's the matter?"

"The matter is quite clear to me. You cancelled our lunch plans to make sure you made your one o'clock appointment on time, remember?"

Britain stared at her trying to process what she was referring to and when he didn't reply she felt she had him redhanded.

"No comment now? After you cancelled our lunch, so you could be on time to for your visit to see Courtney Ross at one o'clock!"

Britain raised an eyebrow with surprise. "Is that what you're upset about, my visit to Courtney's house?" Britain asked surprised.

"Don't try to deny it, Britain Franklin. I was there too, and I saw you in her bedroom! Remember! You showed up at Courtney's house at one o'clock on the button!" she fussed.

"Sabrina." He raised one hand. "I'm not denying it, I'm just trying to be clear about why you're so touchy with me. I'm surprised you would be so peeved and bent out of shape with me due to a visit I made to Courtney's house?" he confusedly asked. "But is my visit to Courtney's house the reason you're so touchy and irritable? Is that what you're upset about?" he asked.

Sabrina didn't answer as she stood there looking in his eyes. She didn't know how to feel or what to believe. He seemed so casual and calm about his reasons for visiting Courtney's house.

"Sabina, are you going to answer me? Is my visit to Courtney's house the reason for you being in such an emotional state? You didn't speak to me, you just ran out of Courtney's house as if the place was on fire. You wouldn't let me say one word. You just ran to your car and drove off."

"Of course, I ran out and drove away. I was stunned to see you there. Why were you there, Britain? I know I shouldn't have been there. But she dared me to show up at her house at one o'clock," Sabrina tearfully admitted and then grabbed her cheeks with both hands, standing there staring at him as tears rolled down her face.

"Courtney dared you to show up at her house at one o'clock?" Britain asked with a surprise expression and a puzzled look in his eyes. "Sabrina, I guess I'm not following you. Please calm down and explain yourself."

"I wasn't there because I thought you would come to her house. I was there because I was sure you wouldn't show up. I wanted to prove to her that she was lying when she announced you would be dropping by to visit her!" Sabrina sadly explained. "But you did show up just as she said you would!"

"Let me see if I'm following you correctly," Britain said and pointed toward the settee in her room. "Is it okay if I be seated over there?"

"Sure, why not," Sabrina mumbled as she walked across the room behind him and took a seat in a chair near the settee. She folded her arms in her lap and looked toward Britain.

He looked toward Sabrina with a serious expression on his face as he took a seat on the settee. "Sabrina, you're upset with me and torn up inside because I paid a visit to Courtney Ross's house?"

Sabrina nodded. "Yes, that's why I'm upset."

"You're upset because I showed up at Courtney's house, but you thought I wouldn't show up there. You only showed up because you wanted to prove to her that I wouldn't show up. But I did show up and you're beside yourself with distraught and I cannot remember a time when you were touchier and so unwilling to listen." He held up both arms. "Nevertheless, I'm still lost because I don't know why you're so distressed that I paid a visit to Courtney Ross's house," he said to her. "The young woman does work for me. Granted, she had a crush on me and may still do, but that's in the past. Besides, Courtney mentioned that you two are friends now," Britain told her.

Sabrina sadly shook her head. "Courtney Ross is not my friend."

He nodded with surprised eyes. "Okay, she's not your friend. However, I accepted her at her word about the friendship since I have seen her coming and going paying you visits at the Taylor mansion a few times."

"Courtney is not my friend and what she felt for you is not in the past!" Sabrina relayed strongly. Courtney Ross still loves you. So, what was I supposed to think when you showed up at her house just as she said you would?" Sabrina softly asked.

He looked at her lost for words since they both were dealing with two different realities. He thought Courtney was a new friend of Sabrina's and had moved on from him. Now he's being told she's still in love with him and is not Sabrina's friend. Plus, he's thinking about the odd situation that occurred at Courtney's house.

"Sabrina, you are visibly trembling, and I can see tears in your eyes as if the world is ending. Your irritation is centered at me when frankly I'm not sure I get a clear picture of what's going on between you and Courtney. Clearly, there's some bad blood between you two that I'm probably not aware of. However, we'll get to the bottom of this particular situation!" He assured her as he got out of his seat and hurried across her large room toward her open bedroom door.

Sabrina looked at Britain wondering what he was doing as he stepped out into the long hallway and looked to his right and then called out.

"Kenny, please come upstairs to Sabrina's room and bring your sister with you! Just come straight down the hallway to the first open door."

Sabrina grabbed her face with both hands in shock. "You mean Courtney Ross is here in my house?"

Britain looked toward her while standing in the doorway waiting for Kenny and Courtney. "Yes, I brought them with me. We all came in together."

"Why would you do that?" Sabrina asked not pleased.

"I had my reasons for bringing them along," he politely told her.

"Maybe you had your reasons, but why didn't you tell me you brought them with you? You should have told me that Courtney and Kenny were downstairs in my living room." Sabrina shook her head in distress. "You have no idea the things she said to me this morning. I don't want Courtney Ross in my house. Believe me, she is not well."

Britain glanced toward Sabrina and nodded. "You don't have to convince me of that. That's why I asked Kenny to come and bring Courtney along. I felt something was off with this whole situation; and I'm right. Something is very off but I intend to get to the bottom of it just as soon as Kenny and Courtney makes it upstairs," Britain assured her.

"Britain, this isn't going to work. You want answers from them. But you still haven't given me any answers about why you were visiting Courtney. All I have is her explanation which is too revolting and despicable to repeat. So, I definitely do not want her in my house; and without an explanation from you, you should leave as well," Sabrina sadly urged.

Propped with his back against the doorframe with his arms folded, Britain looked toward Sabrina with compassionate eyes. "Sweetheart, whatever you think I have done is just a big misunderstanding that will be cleared up soon. When Courtney and Kenny get upstairs, hopefully we can get some answers out of them and get to the bottom of this one bizarre afternoon," he said and then glanced toward the end of the long marble hallway wondering what was keeping Kenny and Courtney. It had been enough time that they should have made it upstairs. Looking toward the end of the hallway, Britain realized Kenny hadn't answered him when he first called to him. It dawned on Britain that Kenny and Courtney probably couldn't hear him from the location of the second level middle ways the solid hallway. Therefore, Britain figured he needed to walk down to the edge of the hallway and call out to them. But before doing so, he looked around the doorframe at Sabrina. "I'm sure they didn't hear me the first time. I'm going to the edge of hallway and ask them to come up," Britain said and headed down the hallway.

Moments later, Britain stepped back into Sabrina's room and nodded toward her. "They're coming upstairs now. But I just want you to know. I'm deeply sorry that you're going through this and I respect your wishes that you want me to leave and you don't want Courtney in your home. Nevertheless, Sabrina. Just sit tight until we get to the bottom of this disarray. I need to find out why you're so dismayed with me. Something tells me that it has a lot more to do with than just the fact that I showed up at Courtney's house."

"Britain, of course, you're right. It does have to do with a lot more than just that. But I'm disappointed and upset about all of it," Sabrina mumbled.

"I don't know what you mean by that," Britain said, filled with frustration but he kept his composure. "However, I intend to get some more answers from Courtney and Kenny," he said. "I heard you and respect the fact that you no longer for whatever reason want her in your home. Soon as I get some answers from her and vindicate myself in your eyes, Courtney Ross can leave," Britain humbly assured her. "I'll also leave after I get my answers if that's what you want," Britain respectfully relayed to her as he stepped over to one of her bedroom windows, pulled the curtains back and looked out.

Before Sabrina could reply, she and Britain clearly heard Kenny and Courtney's loud voices fussing their way down the long hallway toward Sabrina's room. Britain exchanged looks with Sabrina and she nodded.

"Its okay, show them to my room and ask your questions," she hesitantly mumbled.

Britain nodded at Sabrina and then hurried across her bedroom floor to stand at the door. He saw them at the end of the hallway and they were clearly unaware of which room belonged to Sabrina as they headed toward the first door on the left.

Britain called out to them. "Kenny, bring your sister this way," he said, beckoning them to continue down the hallway to Sabrina's room.

When Courtney and Kenny walked into Sabrina's room, Sabrina screamed out and grabbed her mouth and held it tight with both hands. Bloodstains were splattered all over Kenny's white shirt. The left side of his face was slightly swollen. He looked like he had been in a fight with someone who had gotten the best of him. But when Sabrina eyes caught Courtney, she screamed louder. Courtney looked worse than Kenny. Her clothes were ripped and torn, her long shoulder length hair had been chopped to the ears and she had two black eyes and a swollen lip.

Sabrina felt the nightmare wouldn't end. She was home but none of her family or staff was there. It dawned on her that they were all still at the fundraiser. Observing how shaken Sabrina appeared, Britain stepped near her and put his arm around her waist. She didn't push him away as she trembled in her tracks as a cold chill ripped through her. Suddenly her instincts told her Britain was a victim too.

"Start talking, Kenny!" Britain demanded in a sharp tone.

Kenny stood there staring at Sabrina with confusion in his sad eyes. He held up both hands and shook his head.

"I said, start talking, Kenny! What are you waiting for?" Britain strongly urged, with a serious look on his face.

"Sure, I'll start talking," Kenny said with a crushed look on his face. "But like I was telling you earlier, I'm halfway in the dark here myself."

"Just tell us the part where you're not in the dark," Britain demanded.

"I don't know where to start." Kenny grabbed the back of his neck with his right hand and paused up at the ceiling for a moment; and then looked at Britain. "So, where do you want me to start? I agreed to come over here and I dragged Courtney with me because I wanted to clear up that closet incident that you punched me in the nose about. But I'll be damned if I know anymore about what's going on than you do! Courtney is the only one who really knows what this was all about!" Kenny pointed toward his sister. "But look at my spaced-out sister. She's completely off her rocker. She's in no condition to answer any questions. I have to get her back home and stay there with her until Trina or Mom gets home. She has to be admitted that's for sure. Man, after what we just witnessed, there's no doubt in my head that my sister has cracked up and lost touched with all reality."

Britain nodded in agreement with Kenny, but he still wanted to clear the air with Sabrina and needed Courtney to explain to Sabrina why he had visited her. Britain rubbed his chin and then paused in Kenny's eyes.

"Kenny, to be completely honest, I feel sympathy and compassion for what has happened to Courtney and her state of mind, but my main priority at the moment is to clear the air with Sabrina. It's becoming apparently clear that Courtney has connived and manipulated Sabrina in some way and I want to get to the bottom of it!" Britain glanced at Courtney and shook his head.

"What a difference a few months can make," he said sincerely and then looked toward Kenny. "Your sister was a completely different young lady when we first hired her at the company. She was smart and very polite, and all the customers loved her," Britain stressed. "She had a bright future ahead of her."

"Then she hit the bottle again," Kenny quickly added. "Suddenly she started being sneaky and untruthful and went straight downhill from there," Kenny said with deep disappointment, shaking his head. "Now it deeply pains me to say that she has reached the bottom." He held out both hands. "But she brought all this misery and chaos on herself!"

Britain nodded. "It's obvious that she's quite ill and needs to see a doctor. But she has managed to single-handedly push all of our buttons! She has all three of us at each other's throat! Sabrina is upset with me! I'm pissed at you, and Courtney had a hand in it all," Britain said disappointedly.

Kenny agreed. "You are hundred percent right that my messed up in the head, little devious, scheming, calculating sister had a hand in it all!" Kenny said firmly. "But you both should take a good look at her." He pointed toward Courtney. "You can see how she has flipped out. I need to get her back home and to a doctor as soon as possible. Don't you think? She's in no condition to talk or explain anything," Kenny told them.

"I agree that she does need to see a doctor as soon as possible," Britain agreed. "Nevertheless, a few more minutes here isn't going to make that big of a difference. Therefore, before the two of you walk out of this room, Courtney needs to open her mouth and do a little explaining to Sabrina!"

Kenny understood Britain's request, but he felt his sister wasn't in a state to comply. "But she's in no condition to explain herself," Kenny said. "As you suggested, I drove her around in my car with the windows down for nearly an hour and supplied her with three cups of coffee. But you know all of that because you trailed us. You felt we should try to sober Courtney up before we met over here to face Sabrina. But as you can see, none of that helped. She's still out of it. Maybe a glass of cold water will help," Kenny suggested.

Britain glanced at Sabrina and she nodded. "You'll have to wait here while I get a bottle of water from the kitchen, all the servants are out."

"You don't have to do that. Faucet water will do," Kenny suggested.

"Okay, I'll grab her a cup of water from my bathroom," Sabrina said as she headed across the room toward her connected bathroom.

She returned and handed Kenny the cup of water and a few minutes after she gave Kenny the water for Courtney to drink, Courtney was still mostly dead weigh hanging on Kenny's shoulder. He had only gotten her to sip a fourth of the cup of water. "I'm sorry, Britain. She is still incoherent, and I need to get her home. Clearly, she has experienced some kind of mental break," Kenny urged.

Britain nodded. "I can see that you are most likely correct; and I deeply sympathize. However, I will not back down. It's crucially important that Courtney corrects this colossal misunderstanding that she set in motion," Britain seriously relayed to Kenny. "I can see she's mostly out of it, but I need her to at least attempt to explain herself; and make herself just clear enough to take back whatever untruths she planted in Sabrina's head," Britain firmly insisted. "It's obvious that she manufactured some scheme to get Sabrina to her home and upstairs in that closet," Britain heatedly stated.

Kenny exchanged looks with Sabrina; and then Kenny and Sabrina looked toward Britain who continued. "Your little sister who you say is in no condition to talk or explain herself, asked me to come over to your home today to see her at 1:00 o'clock. I never would have bothered, but she said she wanted to make amends and throw Sabrina a surprise bridal shower," Britain explained. "Why she needed to see me if she wanted to throw a bridal shower for Sabrina, I wasn't sure. But at the time her request sounded like a worthwhile effort. But I was in the dark to what she was really up to. I was also under the impression that she and Sabrina had become friends."

Sabrina jaw dropped as she grabbed her face with both hands. She realized how Courtney had conned Britain into playing into her game as well. Suddenly her heart sunk, and she knew she had no reason to be upset with Britain. She immediately felt ashamed of herself for her ill behavior toward him, which he didn't deserve.

Kenny shook his head and held up both hands. "I hear you talking, but I can't make her talk or sober her up. Besides, I'm sort of worried about her at this moment. Something is deeply wrong with my sister and she needs a doctor," Kenny strongly suggested.

Britain nodded with compassionate in his eyes. "Kenny, I can tell you are restless and need to get Courtney home and to a doctor as soon as possible; and I won't hold you long." Britain inhaled sharply and exchanged looks with Sabrina. "Because from the way she behaved earlier, she has lost all logic of reality," Britain said sincerely as his eyes glowed with sadness. "I sensed something was off when I first arrived at your house and walked inside. She immediately wasn't herself and started talking fast and acting strange right off," Britain explained. "She said something bizarre about getting it on later, which really went over the top of my head. It didn't dawn on me at the time that she was saying things for the sole purpose of having Sabrina overhear her. She wasn't being logical or making any sense and before I could process the fact that something was really off with her behavior, she had hurried me along by the arm up the short stairs to her bedroom. Enroot to her room while I was trying to figure out why we were headed upstairs to her bedroom, I could clearly see the open door to her room and we had stepped into her room before it registered with me that something wasn't right," Britain calmly explained. "Nevertheless, I didn't comment as I stepped inside her room. However, once we were inside her room, the only thing she wanted me to know and I quote: "It's not a good time to talk." Therefore, when she looked at me and said that, it dawned on me that what she had said didn't make any sense," Britain explained. "She had just gone to the trouble of taking me upstairs to her room, and the moment we stepped into her room she tells me that. I just looked at her waiting for her to explain herself. I thought it was odd that she led me into her bedroom to say such non-sense. However, once again, I brushed aside how odd her behavior seemed and turned to head out of her room. But just as I reached the door, she shouted loudly that she had something she wanted me to see. Before I could anticipate about what the something could be, she pulled open the closet door and there stood you and Sabrina! For a moment I was speechless as Sabrina tore out of the closet and headed out of the room. Stunned, I stood there for a moment trying to collect myself as my brain went into overdrive trying to figure out what had just happened. I looked toward Courtney who was propped against the doorframe holding both cheeks, bent over laughing as she watched Sabrina run out of her room crying. When I headed out of the room to chase after Sabrina, Courtney grabbed my shirt and stopped me. She shouted that she had really wanted me to drop by to catch you and Sabrina in the closet making out."

Kenny raised both arms and shook his head but kept silent as Sabrina stood holding her face with her mouth open.

"I regretful lost my poise when she screamed such an outrageous accusation in my face," Britain looked apologetically toward Kenny. "You stood there speechless, that's when I lost my composure and punched you in the face," Britain said remorsefully with much regret. "Kenny, I want you to know I'm deeply sorry and I'm not pleased with myself one bit for striking you, especially when you were innocent to Courtney's trumped-up story," Britain said humbly. "Even if you were not innocent, violence is never the answer and something I'm totally against and frown upon. Nevertheless, I struck you before it dawned on me that everything out of her mouth were lies. Therefore, Kenny, once again I apologize and can't stressed how sorry I am."

Sabrina walked over to Britain and threw her arms around him. "I'm the one who's sorry. I'm deeply shamefully sorry," Sabrina pleading said in tears as she touched Britain's face. "It's partly my fault. I know Courtney and should have known she was scheming and playing a sick game. I should have been stronger and not allowed myself to fall into her web of lies! She told me the two of you were lovers and you had been making out with her for months," Sabrina said, hating the sound of the words as they came from her mouth.

Britain looked at her with disbelief and shock in his eyes. "My goodness, I had no idea Courtney had reached such a level of manipulation. Something is seriously the matter with that young woman," Britain sadly admitted.

Sabrina wiped a tear from her left eye with the back of her fingers. "She told me you spent the night together and that I could see the both of you together today at her house with my own eyes at 1:00 o'clock if I dared to show up," Sabrina sadly explained. "Courtney lies bothered me and knocked the wind out of me. But deep down I knew she was lying. But I made a huge error in judgement when I decided against my better judgement to see her scheme through."

"Her untruths were so outlandish; how could you have given them an ounce of credence?" Britain asked. "Just the mere accusation that I spent the night with her. It's all too unreal and not me. I love you like no tomorrow and we're engaged and about to be married very soon. Besides, even if we were not about to me married. It's still not in me to do what she accused me of."

Sabrina stood there facing him with no real good explanation of why she allowed herself to get swept up into Courtney's web of lies. She felt it wouldn't be appropriate to say she wanted to catch Courtney in a lie. However, that was her real reason for playing along with Courtney's game. Therefore, she stayed mute as they all felt duped by Courtney, trying to figure out what was going on in Courtney's mind.

"Sweetheart, this is turning into a real live nightmare," Britain said to Sabrina. "But I must admit, I'm thrown that you played into her web," Britain admitted. "Especially, if you knew she was lying, which you just said you knew she was lying. I have to ask, what made you go over to her house to be a part of such a farce?" Britain calmly asked.

Sabrina humbly looked Britain in the face. "Honestly, I'm ashamed of why I followed through with her invitation. I did it because I knew deep down she was lying, and I needed to prove to her face that she was lying. The way I expected to do that was by you not showing up after she told me you would," Sabrina softly anxiously explained.

"By saying deep down you felt she was lying, that indicates that you were not one hundred percent sure of her lies," Britain inquired.

Sabrina nodded. "I deeply apologize for my moment of doubt. It was just a sliver of a moment," Sabrina regretfully admitted.

"A sliver of a moment is a lot when there should be zero doubt between us," Britain firmly stated. "We're about to be married. "There's no room for doubt in our relationship," Britain seriously stated. "It pains me that you had even a sliver of doubt," he sadly admitted.

Sabrina grabbed his arm. "Please, forgive me for being so foolish and getting myself caught up in such a bizarre mess; and most of all, please forgive me for making you think I doubted you in any way."

"Of course, I forgive you. But, you did just say you had a sliver of doubt toward me," Britain reminded her.

"I know I said that. But I don't doubt you not even a sliver. I say that because the doubt I felt wasn't real. It was all under false pretense. Remember earlier when you came over and wanted to grab a sandwich?" Sabrina asked.

"Yes, I remember. What does that have to do with this?"

"It has everything to do with this. It ignited my false doubt since the incident caused me to lose some of my faith when you came over and suggested a quick sandwich because you had an appointment at 1:00 o'clock. I'm only human and when you told me that you had an appointment at the same time Courtney had said you would be at her house; my imagination went crazy and I lost my composure and thought all kinds of ridiculous thoughts. I didn't want to believe her, and as I said, deep down I didn't really believe her. But I drove to her house and you showed up just like she said you would. Being in the dark of her setup, what else could I believe? She manipulated me just as she did you and Kenny. Furthermore, she darned me to show up. I had to go to her house to prove to her that she was a liar," Sabrina tearfully told him. "So, please believe me." Sabrina held up both hands. "I know you deep down in my soul and I would trust you with my life and the life of everyone dear to me. I know you are the epitome of what a gentleman should be and there's not a splinter of doubt in my heart about your impeccable character," Sabrina said with conviction.

Britain nodded and then shook his head as he stepped up to Sabrina and grabbed her in his arms and kissed her on the lips. He pulled away and looked at her. "I believe you and would like to offer my apologies for questioning your belief in me. Things are just a bit intense right now. I'm quite disappointment that Courtney won't speak and admit she orchestrated this whole charade. I know you believe me. Yet, I would still like for you to hear her admit she set me up," Britain said frustrated.

"I knew she had issues, but I didn't think she would go this far," Sabrina admitted. "I was trying to help her by being her friend. I should have known my friendship wasn't what she really needed. She needed professional help and that's what I should have encouraged her toward," Sabrina said, concerned about Courtney's spaced out condition.

Kenny looked at Sabrina and shook his head as he hit his fist in his hand. "Don't feel sorry for her. She didn't feel sorry for us. It's clear how devious my sister turned out to be. She manipulated and played us all for fools," Kenny firmly reminded them, as his expression went from concern to disgust. He took both hands and shoved Courtney away from leaning on his shoulder as he continued with distress in his voice. "She is certifiable, and with everything you two have just said, and the lies she told me to get me inside the house, I wouldn't put it past her to be faking now! Maybe she's purposely carrying on as if she has lost it just to keep from facing the music," Kenny suggested.

Britain and Sabrina exchanged looks, knowing his suggestion could be true. Yet, they both could see that Courtney looked spaced out and completely out of touch with reality as she stood there with her eyes half open as if she didn't know where she was.

Kenny grabbed Courtney by the shoulders and placed her back firmly against the bedroom wall. "Let us know if we are right about you! We want to know if you're faking it girl?" he yelled angrily in her face. "Open your conniving mouth and answer me! I want to know if you're completely finished with your scheming lies! You have lied to me for weeks! Feeding me that garbage about Samantha having a thing for me, and to think I bought into your lies when you said Samantha was inside the house and wanted to see me. I was a bigger fool than you to buy into that lie! But you knew exactly what you were doing! You played on my weakness! Knowing how I have always felt about Samantha. Damn you, Courtney! You schemed and lied and played on my feelings and emotions to set all three of us up! I'm ashamed to call you my sister!" Kenny roared angrily in her face, giving her a slight shove in the chest as she stumbled about with a dazed look on her face.

Courtney started talking to herself. "Britain, I know you love me, but I understand the situation you're in. You can't let Sabrina know how much you want me. Sabrina might find out. But we can't let her know."

Sabrina clung tighter to Britain and looked toward Kenny.

"What happened to her face and hair?"

"She happened to her face and hair! Nobody laid a finger on her. She flipped her lid when Britain threw a punch to me, and then looked at her and told her he didn't buy her lies. She ripped her own clothes and cropped off her hair; and then went as far as to punch herself in each eye with her own fist," Kenny confessed.

"Why would she do that?" Sabrina asked.

"Why does she do any of the whacked-out stuff she does?" Kenny pointed to her head. "She's hitting the bottle again heavy, but it's more than the liquor this time. She went too far and has clearly lost touch with reality. She's completely off her rocker," Kenny sadly admitted, choked up with disappointment. "Her plan was to frame Britain for rape."

"Kenny are you kidding?" Sabrina asked stunned. "Is that what she told you that she intended to frame Britain for rape?" Sabrina looked at Kenny and shook her head. She could see from the deeply sadden expression on Kenny's face and his anxious manner that he was crushed and beside himself from Courtney's behavior and actions.

Kenny nodded. "Yeah, it's what she told me. I'm not pleased to say, but that was her plan after Britain didn't buy into her garbage after you ran out of the house," Kenny shared. "But after her well-played frame-up, there was a minor problem she hadn't considered."

"And what was that?" Sabrina asked.

"It was me. I was a witness to her madness."

"This is all so unbelievable," Sabrina grabbed her cheeks and looked toward Courtney who seemed lost in another world. "And to think, I thought she was my friend for awhile. But I caught on to her real quick." Sabrina grabbed her head and looked up at the ceiling in disbelief. Then she looked at Britain, shaking her head in disbelief as she took her fingers and continued to wipe tears from her eyes. "When you two first walked in my room I was so beside myself about the issue Britain and I was trying to resolve until I didn't really notice her face and hair. I'm stunned by what she did to herself. "Is this really happening? Is that really Courtney?" Sabrina pointed toward Courtney.

Britain nodded. "This is really happening and that's really Courtney."

"This is all so sad that it had to come to this. I'm highly disappointed and upset by her treachery. However, I'm more upset by her condition. I hate this happened to Courtney. It's obvious she has suffered a breakdown. When Kenny said that when they first walked in the room, I wasn't sure he was sure. But just observing her behavior, there's no doubt in my mind. She needs to see a doctor as soon as possible." Sabrina grabbed her face, shaking her head. "I'm deeply sorry about her condition, aren't you Britain?"

Britain held Sabrina tight and nodded with sad eyes. "Yes, I'm deeply sadden. She is obvious sick and needed help. I guess we all missed the big picture. If we had seen the serious signals, other than just assuming she was filled with vodka, we could have helped her get the help she needed," Britain compassionately stated.

"It's so sad to see her in such a state. I remember when you and I first met, you were telling me how nice and polite Courtney was and I remember back when she was dating your brother for awhile," Sabrina recalled. "She was like night and day from the woman I'm looking at now. It was as if overnight, she became jealous, scheming and manipulative," Sabrina said and squeezed her hands together. "When before she was so nice and sweet; what happened to that girl? People don't just suddenly lose their minds overnight."

"It didn't happen overnight," Kenny quickly weighed in. "I noticed a change in her right after the holidays."

"I noticed a change in her also at work," Britain added. "I couldn't put my finger on it, but her behavior wasn't what I had remembered it to be. She seemed restless and rude."

"I noticed the same," Kenny said. "I remember how depressed she became right after the Christmas holidays when your brother stopped seeing her and she lost her job. Your company rehired her back with a job offsite, but she still didn't perk up. It was only after you eventually gave her a job back onsite that she seemed a little less down. But Courtney never seemed like herself again after all that," Kenny shared. "I didn't think too much of it because I just figured she was grumpy and upset with herself for messing things up with your brother. I figured she would get over it. But I guess she never did. I think she's been headed downhill since the first of the year. She started back to drink heavy around that time and she also started behaving somewhat indifferent about stuff around then as if nothing really mattered. Trina also mentioned how Courtney wasn't eating or sleeping well," Kenny shared. "Thinking back, I recall that Trina also mentioned that she had noticed a shift in Courtney's behavior before I moved from home into my own apartment. But again, when Trina mentioned her insight on Courtney, I didn't give it any credit. I chalked it up to be mostly about the heavy drinking and figured she would soon get off the booze as she had done in the past," Kenny respectfully explained. "But it blows me away that she ended up this way. The folks always held Courtney up as an example for me and Trina. They felt she would be the one to make something out of her life; and that Trina and I would just be in her shadow," Kenny told them.

"That's a tough pill to swallow," Britain commented. "Your parents should've made all three of you feel like number one. That was always my parents' mode," Britain said, stepped over and patted Kenny's shoulder. "Sorry, you felt like your parents had you living in your sister's shadow."

Kenny nodded. "That's just the way it always was in my household. Courtney was their favorite because of her smarts and good looks mostly. They always said Trina and I were always just average in everything; and that's probably because she's the one who dated and had the love of a rich Franklin," Kenny explained and paused. "I know I'm referring to your family, but there's no way around it. Because it is your family," Kenny said, as if his mind was in deep thought. "Trina and I never had a chance with a Franklin. She once had a slight crush on Sydney, who never knew about her slight crush and I have always been in love with Samantha and never had a chance with her. However, Courtney was different; she could have who she wanted but she just didn't have the good sense to keep that person," Kenny sadly stated, and then looked at Courtney and shook his head. "Let's get out of here, Courtney. I need to get you home to Mom, so we can get you to one of those mental facilities," Kenny sadly mumbled.

"Kenny, I know your family cannot afford medical treatment for Courtney at a mental facility. So, please, have your mother take Courtney to the facility of her choice and my family will foot the bill," Britain assured him. "Your family won't have to worry about the medical cost."

"I thought she had health coverage with Franklin Gas?" Kenny inquired.

Britain shook his head. "We offer it with a $10 deduction from each paycheck. She declined the health coverage. But nevertheless, we'll cover it."

It was a moment of silence after Britain offered to foot Courtney's medical care at any mental facility of her family's choice. Kenny was surprised but exceedingly pleased with Britain's unexpected generous offer.

Kenny exchanged smiles with Sabrina and then nodded at Britain. "Thanks Britain. I'm overwhelmed with gratitude and I know my mother will be as well. It will take a huge financial burden off of my mother's shoulders." He held out both arms. "However, I can't believe your generous donation to foot Courtney's medical bill. That's more than generous of you, considering the scheme Courtney just pulled on you and Sabrina today."

"I know. It was unfortunate the game she played. We're all disappointed and upset with her, but we can afford to be compassionate since we're not the ones ill. We have to keep in mind that she's not herself. She's a very sick young lady," Britain reminded him.

"Of course, you're right," Kenny agreed. "My mind just hasn't processed it all. I can't get over how pissed I am at her for duping us into this mess. But I better get her home, so we can get her the medical attention she needs." Kenny gripped her arm to lead her out of the room. "Courtney let's get out of here and get you home," Kenny said, heading out of Sabrina's bedroom.

Courtney resisted and wouldn't follow along with him. "Kenny, get away from me!" Courtney angrily shouted and jerked her arm away.

He grabbed her arm again and gave her a slight nudge toward the door. She staggered and landed up against the doorframe. Colliding against the doorframe seemed to unleash another personality from within her. Suddenly, Courtney looked wildly about the room and then slowly reached into her bosom and pulled out a switchblade. Before Kenny realized her state of mind, she quickly charged up to him and sliced his hand.

"I said get away from me and I meant that Kenny Ross!" She shouted.

Kenny jumped back in horrible pain, grabbed his hand and yelled. "You really have gone mad!"

"Stay where you are!" Courtney shouted toward the three of them, pointing and swinging the switchblade.

"Don't worry guys! I don't plan to hurt either one of you! It's that skinny bastard Sabrina I'm after! She has to pay for taking my Britain from me! She has some nerves to think she can sail into this town and take my man without a fight or any efforts on my part!" Courtney pointed her switchblade toward Sabrina. "You have another thought coming, you back-stabbing bitch!"

Courtney was totally out of control. They didn't mumble a word as they all exchanged shock looks with each other. Kenny had disbelief on his face and tears in his eyes. His expression told Sabrina that he was just moments from tackling his sister and her knife head on. Then he made a couple steps toward her and she swung the blade at him and sliced his other hand. Now he stood there with blood gushing from both hands, spilling out on Sabrina's plum bedroom carpeting. He was obviously in a lot of pain as he dropped to his knees in the corner of the Sabrina's room.

Britain made one step toward Courtney, and Sabrina grabbed his arm. "Don't go near her. She's mad and out of her head. She'll cut you too."

Britain nodded. "Just be calm. I'll be careful, but Kenny needs medical attention. My cell phone is in my jacket in my car. Where's your phone?"

"It's in my purse on my dresser," Sabrina pointed toward the dresser.

Courtney looked at Britain with the look of a sick love gone mad. For a moment, Sabrina thought Britain would get through to Courtney, but as Britain headed toward Kenny to check on him and to try to step toward the dresser for Sabrina's purse, Courtney shouted. "Don't make another step toward that damn dresser or my deceitful ass brother! Don't you touch that disloyal bastard! I don't care if he bleeds too death!"

"You don't mean that, Courtney," Britain pleaded calmly. "Just put the knife away, Courtney! Everything is going to work out, but right now Kenny needs a doctor. You need to let me help him, or at least let us call 911. He's losing a lot of blood!"

Courtney didn't reply. She just stared at Britain in somewhat of a daze as if her mind was a million miles away. Britain walked closer, waved both hands across her face, and then took another step toward her, but just at that moment she snapped out of her daze and swung her switchblade toward him, trying to cut him.

"Don't come any closer! You just lied to me! Nothing is going to work out! And how can it as long as Sabrina is in the picture! She is the reason for all our pain! You know that, Britain. I have no other choice but to make her pay! I should have followed my first mind and gotten rid of her right after Christmas! Why was I such a fool to wait all this time, allowing her to get her hooks so deep in you? But it will all work out now because I plan to finish her off!"

Sabrina grabbed her mouth and screamed. "This nightmare is getting worse! If you can't get through to her, nobody can!"

Britain glanced around at Sabrina and touched her face to comfort her. "It's going to be alright," he said, trying to assure her.

Sabrina covered her face and shook her head. "Nothing is going to be alright. She just cut her own brother. I doubt if she's going to hesitate to do the same or worse to you and I," Sabrina strongly suggested.

Britain glanced at his watch. "Where is everybody? The house seems deserted. I remember you mentioned when you fetched that cup of water for Courtney that all the staff was out," Britain anxiously inquired.

Sabrina nervously nodded. "Yes, the house is deserted. It's never completely deserted like this, but Father, Starlet, Samantha, and all the staff are out at the WJJ Theater for that fundraiser to hear Starlet sing." Sabrina grabbed her face. "It had slipped my mind earlier, but that's where they all are. If I hadn't overslept, I probably would have called and cancelled our lunch to attend the fundraiser. Then I wouldn't have ended up in this jam."

"That's right, my house is empty as well," Britain recalled. "I recall mother mentioning the fundraiser and all the staff would also attend to hear Starlet sing. I had informed her that you and I had other plans," Britain said.

"That's too bad. Both homes are empty while we're on our own trying to talk down a mental person." Sabrina trembled with frightened nerves.

Sabrina screamed when they both looked toward Courtney just in time to see her pull a small silver pistol from her bosom. Sabrina grabbed her mouth with both hands and stopped her scream as she swallowed hard. She and Britain exchanged looks with each other and stared at each other for a moment. They were stunned and at a standstill. Then Britain called out to Kenny who was down on his knees near the bed in obvious pain.

"Kenny! You have to do something! You have to try to get through to your sister! She has a gun!"

Sabrina shook her head as tears poured down her face. "Britain, what can he do? Kenny is in too much pain to help us. He'll probably go into shock and pass out if we can't call an ambulance and rush him to a hospital soon."

"I know you're right, but we have to think of something. We need to get through to Courtney, so she'll allow us to grab your purse from the dresser to call for help for Kenny. He needs to be rushed to an Emergency Room now!" Britain urgently relayed.

"But she won't listen to you, Britain," Sabrina cried. "What do I have to lose, maybe she'll listen to me," Sabrina said and then stared at Courtney with humble eyes. "Courtney, please, let us out of here! Your brother needs medical attention." She pointed toward Kenny. "Can't you see how he's bleeding out on the carpet? Do you want him to bleed too death? What has happened to you? Where is that girl who used to hang out at Franklin House months ago? I would see you there and you were nice and quiet. Be that girl again and open your eyes to what you're doing right now! I beg of you!" Sabrina pleaded.

Courtney laughed. "You're one to talk about Franklin House. What a short memory you have! I'm no longer hanging out at Franklin House because you put an end to that! That's why I plan to put an end to your little sweet life now!" Courtney laughed and waved her gun in the air.

"Courtney, open your eyes to what you are saying and doing! Something is wrong with you! You need professional help!" Sabrina strongly suggested. "What you're doing is not just wrong, it's criminal. You're committing a crime by holding us in this room against our will! You'll also go down for murder one if Kenny doesn't make it!"

"Who cares if a disloyal traitor doesn't make it?" Courtney shouted.

Sabrina shook her head in dismay. "I finally put two and two together and figured out that you were manipulative, conniving and untruthful. But I never figured you would go as far as to cut or shoot someone!" Sabrina cried.

Britain had a solemn look on his face as he caressed Sabrina's shoulder to calm her down. "Sabrina, she's over the edge. She's not going to listen to reason," he said.

"He's right, you know! I would never listen to anything out of your mouth! You're a gullible little fool! You might as well save your breath." She kept waving the gun in the air over her head. "I don't know who Britain is trying to fool but I know he's not really into you. How could he be into someone like you? You're too bony and whiny, crying every minute. Why cry, just face your fate and be done with it." Courtney glanced in the corner at Kenny and stared at him for a moment as if she was noticing his wounds for the first time. Then she glanced away from him with a robot stare straight at the gun in her hand. But it was only a split second before she focused her spaced out, cold piercing eyes back toward Sabrina and Britain. "I'll tell you right now!" she hatefully shouted. "Calling me all those disgusting names like manipulative and conniving won't get you any mercy from where I'm standing!" Courtney bitterly shouted, slightly rocking from side to side. "How stupid can you get? I have the gun with my finger on the trigger and you have the nerve to call me bad names! You are one dense billion-dollar baby!" She bent over laughing before she stared at Sabrina and coldly shouted. "Oh, well, I guess it doesn't matter since your dense days are over!"

"Why is that, Courtney?" Sabrina trembling with nerves asked.

"I'll tell you why your dense days are over, Sabrina Taylor! They are over because you have a snowball's chance in hell of leaving this stylish pink room alive! You couldn't give up Britain, now you have to give up yourself!"

Sabrina reached out and grabbed Britain's shirttail, pulling him back near her. She was trembling as Courtney spoke with bitterness and demented anger. They knew she meant every word and definitely wanted Sabrina dead.

"Britain, I'm so scared right now. I feel we're trapped by her. What can we do? I know she's just that far gone to shoot me."

"Don't worry, most beautiful. I love you more than anything! She'll have to get through me before she can harm you. She can only fire one bullet at a time. When I approach her, and she fires, I want you to run out of this room as fast as you can," Britain demanded in a worried voice. "Don't stop anywhere in the house to use the phone, run to your car and drive away. Then you can use your car phone and call for help."

"But, Britain, I can't let you throw yourself in front of a bullet. You could lose your life. I won't do it. I would rather die than see you killed. I can't do it. I won't do it," Sabrina firmly stated between tears.

Sabrina and Britain were standing not far from the corner of the bed where a weak injured Kenny was bend over on his knees in excruciating pain. Nevertheless, after hearing Sabrina's defeated words that she would rather die than see Britain killed, those words miraculously gave Kenny incredible roaring strength that he didn't even know was within him. He sprang swiftly to his feet. His eyes were sad and wet, and he was in obvious agonizing pain, but with the determination and added strength of three men, he wrapped his wounded hands around himself and yelled with conviction. "Sabrina, you won't have to watch Britain sacrifice himself for you! My screwy sister might be packing a piece, but it won't stop me from stopping her whacked out ass!" Kenny assured them with conviction. "This show is over!" He roared angrily and charged into Courtney quicker than she could blink. He caught her off guard as her back landed hard against the bedroom wall. She stumbled, almost losing her balance.

"Get out of here guys!" Kenny hollered toward Britain and Sabrina.

Britain and Sabrina tore out of the bedroom, but by the time they made it down the hallway to the staircase and across the enormous living room floor; they paused in their tracks when they heard a shot. Sabrina looked back, but Britain swung open the front door and pushed her through it. Then there was another shot just as Sabrina ran through the door and across the front porch and down the front steps. Sabrina glanced over her shoulder and didn't see Britain. She paused and turned to head back up the steps, but just as she did, she caught the third bullet from Courtney's gun. She fell backward off the steps into her family's big front yard.

Moments later, as Sabrina laid there on the ground, flat on her back with her eyes half open, Courtney walked up and stood over her. She could see clear enough to see that Courtney was bending over laughing. It reminded her of the scene in the cemetery a month earlier. She should have seen Courtney for the mentally ill young lady she was during that eerie bizarre episode, but no, she figured Courtney deserved her sympathy and a break. Now Courtney had broken them all after freaking into a full-fledged psychopath.

"Sabrina Taylor! Can you hear me? You aren't quite dead yet but soon you will be! Just as dead as a doorknob! And you know what? It does my heart good to look down at you suffering and crying as your life slips right through your fingers, and there isn't a damn thing you can do about it! Yes, Sabrina Taylor! You had it all. You had good looks and lots of friends! But most of all you had the love of my man! Britain Franklin was my man and you strolled into town and took him away from me! That wasn't right. I had him first. He was mine. But you stole him and made me a loser! But now, who's the loser? Who's lying flat on their back holding on for dear life by the skin of their teeth?" She yelled down at Sabrina.

"You little rich sucker! From the moment I first knocked on your door and pretended to be sorry about the loss of your mother, it was all a scheme!" She laughed. "It's unbelievable how easy it was to pull the wool over your eyes. I thought you had more brains. But I guess you consider yourself smart. You better think again. You're closer to dumb than most. You think I'm loony but not even I would have fallen for all the cons I pulled on you," Courtney bent over laughing. "Britain is the best looking, smartest man in this town. I don't blame him for hooking up with a dummy like you! He just made a mistake. He was taken with you not realizing how brainless you are," she bitterly roared. "Because if you were so damn smart, you wouldn't be lying flat on your back right now in your own front yard. You were so easy to con, so now here you lie; a real goner!"

Courtney paced a bit and then kicked a nearby bush. She was silent for a moment staring into space, and then she turned around and looked down at Sabrina with even more rage in her red, wet eyes.

"It's a shame and a real pity that two other people had to lose their lives because of you, Sabrina Taylor!" She screamed down at her, kicking her twice in the ribs and once in the shoulder.

The pain was unbearable as Sabrina lay there silently screaming inside. Sabrina could only grit her teeth and frown in excruciating pain, but it didn't seem to matter. Courtney had taken Britain's life. Now Sabrina suddenly felt numb and indifferent as if her entire world had crushed down around her. Deep down inside she felt as if she wanted to die too. She was extremely weak as she was going in and out of consciousness and she felt each second bringing her closer to death and closer to being with Britain and her two mothers. Somehow that thought gave her peace and took away some of her fear.

"I hate you so much, Sabrina Taylor! I should shoot you again in the middle of your forehead and put you out of your misery! But I have no compassion for you, none! It was you who forced me to put a bullet in Britain! Poor guy! He was such a blind fool to hook up with you. He would have been so much better off with me, but he couldn't see that! So now he's stone-cold too. I didn't want to do that to my Britain. I tell you, it seems like such a waste to take the life of such a perfect man. You know what I mean. You saw it with your own damn eyes. He left me no other choice. He didn't stand up for me. He stayed right by your side and looked at me like I was the plagued or a monster! So, I killed him. Sorry, but life's a bitch and then you die, especially if you try to play me! He had no right to look at me like that. He was supposed to look at me with love in his eyes. I just want you to know that's why I killed him." Courtney grabbed her head with one hand and screamed. "Oh! No! That means he's gone forever! That's not what I wanted! Only you were supposed to die! Not my Britain," she humbly stated in a dazed manner, wiping tears with her torn dress.

"Kenny, on the other hand, he had it coming! He got in the way too many times. Over at the house he wouldn't back up my stories. Then the stupid fool tried to take my gun! You know he tried to take my gun. Can you believe the nerve of that damn lush! Some big brother he turned out to be! You would never know he has me by three years since he has peanuts for brains! I have always been the smarter sibling. Where was his loyalty when I needed it? I hope he rots in Hell!"

Courtney dropped down to her knees beside Sabrina and placed the little pistol against Sabrina's head. Sabina didn't blink as she laid there staring up at the bluest sky ever observed. There wasn't a cloud in the endless view of space. It was clear peacefulness in the air as the sun was very bright. She could smell the cedar bush near her head that she watched the gardener plant right after they moved there. Sabrina could smell the evergreen near her feet. With all the familiar smells of home, her front yard seemed like hell and she was staring the devil straight in the face.

"Sabrina Taylor! If I had more than one bullet left in this gun, I would put a bullet right between your eyes and watch as your brains spilled out on the lawn; and I would watch you die a horrifying death! But you'll just have to die slowly and painfully because this last bullet is for me. You didn't think I was going to hang around in this poor, pitiful world without Britain? Did you? No way! As much as I hate you and would love to plant this last bullet in your brains, I must refrain myself because I must be with my Britain."

Courtney placed the gun on her stomach and pulled the trigger. She fell on the ground beside Sabrina. Blood scattered from Courtney's gunshot wound onto Sabrina's arm. Sabrina trembled beside Courtney's injured body as she felt herself becoming weaker and weaker. Her heart would soon stop, but she had to try and make her way up the front steps and get inside to see Britain and kiss his beautiful face before she took her last breath.

Sabrina grabbed her right side and rolled herself over on my stomach. She looked toward the front steps that were only a few feet away, but they seemed to be miles from her. "I'm too weak," she cried. "How will I manage to get to Britain? I have to see his face one last time."

Sabrina dropped her face in the grass and noticed that it was just long enough to grip, but she wondered could she find the strength to grab onto the grass and pull her own weight? She thought to herself and knew that deep down somehow, she would have to find the strength to get to Britain; and she knew her determination wouldn't fail her. She knew she had to get to Britain no matter how much pain and suffering she had to endure. She reached out both hands as far as she could and gripped two handfuls of grass and started crawling on her stomach. Inch by throbbing inch with each agonizing breath she took, she made it closer to the front steps. Then, between her heavy breathing and sobbing, she heard the sound of a car passing down the exclusive street. She silently cried and thought to herself that if only they would have stopped. Then it dawned on her that why would they stop when they had no idea there were two people lying dead on the huge estate and two more slipping away swiftly.

Sabrina had come to love their elite estate that was tucked away off the main road in a secluded affluence section with other priceless homes just as grand. The area mirrored a fairytale wonderland of immaculate landscaping with shapely evergreen trees and bushes; and while Sabrina laid surrounded by all the exclusiveness of her home. She thought how she was in unbearable pain lying helpless in her own front yard, thinking that each breath would be her last. It felt unreal as if she was wide awake in a nightmare, then her mind flashed back on when her parents purchased the Taylor mansion and how she instantly fell in love with the estate. Now lying on the front lawn fighting for her life, she didn't love the seclusion as much. She wondered if anyone was home at Franklin House or the Coleman mansion. Her hopeful thoughts faded when it dawned on her that all of Franklin House and the Coleman mansion were most likely at the fundraiser, otherwise someone would have rushed to their rescue after hearing the gunfire.

She gripped another fistful of grass, pulling herself right up to the steps, and between her heavy breathing and sniffling, she heard a squeaking noise.

Her left hand gripped the bottom step and she paused and listened. This time all she could hear was an airplane in the distance. Her right hand grabbed the other edge of the step and she struggled in excruciating pain to pull herself up the bottom step, but she couldn't muscle up enough strength from her agonizing painful weaken body. She laid her face on the step and tried to catch her breath.

"Britain, I'm trying," she cried out in a low weak voice. "God knows I'm trying. I love you, Britain; and I just need to see you one last time. Then I'll give up and let the suffering stop," she cried in a low feeble voice.

"Sabrina, Sabrina, is that you, my darling beautiful Sabrina?" Britain asked in a low weak voice. "Are you okay?" he said breathless.

It was Britain's voice and it meant he was still holding on. Sabrina's weak heart raced with joy from the sound of his voice. Hearing his voice was like a voice from Heaven to her as her half-closed eyes sparkled with admiration with the thought of him being okay. "Sabrina, I need to see your beautiful face. I need to hold you just one last time," Britain called in a low weakened voice.

Knowing he was still alive and holding on gave Sabrina instant strength to move. She screamed inside with each breath she took as the horrific pain ripped through her as she pushed herself. It was pure determination up against horrendous pain. She closed her eyes with a tight frown as she somehow gathered up enough strength to push herself up the bottom step. Then she opened her eyes, and through her cloudy, wet eyes, she saw his magnificent face. He was crawling on his stomach through the front door. Agonizing pain and determination showed on his face.

He managed to crawl almost to the edge of the porch, reached one hand, fully stretched out to Sabrina. Her hand managed to reach his. He grabbed her hand and gripped it with all his strength. He had no more strength to crawl. She had no more strength to move. She laid at the bottom of the steps with her hand in his. He laid across the porch with his hand in her.

He gripped her hand tighter as he managed in a weak voice, "I love you."

Sabrina managed with her last ounce of strength. "Britain, I love you."

Made in the USA
Monee, IL
16 March 2020

23271877R00182